More Annotated Alice

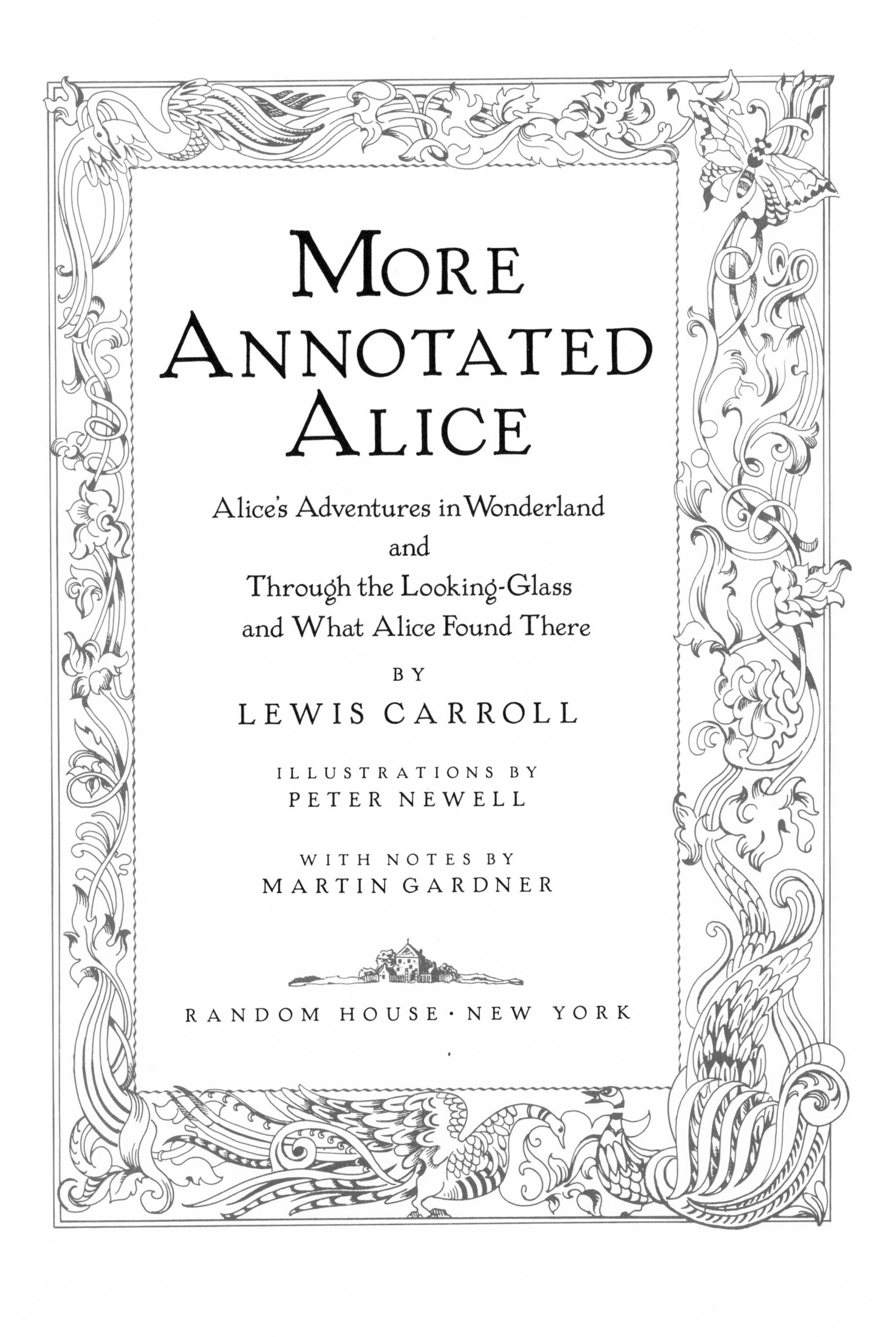

MORE ANNOTATED ALICE

Alice's Adventures in Wonderland
and
Through the Looking-Glass
and What Alice Found There

BY

LEWIS CARROLL

ILLUSTRATIONS BY
PETER NEWELL

WITH NOTES BY
MARTIN GARDNER

RANDOM HOUSE · NEW YORK

 Published in the United States
by Random House, Inc., New York, and simultaneously by
Random House of Canada Limited, Toronto.

"Alice's Adventures in Wonderland from an Artist's Stand-point"
by Peter Newell was originally published in the October 1901
issue of *Harper's Monthly* magazine.

Owing to limitations of space, all other acknowledgments of permission
to use previously published material will be found on page 363.

Library of Congress Cataloging-in-Publication Data

Carroll, Lewis, 1832–1898.
[Alice's adventures in wonderland]
More annotated Alice : Alice's adventures in wonderland & Through
the looking-glass / by Lewis Carroll; illustrated by Peter Newell;
with notes by Martin Gardner.
p. cm.
ISBN 0-394-58571-2
1. Fantastic fiction, English. 2. Carroll, Lewis, 1832–1898.
Alice's adventures in wonderland. 3. Carroll, Lewis, 1832–1898.
Through the looking-glass. 4. Fantastic fiction, English—History
and criticism. I. Gardner, Martin. II. Newell, Peter,
1862–1924. III. Carroll, Lewis, 1832–1898. Through the looking-
glass. 1990. IV. Title.
PR4611.A7 1990b 823'.8—dc20 90-53123

Manufactured in the United States of America
Book design by Jo Anne Metsch

To the thousands of readers of my
Annotated Alice
who took the time to send letters of appreciation,
and to offer corrections and suggestions
for new notes. Without those letters,
this sequel could never have been written.

Ye golden hours of Life's young spring,
  Of innocence, of love and truth!
Bright, beyond all imagining,
  Thou fairy-dream of youth!

I'd give all wealth that years have piled,
  The slow result of Life's decay,
To be once more a little child
  For one bright summer-day.

From "Solitude," written by
Lewis Carroll when he was twenty-one

PREFACE

Charles Lutwidge Dodgson, better known as Lewis Carroll, was a shy, eccentric bachelor who taught mathematics at Christ Church, Oxford. He had a great fondness for playing with mathematics, logic, and words, for writing nonsense, and for the company of attractive little girls. Somehow these passions magically fused to produce two immortal fantasies, written for his most-loved child-friend, Alice Liddell, daughter of the Christ Church dean. No one suspected at the time that those two books would become classics of English literature. And no one could have guessed that Carroll's fame would eventually surpass that of Alice's father and of all Carroll's colleagues at Oxford.

No other books written for children are more in need of explication than the *Alice* books. Much of their wit is interwoven with Victorian events and customs unfamiliar to American readers today, and even to readers in England. Many jokes in the books could be appreciated only by Oxford residents, and others were private jokes intended solely for Alice. It was to throw as much light as I could on these obscurities that thirty years ago I wrote *The Annotated Alice.*

There was little in that volume that could not be found scattered among the pages of books about Carroll. My task then was not to do original research but to take all I could find from the existing literature that would make the *Alice* books more enjoyable to contemporary readers.

During the thirty years that followed, public and scholarly interest in Lewis Carroll has grown at a remarkable rate. The Lewis Carroll Society was formed in England, and its lively periodical, *Jabberwocky*, has appeared quarterly since its first issue in 1969. The Lewis Carroll Society of North America, under the leadership of Stan Marx, came into existence in 1974. New biographies of Carroll—and one of Alice Liddell!—as well as books about special aspects of Carroll's life and writings have been published. That indispensable guide for collectors, *The Lewis Carroll Handbook,* was revised and updated in 1962 by the late Roger Green, and updated again in 1979 by Denis Crutch. Papers about Carroll turned up with increasing frequency in academic journals. There were new collections of essays about Carroll, and new bibliographies. The two-volume *Letters of Lewis Carroll*, edited by Morton H. Cohen, was published in 1979. Michael Hancher's *The Tenniel Illustrations to the "Alice" Books* came out in 1985.

New editions of *Alice,* as well as reprintings of *Alice's Adventures Under Ground* (the original story hand-lettered and illustrated by Carroll as a gift to Alice Liddell), and *The Nursery "Alice"* (Carroll's retelling of the story for very young readers) rolled off presses around the world. Several editions of *Alice* were newly annotated—one by the British philosopher Peter Heath. Other editions were given new illustrations by distinguished graphic artists. Some notion of the vastness of this literature can be gained by leafing through the 253 pages of Edward Guiliano's *Lewis Carroll: An Annotated International Bibliography, 1960–77*, already more than a decade behind the times.

Since 1960 Alice has been the star of endless screen, television, and radio productions around the world. Poems and songs in the *Alice* books have been given new melodies by modern composers—one of them Steve Allen, for CBS's 1985 musical. David Del Tredici has been writing his brilliant symphonic works based on *Alice* themes. Glen Tetley's "Alice" ballet, featuring Del Tredici's music, was produced in Manhattan in 1986. Morton Cohen, who knows more about Dodgson than any other living person, is completing a biography that will contain startling new revelations.

While all this was going on, hundreds of readers of *AA* sent me letters that called attention to aspects of Carroll's text I had failed to appreciate and that suggested where old notes could be improved and new ones added. When those letters reached the top of a large carton, I said to myself that the time had come to publish this new material. Should I try to revise and update the original book? Or should I write a sequel called *More Annotated Alice*? I finally decided that a sequel would be better. Readers who owned the original would not find it obsolete. There would be no need to compare its pages with those in a revised edition to see where fresh notes had been added. And it would have been a horrendous task to squeeze all the new notes into the marginal spaces of the original book.

A sequel also offered an opportunity to introduce readers to different illustrations. It is true that Tenniel's drawings are eternally part of the *Alice* "canon," but they are readily accessible in *The Annotated Alice*, as well as in scores of other editions currently in print. Peter Newell was not the first graphic artist after Tenniel to illustrate *Alice,* but he was the first to do so in a memorable way. An edition of the first *Alice* book with forty plates by Newell was published by Harper and Brothers in 1901, followed by the second *Alice* book, again with forty plates, in 1902. Both volumes are now costly collector's items. Whatever readers may think of Newell's art, I believe they will find it refreshing to see Alice and her friends through another artist's imagination.

Newell's fascinating article on his approach to *Alice* is reprinted here, followed by the latest and best of several essays about Newell and his work. I had planned to discuss Newell in this preface until I discovered that my friend Michael Hearn, author of *The Annotated Wizard of Oz* and other books, had said everything in an essay that I could have said and much more.

The famous lost episode about a wasp in a wig—Carroll deleted it from the second *Alice* book after Tenniel complained that he couldn't draw a wasp and thought the book would be better without the episode—is included here at the back of the book, rather than in the chapter about the White Knight where Carroll had intended it to go. The episode was first published in 1977 as a chapbook by the Lewis Carroll Society of North America, with my introduction and notes. This book is now out of print, and I am pleased to have obtained permission to include the entire volume here.

A few errors in the introduction to *The Annotated Alice* need correcting. I spoke of Shane Leslie's essay "Lewis Carroll and the Oxford Movement" as though it were serious criticism. Readers were quick to inform me it is no such thing. It was intended to spoof the compulsion of some scholars to search for improbable symbolism in *Alice.* I said that none of Carroll's photographs of naked little girls seemed to have survived. Four such pictures, hand colored, later turned up in the Carroll collection of the Rosenbach Foundation in Philadelphia. They are reproduced in *Lewis Carroll's Photographs of Nude Children,* a handsome monograph published by the foundation in 1979, with an introduction by Professor Cohen.

There has been considerable speculation among Carrollians about whether Carroll was "in love" with the real Alice. We know that Mrs. Liddell sensed something unusual in his attitude toward her daughter, took steps to discourage his attentions, and eventually burned all his early letters to Alice. My introduction mentioned a cryptic reference in Carroll's diary (October 28, 1862) to his being out of Mrs. Liddell's good graces "ever since Lord Newry's business." When Viscount Newry, age eighteen, was an undergraduate at Christ Church, Mrs. Liddell hoped he might marry one of her daughters. In 1862 Lord Newry wanted to give a ball, which was against college rules. He petitioned the faculty for permission, with Mrs. Liddell's support, but was turned down. Carroll had voted against him. Does this fully explain Mrs. Liddell's antagonism? Or was her anger reinforced by a feeling that Carroll himself wished someday to marry Alice? For Mrs. Liddell this was out of the question, not only because of the large age difference, but also because she considered Carroll too low on the social scale.

The page in Carroll's diary that covered the date of his break with Mrs. Liddell was cut from the volume by an unknown member of the Carroll family and was presumably destroyed. Alice's son Caryl Hargreaves is on record as having said he thought Carroll was romantically in love with his mother, and there are other indications, not yet made public, that Carroll may have expressed marital intentions to Alice's parents. Anne Clark, in her biographies of Carroll and of Alice, is convinced that some sort of proposal was made.

The question will be thoroughly dealt with in Morton Cohen's forthcoming biography of Carroll. Professor Cohen originally thought Carroll never considered marrying anyone, but Cohen later altered his opinion. Here is how he explained it in an interview published in *Soaring with the Dodo* (Lewis Carroll Society of North America, 1982), a collection of essays edited by Edward Guiliano and James Kinkaid:

> Actually, I didn't change my mind recently; I changed it in 1969 when I first got a photocopy of the diaries from the family. When I sat down and read through the diaries—the complete diaries not just the published excerpts—somewhere between 25 and 40% was never published, and naturally those unpublished bits and pieces are enormously significant. Those were the parts that the family decided should not be published. Roger Lancelyn Green, who edited the diaries, actually never even saw the full unpublished diaries because he worked from an edited typescript. When I first read through the unpublished portions of the diaries, however, I realized that another dimension to Lewis Carroll's "romanticism" existed. Of course it is pretty hard to reconcile the stern Victorian clergyman with the man who favored little girls to a point where he would want to propose marriage to one or more of them. I believe now that he made some sort of proposal of marriage to the Liddells, not saying "may I marry your eleven-year-old daughter," or anything like that, but perhaps advancing some meek suggestion that after six or eight years, if we feel the same way that we feel now, might some kind of alliance be possible? I believe also that he went on later on to think of the possibility of marrying other girls, and I think that he would have married. He was a marrying man. I very firmly believe that he would have been happier married than as a bachelor, and I think one of the tragedies of his life was that he never managed to marry.

Some critics have likened Carroll to Humbert Humbert, the narrator of Vladimir Nabokov's novel *Lolita.* Both were indeed attracted to what Nabokov called nymphets, but their motives were quite different. Lewis Carroll's little girls may have appealed to him precisely because he felt sexually secure with them. There was a tendency in Victorian England, reflected in much of its literature and art, to idealize the beauty and virginal purity of little girls. This surely made it easier for Carroll to take for granted that his fondness for them was on a high spiritual plane. Carroll was a devout Anglican, and no scholar has suggested that he was conscious of anything but the noblest intentions, nor is there a hint of impropriety in the recollections of his many child-friends.

Although *Lolita* has many allusions to Edgar Allan Poe, who shared Humbert's sexual preferences, it contains no references to Carroll. Nabokov spoke in an interview about Carroll's "pathetic affinity" with Humbert, adding that "some odd scruple prevented me from alluding in *Lolita* to his wretched perversion and to those ambiguous photographs he took in dim rooms."

Nabokov was a great admirer of the *Alice* books. In his youth he translated *Alice's Adventures in Wonderland* into Russian—"not the first translation," he once remarked, "but the best." He wrote one novel about a chess player (*The Defense*) and another with a playing-card motif (*King, Queen, Knave*). Critics have also noticed the similarity of the endings of *Alice's Adventures in Wonderland* and Nabokov's *Invitation to a Beheading*.*

Several reviewers of *AA* complained that its notes ramble too far from the text, with distracting comments more suitable for an essay. Yes, I often ramble, but I hope that at least some readers enjoy such meanderings. I see no reason why annotators should not use their notes for saying anything they please if they think it will be of interest, or at least amusing. Many of my long notes in *AA*—the one on chess as a metaphor for life, for example—were intended as mini-essays.

More Annotated Alice is designed strictly as a supplement to *The Annotated Alice*. The two books have almost nothing in common except Carroll's text. All the notes in *MAA* are new, except for a few that made it into the last hardcover edition of *AA* and its Penguin softcover version. Because the only edition of *AA* available in the United States at the moment is a Meridian paperback, which contains none of these recent notes, I have included them here.

The names of readers who provided material for this book are given in the notes, but here I wish to acknowledge a special debt to Dr. Selwyn H. Goodacre, current editor of *Jabberwocky* and a noted Carrollian scholar. Not only did he provide numerous insights, but he also gave generously of his time in reading a first draft of my notes and offering valuable corrections and suggestions. Needless to say, I welcome letters from readers who spot mistakes or who propose additional notes. Perhaps ten years from now I may have the pleasure of editing *Still More Annotated Alice*.

*For the many allusions to *Alice* in Nabokov's fiction, see note 133 (pages 377–78, Chapter 29) of *The Annotated Lolita*, edited by Alfred Appel, Jr. (McGraw-Hill, 1970).

CONTENTS

ALICE'S ADVENTURES IN WONDERLAND

FROM AN ARTIST'S STAND-POINT

by Peter Newell

The dominant note in the character of Alice is childish purity and sweetness, and this characteristic Sir John Tenniel has caught and fixed in a way none may rival. His appreciation of the many grotesque personages peopling this wonderland is broad and sympathetic, and his work will live as long as Alice. It may appear presumptuous therefore on my part to attempt to portray what Alice means to me. But the kindness with which the public has received my other work, together with the encouragement of certain friends (to whom the inception of this undertaking is due), has inspired the hope in me that this more serious effort will not be altogether unwelcome.

To me, Alice has a very distinct personality, so that my conception of her is almost as convincing as would have been a personal acquaintance with her in real life. Alice in Wonderland, and yet not wonderstruck!

A sweet, childish spirit at home in the midst of mystery! An exile of that faraway Stork Country—the prenatal wonderland—with its atmosphere still clinging to her and coloring her fancy. And yet a little girl is she, with lessons to learn and duties to perform—a demure, quaint little girl, with a strict regard for the proprieties of life, and a delicate sense of consideration for the feelings of others, even when her companions happen to be Mice, Dodos, Gryphons, and various other strange and awe-inspiring things. And underlying all this is that simple, sincere faith which seems to be the peculiar property of childhood, and which upon all occasions induces in her a respectful attitude, however absurd may be the situation. Such is my impression of Alice as she lies asleep on the green bank of a vagrant brook on a pleasant summer afternoon; and if dreams are but projections of our waking thoughts, like this must she be when her gray eyes are open in wakefulness. Gray eyes, did I say? Yes, surely she must have gray eyes, and large, through which her soul looks out flutteringly, like a white butterfly just issued from its cocoon into the air and sunshine.

And yet there is a self-reliance about her as pronounced as the confidence of the palpitating insect when it spreads its untried wings to soar above the roses or the flowers of the field. Her face, wreathed in a wealth of brown hair, is delicately modelled, with the roundness and dimples of babyhood still modifying its contour and shaping the outlines of her petite figure. And as other summers come and go I think I can see her develop into a woman, with delicately chiselled features and a form of modest grace, and the concern of life gradually creeping into her eyes. And the same tenderness of the little Alice of long ago will abide in her heart, happily adjusting her to home and the ever-widening circle about her. And in the quiet evening hours she will again wander through the mystic world of a more mature fancy, until in the twilight of life she will enter into that Wonderland the glorious vistas of which lead the traveller on and on in a never-ending pilgrimage.

Quite as delightful, though in a different way, are the companions of Alice in her remarkable adventures. The personification of the dumb animals and the inanimate things is so skilfully done as to appear quite natural and appropriate. One would not be greatly surprised to hear a Rabbit or a Gryphon speak, if their words produced an impression similar to that created by their inarticulate or immobile expression.

And so, in the mind of the reader, there is no classification of her friends into their various orders, but all are real characters on a common plane of human action and interest. What an excellent idea we obtain of that extinct specimen of the pigeon tribe, the Dodo, after witnessing its extraordinary exhibition of liberality in awarding prizes (from the pocket of another) to all the participants in the Caucus Race, and Alice in particular! And how well does the contradictory, crusty manner of the Caterpillar seem to be adapted to that singular worm as it sits, wreathed in a cloud of smoke from its hookah, on the top of a toadstool, where Alice chances to encounter it! And what a droll scene is that where the Fish Footman ceremoniously delivers the Queen's invitation to the Duchess to play croquet to the equally pompous Frog Footman! How well suited to each other do the Hatter and the March Hare appear to be as they sip their tea and wrangle over the half-recumbent form of their comfortable friend, the drowsy Door Mouse!

The Cheshire Cat, the Queen, the Gryphon, the Mock Turtle—all are bits of realism from the world of fancy, to use terms apparently contradictory, but which seem to me to be peculiarly appropriate to a description of these creatures, so admirable in every respect. *Alice's Adventures in Wonderland* is a play in which the subordinate actors are quite as excellent in their way as the leading character. They are differentiated from each other by a variation in their personalities, rather than by an inequality in their ability to entertain. Creatures are they of a vagrant fancy, which, like a rushing mountain stream, of times reflects distorted images, but is ever pure, with the sunlight glancing from its bosom. But, like the rapid-flowing brook, there are placid pools in its course, and in one crystal, reposeful spot is the face of Alice. *Alice's Adventures in Wonderland* is a book which appeals alike to young and old. It is an object-lesson that tends to make us realize the truth of the adage, "Men are but boys grown tall."

And what more healthy influence can be at work in the world than that which inclines busy, careworn men to identify themselves with an eternal youth? Genial, kind-hearted, loving Lewis Carroll! What better tribute can be paid to his excellence than to say that it was his mission in life not only to popularize purity in child literature, but to incite an emulation in other writers, productive of results the extent of the beneficent effects of which it is impossible to estimate.

Peter Newell

PETER NEWELL

(1862–1924)

by Michael Patrick Hearn

During the Golden Age of American illustration, when work by such distinguished artists as Charles Dana Gibson, Howard Pyle, and Maxfield Parrish graced many of the nation's books and periodicals, one of the most original of the country's designers was Peter Newell. An illustrator of Mark Twain, Stephen Crane, and Lewis Carroll, Newell was famous for his gentle cartoons in rich, velvety flat tones which enlivened the Harper's family of magazines—the *Monthly,* the *Weekly, Harper's Bazar, Harper's Young People*—and other national publications. However, perhaps his most enduring work was that for children: in particular *The Hole Book, The Slant Book,* and other novelty picture books which he both wrote and illustrated.

Peter Sheaf Hersey Newell was born on March 5, 1862, in rural Illinois, the last of four children of George Frederick Newell, a wagon-maker, and Louisa N. Newell. "I broke out," he later recalled, "the same time as the Civil War did, in a crossroads in the country in MacDonough County, Illinois. The place hadn't any name, but its nickname was 'Gungiwam.' Our house was the only frame house in the place (the rest were log huts), and it was clapboarded with walnut." Even as a little boy, Newell showed a passion for drawing. He was known to draw on anything, the barn door, wagon wheels, the school blackboard. Evidently his parents encouraged his early interest in art, for while he was still in school, he entered a large oil painting, *The Good Samaritan,* in the annual Bushnell fair and won the blue ribbon.

On graduating from high school at age sixteen, the amateur artist was apprenticed in a local cigar factory. He stayed only three months. Fortunately a local entrepreneur took a personal interest in the boy's artistic talent and found employment for his young protégé in a studio in nearby Jacksonville, Illinois. Here Newell made large crayon portraits by copying his subjects' photographs. Although uninspiring, this labor must have schooled the young artist in the subtleties of shading, modeling, and tonal progressions, which served him well when he began to draw for the half-tone process of the national magazines.

But Newell did not want to draw portraits. He wanted to be a cartoonist. Bored with his work in Jacksonville, he found the courage to submit a sketch to the editor of an Eastern magazine, *Harper's Bazar.* The reply was swift and confusing: while the note read, "No talent indicated," a check was enclosed. Encouraged by this paradoxical evaluation of his work, Newell set off for New York City in 1882 to seek his fortune.

He immediately enrolled at the Art Students League but barely survived a semester. Evidently he was restless with his studies. Once, when a waiter was brought in to pose for the sketch class, Newell's drawing aroused the most comment: he had drawn a dead cat on the waiter's tray. While at school, he continued to submit his drawings to the popular illustrated journals. "When I first began to draw for the magazines," he once told a reporter, "there were very few magazines that used pictures. There was *Harper's, Scribner's,* and *Godey's*—that was about all." Nevertheless, this young, largely self-taught artist succeeded in placing some of his comic designs with their editors. "When I was starting," Newell later admitted, "I cultivated not only my drawing, but my imagination. I tried to develop my power of conceiving humorous situations. . . . If an artist had an idea that caught the editor's fancy, he would receive more favorable attention than an artist who had nothing but a good drawing." Eventually Newell's cartoons began appearing regularly in the national periodicals, including the children's magazines *St. Nicholas* and *Harper's Young People* (later *Harper's Round Table*).

Newell earned his earliest recognition as an illustrator from his amusing pen-and-ink sketches. Magazine and book publishing was then replacing the old, laborious method of reproduction by wood engraving with the relatively cheaper and easier new process of photomechanical printing of illustrations. Unfortunately this new technology took some time to perfect, and in its early days, it did not allow for a variety of tone. Artists were required to work almost exclusively in line. Fortunately, because the camera as yet could not pick up the subtleties in gradation, errors could easily be corrected with white paint and then reworked in India ink. Another result of the limitations of this method of reproduction was that artists too frequently employed several lines where only one was needed, and so these illustrations were often overwrought.

Newell, however, was drawn to the work of the masters. His early published sketches in line betray a great debt to A. B. Frost and E. W. Kemble, two of the most popular and admired of American illustrators of their day. Newell learned as much from their subjects as from their clean, crisp

pen-and-ink styles. Newell, too, became known for his cartoons of rural life, particularly Negro scenes; and consequently he, like Frost and Kemble, was erroneously thought to be a native of the South.

Encouraged by his initial success with the Eastern magazines, Newell returned to Illinois and established his own illustration studio. Now confident of his chosen profession, Newell married his sweetheart, Leona Dow Ashcroft, on February 5, 1884. But Springfield did not prove to be the best place for an illustrator once he had a family to support, and so Newell became an itinerant artist who traveled through the Midwest and West, giving chalk talks when he could not get commissions for book and magazine work. In 1888, he and his family spent the summer in a tent, in Manitou, Colorado, not far from Colorado Springs. Life in the West was still rugged, and several homes near the Newells' were robbed. One morning while walking about the springs, the artist discovered a piece of zinc, covered with blood, in the road near his home. Worried for the safety of his wife and daughter, he went back to the tent and drew on a large piece of stiff paper the silhouettes of several fierce, rough-looking men. He then cut these out and arranged them along the side of the tent so that the light of the candle outlined them sharply against the canvas. Newell figured that anyone who passed by the tent would suspect that it

was inhabited by a band of formidable men and not by the gentle artist, his wife, and their little girl. Apparently this ruse succeeded in discouraging burglars, for the Newells, unlike their neighbors, were never bothered by the thieves.

Although he enjoyed the scenery of Manitou and the other places that he visited, Newell realized that if he was to continue as an illustrator he would have to return to New York. Since his last stay in the city, the publishing industry had begun to depend more and more on the halftone for book and magazine pictures. Although still limited to black and white, this new sensitive photomechanical process nevertheless was liberating to artists, for it gave them a wide range of tone for their designs. Many illustrators now turned from line to wash, and Newell followed the fashion.

One of his earliest experiments with the halftone was the little cartoon "Wild Flowers" (*Harper's Monthly,* August 1893), depicting a bug-eyed little girl being consoled by an elderly gentleman in a garden and accompanied by the following nonsense verse: " 'Of what are you afraid, my child?' inquired the kindly teacher. / 'Oh, sir, the flowers, they are wild,' replied the timid creature." This simple little design made Newell famous; and just like Gelett Burgess and his bit of nonsense "The Purple Cow," Newell could not avoid the great notoriety of "Wild Flowers." Its verse was widely quoted and memorized by his admirers, and Newell never knew when he might meet up with one of them. "Not long ago," he told Joyce Kilmer in 1916, "I was to speak at a little dinner, and I admit that I was not very comfortable in my mind about it. A lady who sat near me watched me for a few moments and then wrote something on her menu, folded it up, and passed it on to me. I opened it and found my wild flower verse."

"Wild Flowers" was only the first of a series of cartoons with comic verses which appeared sporadically in the back pages of *Harper's Monthly* and which were eventually collected as *Peter Newell's Pictures & Rhymes* (1899). This delightful volume proved to be as popular with children as with their parents. Newell possessed a gentle, innocent sense of humor like that of Edward Lear; and although he lacked the Englishman's ability as a poet, Newell nevertheless could make a clever turn of phrase, as in the following verse from his *Pictures & Rhymes:* "From Foxe's *Book of Martyrs,* Aunt Matilda slowly read. / 'O aunt, turn over a new leaf,' her youthful nephew said." And like the humor in Lear's limericks, the comedy in Newell's cartoons was as dependent upon the pictures as on the texts. However, Newell denied that he had ever seen or read Lear's *Book of Nonsense.*

In the halftone, Newell found the proper medium through which to express his particular kind of comedy. He was well aware of what the camera could and could not do; he knew its limitations and profited by them. Indeed, Newell was one of only a few artists of the period who did not sacrifice the distinctive character of their illustrations when transforming their styles from line to wash. Newell now simplified his compositions by containing the forms within bold outlines, which in turn he filled in with richly varied flat tones. "I didn't do the first flat tones that were done in this country," he admitted. "Of course, the Japanese had done them before, and so had Boutet de Monvel." Also from the Japanese, Newell learned new forms of dramatic composition and the internal rhythms of intertwining curved lines and contrasting flat colors and patterns. From Oriental art, he learned to simplify to get the maximum effect desired; now his designs gained in strength as he dropped all superfluous detail, aware that the point of a cartoon must be immediately understood for it to have any impact. "Every man has his own individuality," he argued. "Some men have been influenced by other artists, but their personality must sooner or later appear in their work if they are to succeed." And succeed he did, in allowing his own personality to emerge through the flat, rhythmic style of his halftone illustrations.

The deceptively simple, almost naïve manner of his illustrations should not suggest that Newell was careless with their preparation. On the contrary, Newell labored on each design until it created just the effect that the artist intended. For each drawing, he made a careful preliminary sketch and then transferred this composition to a clean sheet of paper for the final version. He then finished the art with mixed media, sometimes reworking the drawing with pencil, India ink, crayon, wash, watercolor, and white paint for highlights. Many of his illustrations which were reproduced in black and white were originally done in full color. And so painstaking an artist was Newell that if a drawing did not come up to his standards, he did not hesitate to discard it and begin anew.

The Peter Newell manner had its admirers, but the original had no equal among its imitators. One of Newell's most ardent followers was the young Lyonel Feininger, the modern American painter and teacher at the famous Bauhaus. In his early years as a professional illustrator, he contributed to *Harper's Young People* charming pictures for fairy tales, drawings which sported the flat tones and bounding outlines of Newell's work in the same periodical. Other artists were able to capture some of the technical grace of Newell's art, but none quite caught the distinctive comic spirit of Newell's famous cartoons.

Editors were drawn to Newell as much for his dependability as for his infectious good humor. He was given all kinds of texts to illustrate. Among the many books which he illustrated (many of which were originally serialized in magazines) were Mark Twain's *Following the Equator* (1897) and Stephen Crane's *Whilomville Stories* (1900). Perhaps his most famous book illustrations in his day were those for John Kendrick Bangs's *A House-Boat on the Styx* (1896) and its several sequels, and the success of these best-selling books was credited as much to the pictures as to their texts.

No matter what the commission, whether it was his own nonsense verses or Ivory Soap ads in the back pages of *St. Nicholas,* Newell was always conscientious in his labors. "An illustrator should be fully familiar with the story for which he is making the pictures," he believed. "I always read a story three or four times, so as to be thoroughly acquainted with it before I make any pictures for it. Accuracy in the representations of characters in fiction is an important part of an illustrator's equipment." He was known to take considerable time to authenticate little points in costumes and settings for his illustrations, though he never worked directly from the model. Instead, he relied on his own imagination and powers of invention. "An artist who is to make a success of illustrating must possess the qualities necessary for success on the stage," he said. "A successful illustrator must be able to reproduce characters and to produce the emotion present in the incident which he is depicting. All great illustrators have had this power—it is the only way in which an artist can give the text a correct interpretation. . . . He must be able to project himself into the scene he is drawing. He must identify himself with the characters of the situation. He must be able to induce the emotions which those characters are supposed to feel. . . . Many times I have found myself with my face distorted like those of the characters I was drawing." Indeed, many of his bug-eyed, spindly-legged grotesques look much like the artist himself, a tall, gawky gentleman with bushy eyebrows, mustache, and abundant curly hair. "If an artist has this sort of imaginative power, this power of projecting himself into his work, and is a good draftsman," he concluded, "I think that he will be a successful illustrator."

Another reason for Newell's success in the field was that he was always working, for books, magazines, and newspapers, and he knew well some of the problems created by unreasonable deadlines. He once admitted, "I have seen a few illustrations in which the artist has departed from the text—representing the hero of a story as smooth-shaven when the author gave him a beard, for instance. But sometimes this is really not the artist's fault; it is the fault of the editor, who has given him an order for a lot of work to be done in a hurry, and has not given him sufficient time to read the story carefully." And Newell had no patience with the artist who did not diligently do his work. "I never could understand this bohemian business very well," he complained. "There are some writers and painters who do their work right along, like masons and carpenters. That's the way I do it. I don't see any reason why an artist shouldn't be an honest, hardworking citizen like anybody else. As a matter of fact, I am inclined to think that these people who sit around waiting for inspiration are lazy. The position that they take is nothing but a pose. If they got married and had responsibilities resting on them they'd speedily be cured. . . . Some of my best work has been done while I had a baby in my lap."

It is surprising that this hardworking father did find time to be with his own two girls and little boy. He became something of a local celebrity in Leonia, the New Jersey town named for Mrs. Newell; and he did all he could to contribute to the community. He served as a Sunday school superintendent and on the local boards of education and health; he was a founder and first president of the Men's Neighborhood Club of Leonia. He played the piano, flute, and cello, and sang in the church choir; he enjoyed fishing and tennis, but his particular passion was chess. And what little spare time he had left, he spent carving little wooden figures. He was also a great favorite with the local boys and girls for his simple sleight-of-hand tricks, and all of them knew him as Uncle Peter.

The proud father was often inspired by his own children. Once, when he found one of them struggling with a picture book which was turned upside down, Newell decided to create a children's book which could be read at either angle. The two volumes of *Topsys & Turvys* (1893 and 1894) were the results. A child need only turn over this book of chromolithographed pictures to transform an elephant into an ostrich, a farmer into his pig, some ladies into butterflies, plates of ice cream into little boys. Newell explained in the second volume: "This book is like a tumbler. It's thus that you begin it, / but till it is inverted, there's always more within it." The concept of

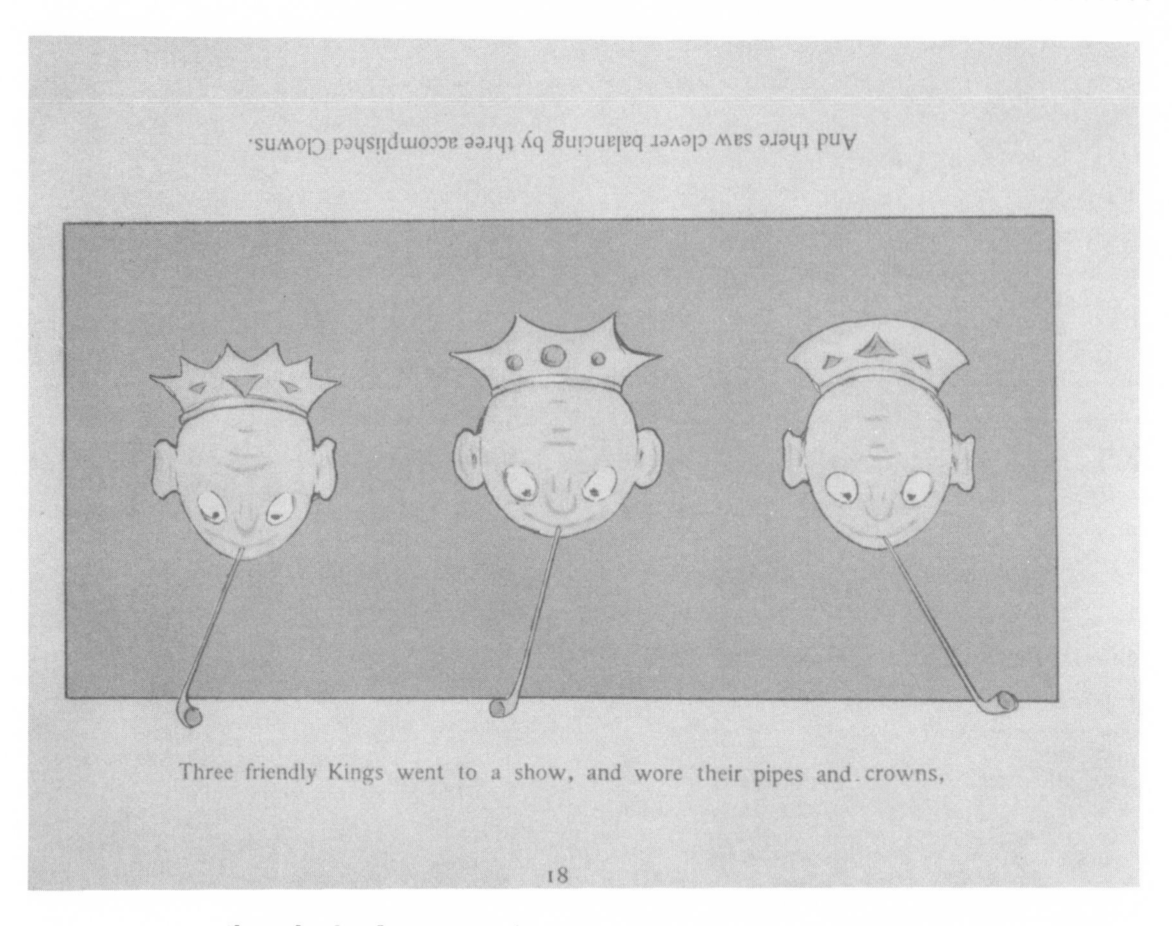

these books does seem simple enough, but surprisingly few other artists—notably Rex Whistler in *Oho!* (1946), Hilary Knight in *Sylvia the Sloth* (1969), and Gustave Verbeck in his early comic strip "The Upside-Downs of Lady Lovekins and Old Man Muffaroo"—have attempted this clever and challenging form of pictorial storytelling. Newell followed his popular *Topsys & Turvys* with another ingenious picture book, *A Shadow Show* (1896), an obvious imitation of Charles Henry Bennett's *Shadows* (two volumes, 1857 and 1858). Like its Victorian prototype, *A Shadow Show* reveals the true nature of each of its subjects by the shape of its outline.

More than any other American illustrator of the day, Newell explored the possibilities of the form of the picture book. So inventive were his novelty books that he sometimes had to take out a patent rather than the usual copyright to protect his literary curiosities. In both *The Hole Book* (1908) and its sequel *The Rocket Book* (1912), a hole was actually cut through the pages to show the humorous consequences of little Tom Potter's accidental shooting of his father's pistol in the first volume and, in the second, naughty Fritz's launching of a rocket, which goes from the basement through the floors of an apartment building. Even more eccentric than this pair of "hole books" is *The Slant Book* (1910), trimmed on an angle to

THE ROCKET BOOK

depict the adventures of a runaway baby carriage as it races down a steep hill. In each of these clever volumes, the silly two-color pictures are accompanied by doggerel, which perhaps was not necessary, for the humor of each situation is so completely communicated by the illustrations.

The most ambitious (and controversial) of Newell's children's books were his editions of *Alice's Adventures in Wonderland* (1901), *Through the Looking-Glass* (1902), and *The Hunting of the Snark* (1903). It is difficult to imagine Lewis Carroll's classic Alice books without the original illustrations by John Tenniel, but Harper and Brothers decided that the famous children's stories should be updated. It must have been an honor for Peter Newell to be chosen for this commission, but he also had to be prepared to defend the apparent audacity of his trying to replace Tenniel. Certainly

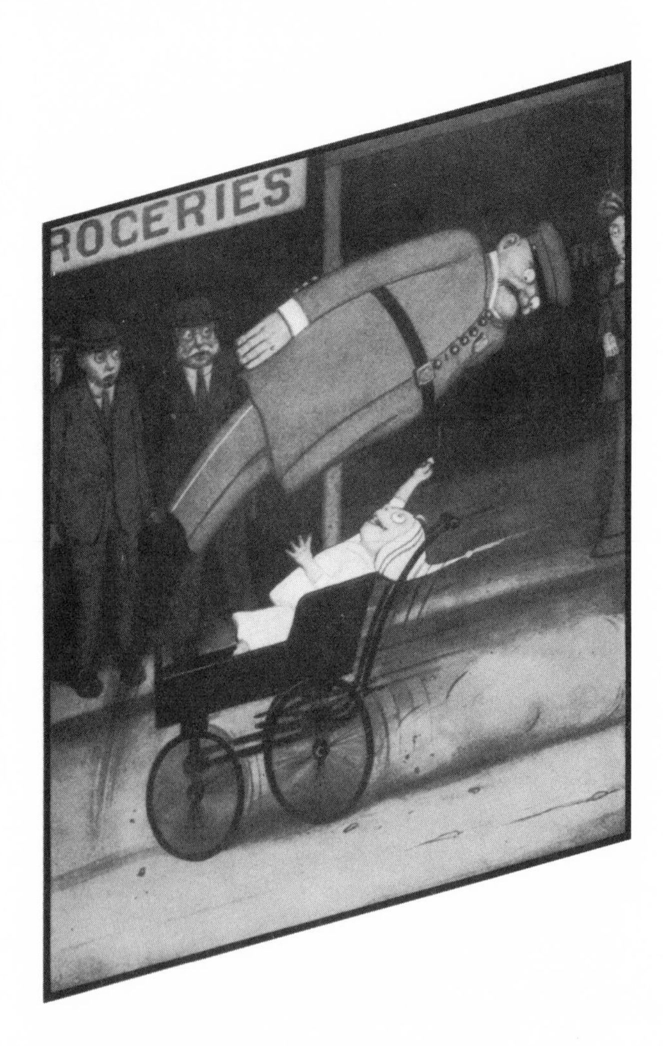

THE SLANT BOOK

Newell was somewhat restricted by Tenniel's original conceptions of the Mad Hatter, the March Hare, the Mock Turtle, the Cheshire Cat, and all the other odd personages; but the American brought them all to life vividly. The books were crammed with full-page halftone plates, and Newell had the luxury of depicting incidents that Tenniel, firmly under Lewis Carroll's thumb, had not had the opportunity to illustrate; even the least important subject was sympathetically treated by the new artist. Newell argued that all of Carroll's absurd creatures were "real characters on a common plane of humor, action, and interest," that *Alice's Adventures in*

Wonderland was a play in which each subordinate actor was as excellent in his way as the lead.

Newell's *Alice* was not to everyone's taste (he had chosen his daughter Josephine as his model), but Harper and Brothers was pleased enough with the new Carroll volumes to hire Newell to illustrate *Favorite Fairy Tales* (1907). This project, in the same elegant format as *Alice's Adventures in Wonderland,* collected classic children's stories recommended by such prominent public figures as Mark Twain, Henry James, Howard Pyle, Grover Cleveland, William Jennings Bryan, and Jane Addams. Although the text did have errors (for example, Charles Perrault is credited as the author of the English fairy tales "Jack the Giant Killer" and "Jack and the Beanstalk"), no such carelessness marred the fine illustrations. Known primarily as a humorist, Newell on occasion had illustrated travesties of nursery books; for example, Guy Wetmore Carryl's *Fables for the Frivolous* (1898) was an elaborate parody of La Fontaine's work, his *Mother Goose for Grown-Ups* (1900), a take-off of traditional nursery rhymes. Newell, however, in interpreting such selections as "The Gastronomic Guile of Simple Simon" and "The Opportune Overthrow of Humpty Dumpty," played it straight; his pictures in *Mother Goose for Grown-Ups* were appropriate for any conventional edition of Mother Goose rhymes. Likewise, in *Favorite Fairy Tales,* Newell successfully interpreted the histories of such nursery celebrities as Aladdin, Snow White and Rose Red, and Beauty and her Beast with uncommon grace and affection. The only disappointment with *Favorite Fairy Tales* is that, because the artist was restricted to one picture a story, there are far fewer plates in this collection than in the earlier *Alice* books.

With the growth of the Sunday comic strip at the turn of the century, Newell, one of the country's most talented comic illustrators, tried his hand at the new form. In "The Naps of Polly Sleepyhead," which appeared in the *New York Sunday Herald* beginning in 1906, Newell turned back to Lewis Carroll. Like Alice in Wonderland, Polly Sleepyhead went through marvelous adventures from which she awoke in the last frame. Newell's strip had been anticipated by Winsor McCay's classic "Little Nemo in Slumberland," which preceded "The Naps of Polly Sleepyhead" in the *Herald*'s Sunday funny papers. Although Newell's effort lacked the architectural extravagance of McCay's more famous dream series, "The Naps of Polly Sleepyhead" was beautifully drawn and possessed a simple, childlike humor. Perhaps too fragile to survive in the rough-and-tumble world of Buster Brown and the Katzenjammer Kids, Newell's delightful strip lasted only about a year.

Since his death on January 15, 1924, in Little Neck, Long Island, Peter Newell has been largely forgotten. He now receives scant mention in the popular studies of American illustration and children's book artists. Perhaps his gentle slapstick now seems dated, while the anarchistic violence of the Katzenjammer Kids remains au courant. Nevertheless, Newell was an original, and his contribution to American illustration is inestimable. Fortunately a few of Newell's picture books have recently been republished, so new readers may find amusement in the charming wit of one of America's most inventive illustrators.

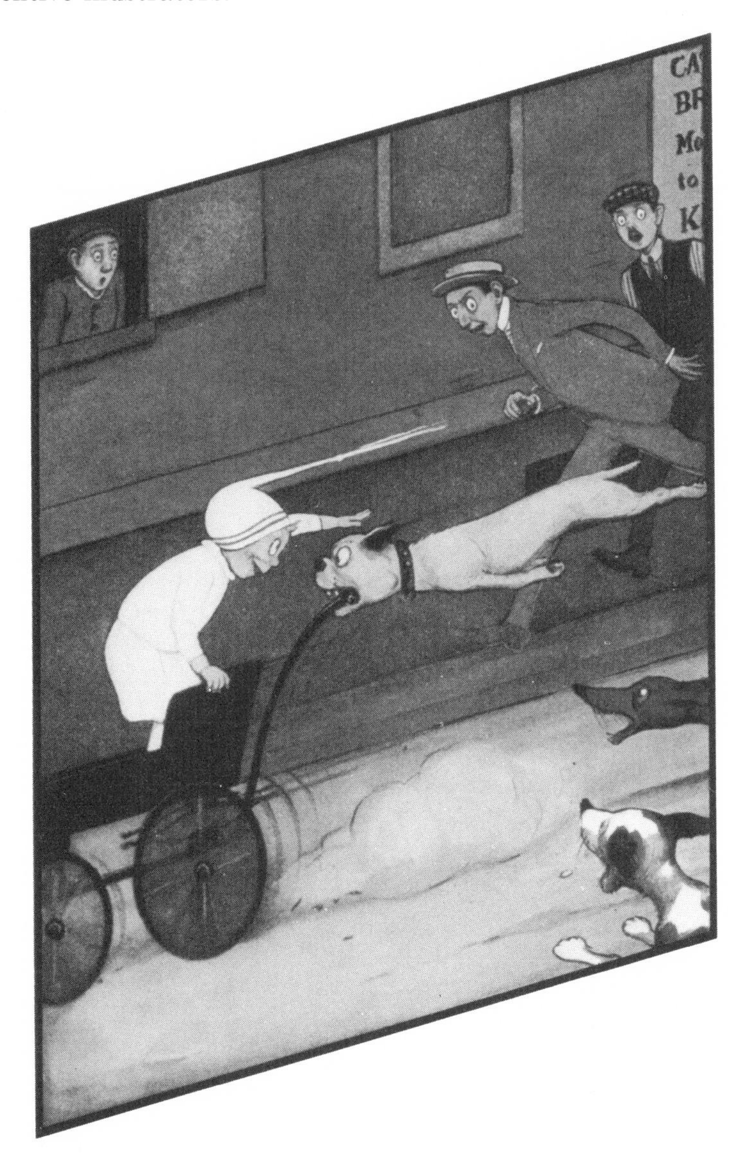

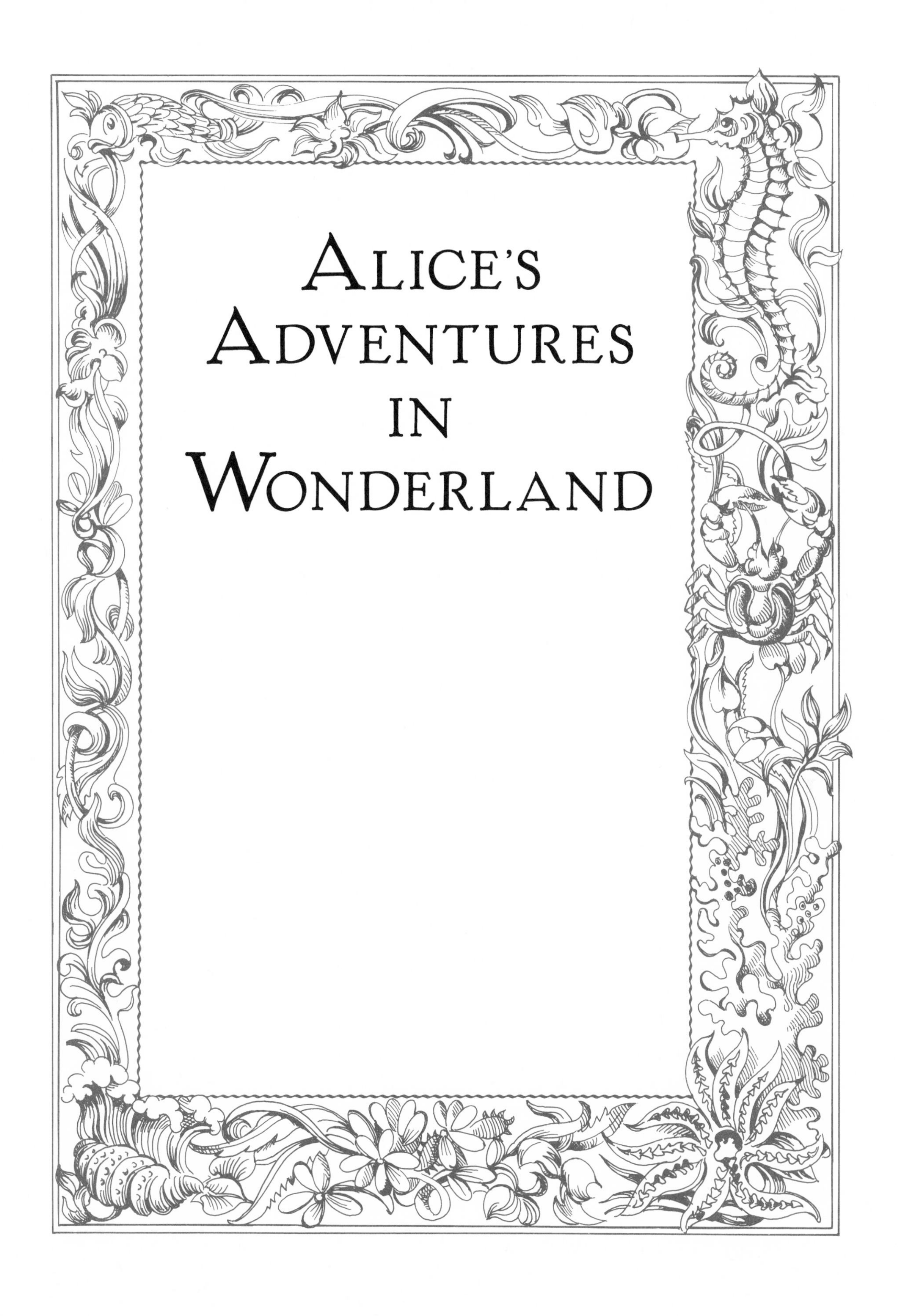

Alice's Adventures in Wonderland

ALICE'S ADVENTURES IN WONDERLAND

All in the golden afternoon[1]
Full leisurely we glide;
For both our oars, with little skill,
By little arms are plied,
While little hands make vain pretence
Our wanderings to guide.

Ah, cruel Three! In such an hour,
Beneath such dreamy weather,
To beg a tale of breath too weak
To stir the tiniest feather!
Yet what can one poor voice avail
Against three tongues together?

Imperious Prima flashes forth
Her edict "to begin it":
In gentler tones Secunda hopes
"There will be nonsense in it!"
While Tertia interrupts the tale
Not more *than once a minute.*

Anon, to sudden silence won,
In fancy they pursue
The dream-child moving through a land
Of wonders wild and new,
In friendly chat with bird or beast—
And half believe it true.

And ever, as the story drained
The wells of fancy dry,
And faintly strove that weary one
To put the subject by,
"The rest next time—" "It is *next time!"*
The happy voices cry.

1. July 4, 1862, was the "golden afternoon" on which Carroll and his friend the Reverend Robinson Duckworth took the three Liddell sisters on a rowing trip up the Thames. It was the occasion on which Carroll, amusing the children with extemporaneous yarns, first sent his "dream-child" (Secunda in the poem because she was the second oldest) down the rabbit hole. Note how the poem's first stanza puns three times on the word "little" ("Liddell" was pronounced to rhyme with "fiddle").

Carroll later spoke of the "cloudless blue above." Alice recalled the sun as "so burning" that they landed the boat to take refuge in some shade. In my note on this poem, in *The Annotated Alice,* I mentioned the distressing fact that a London meteorological office had recorded that on July 4, 1862, the weather near Oxford was "cool and rather wet." This was later confirmed by Philip Stewart, of Oxford University's Department of Forestry. He informed me in a letter that the *Astronomical and Meteorological Observations Made at the Radcliffe Observatory, Oxford,* Vol. 23, gives the weather on July 4 as rain after two P.M., cloud cover 10/10, and maximum shade temperature of 67.9 degrees Fahrenheit. These records support the view that Carroll and Alice confused their memories of the occasion with similar boating trips made on sunnier days.

The question remains controversial, however. For a well-argued defense of the conjecture that the day may have been dry and sunny after all, see "The Weather on Alice in Wonderland Day, 4 July 1862," by H. B. Doherty, of the Dublin Airport, in *Weather,* Vol. 23 (February 1968), pages 75–78.

Thus grew the tale of Wonderland:
Thus slowly, one by one,
Its quaint events were hammered out—
And now the tale is done,
And home we steer, a merry crew,
Beneath the setting sun.

Alice! A childish story take,
And, with a gentle hand,
Lay it where Childhood's dreams are twined
In Memory's mystic band.
Like pilgrim's wither'd wreath of flowers[2]
Pluck'd in a far-off land.

2. Pilgrims to the Holy Land often wore wreaths of flowers on their heads. Reader Howard Lees sent this quotation from the Prologue of Chaucer's *Canterbury Tales,* where the Summoner is described as follows:

> *He wore a garland set upon his head*
> *Large as the holly-bush upon a stake*
> *Outside an ale house. . . .*

Is not Carroll suggesting, Lees asks, "that Alice should store these tales in her childhood memory; the memory that, when she becomes an adult, is like a withered bunch of flowers plucked in the far-off land of childhood?"

A few years before writing this prefatory poem, Carroll photographed Alice with a wreath of flowers on her head. The picture is reproduced in Anne Clark's *Lewis Carroll: A Biography* (Schocken, 1979), opposite page 65.

Christmas-Greetings

[FROM A FAIRY TO A CHILD]

Lady dear, if Fairies may
For a moment lay aside
Cunning tricks and elfish play,
'Tis at happy Christmas-tide.

We have heard the children say—
Gentle children, whom we love—
Long ago, on Christmas Day,
Came a message from above.

Still, as Christmas-tide comes round,
They remember it again—
Echo still the joyful sound
"Peace on earth, good-will to men!"

Yet the hearts must childlike be
Where such heavenly guests abide;
Unto children, in their glee,
All the year is Christmas-tide!

Thus, forgetting tricks and play
For a moment, Lady dear,
We would wish you, if we may,
Merry Christmas, glad New Year!

Christmas, 1867

CHAPTER I
DOWN THE RABBIT-HOLE

lice was beginning to get very tired of sitting by her sister on the bank and of having nothing to do: once or twice she had peeped into the book her sister was reading, but it had no pictures or conversations in it, "and what is the use of a book," thought Alice, "without pictures or conversations?"

So she was considering, in her own mind (as well as she could, for the hot day made her feel very sleepy and stupid), whether the pleasure of making a daisy-chain would be worth the trouble of getting up and picking the daisies, when suddenly a White Rabbit with pink eyes ran close by her.

There was nothing so *very* remarkable in that; nor did Alice think it so *very* much out of the way to hear the Rabbit say to itself "Oh dear! Oh dear! I shall be too late!" (when she thought it over afterwards it occurred to her that she ought to have wondered at this, but at the time it all seemed quite natural); but, when the Rabbit actually *took a watch out of its waistcoat-*

pocket, and looked at it, and then hurried on, Alice started to her feet, for it flashed across her mind that she had never before seen a rabbit with either a waistcoat-pocket, or a watch to take out of it, and burning with curiosity, she ran across the field after it, and was just in time to see it pop down a large rabbit-hole under the hedge.

In another moment down went Alice after it, never once considering how in the world she was to get out again.

The rabbit-hole went straight on like a tunnel for some way, and then dipped suddenly down, so suddenly that Alice had not a moment to think about stopping herself before she found herself falling down what seemed to be a very deep well.

Either the well was very deep, or she fell very slowly, for she had plenty of time as she went down to look about her, and to wonder what was going to happen next. First, she tried to look down and make out what she was coming to, but it was too dark to see anything: then she looked at the sides of the well, and noticed that they were filled with cupboards and book-shelves: here and there she saw maps and pictures hung upon pegs. She took down a jar from one of the shelves as she passed: it was labeled "ORANGE MARMALADE," but to her great disappointment it was empty: she did not like to drop the jar, for fear of killing somebody underneath, so managed to put it into one of the cupboards as she fell past it.

"Well!" thought Alice to herself. "After such a fall as this, I shall think nothing of tumbling down-stairs! How brave they'll all think me at home! Why, I wouldn't say anything about it, even if I fell off the top of the house!" (Which was very likely true.)

Down, down, down. Would the fall *never* come to an end? "I wonder how many miles I've fallen by this time?" she said aloud. "I must be getting somewhere near the centre of the earth. Let me see: that would be four thousand miles down, I think—" (for, you see, Alice had learnt several things of this sort in her lessons in the school-room, and though this was not a *very* good opportunity for showing off her knowledge, as there was no one to listen to her, still it was good practice to say it over) "—yes, that's about the right distance—but then I wonder what Latitude or Longitude I've got to?" (Alice had not the slightest idea what Latitude was, or Longitude either, but she thought they were nice grand words to say.)

Presently she began again. "I wonder if I shall fall right *through* the earth! How funny it'll seem to come out among the people that walk with their heads downwards! The antipathies, I think—" (she was rather glad there *was* no one listening, this time, as it didn't sound at all the right word) "—but I shall have to ask them what the name of the country is, you know. Please, Ma'am, is this New Zealand? Or Australia?" (and she tried to curtsey as she spoke—fancy, *curtseying* as you're falling through the air! Do you think you could manage it?) "And what an ignorant little girl she'll think me for asking! No, it'll never do to ask: perhaps I shall see it written up somewhere."

Down, down, down. There was nothing else to do, so Alice soon began talking again. "Dinah'll miss me very much to-night, I should think!" (Dinah was the cat.)[1] "I hope they'll remember her saucer of milk at tea-time. Dinah, my dear! I wish you were down here with me! There are no mice in the air, I'm afraid , but you might catch a bat, and that's very like a mouse, you know. But do cats eat bats, I wonder?" And here Alice began to get rather sleepy, and went on saying to herself, in a dreamy sort of way, "Do cats eat bats? Do cats eat bats?" and sometimes "Do bats eat cats?" for, you see, as she couldn't answer either question, it didn't much matter which way she put it. She felt that she was dozing off, and had just begun to dream that she was walking hand in hand with Dinah, and was saying to her, very earnestly, "Now, Dinah, tell me the truth: did you ever eat a bat?" when suddenly, thump! thump! down she came upon a heap of sticks and dry leaves, and the fall was over.

Alice was not a bit hurt, and she jumped up on to her feet in a moment: she looked up, but it was all dark overhead: before her was another long passage, and the White Rabbit was still in sight, hurrying down it. There was not a moment to be lost: away went Alice like the wind, and was just in time to hear it say, as it turned a corner, "Oh my ears and whiskers, how late it's getting!" She was close behind it when she turned the corner, but the Rabbit was no longer to be seen: she found herself in a long, low hall, which was lit up by a row of lamps hanging from the roof.

There were doors all round the hall, but they were all locked; and when Alice had been all the way down one side and up the other, trying

1. The Liddell sisters were fond of the family's two tabby cats, Dinah and Villikens, named after a popular song, "Villikens and His Dinah." Dinah and her two kittens, Kitty and Snowdrop, reappear in the first chapter of the second *Alice* book, and later, in Alice's dream, as the red and white queens.

"Down she came upon a heap of dry leaves"

every door, she walked sadly down the middle, wondering how she was ever to get out again.

Suddenly she came upon a little three-legged table, all made of solid glass: there was nothing on it but a tiny golden key, and Alice's first idea was that this might belong to one of the doors of the hall; but, alas! either the locks were too large, or the key was too small, but at any rate it would not open any of them. However, on the second time round, she came upon a low curtain she had not noticed before, and behind it was a little door about fifteen inches high: she tried the little golden key in the lock, and to her great delight it fitted![2]

Alice opened the door and found that it led into a small passage, not much larger than a rat-hole: she knelt down and looked along the passage into the loveliest garden you ever saw.[3] How she longed to get out of that dark hall, and wander about among those beds of bright flowers and those cool fountains, but she could not even get her head through the doorway; "and even if my head *would* go through," thought poor Alice, "it would be of very little use without my shoulders. Oh, how I wish I could shut up like a telescope! I think I could, if I only knew how to begin." For, you see, so many out-of-the-way things had happened lately, that Alice had begun to think that very few things indeed were really impossible.

There seemed to be no use in waiting by the little door, so she went back to the table, half hoping she might find another key on it, or at any rate a book of rules for shutting people up like telescopes: this time she found a little bottle on it ("which certainly was not here before,"

2. A gold key that unlocked mysterious doors was a common object in Victorian fantasy. Here is the second stanza of Andrew Lang's "Ballade of the Bookworm":

> *One gift the fairies gave me (three*
> *They commonly bestowed of yore):*
> *The love of books, the golden key*
> *That opens the enchanted door.*

In his notes for an Oxford edition of the *Alice* books, Roger Green links this gold key to the magic key to Heaven in George MacDonald's famous fantasy tale "The Golden Key." The story first appeared in an 1867 book, *Dealings with Fairies,* two years after the publication of *Alice in Wonderland,* but Carroll and MacDonald were good friends and it is possible, Green writes, that Carroll saw the story in manuscript. MacDonald also wrote a poem titled "The Golden Key" that was published early enough (1861) for Carroll to have read it. The story is reprinted in Michael Hearn's splendid anthology *The Victorian Fairy Tale Book* (Pantheon, 1988).

3. T. S. Eliot revealed to the critic Louis L. Martz that he was thinking of this episode when he wrote the following lines for "Burnt Norton," the first poem in his *Four Quartets:*

> *Time present and time past*
> *Are both perhaps present in time future,*
> *And time future contained in time past.*
> *If all time is eternally present*
> *All time is unredeemable.*
> *What might have been is an abstraction*
> *Remaining a perpetual possibility*
> *Only in a world of speculation.*
> *What might have been and what has been*
> *Point to one end, which is always present.*
> *Footfalls echo in the memory*
> *Down the passage which we did not take*
> *Towards the door we never opened*
> *Into the rose-garden.*

The little door to a secret garden also appears in Eliot's *The Family Reunion.* It was for him a metaphor for events that might have been, had one opened certain doors.

said Alice), and tied around the neck of the bottle was a paper label, with the words "DRINK ME" beautifully printed on it in large letters.[4]

It was all very well to say "Drink me," but the wise little Alice was not going to do *that* in a hurry. "No, I'll look first," she said, "and see whether it's marked *'poison'* or not"; for she had read several nice little stories about children who had got burnt, and eaten up by wild beasts, and other unpleasant things, all because they *would* not remember the simple rules their friends had taught them:[5] such as, that a red-hot poker will burn you if you hold it too long; and that, if you cut your finger *very* deeply with a knife, it usually bleeds; and she had never forgotten that, if you drink much from a bottle marked "poison," it is almost certain to disagree with you, sooner or later.

However, this bottle was *not* marked "poison," so Alice ventured to taste it, and, finding it very nice (it had, in fact, a sort of mixed flavour of cherry-tart, custard, pine-apple, roast turkey, toffy, and hot buttered toast), she very soon finished it off.

*   *   *   *   *
  *   *   *   *
*   *   *   *   *

"What a curious feeling!" said Alice. "I must be shutting up like a telescope!"[6]

And so it was indeed: she was now only ten inches high, and her face brightened up at the thought that she was now the right size for going through the little door into that lovely garden. First, however, she waited for a few minutes to see if she was going to shrink any further: she felt a little nervous about this; "for it might end, you know," said Alice to herself,

4. The Victorian medicine bottle had neither a screw top nor a label on the side. It was corked, with a paper label tied to the neck.

5. The "nice little stories," Charles Lovett reminded me, were not so nice. They were the traditional fairy tales, filled with episodes of horror and usually containing a pious moral. By doing away with morals, the *Alice* books opened up a new genre of fiction for children.

6. This is the first of twelve occasions in the book on which Alice alters in size. Richard Ellmann has suggested that Carroll may have been unconsciously symbolizing the great disparity between the small Alice whom he loved but could not marry and the large Alice she would soon become. See "On Alice's Changes in Size in Wonderland," by Selwyn Goodacre, in *Jabberwocky* (Winter 1977), for many discrepancies in Tenniel's pictures with respect to Alice's size.

"The poor little thing sat down and cried"

"in my going out altogether, like a candle.[7] I wonder what I should be like then?" And she tried to fancy what the flame of a candle looks like after the candle is blown out, for she could not remember ever having seen such a thing.

After a while, finding that nothing more happened, she decided on going into the garden at once; but, alas for poor Alice![8] when she got to the door, she found she had forgotten the little golden key, and when she went back to the table for it, she found she could not possibly reach it: she could see it quite plainly through the glass, and she tried her best to climb up one of the legs of the table, but it was too slippery; and when she had tired herself out with trying, the poor little thing sat down and cried.

"Come, there's no use in crying like that!" said Alice to herself rather sharply. "I advise you to leave off this minute!" She generally gave herself very good advice (though she very seldom followed it), and sometimes she scolded herself so severely as to bring tears into her eyes; and once she remembered trying to box her own ears for having cheated herself in a game of croquet she was playing against herself, for this curious child was very fond of pretending to be two people.[9] "But it's no use now," thought poor Alice, "to pretend to be two people! Why, there's hardly enough of me left to make *one* respectable person!"

Soon her eye fell on a little glass box that was lying under the table: she opened it, and found in it a very small cake, on which the words "EAT ME" were beautifully marked in currants. "Well, I'll eat it," said Alice, "and if it makes me grow larger, I can reach the key; and

7. Note Tweedledum's use of the same candle-flame metaphor in the fourth chapter of the second *Alice* book.

8. "alas for poor Alice!": Did Carroll intend a pun on "alas"? It is hard to be sure, but there is no question about the intent in *Finnegans Wake* (Viking revised edition, page 528) when James Joyce writes: "Alicious, twinstreams twinestraines, through alluring glass or alas in jumboland?" And again (page 270): "Though Wonderlawn's lost us for ever. Alis, alas, she broke the glass! Liddell lokker through the leafery, ours is mistery of pain."

For the hundreds of references to Dodgson and the *Alice* books in *Finnegans Wake,* see Ann McGarrity Buki's excellent paper "Lewis Carroll in *Finnegans Wake,*" in *Lewis Carroll: A Celebration* (Clarkson N. Potter, 1982), edited by Edward Guiliano, and J. S. Atherton's earlier paper "Lewis Carroll and *Finnegans Wake,*" in *English Studies* (February 1952). Most of the allusions are not in dispute, though what is one to make of such oddities as the identical initial letters of the names Alice Pleasance Liddell and Anna Livia Plurabelle? Is it a coincidence, like the correspondences in the names of Carroll and Alice (noticed by reader Dennis Green) with respect to word lengths, and the positions of vowels, consonants, and double letters in the last names?

ALICE LIDDELL
LEWIS CARROLL

More letterplay: Consider the initial consonants of "Dear Lewis Carroll." Backwards they are the initials of Charles Lutwidge Dodgson.

Of more serious interest is the fact that Alice had a son named Caryl Liddell Hargreaves. Another coincidence? Alice's one major romance, before she married Reginald Hargreaves, was with England's Prince Leopold. They met when he was a Christ Church undergraduate. Queen Victoria considered unthinkable his marrying anyone other than a princess, and Mrs. Liddell agreed. Alice wore a gift from the prince on her wedding gown, and she named her second son Leopold. A few weeks later, Prince Leopold, married to a princess, named a daughter Alice. It is hard to believe that when Alice called her third son Caryl she did not have her old mathema-

if it makes me grow smaller, I can creep under the door: so either way I'll get into the garden, and I don't care which happens!"

She ate a little bit, and said anxiously to herself "Which way? Which way?", holding her hand on the top of her head to feel which way it was growing; and she was quite surprised to find that she remained the same size. To be sure, this is what generally happens when one eats cake; but Alice had got so much into the way of expecting nothing but out-of-the-way things to happen, that it seemed quite dull and stupid for life to go on in the common way.

So she set to work, and very soon finished off the cake.

tician friend in mind, but according to Anne Clark, in her marvelous book *The Real Alice* (Stein & Day, 1982), Alice always insisted that the name came from a novel. The novel's identity is unknown.

9. There is no evidence, Denis Crutch and R. B. Shaberman maintain in their booklet *Under the Quizzing Glass* (Magpie Press, 1972), that Alice Liddell liked to pretend she was two people. However, in keeping with their contention that Carroll injected much of himself into his fictional Alice, they remind us that Carroll was always careful to keep separate Charles Dodgson, the Oxford mathematician, and Lewis Carroll, writer of children's books and lover of little girls.

CHAPTER II

THE POOL OF TEARS

"Curiouser and curiouser!" cried Alice (she was so much surprised, that for the moment she quite forgot how to speak good English). "Now I'm opening out like the largest telescope that ever was! Good-bye, feet!" (for when she looked down at her feet, they seemed to be almost out of sight, they were getting so far off). "Oh, my poor little feet, I wonder who will put on your shoes and stockings for you now, dears? I'm sure *I* sha'n't be able! I shall be a great deal too far off to trouble myself about you: you must manage the best way you can—but I must be kind to them," thought Alice, "or perhaps they wo'n't walk the way I want to go! Let me see. I'll give them a new pair of boots every Christmas."

And she went on planning to herself how she would manage it. "They must go by the carrier," she thought; "and how funny it'll seem, sending presents to one's own feet! And how odd the directions will look!

" 'Now I'm opening out like the largest telescope that ever was!' "

Alice's Right Foot, Esq.[1]
Hearthrug,
near the Fender,
(with Alice's love).

1. Selwyn Goodacre suspects that when Alice addresses her right foot as "Esquire," Carroll may have intended a subtle English/French joke. The French word for "foot" is *pied.* Its gender is masculine regardless of the owner's sex.

Oh dear, what nonsense I'm talking!"

Just at this moment her head struck against the roof of the hall: in fact she was now rather more than nine feet high, and she at once took up the little golden key and hurried off to the garden door.

Poor Alice! It was as much as she could do, lying down on one side, to look through into the garden with one eye; but to get through was more hopeless than ever: she sat down and began to cry again.

"You ought to be ashamed of yourself," said Alice, "a great girl like you," (she might well say this), "to go on crying in this way! Stop this moment, I tell you!" But she went on all the same, shedding gallons of tears, until there was a large pool around her, about four inches deep, and reaching half down the hall.

After a time she heard a little pattering of feet in the distance, and she hastily dried her eyes to see what was coming. It was the White Rabbit returning, splendidly dressed, with a pair of white kid-gloves in one hand and a large fan in the other: he came trotting along in a great hurry, muttering to himself, as he came, "Oh! The Duchess, the Duchess! Oh! *Wo'n't* she be savage if I've kept her waiting!" Alice felt so desperate that she was ready to ask help of any one: so, when the Rabbit came near her, she began, in a low, timid voice, "If you please, Sir—" The Rabbit started violently, dropped

2. In his original story, *Alice's Adventures Under Ground,* the names are Gertrude and Florence; these were cousins of Alice Liddell.

the white kid-gloves and the fan, and scurried away into the darkness as hard as he could go.

Alice took up the fan and gloves, and, as the hall was very hot, she kept fanning herself all the time she went on talking. "Dear, dear! How queer everything is to-day! And yesterday things went on just as usual. I wonder if I've changed in the night? Let me think: was I the same when I got up this morning? I almost think I can remember feeling a little different. But if I'm not the same, the next question is 'Who in the world am I?' Ah, *that's* the great puzzle!" And she began thinking over all the children she knew that were of the same age as herself, to see if she could have been changed for any of them.

"I'm sure I'm not Ada," she said, "for her hair goes in such long ringlets, and mine doesn't go in ringlets at all; and I'm sure I ca'n't be Mabel,[2] for I know all sorts of things, and she, oh, she knows such a very little! Besides, *she's* she, and *I'm* I, and—oh dear, how puzzling it all is! I'll try if I know all the things I used to know. Let me see: four times five is twelve, and four times six is thirteen, and four times seven is—oh dear! I shall never get to twenty at that rate! However, the Multiplication-Table doesn't signify: let's try Geography. London is the capital of Paris, and Paris is the capital of Rome, and Rome—no, *that's* all wrong, I'm certain! I must have been changed for Mabel! I'll try and say *'How doth the little—',*" and she crossed her hands on her lap as if she were saying lessons, and began to repeat it, but her voice sounded hoarse and strange, and the words did not come the same as they used to do:—

"The Rabbit started violently"

3. Almost all the poems in the *Alice* books are parodies of poems or songs well known in Carroll's day. (The originals are given in full in my *AA.*) Here Carroll has selected the lazy crocodile, an animal far removed from the ever-busy bee, to parody "Against Idleness and Mischief," a poem by Isaac Watts that begins:

How doth the little busy bee
Improve each shining hour,
And gather honey all the day
From every opening flower!

"How doth the little crocodile[3]
Improve his shining tail,
And pour the waters of the Nile
On every golden scale!

"How cheerfully he seems to grin,
How neatly spreads his claws,
And welcomes little fishes in,
With gently smiling jaws!

"I'm sure those are not the right words," said poor Alice, and her eyes filled with tears again as she went on, "I must be Mabel after all, and I shall have to go and live in that poky little house, and have next to no toys to play with, and oh, ever so many lessons to learn! No, I've made up my mind about it: if I'm Mabel, I'll stay down here. It'll be no use their putting their heads down and saying 'Come up again, dear!' I shall only look up and say 'Who am I, then? Tell me that first, and then, if I like being that person, I'll come up: if not, I'll stay down here till I'm somebody else'—but, oh dear!" cried Alice, with a sudden burst of tears, "I do wish they *would* put their heads down! I am so *very* tired of being all alone here!"

As she said this she looked down at her hands, and was surprised to see that she had put on one of the Rabbit's little white kid-gloves while she was talking. "How *can* I have done that?" she thought. "I must be growing small again." She got up and went to the table to measure herself by it, and found that, as nearly as she could guess, she was now about two feet high, and was going on shrinking rapidly: she soon found out that the cause of this was the fan she was holding, and she dropped it hastily, just in time to save herself from shrinking away altogether.

"That *was* a narrow escape!" said Alice, a good deal frightened at the sudden change, but very glad to find herself still in existence. "And now for the garden!" And she ran with all speed back to the little door; but, alas! the little door was shut again, and the little golden key was lying on the glass table as before, "and things are worse than ever," thought the poor child, "for I never was so small as this before, never! And I declare it's too bad, that it is!"

As she said these words her foot slipped, and in another moment, splash! she was up to her chin in saltwater. Her first idea was that she had somehow fallen into the sea, "and in that case I can go back by railway," she said to herself. (Alice had been to the seaside once in her life, and had come to the general conclusion that wherever you go to on the English coast, you find a number of bathing-machines in the sea, some children digging in the sand with wooden spades, then a row of lodging-houses, and behind them a railway station.) However, she soon made out that she was in the pool of tears which she had wept when she was nine feet high.

"I wish I hadn't cried so much!" said Alice, as she swam about, trying to find her way out. "I shall be punished for it now, I suppose, by being drowned in my own tears! That *will* be a queer thing, to be sure! However, everything is queer to-day."

Just then she heard something splashing about in the pool a little way off, and she swam nearer to make out what it was: at first she thought it must be a walrus or hippopotamus, but then she remembered how small she was now, and she soon made out that it was only a mouse, that had slipped in like herself.

"Would it be of any use, now," thought Alice, "to speak to this mouse? Everything is so out-of-the-way down here, that I should think very likely it can talk: at any rate, there's no harm in trying." So she began: "O Mouse, do you know the way out of this pool? I am very tired of swimming about here, O Mouse!" (Alice thought this must be the right way of speaking to a mouse: she had never done such a thing before, but she remembered having seen, in her brother's Latin Grammar,[4] "A mouse—of a mouse—to a mouse—a mouse—O mouse!") The mouse looked at her rather inquisitively, and seemed to her to wink with one of its little eyes, but it said nothing.

"Perhaps it doesn't understand English," thought Alice. "I daresay it's a French mouse, come over with William the Conqueror." (For, with all her knowledge of history, Alice had no very clear notion how long ago anything had happened.) So she began again: "Où est ma chatte?" which was the first sentence in her French lesson-book.[5] The Mouse gave a sudden leap out of the water, and seemed to quiver all over with fright. "Oh, I beg your pardon!" cried Alice hastily, afraid that she had hurt the poor animal's feelings. "I quite forgot you didn't like cats."

"Not like cats!" cried the Mouse in a shrill passionate voice. "Would *you* like cats, if you were me?"

"Well, perhaps not," said Alice in a soothing

4. In his article "In Search of Alice's Brother's Latin Grammar," in *Jabberwocky* (Spring 1975), Selwyn Goodacre argues that the book may have been *The Comic Latin Grammar* (1840). It was anonymously written by Percival Leigh, a writer for *Punch,* with illustrations by *Punch* cartoonist John Leech. Carroll owned a first edition.

Only one noun in the book is declined in full: *musa,* the Latin word for "muse." Goodacre suggests that Alice, "looking over her brother's shoulder at his Latin Grammar, mistook *musa* for *mus,*" the Latin word for "mouse." Further comments on this speculation appear in *Jabberwocky* (Spring 1977).

5. Hugh O'Brien, writing on "The French Lesson Book" in *Notes and Queries* (December 1963), identified the book as *La Bagatelle* (1804).

"The Mouse gave a sudden leap out of the water"

tone: "don't be angry about it. And yet I wish I could show you our cat Dinah. I think you'd take a fancy to cats, if you could only see her. She is such a dear quiet thing," Alice went on, half to herself, as she swam lazily about in the pool, "and she sits purring so nicely by the fire, licking her paws and washing her face—and she is such a nice soft thing to nurse—and she's such a capital one for catching mice—oh, I beg your pardon!" cried Alice again, for this time the Mouse was bristling all over, and she felt certain it must be really offended. "We wo'n't talk about her any more, if you'd rather not."

"We, indeed!" cried the Mouse, who was trembling down to the end of its tail. "As if *I* would talk on such a subject! Our family always *hated* cats: nasty, low, vulgar things! Don't let me hear the name again!"

"I wo'n't indeed!" said Alice, in a great hurry to change the subject of conversation. "Are you—are you fond—of—of dogs?" The Mouse did not answer, so Alice went on eagerly: "There is such a nice little dog, near our house, I should like to show you! A little bright-eyed terrier, you know, with oh, such long curly brown hair! And it'll fetch things when you throw them, and it'll sit up and beg for its dinner, and all sorts of things—I ca'n't remember half of them—and it belongs to a farmer, you know, and he says it's so useful, it's worth a hundred pounds! He says it kills all the rats and—oh dear!" cried Alice in a sorrowful tone. "I'm afraid I've offended it again!" For the Mouse was swimming away from her as hard as it could go, and making quite a commotion in the pool as it went.

So she called softly after it, "Mouse dear! Do come back again, and we wo'n't talk about cats, or dogs either, if you don't like them!" When the Mouse heard this, it turned round and swam slowly back to her: its face was quite pale (with passion, Alice thought), and it said, in a low trembling voice, "Let us get to the shore, and then I'll tell you my history, and you'll understand why it is I hate cats and dogs."

It was high time to go, for the pool was getting quite crowded with the birds and animals that had fallen into it: there was a Duck and a Dodo, a Lory and an Eaglet, and several other curious creatures.[6] Alice led the way, and the whole party swam to the shore.

6. Note the ape in Newell's pictures of the "curious creatures" in Chapter 3. It is nowhere mentioned in the text of this book or in the original manuscript, *Alice's Adventures Under Ground,* although Carroll did put an ape in his own drawing of the creatures, and Tenniel has an ape in two of his illustrations. It has been suggested that Tenniel intended his ape to be a caricature of Charles Darwin. This seems unlikely. The face of Tenniel's ape, in his second picture, exactly duplicates that of an ape in his political cartoon in *Punch* (October 11, 1856), where the ape represents "King Bomba," the nickname for Ferdinand II, King of the Two Sicilies.

The flightless dodo became extinct about 1681. Charles Lovett informed me that the Oxford University Museum, which Carroll often visited with the Liddell children, contained (and still does) the remains of a dodo, and a famous painting of the bird by John Savory. The dodo was native to the island of Mauritius in the Indian Ocean. Dutch sailors and colonists killed the "disgusting birds," as they called them, for food, and their eggs (just one to a nest) were eaten by the farm animals of the early settlers. The dodo is one of the earliest examples of an animal species totally exterminated by the human species.

Carroll's Dodo was intended as a caricature of himself—his stammer is said to have made him pronounce his name "Do-do-Dodgson." The Duck is the Reverend Robinson Duckworth, who often accompanied Carroll on boating expeditions with the Liddell sisters. The Lory, an Australian parrot, is Lorina, who was the eldest of the sisters (this explains why, in the second paragraph of the next chapter, she says to Alice, "I'm older than you, and must know better"). Edith Liddell is the Eaglet. The episode that follows draws on an actual boating trip when the "curious party" was caught in a rainstorm (see my note in *AA*).

CHAPTER III

A CAUCUS-RACE AND A LONG TALE

They were indeed a queer-looking party that assembled on the bank—the birds with draggled feathers, the animals with their fur clinging close to them, and all dripping wet, cross, and uncomfortable.

The first question of course was, how to get dry again: they had a consultation about this, and after a few minutes it seemed quite natural to Alice to find herself talking familiarly with them, as if she had known them all her life. Indeed, she had quite a long argument with the Lory, who at last turned sulky, and would only say, "I'm older than you, and must know better." And this Alice would not allow, without knowing how old it was, and as the Lory positively refused to tell its age, there was no more to be said.

At last the Mouse, who seemed to be a person of some authority among them, called out "Sit down, all of you, and listen to me! *I'll* soon make you dry enough!" They all sat down at once, in a large ring, with the Mouse in the middle. Alice kept her eyes anxiously fixed on it, for she felt sure she would catch a bad cold if she did not get dry very soon.

"Ahem!" said the Mouse with an important air. "Are you all ready? This is the driest thing I know. Silence all round, if you please! 'William the Conqueror, whose cause was favoured by the pope, was soon submitted to by the English, who wanted leaders, and had been of late much accustomed to usurpation and conquest. Edwin and Morcar, the earls of Mercia and Northumbria—' "

"Ugh!" said the Lory, with a shiver.

"I beg your pardon!" said the Mouse, frowning, but very politely. "Did you speak?"

"Not I!" said the Lory, hastily.

"I thought you did," said the Mouse. "I proceed. 'Edwin and Morcar, the earls of Mercia and Northumbria, declared for him; and even Stigand, the patriotic archbishop of Canterbury, found it advisable—' "

"Found *what*?" said the Duck.

"Found *it,*" the Mouse replied rather crossly: "of course you know what 'it' means."

"I know what 'it' means well enough, when *I* find a thing," said the Duck: "it's generally a frog, or a worm. The question is, what did the archbishop find?"

The Mouse did not notice this question, but hurriedly went on, "—found it advisable to go with Edgar Atheling to meet William and offer him the crown. William's conduct at first was moderate. But the insolence of his Normans—' How are you getting on now, my dear?" it continued, turning to Alice as it spoke.

"As wet as ever," said Alice in a melancholy tone: "it doesn't seem to dry me at all."

"In that case," said the Dodo solemnly, rising to its feet, "I move that the meeting adjourn, for the immediate adoption of more energetic remedies—"

"Speak English!" said the Eaglet. "I don't know the meaning of half those long words, and, what's more, I don't believe you do either!" And the Eaglet bent down its head to hide a smile: some of the other birds tittered audibly.

"What I was going to say," said the Dodo in an offended tone, "was that the best thing to get us dry would be a Caucus-race."

"What *is* a Caucus-race?" said Alice; not that she much wanted to know, but the Dodo had paused as if it thought that *somebody* ought to speak, and no one else seemed inclined to say anything.

"Why," said the Dodo, "the best way to explain it is to do it." (And, as you might like to try the thing yourself some winter-day, I will tell you how the Dodo managed it.)

First it marked out a race-course, in a sort of circle, ("the exact shape doesn't matter," it said,) and then all the party were placed along the course, here and there. There was no "One, two, three, and away!", but they began running when they liked, and left off when they liked, so that it was not easy to know when the race was over. However, when they had been running half an hour or so, and were quite dry again, the Dodo suddenly called out "The race is over!" and they all crowded round it, panting, and asking "But who has won?"

This question the Dodo could not answer without a great deal of thought, and it stood for

The Caucus-Race

a long time with one finger pressed upon its forehead (the position in which you usually see Shakespeare, in the pictures of him), while the rest waited in silence. At last the Dodo said "*Everybody* has won, and *all* must have prizes."

"But who is to give the prizes?" quite a chorus of voices asked.

"Why, *she,* of course," said the Dodo, pointing to Alice with one finger; and the whole party at once crowded round her, calling out, in a confused way, "Prizes! Prizes!"

Alice had no idea what to do, and in despair she put her hand in her pocket, and pulled out a box of comfits (luckily the saltwater had not got into it), and handed them round as prizes. There was exactly one a-piece, all round.

"But she must have a prize herself, you know," said the Mouse.

"Of course," the Dodo replied very gravely. "What else have you got in your pocket?" it went on, turning to Alice.

"Only a thimble," said Alice sadly.

"Hand it over here," said the Dodo.

Then they all crowded round her once more, while the Dodo solemnly presented the thimble, saying "We beg your acceptance of this elegant thimble";[1] and, when it had finished this short speech, they all cheered.

Alice thought the whole thing very absurd, but they all looked so grave that she did not dare to laugh; and, as she could not think of anything to say, she simply bowed, and took the thimble, looking as solemn as she could.

The next thing was to eat the comfits: this caused some noise and confusion, as the large birds complained that they could not taste

1. In my note on the Caucus-race in *AA,* I argue that Carroll intended the race to satirize the behavior of political parties in England. If so, the thimble, taken from Alice and then returned to her, may symbolize the way governments take taxes from the pockets of citizens, then return the money in the form of political projects. See "The Dodo and the Caucus Race," by Narda Lacey Schwartz, in *Jabberwocky* (Winter 1977), and "The Caucus-Race in *Alice in Wonderland:* A Very Drying Exercise," by August Imholtz, Jr., in *Jabberwocky* (Autumn 1981). The running in the Caucus-race, according to Alfreda Blanchard in *Jabberwocky* (Summer 1982), may signify the running of politicians for office.

In his drawing of this scene Tenniel was forced to put human hands under the Dodo's small, degenerate wings. How else could it hold a thimble? Newell solves the problem by attaching five fingers to the ends of the wings. The symbol at the lower right corner, which you see on all of Tenniel's drawings, is a monogram of his initials, J. T.

"The Dodo solemnly presented the thimble"

theirs, and the small ones choked and had to be patted on the back. However, it was over at last, and they sat down again in a ring, and begged the Mouse to tell them something more.

"You promised to tell me your history, you know," said Alice, "and why it is you hate—C and D," she added in a whisper, half afraid that it would be offended again.

"Mine is a long and sad tale!" said the Mouse, turning to Alice, and sighing.

"It *is* a long tail, certainly," said Alice, looking down with wonder at the Mouse's tail; "but why do you call it sad?" And she kept on puzzling about it while the mouse was speaking, so that her idea of the tale was something like this:—[2]

"Fury said to
a mouse, That
he met in the
house, 'Let
us both go
to law: *I*
will prose-
cute *you.*—
Come, I'll
take no de-
nial: We
must have
the trial;
For really
this morn-
ing I've
nothing
to do.'
Said the
mouse to
the cur,
'Such a
trial, dear
sir, With
no jury
or judge,
would
be wast-
ing our
breath.'
'I'll be
judge,
I'll be
jury,'
said
cun-
ning
old
Fury:
'I'll
try
the
whole
cause,
and
con-
demn
you to
death."

2. See the note in *AA* for the original version of the mouse-tail poem as it appeared in *Alice's Adventures Under Ground,* and for comments on the tail in general. I did not know, until I read about it in *Under the Quizzing Glass,* by R. B. Shaberman and Denis Crutch, that Carroll once proposed an additional change in the poem's final quatrain. It was among thirty-seven corrections that he listed in his copy of the 1866 edition of the book. The revised stanza would have been:

Said the mouse to the cur, "Such a trial, dear sir,
With no jury or judge, would be tedious and dry."
"I'll be judge, I'll be jury," said cunning old Fury;
"I'll try the whole cause, and condemn you to die."

For some reason the change was never made. The tail's shape has varied widely, and still does, from printing to printing, both in English and in translations. See David H. Schaeffer's monograph *Lewis Carroll's Mouse's Tail: The Saga of Its Journey Around the World and Through a Computer* (privately printed, 1970).

Fury was the name of a fox terrier owned by Carroll's child-friend Eveline Hull. Morton Cohen, in a note on page 358 of *The Letters of Lewis Carroll* (Oxford, 1979), speculates that the dog was named after the cur in the mouse's tale. He quotes an entry from Carroll's diary (omitted from the published version) telling how Fury developed hydrophobia and had to be shot, which was done in Carroll's presence.

" 'Mine is a long and sad tale,' said the Mouse"

"You are not attending!" said the Mouse to Alice, severely. "What are you thinking of?"

"I beg your pardon," said Alice very humbly: "you had got to the fifth bend, I think?"

"I had *not*!" cried the Mouse, sharply and very angrily.

"A knot!" said Alice, always ready to make herself useful, and looking anxiously about her. "Oh, do let me help to undo it!"

"I shall do nothing of the sort," said the Mouse, getting up and walking away. "You insult me by talking such nonsense!"

"I didn't mean it!" pleaded poor Alice. "But you're so easily offended, you know!"

The Mouse only growled in reply.

"Please come back, and finish your story!" Alice called after it. And the others all joined in chorus "Yes, please do!" But the Mouse only shook its head impatiently, and walked a little quicker.

"What a pity it wouldn't stay!" sighed the Lory, as soon as it was quite out of sight. And an old Crab took the opportunity of saying to her daughter "Ah, my dear! Let this be a lesson to you never to lose *your* temper!" "Hold your tongue, Ma!" said the young Crab, a little snappishly. "You're enough to try the patience of an oyster!"

"I wish I had our Dinah here, I know I do!" said Alice aloud, addressing nobody in particular. "*She'd* soon fetch it back!"

"And who is Dinah, if I might venture to ask the question?" said the Lory.

Alice replied eagerly, for she was always ready to talk about her pet: "Dinah's our cat. And she's such a capital one for catching mice,

"On various pretexts they all moved off"

you ca'n't think! And oh, I wish you could see her after the birds! Why, she'll eat a little bird as soon as look at it!"

This speech caused a remarkable sensation among the party. Some of the birds hurried off at once: one old Magpie began wrapping itself up very carefully, remarking "I really must be getting home: the night-air doesn't suit my throat!" And a Canary called out in a trembling voice, to its children, "Come away, my dears! It's high time you were all in bed!" On various pretexts they all moved off, and Alice was soon left alone.

"I wish I hadn't mentioned Dinah!" she said to herself in a melancholy tone. "Nobody seems to like her, down here, and I'm sure she's the best cat in the world! Oh, my dear Dinah! I wonder if I shall ever see you any more!" And here poor Alice began to cry again, for she felt very lonely and low-spirited. In a little while, however, she again heard a little pattering of footsteps in the distance, and she looked up eagerly, half hoping that the Mouse had changed his mind, and was coming back to finish his story.

CHAPTER IV

THE RABBIT SENDS IN A LITTLE BILL

It was the White Rabbit, trotting slowly back again, and looking anxiously about as it went, as if it had lost something; and she heard it muttering to itself, "The Duchess! The Duchess! Oh my dear paws! Oh my fur and whiskers! She'll get me executed, as sure as ferrets are ferrets![1] Where *can* I have dropped them, I wonder?" Alice guessed in a moment that it was looking for the fan and the pair of white kid-gloves, and she very good-naturedly began hunting about for them, but they were nowhere to be seen—everything seemed to have changed since her swim in the pool; and the great hall, with the glass table and the little door, had vanished completely.

Very soon the Rabbit noticed Alice, as she went hunting about, and called out to her, in an angry tone, "Why, Mary Ann,[2] what *are* you doing out here? Run home this moment, and fetch me a pair of gloves and a fan! Quick, now!" And Alice was so much frightened that she ran off at once in the direction it pointed to,

1. In *Alice's Adventures Under Ground* the White Rabbit exclaims: "The Marchioness! The Marchioness! oh my dear paws! oh my fur and whiskers! She'll have me executed as sure as ferrets are ferrets!" There is no Duchess in this first version of the story; we later learn from the White Rabbit: "The Queen's the Marchioness: didn't you know that?" And he adds: "Queen of Hearts and Marchioness of Mock Turtles."

We learn in the "Pig and Pepper" chapter that the White Rabbit's fear is justified, because the Duchess shouts at Alice, "Talking of axes, chop off her head!" Selwyn Goodacre thinks it out of character for a duchess to order executions. He suggests that Carroll introduced the Duchess's remark in an effort to harmonize the story with the White Rabbit's exclamation in the earlier version.

Ferrets are a semidomesticated variety of the English polecat, used mainly for hunting rabbits and mice. They are usually yellowish white, with pink eyes. The White Rabbit had good reason to refer to ferrets in his fear of being "executed." Here is a passage from Oliver Goldsmith's section on "The Ferret" in his *History of the Earth and Animated Nature:*

> It is naturally such an enemy of the rabbit kind, that if a dead rabbit be presented to a young ferret, although it has never seen one before, it instantly attacks and bites it with an appearance of rapacity. If the rabbit be living, the ferret is still more eager, seizes it by

“ ‘Why, Mary Ann, what *are* you doing here?’ ”

without trying to explain the mistake that it had made.

"He took me for his housemaid," she said to herself as she ran. "How surprised he'll be when he finds out who I am! But I'd better take him his fan and gloves—that is, if I can find them." As she said this, she came upon a neat little house, on the door of which was a bright brass plate with the name "W. RABBIT" engraved upon it. She went in without knocking, and hurried upstairs, in great fear lest she should meet the real Mary Ann, and be turned out of the house before she had found the fan and gloves.

"How queer it seems," Alice said to herself, "to be going messages for a rabbit! I suppose Dinah'll be sending me on messages next!" And she began fancying the sort of thing that would happen: " 'Miss Alice! Come here directly, and get ready for your walk!' 'Coming in a minute, nurse! But I've got to watch this mouse-hole till Dinah comes back, and see that the mouse doesn't get out.' Only I don't think," Alice went on, "that they'd let Dinah stop in the house if it began ordering people about like that!"

By this time she had found her way into a tidy little room with a table in the window, and on it (as she had hoped) a fan and two or three pairs of tiny white kid-gloves: she took up the fan and a pair of the gloves, and was just going to leave the room, when her eye fell upon a little bottle that stood near the looking-glass. There was no label this time with the words "DRINK ME," but nevertheless she uncorked it and put it to her lips. "I know *something* interesting is sure to happen," she said to herself, "whenever

> the neck, winds itself round it, and continues to suck its blood, till it be satiated.

In addition to the use of "ferret" as a verb, the word was colloquially applied in England to thieving moneylenders. According to Peter Heath's note in *The Philosopher's Alice* (St. Martin's, 1974), the phrase "as sure as ferrets are ferrets" was current in Carroll's day. Heath cites its use in one of Anthony Trollope's novels.

As Carroll notes in his *Nursery "Alice,"* Tenniel drew a ferret among the twelve jurors for the trial of the Knave of Hearts. In Newell's picture of the jurors (Chapter 12), the tail you see at the lower left is, I think, that of a ferret.

2. According to Roger Green, "Mary Ann" was at the time a British euphemism for "servant girl." Dodgson's friend Mrs. Julia Cameron, a passionate amateur photographer, actually had a fifteen-year-old housemaid named Mary Anne, and there is a photograph of her in Anne Clark's biography of Carroll to prove it. Mary Anne Paragon was the dishonest servant who took care of David Copperfield's house (see Chapter 44 of the Dickens novel). Her nature, we are told, was "feebly expressed" by her last name.

Slang dictionaries give other meanings to "Mary Ann" that were current in Carroll's day. A dressmaker's dress-stand was called a Mary Ann. Later the name became attached to women, especially in Sheffield, who attacked sweat-shop owners. Still later it became a vulgar term for sodomites.

Before the French Revolution "Mary Anne" was a generic term for secret republican organizations, as well as a slang term for the guillotine. "Marianne" became and still is a mythic female symbol of republican virtues, a French symbol comparable to England's John Bull and our Uncle Sam. She is traditionally depicted, in political cartoons and statuettes, as wearing the red Phrygian, or liberty, bonnet worn by republicans in the French Revolution. It is probably coincidental that Carroll's use of the name anticipates the obsession with beheading shared by the Duchess and the Queen of Hearts.

I eat or drink anything: so I'll just see what this bottle does. I do hope it'll make me grow large again, for really I'm quite tired of being such a tiny little thing!"

It did so indeed, and much sooner than she had expected: before she had drunk half the bottle, she found her head pressing against the ceiling, and had to stoop to save her neck from being broken. She hastily put down the bottle, saying to herself "That's quite enough—I hope I sha'n't grow any more—As it is, I ca'n't get out at the door—I do wish I hadn't drunk quite so much!"

Alas! It was too late to wish that! She went on growing, and growing, and very soon had to kneel down on the floor: in another minute there was not even room for this, and she tried the effect of lying down with one elbow against the door, and the other arm curled round her head. Still she went on growing, and, as a last resource, she put one arm out of the window, and one foot up the chimney, and said to herself "Now I can do no more, whatever happens. What *will* become of me?"

Luckily for Alice, the little magic bottle had now had its full effect, and she grew no larger: still it was very uncomfortable, and, as there seemed to be no sort of chance of her ever getting out of the room again, no wonder she felt unhappy.

"It was much pleasanter at home," thought poor Alice, "when one wasn't always growing larger and smaller, and being ordered about by mice and rabbits. I almost wish I hadn't gone down that rabbit-hole—and yet—and yet—it's rather curious, you know, this sort of life! I do wonder what *can* have happened to me! When I used to read fairy tales, I fancied that kind of thing never happened, and now here I am in the middle of one! There ought to be a book written about me, that there ought! And when I grow up, I'll write one—but I'm grown up now," she added in a sorrowful tone: "at least there's no room to grow up any more *here.*"

"But then," thought Alice, "shall I *never* get any older than I am now? That'll be a comfort, one way—never to be an old woman—but then—always to have lessons to learn! Oh, I shouldn't like *that!*"[3]

"Oh, you foolish Alice!" she answered herself. "How can you learn lessons in here? Why, there's hardly room for *you,* and no room at all for any lesson-books!"

And so she went on, taking first one side and then the other, and making quite a conversation of it altogether; but after a few minutes she heard a voice outside, and stopped to listen.

"Mary Ann! Mary Ann!" said the voice. "Fetch me my gloves this moment!"[4] Then came a little pattering of feet on the stairs. Alice knew it was the Rabbit coming to look for her, and she trembled till she shook the house, quite forgetting that she was now about a thousand times as large as the Rabbit, and had no reason to be afraid of it.

Presently the Rabbit came up to the door, and tried to open it; but, as the door opened inwards, and Alice's elbow was pressed hard against it, that attempt proved a failure. Alice heard it say to itself "Then I'll go round and get in at the window."

"*That* you wo'n't!" thought Alice, and after

3. In the Pennyroyal edition of *Alice in Wonderland* (University of California, 1982), James Kincaid glosses Alice's remark this way:

> This is a double-edged line and perhaps a poignant one, given Carroll's feelings about his child-friends growing up. [His] letters are full of self-pitying jokes on the subject: "Some children have a most disagreeable way of getting grown-up. I hope you won't do anything of that sort before we meet again."

In his "Confessions of a Corrupt Annotator" (*Jabberwocky,* Spring 1982), Kincaid defends the right of annotators to take off in any direction they like. He cites the above note as an example. "The historical context does not call for a gloss, but the passage provides an opportunity to point out the ambivalence that may attend the central figure and her desire to grow up." I thank Mr. Kincaid for supporting my own rambling in *AA*—a practice continued in this sequel.

4. This is the second time the White Rabbit has called for his gloves, but whether he ever obtained them we are not told. Gloves were as important to Carroll as they were to the Rabbit, both in reality and linguistically. "He was a little eccentric in his clothes," Isa Bowman writes in *The Story of Lewis Carroll* (J. M. Dent, 1899). "In the coldest weather he would never wear an overcoat, and he had a curious habit of always wearing, in all seasons of the year, a pair of grey and black cotton gloves."

Gloves are the topic of one of Carroll's most amusing letters, written to Isa Bowman's sister Maggie. Carroll pretended that when Maggie spoke of sending him "sacks full of love and baskets full of kisses," she really meant to write "a sack full of *gloves* and a basket full of *kittens!*" A sack full of 1,000 gloves arrived, he goes on, and a basket of 250 kittens. He was thus able to put four gloves on each kitten to prevent their paws from scratching the schoolgirls to whom he gave the kittens:

> So the little girls went dancing home again, and the next morning they came dancing back to school. The scratches were all healed, and they told me "The kittens *have* been good!" And, when

any kitten wants to catch a mouse, it just takes off *one* of its gloves; and if it wants to catch *two* mice, it takes off two gloves; and if it wants to catch *three* mice, it takes off *three* gloves; and if it wants to catch *four* mice, it takes off all its gloves. But the moment they've caught the mice, they pop their gloves on again, because they know we can't love them without their gloves. For, you see, "gloves" have got "love" *inside* them—there's none *outside.*

5. Carrollians have noticed that in Tenniel's illustration of this scene the White Rabbit's vest, white in an earlier picture, has become checked like his jacket.

6. Is this another French joke? As reader Michael Bergmann pointed out in a letter, "apple" is *pomme* in French, and "potato" is *pomme de terre,* or "apple of the earth."

What kind of animal is Pat, the apple digger? Carroll doesn't say. Denis Crutch and R. B. Shaberman, in *Under the Quizzing Glass,* conjecture that Pat is one of the two guinea pigs who revive Bill after he has been kicked out of the chimney. During the trial of the Knave of Hearts both guinea pigs are in the courtroom, where they are "suppressed" for cheering.

waiting till she fancied she heard the Rabbit just under the window, she suddenly spread out her hand, and made a snatch in the air. She did not get hold of anything, but she heard a little shriek and a fall, and a crash of broken glass, from which she concluded that it was just possible it had fallen into a cucumber-frame, or something of the sort.[5]

Next came an angry voice—the Rabbit's—"Pat! Pat! Where are you?" And then a voice she had never heard before, "Sure then I'm here! Digging for apples, yer honour!"[6]

"Digging for apples, indeed!" said the Rabbit angrily. "Here! Come help me out of *this!*" (Sounds of more broken glass.)

"Now tell me, Pat, what's that in the window?"

"Sure, it's an arm, yer honour!" (He pronounced it "arrum.")

"An arm, you goose! Who ever saw one that size? Why, it fills the whole window!"

"Sure, it does, yer honour: but it's an arm for all that."

"Well, it's got no business there, at any rate: go and take it away!"

There was a long silence after this, and Alice could only hear whispers now and then; such as "Sure, I don't like it, yer honour, at all, at all!" "Do as I tell you, you coward!", and at last she spread out her hand again, and made another snatch in the air. This time there were *two* little shrieks, and more sounds of broken glass. "What a number of cucumber-frames there must be!" thought Alice. "I wonder what they'll do next! As for pulling me out of the window, I

" 'What's that in the window?' "

only wish they *could!* I'm sure I don't want to stay in here any longer!"

She waited for some time without hearing anything more: at last came a rumbling of little cart-wheels, and the sound of a good many voices all talking together: she made out the words: "Where's the other ladder?—Why, I hadn't to bring but one. Bill's got the other—Bill! Fetch it here, lad!—Here, put 'em up at this corner—No, tie 'em together first—they don't reach half high enough yet—Oh, they'll do well enough. Don't be particular—Here, Bill! Catch hold of this rope—Will the roof bear?—Mind that loose slate—Oh, it's coming down! Heads below!" (a loud crash)—"Now, who did that?—It was Bill, I fancy—Who's to go down the chimney?—Nay, I sha'n't! *You* do it!—*That* I wo'n't, then!—Bill's got to go down—Here, Bill! The master says you've got to go down the chimney!"

"Oh! So Bill's got to come down the chimney, has he?" said Alice to herself. "Why, they seem to put everything upon Bill! I wouldn't be in Bill's place for a good deal: this fireplace is narrow, to be sure; but I *think* I can kick a little!"

She drew her foot as far down the chimney as she could, and waited till she heard a little animal (she couldn't guess of what sort it was) scratching and scrambling about in the chimney close above her: then, saying to herself "This is Bill", she gave one sharp kick, and waited to see what would happen next.

The first thing she heard was a general chorus of "There goes Bill!" then the Rabbit's voice alone—"Catch him, you by the hedge!" then silence, and then another confusion of

" 'Catch him, you by the hedge' "

voices—"Hold up his head—Brandy now—Don't choke him—How was it, old fellow? What happened to you? Tell us all about it!"

Last came a little feeble, squeaking voice ("That's Bill," thought Alice), "Well, I hardly know—No more, thank ye; I'm better now—but I'm a deal too flustered to tell you—all I know is, something comes at me like a Jack-in-the-box, and up I goes like a sky-rocket!"

"So you did, old fellow!" said the others.

"We must burn the house down!" said the Rabbit's voice. And Alice called out, as loud as she could, "If you do, I'll set Dinah at you!"

There was a dead silence instantly, and Alice thought to herself "I wonder what they *will* do next! If they had any sense, they'd take the roof off." After a minute or two they began moving about again, and Alice heard the Rabbit say "A barrowful will do, to begin with."

"A barrowful of *what?*" thought Alice. But she had not long to doubt, for the next moment a shower of little pebbles came rattling in at the window, and some of them hit her in the face. "I'll put a stop to this," she said to herself, and shouted out "You'd better not do that again!", which produced another dead silence.

Alice noticed, with some surprise, that the pebbles were all turning into little cakes as they lay on the floor, and a bright idea came into her head. "If I eat one of these cakes," she thought, "it's sure to make *some* change in my size; and, as it ca'n't possibly make me larger, it must make me smaller, I suppose."

So she swallowed one of the cakes, and was delighted to find that she began shrinking directly. As soon as she was small enough to get through the door, she ran out of the house, and found quite a crowd of little animals and birds waiting outside. The poor little Lizard, Bill, was in the middle, being held up by two guinea-pigs, who were giving it something out of a bottle. They all made a rush at Alice the moment she appeared; but she ran off as hard as she could, and soon found herself safe in a thick wood.

"The first thing I've got to do," said Alice to herself, as she wandered about in the wood, "is to grow to my right size again; and the second thing is to find my way into that lovely garden. I think that will be the best plan."

It sounded an excellent plan, no doubt, and very neatly and simply arranged: the only difficulty was, that she had not the smallest idea how to set about it; and, while she was peering about anxiously among the trees, a little sharp bark just over her head made her look up in a great hurry.

An enormous puppy was looking down at her with large round eyes, and feebly stretching out one paw, trying to touch her.[7] "Poor little thing!" said Alice, in a coaxing tone, and she tried hard to whistle to it; but she was terribly frightened all the time at the thought that it might be hungry, in which case it would be very likely to eat her up in spite of all her coaxing.

Hardly knowing what she did, she picked up a little bit of stick, and held it out to the puppy: whereupon the puppy jumped into the air off all its feet at once, with a yelp of delight, and rushed at the stick, and made believe to worry it: then Alice dodged behind a great thistle, to keep herself from being run over; and, the mo-

7. Many commentators have felt that this puppy is out of place in Wonderland, as if it had wandered into Alice's dream from the real world. Denis Crutch has observed that it is the only important creature in Wonderland who does not speak to Alice.

"The poor little Lizard, Bill, was in the middle, being held up"

ment she appeared on the other side, the puppy made another rush at the stick, and tumbled head over heels in its hurry to get hold of it: then Alice, thinking it was very like having a game of play with a cart-horse, and expecting every moment to be trampled under its feet, ran round the thistle again: then the puppy began a series of short charges at the stick, running a very little way forwards each time and a long way back, and barking hoarsely all the while, till at last it sat down a good way off, panting, with its tongue hanging out of its mouth, and its great eyes half shut.

This seemed to Alice a good opportunity for making her escape: so she set off at once, and ran till she was quite tired and out of breath, and till the puppy's bark sounded quite faint in the distance.

"And yet what a dear little puppy it was!" said Alice, as she leant against a buttercup to rest herself, and fanned herself with one of the leaves. "I should have liked teaching it tricks very much, if—if I'd only been the right size to do it! Oh dear! I'd nearly forgotten that I've got to grow up again! Let me see—how *is* it to be managed? I suppose I ought to eat or drink something or other; but the great question is 'What?' "

The great question certainly was "What?" Alice looked all round her at the flowers and the blades of grass, but she could not see anything that looked like the right thing to eat or drink under the circumstances. There was a large mushroom growing near her, about the same height as herself; and, when she had looked under it, and on both sides of it, and behind it,

"The puppy jumped into the air"

it occurred to her that she might as well look and see what was on top of it.

She stretched herself up on tiptoe, and peeped over the edge of the mushroom, and her eyes immediately met those of a large blue caterpillar, that was sitting on the top, with its arms folded, quietly smoking a long hookah, and taking not the smallest notice of her or of anything else.

CHAPTER V

ADVICE FROM A CATERPILLAR

The Caterpillar and Alice looked at each other for some time in silence: at last the Caterpillar took the hookah out of its mouth, and addressed her in a languid, sleepy voice.

"Who are *you*?" said the Caterpillar.

This was not an encouraging opening for a conversation. Alice replied, rather shyly, "I—I hardly know, Sir, just at present—at least I know who I *was* when I got up this morning, but I think I must have been changed several times since then."

"What do you mean by that?" said the Caterpillar, sternly. "Explain yourself!"

"I ca'n't explain *myself,* I'm afraid, Sir," said Alice, "because I'm not myself, you see."

"I don't see," said the Caterpillar.

"I'm afraid I ca'n't put it more clearly," Alice replied, very politely, "for I ca'n't understand it myself, to begin with; and being so many different sizes in a day is very confusing."

"It isn't," said the Caterpillar.

"Well, perhaps you haven't found it so yet,"

"The Caterpillar and Alice looked at each other"

said Alice; "but when you have to turn into a chrysalis—you will some day, you know—and then after that into a butterfly, I should think you'll feel it a little queer, wo'n't you?"

"Not a bit," said the Caterpillar.

"Well, perhaps *your* feelings may be different," said Alice: "all I know is, it would feel very queer to *me.*"

"You!" said the Caterpillar contemptuously. "Who are *you*?"

Which brought them back again to the beginning of the conversation. Alice felt a little irritated at the Caterpillar's making such *very* short remarks, and she drew herself up and said, very gravely, "I think you ought to tell me who *you* are, first."

"Why?" said the Caterpillar.

Here was another puzzling question; and, as Alice could not think of any good reason, and the Caterpillar seemed to be in a *very* unpleasant state of mind, she turned away.

"Come back!" the Caterpillar called after her. "I've something important to say!"

This sounded promising, certainly. Alice turned and came back again.

"Keep your temper," said the Caterpillar.

"Is that all?" said Alice, swallowing down her anger as well as she could.

"No," said the Caterpillar.

Alice thought she might as well wait, as she had nothing else to do, and perhaps after all it might tell her something worth hearing. For some minutes it puffed away without speaking; but at last it unfolded its arms, took the hookah out of its mouth again, and said "So you think you're changed, do you?"

Old Father William standing on his head

"I'm afraid I am, Sir," said Alice. "I ca'n't remember things as I used—and I don't keep the same size for ten minutes together!"

"Ca'n't remember *what* things?" said the Caterpillar.

"Well, I've tried to say *'How doth the little busy bee,'* but it all came different!" Alice replied in a very melancholy voice.

"Repeat *'You are old, Father William,'* " said the Caterpillar.

Alice folded her hands, and began:—[1]

"You are old, Father William," the young man said,
"And your hair has become very white;
And yet you incessantly stand on your head—
Do you think, at your age, it is right?"

"In my youth," Father William replied to his son,
"I feared it might injure the brain;
But, now that I'm perfectly sure I have none,
Why, I do it again and again."

"You are old," said the youth, "as I mentioned before,
And have grown most uncommonly fat;
Yet you turned a back-somersault in at the door—
Pray, what is the reason of that?"

"In my youth," said the sage, as he shook his grey locks,
"I kept all my limbs very supple
By the use of this ointment—one shilling the box—
Allow me to sell you a couple?"

"You are old," said the youth, "and your jaws are too weak
For anything tougher than suet;
Yet you finished the goose, with the bones and the beak—
Pray, how did you manage to do it?"

"In my youth," said his father, "I took to the law,
And argued each case with my wife;
And the muscular strength, which it gave to my jaw
Has lasted the rest of my life."

"You are old," said the youth, "one would hardly suppose
That your eye was as steady as ever;
Yet you balanced an eel on the end of your nose—[2]
What made you so awfully clever?"

"I have answered three questions, and that is enough,"
Said his father. "Don't give yourself airs!
Do you think I can listen all day to such stuff?
Be off, or I'll kick you down-stairs!"

1. Selwyn Goodacre (in *Jabberwocky,* Spring 1982) has an interesting comment on Alice's folded hands here, and her crossed hands in Chapter 2 ("as if she were saying lessons") when she repeated "How doth the little crocodile . . .":

> I discussed these passages with a retired primary school headmaster . . . and he confirmed to me that that is *exactly* how children were taught—i.e., they had to repeat their lessons (note that the word is not "recite"—that refers to house parties and home entertainment), this means learning by rote; she would have been expected to know the lessons by heart—and to cross her hands if sitting, to fold them if standing, both systems intended to concentrate the mind and prevent fidgeting.

2. In Tenniel's illustration for this line *(below)* you see in the background what looks like a bridge. Philip Benham, writing in *Jabberwocky* (Winter 1970), says: "The 'bridge' is in fact an eel trap, built across a stream or river, and consists of a barrier of conical baskets woven out of rushes or sometimes willow."

Robert Wakeman adds that one made of iron still exists near Guildford. "A small hole at the end of each basket enables the eels to escape into a separate pond, while other types of fish are unable to go through the holes." For more details and other pictures of eel traps, see Michael Hancher's *The Tenniel Illustrations to the "Alice" Books* (Ohio State University Press, 1985).

Old Father William balancing an eel on the end of his nose

"That is not said right," said the Caterpillar.

"Not *quite* right, I'm afraid," said Alice, timidly: "some of the words have got altered."

"It is wrong from beginning to end," said the Caterpillar, decidedly; and there was silence for some minutes.

The Caterpillar was the first to speak.

"What size do you want to be?" it asked.

"Oh, I'm not particular as to size," Alice hastily replied; "only one doesn't like changing so often, you know."

"I *don't* know," said the Caterpillar.

Alice said nothing: she had never been so much contradicted in all her life before, and she felt that she was losing her temper.

"Are you content now?" said the Caterpillar.

"Well, I should like to be a *little* larger, Sir, if you wouldn't mind," said Alice: "three inches is such a wretched height to be."

"It is a very good height indeed!" said the Caterpillar angrily, rearing itself upright as it spoke (it was exactly three inches high).

"But I'm not used to it!" pleaded poor Alice in a piteous tone. And she thought to herself "I wish the creatures wouldn't be so easily offended!"

"You'll get used to it in time," said the Caterpillar; and it put the hookah into its mouth, and began smoking again.

This time Alice waited patiently until it chose to speak again. In a minute or two the Caterpillar took the hookah out of its mouth, and yawned once or twice, and shook itself. Then it got down off the mushroom, and crawled away into the grass, merely remarking, as it went,

"One side will make you grow taller, and the other side will make you grow shorter."[3]

"One side of *what?* The other side of *what?*" thought Alice to herself.

"Of the mushroom," said the Caterpillar, just as if she had asked it aloud;[4] and in another moment it was out of sight.

Alice remained looking thoughtfully at the mushroom for a minute, trying to make out which were the two sides of it; and, as it was perfectly round, she found this a very difficult question. However, at last she stretched her arms round it as far as they would go, and broke off a bit of the edge with each hand.

"And now which is which?" she said to herself, and nibbled a little of the right-hand bit to try the effect. The next moment she felt a violent blow underneath her chin: it had struck her foot!

She was a good deal frightened by this very sudden change, but she felt that there was no time to be lost, as she was shrinking rapidly: so she set to work at once to eat some of the other bit. Her chin was pressed so closely against her foot, that there was hardly room to open her mouth; but she did it at last, and managed to swallow a morsel of the left-hand bit.

*   *   *   *   *
  *   *   *   *
*   *   *   *   *

"Come, my head's free at last!" said Alice in a tone of delight, which changed into alarm in another moment, when she found that her shoulders were nowhere to be found: all she could see, when she looked down, was an immense length of neck, which seemed to rise like

3. Many readers have referred me to old books, which Carroll could have read, that describe the hallucinogenic properties of certain mushrooms. *Amanita muscaria* (or fly agaric) is most often cited. Eating it produces hallucinations in which time and space are distorted. However, as Robert Hornback makes clear in his delightful "Garden Tour of Wonderland," in *Pacific Horticulture* (Fall 1983), this cannot be the mushroom drawn by Tenniel:

> *Amanita muscaria* has bright red caps that appear to be splattered with bits of cottage cheese. The Caterpillar's perch is, instead, a smooth-capped species, very like *Amanita fulva,* which is nontoxic and rather tasty. We might surmise that neither Tenniel nor Carroll wanted children to emulate Alice and end up eating poisonous mushrooms.

4. The Caterpillar has read Alice's mind. Carroll did not believe in spiritualism, but he did believe in the reality of ESP and psychokinesis. In an 1882 letter (see Morton Cohen's *The Letters of Lewis Carroll,* Vol. 1, pages 471–472) he speaks of a pamphlet on "thought reading," published by the Society for Psychical Research, which strengthened his conviction that psychic phenomena are genuine. "All seems to point to the existence of a natural force, allied to electricity and nerve-force, by which brain can act on brain. I think we are close on the day when this shall be classed among the known natural forces, and its laws tabulated, and when the scientific sceptics, who always shut their eyes till the last moment to any evidence that seems to point beyond materialism, will have to accept it as a proved fact in nature."

Carroll was an enthusiastic charter member all his life of the Society for Psychical Research, and his library contained dozens of books on the occult. See "Lewis Carroll and the Society for Psychical Research," by R. B. Shaberman, in *Jabberwocky* (Summer 1972).

a stalk out of a sea of green leaves that lay far below her.

"What *can* all that green stuff be?" said Alice. "And where *have* my shoulders got to? And oh, my poor hands, how is it I ca'n't see you?" She was moving them about, as she spoke, but no result seemed to follow, except a little shaking among the distant green leaves.

As there seemed to be no chance of getting her hands up to her head, she tried to get her head down to *them,* and was delighted to find that her neck would bend about easily in any direction, like a serpent. She had just succeeding in curving it down into a graceful zigzag, and was going to dive in among the leaves, which she found to be nothing but the tops of the trees under which she had been wandering, when a sharp hiss made her draw back in a hurry: a large pigeon had flown into her face, and was beating her violently with its wings.

"Serpent!" screamed the Pigeon.

"I'm *not* a serpent!" said Alice indignantly. "Let me alone!"

"Serpent, I say again!" repeated the Pigeon, but in a more subdued tone, and added, with a kind of sob, "I've tried every way, but nothing seems to suit them!"

"I haven't the least idea what you're talking about," said Alice.

"I've tried the roots of trees, and I've tried banks, and I've tried hedges," the Pigeon went on, without attending to her; "but those serpents! There's no pleasing them!"

Alice was more and more puzzled, but she thought there was no use in saying anything more till the Pigeon had finished.

" 'Serpent!' screamed the Pigeon"

"As if it wasn't trouble enough hatching the eggs," said the Pigeon; "but I must be on the look-out for serpents, night and day! Why, I haven't had a wink of sleep these three weeks!"

"I'm very sorry you've been annoyed," said Alice, who was beginning to see its meaning.

"And just as I'd taken the highest tree in the wood," continued the Pigeon, raising its voice to a shriek, "and just as I was thinking I should be free of them at last, they must needs come wriggling down from the sky! Ugh, Serpent!"

"But I'm *not* a serpent, I tell you!" said Alice. "I'm a—I'm a—"

"Well! *What* are you?" said the Pigeon. "I can see you're trying to invent something!"

"I—I'm a little girl," said Alice, rather doubtfully, as she remembered the number of changes she had gone through, that day.

"A likely story indeed!" said the Pigeon, in a tone of the deepest contempt. "I've seen a good many little girls in my time, but never *one* with such a neck as that! No, no! You're a serpent; and there's no use denying it. I suppose you'll be telling me next that you never tasted an egg!"

"I *have* tasted eggs, certainly," said Alice, who was a very truthful child; "but little girls eat eggs quite as much as serpents do, you know."

"I don't believe it," said the Pigeon; "but if they do, why, then they're a kind of serpent: that's all I can say."

This was such a new idea to Alice, that she was quite silent for a minute or two, which gave the Pigeon the opportunity of adding "You're looking for eggs, I know *that* well enough; and what does it matter to me whether you're a little girl or a serpent?"

"It matters a good deal to *me,*" said Alice hastily; "but I'm not looking for eggs, as it happens; and, if I was, I shouldn't want *yours:* I don't like them raw."

"Well, be off, then!" said the Pigeon in a sulky tone, as it settled down again into its nest. Alice crouched down among the trees as well as she could, for her neck kept getting entangled among the branches, and every now and then she had to stop and untwist it. After a while she remembered that she still held the pieces of mushroom in her hands, and she set to work very carefully, nibbling first at one and then at the other, and growing sometimes taller, and sometimes shorter, until she had succeeded in bringing herself down to her usual height.

It was so long since she had been anything near the right size, that it felt quite strange at first; but she got used to it in a few minutes, and began talking to herself, as usual, "Come, there's half my plan done now! How puzzling all these changes are! I'm never sure what I'm going to be, from one minute to another! However, I've got back to my right size: the next thing is, to get into that beautiful garden—how *is* that to be done, I wonder?" As she said this, she came suddenly upon an open place, with a little house in it about four feet high. "Whoever lives there," thought Alice, "it'll never do to come upon them *this* size: why, I should frighten them out of their wits!" So she began nibbling at the right-hand bit again, and did not venture to go near the house till she had brought herself down to nine inches high.

CHAPTER VI

PIG AND PEPPER

For a minute or two she stood looking at the house, and wondering what to do next, when suddenly a footman in livery came running out of the wood—(she considered him to be a footman because he was in livery: otherwise, judging by his face only, she would have called him a fish)—and rapped loudly at the door with his knuckles. It was opened by another footman in livery, with a round face, and large eyes like a frog; and both footmen, Alice noticed, had powdered hair that curled all over their heads. She felt very curious to know what it was all about, and crept a little way out of the wood to listen.

The Fish-Footman began by producing from under his arm a great letter, nearly as large as himself, and this he handed over to the other, saying, in a solemn tone, "For the Duchess. An invitation from the Queen to play croquet." The Frog-Footman repeated, in the same solemn tone, only changing the order of the words a little, "From the Queen. An invitation for the Duchess to play croquet."

Then they both bowed, and their curls got entangled together.

Alice laughed so much at this, that she had to run back into the wood for fear of their hearing her; and, when she next peeped out, the Fish-Footman was gone, and the other was sitting on the ground near the door, staring stupidly up into the sky.

Alice went timidly up to the door, and knocked.

"There's no sort of use in knocking," said the Footman, "and that for two reasons. First, because I'm on the same side of the door as you are: secondly, because they're making such a noise inside, no one could possibly hear you." And certainly there *was* a most extraordinary noise going on within—a constant howling and sneezing, and every now and then a great crash, as if a dish or kettle had been broken to pieces.

"Please, then," said Alice, "how am I to get in?"

"There might be some sense in your knocking," the Footman went on, without attending to her, "if we had the door between us. For instance, if you were *inside,* you might knock, and I could let you out, you know." He was looking up into the sky all the time he was speaking, and this Alice thought decidedly uncivil. "But perhaps he ca'n't help it," she said to herself; "his eyes are so *very* nearly at the top of his head. But at any rate he might answer questions.—How am I to get in?" she repeated, aloud.

"I shall sit here," the Footman remarked, "till to-morrow—"

At this moment the door of the house opened, and a large plate came skimming out, straight

"Then they both bowed, and their curls got entangled"

at the Footman's head: it just grazed his nose, and broke to pieces against one of the trees behind him.

"—or next day, maybe," the Footman continued in the same tone, exactly as if nothing had happened.

"How am I to get in?" asked Alice again, in a louder tone.

"*Are* you to get in at all?" said the Footman. "That's the first question, you know."

It was, no doubt: only Alice did not like to be told so. "It's really dreadful," she muttered to herself, "the way all the creatures argue. It's enough to drive one crazy!"

The Footman seemed to think this a good opportunity for repeating his remark, with variations. "I shall sit here," he said, "on and off, for days and days."

"But what am *I* to do?" said Alice.

"Anything you like," said the Footman, and began whistling.

"Oh, there's no use in talking to him," said Alice desperately: "he's perfectly idiotic!" And she opened the door and went in.

The door led right into a large kitchen, which was full of smoke from one end to the other: the Duchess[1] was sitting on a three-legged stool in the middle, nursing a baby: the cook was leaning over the fire, stirring a large cauldron which seemed to be full of soup.

"There's certainly too much pepper in that soup!"[2] Alice said to herself, as well as she could for sneezing.

There was certainly too much of it in the *air.* Even the Duchess sneezed occasionally; and as for the baby, it was sneezing and howling alter-

1. Not until Chapter 9, when Alice and the Duchess meet again, are we told that Alice tried to keep her distance from the Duchess because she "was *very* ugly," and because the Duchess kept prodding her shoulder with her "sharp little chin." The sharp chin is mentioned two more times in this episode. The whereabouts of the Duke, if living, is left in mystery.

The chin of Tenniel's Duchess is not very little or sharp, but she is certainly ugly. It seems likely that he copied a painting attributed to the sixteenth-century Flemish artist Quentin Matsys (his name has variant spellings). The portrait is popularly regarded as one of the fourteenth-century duchess Margaret of Carinthia and Tyrol. She had the reputation of being the ugliest woman in history. (Her nickname, "Maultasche," means "pocket-mouthed.") Lion Feuchtwanger's novel *The Ugly Duchess* is about her sad life.

On the other hand, there are numerous engravings and drawings almost identical with Matsys's painting, including a drawing by Francesco Melzi, a pupil of Leonardo da Vinci. Part of the Royal Collection at Buckingham Palace, it is said to be a copy of a lost original by da Vinci! For the confusing history of these pictures, which may have no connection whatever with Duchess Margaret, see Chapter 4 of Michael Hancher's, *The Tenniel Illustrations to the "Alice" Books.*

2. The pepper in the soup and in the air suggests the peppery ill temper of the Duchess. Was it the custom in Victorian England for lower classes to put excessive pepper in their soup to mask the taste of slightly spoiled meat and vegetables?

For Savile Clarke's stage production of *Alice,* Carroll provided the following lines to be spoken by the cook while she stirs the soup: "There's nothing like pepper, says I. . . . Not half enough yet. Nor a quarter enough." The cook then recites, like a witch chanting a charm:

Boil it so easily,
Mix it so greasily,
Stir it so sneezily,
One! Two!! Three!!!

"One for the Missus, two for the cat, and three for the baby," the cook continues, striking the baby's nose.

I quote from Charles C. Lovett's valuable book *Alice on Stage: A History of the Early Theatrical Productions of Alice in Wonderland* (Meckler, 1990). The lines appeared both in the stage production and in the script's published version.

3. In my *AA* I gave two traditional explanations of the origin of "grin like a Cheshire cat," a common expression in Victorian England: Signboards of inns in Cheshire often bore grinning lions; and Cheshire cheese had earlier been molded in the form of a grinning cat.

David Greene sent me this quotation from an 1808 letter of Charles Lamb: "I made a pun the other day, and palmed it upon Holcroft, who grinned like a Cheshire cat. Why do cats grin in Cheshire? Because it was once a county palatine and the cats cannot help laughing whenever they think of it, though I see no great joke in it."

Hans Haverman wrote to suggest that Carroll's vanishing cat might derive from the waning of the moon—the moon has long been associated with lunacy—as it slowly turns into a fingernail crescent, resembling a grin, before it finally disappears.

Did T. S. Eliot have the Cheshire-Cat in mind when he concluded "Morning at the Window" with this couplet?

An aimless smile that hovers in the air
And vanishes along the level of the roofs.

For more on the grin, see "The Cheshire-Cat and Its Origins," by Ken Oultram, in *Jabberwocky* (Winter 1973).

nately without a moment's pause. The only two creatures in the kitchen, that did *not* sneeze, were the cook, and a large cat, which was lying on the hearth and grinning from ear to ear.

"Please would you tell me," said Alice, a little timidly, for she was not quite sure whether it was good manners for her to speak first, "why your cat grins like that?"

"It's a Cheshire-Cat,"[3] said the Duchess, "and that's why. Pig!"

She said the last word with such sudden violence that Alice quite jumped; but she saw in another moment that it was addressed to the baby, and not to her, so she took courage, and went on again:—

"I didn't know that Cheshire-Cats always grinned; in fact, I didn't know that cats *could* grin."

"They all can," said the Duchess; "and most of 'em do."

"I don't know of any that do," Alice said very politely, feeling quite pleased to have got into a conversation.

"You don't know much," said the Duchess; "and that's a fact."

Alice did not at all like the tone of this remark, and thought it would be as well to introduce some other subject of conversation. While she was trying to fix on one, the cook took the cauldron of soup off the fire, and at once set to work throwing everything within her reach at the Duchess and the baby—the fire-irons came first; then followed a shower of saucepans, plates, and dishes. The Duchess took no notice of them even when they hit her; and the baby was howling so much already, that it was quite impossible to say whether the blows hurt it or not.

"Oh, *please* mind what you're doing!" cried Alice, jumping up and down in an agony of terror. "Oh, there goes his *precious* nose!", as an unusually large saucepan flew close by it, and very nearly carried it off.

"If everybody minded their own business," the Duchess said, in a hoarse growl, "the world would go round a deal faster than it does."

"Which would *not* be an advantage," said Alice, who felt very glad to get an opportunity of showing off a little of her knowledge. "Just think what work it would make with the day and night! You see the earth takes twenty-four hours to turn round on its axis—"

"Talking of axes," said the Duchess, "chop off her head!"

Alice glanced rather anxiously at the cook, to see if she meant to take the hint; but the cook was busily stirring the soup, and seemed not to be listening, so she went on again: "Twenty-four hours, I *think;* or is it twelve? I—"

"Oh, don't bother *me*!" said the Duchess. "I never could abide figures!" And with that she began nursing her child again, singing a sort of lullaby to it as she did so, and giving it a violent shake at the end of every line:—[4]

"Speak roughly to your little boy,
And beat him when he sneezes:
He only does it to annoy,
Because he knows it teases."

CHORUS
(in which the cook and the baby joined):—
"Wow! wow! wow!"

4. The Duchess's lullaby parodies "Speak Gently," an enormously popular sentimental poem of the day. For some 150 years there has been controversy over who wrote it. The two principal claimants were David Bates, a Philadelphia broker, and George Washington Langford, an Irish-born resident of Huron, Ohio.

The Langford family tradition is that George wrote the poem while visiting his birthplace in Ireland in 1845. All British printings of the poem prior to 1900 are either anonymous or credited to Langford. No known printing of the poem in England predates 1848. *The Eolian,* a book of verse by David Bates, published in 1849, contains the poem.

Bates's case was strongly boosted by the discovery in 1986 that the poem, signed "D.B.," appeared on the second page of the *Philadelphia Inquirer,* July 15, 1845. Unless an earlier printing can be found in a British or Irish newspaper, it seems highly improbable that Langford could have written it, although a capital mystery remains. How did his name become so firmly attached to the poem in England?

For the original poem, see my note in *AA,* and for a detailed history of the controversy, see my essay "Speak Gently," in *Lewis Carroll Observed* (Clarkson N. Potter, 1976), edited by Edward Guiliano, and reprinted with additions in my *Order and Surprise.*

While the Duchess sang the second verse of the song, she kept tossing the baby violently up and down, and the poor little thing howled so, that Alice could hardly hear the words:—

"I speak severely to my boy,
I beat him when he sneezes;
For he can thoroughly enjoy
The pepper when he pleases!"

CHORUS
"Wow! wow! wow!"

"Here! You may nurse it a bit, if you like!" the Duchess said to Alice, flinging the baby at her as she spoke. "I must go and get ready to play croquet with the Queen," and she hurried out of the room. The cook threw a frying-pan after her as she went, but it just missed her.

Alice caught the baby with some difficulty, as it was a queer-shaped little creature, and held out its arms and legs in all directions, "just like a star-fish," thought Alice. The poor little thing was snorting like a steam-engine when she caught it, and kept doubling itself up and straightening itself out again, so that altogether, for the first minute or two, it was as much as she could do to hold it.

As soon as she had made out the proper way of nursing it (which was to twist it up into a sort of knot, and then keep tight hold of its right ear and left foot, so as to prevent its undoing itself), she carried it out into the open air. "If I don't take this child away with me," thought Alice, "they're sure to kill it in a day or two. Wouldn't it be murder to leave it be-

"Singing a sort of lullaby"

hind?" She said the last words out loud, and the little thing grunted in reply (it had left off sneezing by this time). "Don't grunt," said Alice; "that's not at all a proper way of expressing yourself."

The baby grunted again, and Alice looked very anxiously into its face to see what was the matter with it. There could be no doubt that it had a *very* turn-up nose, much more like a snout than a real nose: also its eyes were getting extremely small for a baby: altogether Alice did not like the look of the thing at all. "But perhaps it was only sobbing," she thought, and looked into its eyes again, to see if there were any tears.

No, there were no tears. "If you're going to turn into a pig, my dear," said Alice, seriously, "I'll have nothing more to do with you. Mind now!" The poor little thing sobbed again (or grunted, it was impossible to say which), and they went on for some while in silence.

Alice was just beginning to think to herself, "Now, what am I to do with this creature, when I get it home?" when it grunted again, so violently, that she looked down into its face in some alarm. This time there could be *no* mistake about it: it was neither more nor less than a pig, and she felt that it would be quite absurd for her to carry it any further.[5]

So she set the little creature down, and felt quite relieved to see it trot away quietly into the wood. "If it had grown up," she said to herself, "it would have made a dreadfully ugly child: but it makes rather a handsome pig, I think." And she began thinking over other children she knew, who might do very well as pigs, and was

5. Frankie Morris, in *Jabberwocky* (Autumn 1985), suggested that the baby's transformation into a pig may derive from a famous prank played on James I by the Countess of Buckingham. She arranged for His Majesty to witness the baptism of what he thought was an infant in arms but was actually a pig, an animal that James I particularly loathed.

"So she set the little creature down"

just saying to herself "if one only knew the right way to change them—" when she was a little startled by seeing the Cheshire-Cat sitting on a bough of a tree a few yards off.

The Cat only grinned when it saw Alice. It looked good-natured, she thought: still it had *very* long claws and a great many teeth, so she felt that it ought to be treated with respect.

"Cheshire-Puss," she began, rather timidly, as she did not at all know whether it would like the name: however, it only grinned a little wider. "Come, it's pleased so far," thought Alice, and she went on. "Would you tell me, please, which way I ought to go from here?"

"That depends a good deal on where you want to get to," said the Cat.

"I don't much care where—" said Alice.

"Then it doesn't matter which way you go," said the Cat.[6]

"—so long as I get *somewhere,*" Alice added as an explanation.

"Oh, you're sure to do that," said the Cat, "if you only walk long enough."

Alice felt that this could not be denied, so she tried another question. "What sort of people live about here?"

"In *that* direction," the Cat said, waving its right paw round, "lives a Hatter: and in *that* direction," waving the other paw, "lives a March Hare. Visit either you like: they're both mad."[7]

"But I don't want to go among mad people," Alice remarked.

"Oh, you ca'n't help that," said the Cat: "we're all mad here. I'm mad. You're mad."

"How do you know I'm mad?" said Alice.

6. I am told there is a passage in the Talmud that says: "If you don't know where you are going, any road will take you there."

7. Two British scientists, Anthony Holley and Paul Greenwood, reported (in *Nature,* June 7, 1984) on extensive observations that fail to support a folk belief that male hares go into a frenzy during the March rutting season. The main behavior of hares throughout their entire eight-month breeding period consists in males chasing females, then getting into boxing matches with them. March is no different from any other month. It was Erasmus who wrote "Mad as a marsh hare." The scientists think "marsh" got corrupted to "March" in later decades.

When Tenniel drew the March Hare he showed wisps of straw on the hare's head. Carroll does not mention this, but at the time it was a symbol, both in art and on the stage, of madness. In *The Nursery "Alice"* Carroll writes, "That's the March Hare with the long ears, and straws mixed up with his hair. The straws showed he was mad—I don't know why." For more on this, see Michael Hancher's chapter on straw as a sign of insanity in *The Tenniel Illustrations to the "Alice" Books.* In Harry Furniss's drawings of the Mad Gardener in Carroll's *Sylvie and Bruno* books you'll see similar straw in the Gardener's hair and clothing.

"Did the Mad Hatter Have Mercury Poisoning?" is the title of an article by H. A. Waldron in *The British Medical Journal* (December 24–31, 1983). The mercury used in curing felt was, in Victorian times, a common cause of mercury poisoning, which could produce psychotic behavior. Dr. Waldron argues that the Mad Hatter was not such a victim, but Dr. Selwyn Goodacre and two other physicians dispute this in the January 28, 1984, issue.

The Hatter and the Hare appear at least twice in *Finnegans Wake:* "Hatters hares" (page 83, line 1, of the Viking revised edition), and "hitters hairs" (page 84, line 28).

"You must be," said the Cat, "or you wouldn't have come here."

Alice didn't think that proved it at all: however, she went on: "And how do you know that you're mad?"

"To begin with," said the Cat, "a dog's not mad. You grant that?"

"I suppose so," said Alice.

"Well, then," the Cat went on, "you see a dog growls when it's angry, and wags its tail when it's pleased. Now *I* growl when I'm pleased, and wag my tail when I'm angry. Therefore I'm mad."

"*I* call it purring, not growling," said Alice.

"Call it what you like," said the Cat. "Do you play croquet with the Queen to-day?"

"I should like it very much," said Alice, "but I haven't been invited yet."

"You'll see me there," said the Cat, and vanished.

Alice was not much surprised at this, she was getting so well used to queer things happening. While she was still looking at the place where it had been, it suddenly appeared again.

"By-the-bye, what became of the baby?" said the Cat. "I'd nearly forgotten to ask."

"It turned into a pig," Alice answered very quietly, just as if the Cat had come back in a natural way.

"I thought it would," said the Cat, and vanished again.

Alice waited a little, half expecting to see it again, but it did not appear, and after a minute or two she walked on in the direction in which the March Hare was said to live. "I've seen hatters before," she said to herself: "the March

"This time it vanished quite slowly"

Hare will be much the most interesting, and perhaps, as this is May, it wo'n't be raving mad—at least not so mad as it was in March." As she said this, she looked up, and there was the Cat again, sitting on a branch of a tree.[8]

"Did you say 'pig', or 'fig'?" said the Cat.

"I said 'pig'," replied Alice; "and I wish you wouldn't keep appearing and vanishing so suddenly; you make one quite giddy!"

"All right," said the Cat; and this time it vanished quite slowly, beginning with the end of the tail, and ending with the grin, which remained some time after the rest of it had gone.

"Well! I've often seen a cat without a grin," thought Alice; "but a grin without a cat! It's the most curious thing I ever saw in all my life!"

She had not gone much farther before she came in sight of the house of the March Hare: she thought it must be the right house, because the chimneys were shaped like ears and the roof was thatched with fur. It was so large a house, that she did not like to go nearer till she had nibbled some more of the left-hand bit of mushroom, and raised herself to about two feet high: even then she walked up towards it rather timidly, saying to herself "Suppose it should be raving mad after all! I almost wish I'd gone to see the Hatter instead!"

8. Selwyn Goodacre has observed that although Alice had "walked on," Tenniel shows the Cheshire-Cat, when it reappears, sitting in the same tree as before. This enabled Carroll, in his *Nursery "Alice,"* to add a bit of paper-folding whimsy. Tenniel's two pictures were placed on left-hand pages so that (in Carroll's words) "if you turn up the corner of this leaf, you'll have Alice looking at the Grin: and she doesn't look a bit more frightened than when she was looking at the Cat, *does* she?"

CHAPTER VII

A MAD TEA-PARTY

There was a table set out under a tree in front of the house, and the March Hare and the Hatter[1] were having tea at it: a Dormouse was sitting between them, fast asleep, and the other two were using it as a cushion, resting their elbows on it, and talking over its head. "Very uncomfortable for the Dormouse," thought Alice; "only as it's asleep, I suppose it doesn't mind."

The table was a large one, but the three were all crowded together at one corner of it. "No room! No room!" they cried out when they saw Alice coming. "There's *plenty* of room!" said Alice indignantly, and she sat down in a large arm-chair at one end of the table.

"Have some wine," the March Hare said in an encouraging tone.

Alice looked all round the table, but there was nothing on it but tea.[2] "I don't see any wine," she remarked.

"There isn't any," said the March Hare.

"Then it wasn't very civil of you to offer it," said Alice angrily.

1. There have been many guesses about whom Carroll may have had in mind when he created the Mad Hatter, or whom Tenniel may have caricatured. As I noted in *AA,* the principal candidate was Theophilus Carter, an eccentric furniture dealer in the Oxford area who always wore a top hat. Ellis Hillman, writing on "Who Was the Mad Hatter?" in *Jabberwocky* (Winter 1973), provides a new candidate: Samuel Ogden, a Manchester hatter known as "Mad Sam," who in 1814 designed a special hat for the tsar of Russia when he visited London.

Hillman also conjectures that "Mad Hatter," if the *H* is dropped, sounds like "Mad Adder." This, he writes, could be taken as describing a mathematician, such as Carroll himself, or perhaps Charles Babbage, a Cambridge mathematician widely regarded as slightly mad in his efforts to build a complicated mechanical calculating machine.

2. Both Carroll and Tenniel apparently forgot that a milk jug was also on the table. We know this because later on in the tea party the Dormouse upsets it.

"It wasn't very civil of you to sit down without being invited," said the March Hare.

"I didn't know it was *your* table," said Alice: "it's laid for a great many more than three."

"Your hair wants cutting,"[3] said the Hatter. He had been looking at Alice for some time with great curiosity, and this was his first speech.

"You should learn not to make personal remarks," Alice said with some severity: "it's very rude."

The Hatter opened his eyes very wide on hearing this; but all he *said* was "Why is a raven like a writing-desk?"[4]

"Come, we shall have some fun now!" thought Alice. "I'm glad they've begun asking riddles—I believe I can guess that," she added aloud.

"Do you mean that you think you can find out the answer to it?" said the March Hare.

"Exactly so," said Alice.

"Then you should say what you mean," the March Hare went on.

"I do," Alice hastily replied; "at least—at least I mean what I say—that's the same thing, you know."

"Not the same thing a bit!" said the Hatter. "Why, you might just as well say that 'I see what I eat' is the same thing as 'I eat what I see'!"

"You might just as well say," added the March Hare, "that 'I like what I get' is the same thing as 'I get what I like'!"

"You might just as well say," added the Dormouse, which seemed to be talking in its sleep, "that 'I breathe when I sleep' is the same thing as 'I sleep when I breathe'!"

3. In *Under the Quizzing Glass,* R. B. Shaberman and Denis Crutch point out that no one would tell a Victorian little girl that her hair was too long, but the remark *would* apply to Carroll. In Isa Bowman's *The Story of Lewis Carroll* (J. M. Dent, 1899), the actress and former child-friend recalls: "Lewis Carroll was a man of medium height. When I knew him his hair was silvery-grey, rather longer than it was the fashion to wear, and his eyes were a deep blue."

4. In a brief preface that Carroll wrote for an 1896 edition of *Alice in Wonderland,* he said he had no answer in mind when he gave this riddle. Many answers have since been suggested, including one by Carroll himself, some of which you will find in my *AA* note. In 1989 England's Lewis Carroll Society announced a contest for new answers, to be published eventually in the society's newsletter, *Bandersnatch.*

Aldous Huxley, writing on "Ravens and Writing Desks" (*Vanity Fair,* September 1928), supplies two nonsense answers: because there's a *b* in both, and because there's an *n* in neither. James Michie sent a similar answer: because each begins with *e.* Huxley defends the view that such metaphysical questions as: Does God exist? Do we have free will? Why is there suffering? are as meaningless as the Mad Hatter's question—"nonsensical riddles, questions not about reality but about words."

"Both have quills dipped in ink" was suggested by reader David B. Jodrey, Jr. Cyril Pearson, in his undated *Twentieth Century Standard Puzzle Book,* suggests, "Because it slopes with a flap."

Denis Crutch (*Jabberwocky,* Winter 1976) reported an astonishing discovery. In the 1896 edition of *Alice,* Carroll wrote a new preface in which he gave what he considered the best answer to the riddle: "Because it can produce a few notes, tho they are *very* flat; and it is nevar put with the wrong end in front." Note the spelling of "never" as "nevar." Carroll clearly intended to spell "raven" backwards. The word was corrected to "never" in all later printings, perhaps by an editor who fancied he had caught a printer's error. Because Carroll died soon after this "correction" destroyed the ingenuity of his answer, the original spelling was never restored. Whether Carroll was aware of the damage done to his clever answer is not known.

"It *is* the same thing with you," said the Hatter, and here the conversation dropped, and the party sat silent for a minute, while Alice thought over all she could remember about ravens and writing-desks, which wasn't much.

The Hatter was the first to break the silence. "What day of the month is it?" he said, turning to Alice: he had taken his watch out of his pocket, and was looking at it uneasily, shaking it every now and then, and holding it to his ear.

Alice considered a little, and then said "The fourth."

"Two days wrong!" sighed the Hatter. "I told you butter wouldn't suit the works!" he added, looking angrily at the March Hare.

"It was the *best* butter," the March Hare meekly replied.

"Yes, but some crumbs must have got in as well," the Hatter grumbled: "you shouldn't have put it in with the bread-knife."

The March Hare took the watch and looked at it gloomily: then he dipped it into his cup of tea, and looked at it again: but he could think of nothing better to say than his first remark, "It was the *best* butter, you know."

Alice had been looking over his shoulder with some curiosity. "What a funny watch!" she remarked. "It tells the day of the month, and doesn't tell what o'clock it is!"

"Why should it?" muttered the Hatter. "Does *your* watch tell you what year it is?"

"Of course not," Alice replied very readily: "but that's because it stays the same year for such a long time together."

"Which is just the case with *mine,*" said the Hatter.

"He dipped it into his cup of tea, and looked at it again"

Alice felt dreadfully puzzled. The Hatter's remark seemed to her to have no sort of meaning in it, and yet it was certainly English. "I don't quite understand you," she said, as politely as she could.

"The Dormouse is asleep again," said the Hatter, and he poured a little hot tea upon its nose.

The Dormouse shook its head impatiently, and said, without opening its eyes, "Of course, of course: just what I was going to remark myself."

"Have you guessed the riddle yet?" the Hatter said, turning to Alice again.

"No, I give it up," Alice replied. "What's the answer?"

"I haven't the slightest idea," said the Hatter.

"Nor I," said the March Hare.

Alice sighed wearily. "I think you might do something better with the time," she said, "than wasting it in asking riddles that have no answers."

"If you knew Time as well as I do," said the Hatter, "you wouldn't talk about wasting *it*. It's *him.*"

"I don't know what you mean," said Alice.

"Of course you don't!" the Hatter said, tossing his head contemptuously. "I dare say you never even spoke to Time!"

"Perhaps not," Alice cautiously replied; "but I know I have to beat time when I learn music."

"Ah! That accounts for it," said the Hatter. "He wo'n't stand beating. Now, if you only kept on good terms with him, he'd do almost anything you liked with the clock. For instance, suppose it were nine o'clock in the morning, just time to begin lessons: you'd only have to whisper a hint to Time, and round goes the clock in a twinkling! Half-past one, time for dinner!"

("I only wish it was," the March Hare said to itself in a whisper.)

"That would be grand, certainly," said Alice thoughtfully; "but then—I shouldn't be hungry for it, you know."

"Not at first, perhaps," said the Hatter: "but you could keep it to half-past one as long as you liked."

"Is that the way *you* manage?" Alice asked.

The Hatter shook his head mournfully. "Not I!" he replied. "We quarreled last March—just before *he* went mad, you know—" (pointing his teaspoon at the March Hare,) "—it was at the great concert given by the Queen of Hearts, and I had to sing[5]

'Twinkle, twinkle, little bat!
How I wonder what you're at!'

You know the song, perhaps?"

"I've heard something like it," said Alice.

"It goes on, you know," the Hatter continued, "in this way:—

'Up above the world you fly,
Like a tea-tray in the sky.
Twinkle, twinkle—' "

Here the Dormouse shook itself, and began singing in its sleep *"Twinkle, twinkle, twinkle, twinkle—"* and went on so long that they had to pinch it to make it stop.

"Well, I'd hardly finished the first verse," said the Hatter, "when the Queen bawled out 'He's murdering the time! Off with his head!' "

"How dreadfully savage!" exclaimed Alice.

"And ever since that," the Hatter went on in a mournful tone, "he wo'n't do a thing I ask! It's always six o'clock now."

A bright idea came into Alice's head. "Is that the reason so many tea-things are put out here?" she asked.

5. The Hatter's song is a parody of the first verse of "The Star," a popular poem by Jane Taylor. (For the entire poem, see my *AA.*) Carroll's parody may also owe something to an incident that Helmut Gernsheim recounts in *Lewis Carroll; Photographer* (Chanticleer, 1950):

> At Christ Church the usually staid don relaxed in the company of little visitors to his large suite of rooms—a veritable children's paradise. There was a wonderful array of dolls and toys, a distorting mirror, a clockwork bear, and a flying bat made by him. This latter was the cause of much embarrassment when, on a hot summer afternoon, after circling the room several times, it suddenly flew out of the window and landed on a tea-tray which a college servant was just carrying across Tom Quad. Startled by this strange apparition, he dropped the tray with a great clatter.

"Yes, that's it," said the Hatter with a sigh: "it's always tea-time, and we've no time to wash the things between whiles."

"Then you keep moving round, I suppose?" said Alice.

"Exactly so," said the Hatter: "as the things get used up."

"But what happens when you come to the beginning again?" Alice ventured to ask.

"Suppose we change the subject," the March Hare interrupted, yawning. "I'm getting tired of this. I vote the young lady tells us a story."

"I'm afraid I don't know one," said Alice, rather alarmed at the proposal.

"Then the Dormouse shall!" they both cried. "Wake up, Dormouse!" And they pinched it on both sides at once.

The Dormouse slowly opened its eyes. "I wasn't asleep," it said in a hoarse, feeble voice, "I heard every word you fellows were saying."

"Tell us a story!" said the March Hare.

"Yes, please do!" pleaded Alice.

"And be quick about it," added the Hatter, "or you'll be asleep again before it's done."

"Once upon a time there were three little sisters," the Dormouse began in a great hurry; "and their names were Elsie, Lacie, and Tillie; and they lived at the bottom of a well—"[6]

"What did they live on?" said Alice, who always took a great interest in questions of eating and drinking.

"They lived on treacle," said the Dormouse, after thinking a minute or two.

"They couldn't have done that, you know," Alice gently remarked. "They'd have been ill."

6. The three little (Liddell) sisters are Lorina Charlotte (L.C., pronounced "Elsie"), Alice, and Edith, whose family nickname was Tillie. "Lacie" is an anagram of "Alice." Newell shows the girls at the bottom of the treacle well, a scene that Tenniel avoided.

Vivien Greene (wife of novelist Graham Greene), who lives in Oxford, was the first to inform me that what is called a treacle well actually existed in Carroll's time at Binsey, near Oxford, and is there today. Before "treacle" became a common term for molasses, it referred to medicinal compounds of varying substances given for snakebites, poisons, and other diseases. Wells that were believed to contain healing waters were called treacle wells. This adds of course to the meaning of the Dormouse's remark, a few lines later, that the sisters were "very ill."

Mavis Batey, in *Alice's Adventures in Oxford* (A Pitkin Pictorial Guide, 1980), tells the eighth-century legend of the Binsey well. It seems that God struck King Algar blind because he pursued the princess Frideswide with the intent to marry her. Her prayer to Saint Margaret for mercy on the king was answered by the appearance of a well at Binsey with miraculous waters that cured Algar's blindness. Saint Frideswide returned to Oxford, where she supposedly founded a nunnery at the spot where Christ Church now stands. The treacle well was a popular healing spot throughout the Middle Ages.

An amusing instance of the earlier meaning of "treacle" is provided by a famous "Curious Bible" printed in 1568 and known as the Treacle Bible. ("Curious Bible" is a generic term for Bibles that contain peculiar printer's errors or strange choices of words made by an editor. In the King James Bible, Jeremiah 8:22 begins: "Is there no balm in Gilead . . . ?" In the Treacle Bible it reads: "Is there not treacle at Gilead?"

In the Latin Chapel of Christ Church Cathedral, a stained-glass window (reproduced in color in Mrs. Batey's booklet) depicts a group of ailing persons on their way to the Binsey treacle well.

"So they were," said the Dormouse; "*very* ill."

Alice tried a little to fancy to herself what such an extraordinary way of living would be like, but it puzzled her too much: so she went on: "But why did they live at the bottom of a well?"

"Take some more tea," the March Hare said to Alice, very earnestly.

"I've had nothing yet," Alice replied in an offended tone: "so I ca'n't take more."

"You mean you ca'n't take *less,*" said the Hatter: "it's very easy to take *more* than nothing."

"Nobody asked *your* opinion," said Alice.

"Who's making personal remarks now?" the Hatter asked triumphantly.

Alice did not quite know what to say to this: so she helped herself to some tea and bread-and-butter, and then turned to the Dormouse, and repeated her question. "Why did they live at the bottom of a well?"

The Dormouse again took a minute or two to think about it, and then said "It was a treacle-well."

"There's no such thing!" Alice was beginning very angrily, but the Hatter and the March Hare went "Sh! Sh!" and the Dormouse sulkily remarked "If you ca'n't be civil, you'd better finish the story for yourself."

"No, please go on!" Alice said very humbly. "I wo'n't interrupt you again. I dare say there may be *one.*"

"One, indeed!" said the Dormouse indignantly. However, he consented to go on. "And

" 'They lived at the bottom of a well' "

so these three little sisters—they were learning to draw, you know—"

"What did they draw?" said Alice, quite forgetting her promise.

"Treacle," said the Dormouse, without considering at all, this time.

"I want a clean cup," interrupted the Hatter: "let's all move one place on."

He moved on as he spoke, and the Dormouse followed him: the March Hare moved into the Dormouse's place, and Alice rather unwillingly took the place of the March Hare. The Hatter was the only one who got any advantage from the change; and Alice was a good deal worse off than before, as the March Hare had just upset the milk-jug into his plate.

Alice did not wish to offend the Dormouse again, so she began very cautiously: "But I don't understand. Where did they draw the treacle from?"

"You can draw water out of a water-well," said the Hatter; "so I should think you could draw treacle out of a treacle-well—eh, stupid?"

"But they were *in* the well," Alice said to the Dormouse, not choosing to notice this last remark.

"Of course they were," said the Dormouse: "well in."

This answer so confused poor Alice, that she let the Dormouse go on for some time without interrupting it.

"They were learning to draw," the Dormouse went on, yawning and rubbing its eyes, for it was getting very sleepy; "and they drew all manner of things—everything that begins with an M—"

"Why with an M?" said Alice.

"Why not?" said the March Hare.[7]

Alice was silent.

The Dormouse had closed its eyes by this time, and was going off into a doze; but, on being pinched by the Hatter, it woke up again with a little shriek, and went on: "—that begins with an M, such as mouse-traps, and the moon, and memory, and muchness—you know you say things are 'much of a muchness'—did you ever see such a thing as a drawing of a muchness!"

"Really, now you ask me," said Alice, very much confused, "I don't think—"

"Then you shouldn't talk," said the Hatter.

This piece of rudeness was more than Alice could bear: she got up in great disgust, and walked off: the Dormouse fell asleep instantly, and neither of the others took the least notice of her going, though she looked back once or twice, half hoping that they would call after her: the last time she saw them, they were trying to put the Dormouse into the teapot.[8]

"At any rate I'll never go *there* again!" said Alice, as she picked her way through the wood. "It's the stupidest tea-party I ever was at in all my life!"[9]

Just as she said this, she noticed that one of the trees had a door leading right into it. "That's very curious!" she thought. "But everything's curious to-day. I think I may as well go in at once." And in she went.

Once more she found herself in the long hall, and close to the little glass table. "Now, I'll manage better this time," she said to herself, and began by taking the little golden key, and unlocking the door that led into the garden.

7. Henry Holiday, who illustrated Carroll's *Hunting of the Snark,* recalled in a letter asking Carroll why all the names of the ship's crew members begin with *B.* Carroll replied, "Why not?"

Note that it is the March Hare, not the Dormouse, who answers Alice's question. As Selwyn Goodacre has pointed out, "his own name begins with an *M* as well, and he wanted to be part of the story."

Selwyn Goodacre also called my attention to the fact that because "molasses" begins with *m,* it was appropriate that the girls "draw" treacle from the well.

8. I am indebted to Roger Green for the surprising information that Victorian children actually had dormice as pets, keeping them in old teapots filled with grass or hay.

9. A scene based on the Mad Tea-Party was one of the earliest to be constructed for a rapidly developing new technology called "virtual reality." A person puts on a helmet with goggles that provide each eye with a video screen connected to a computer program. The subject also wears headphones, and a special suit and gloves fitted with fiber-optic sensors that tell the computer how one's body and hands are moving, and how those motions alter the visual scene. One is thus able to see and move about in a three-dimensional artificial "space." A person can take the role of Alice, or any of the other characters at the Mad Tea-Party, and, as the technology improves, should even be able to interact with the characters. See "On the Road to the Global Village," by Karen Wright (*Scientific American,* March 1990), and "Artificial Reality," by G. Pascal Zachary (*The Wall Street Journal,* January 23, 1990, page 1).

Then she set to work nibbling at the mushroom (she had kept a piece of it in her pocket) till she was about a foot high; then she walked down the little passage: and *then*—she found herself at last in the beautiful garden, among the bright flower-beds and the cool fountains.

CHAPTER VIII

THE QUEEN'S CROQUET-GROUND

1. Bruce Bevan wrote to say that Carroll may have had in mind here an incident described in the chapter on tulip mania in Charles Mackay's 1841 work *Extraordinary Popular Delusions and the Madness of Crowds.* An English traveler in Holland, unaware of the high prices then being paid for rare species of tulips, picked up a tulip root, thinking it an onion, and began to peel it. As it happened, the root was worth four thousand florins. The poor man was arrested and sent to prison until he found the means to pay this sum to the tulip root's owner.

A large rose-tree stood near the entrance of the garden: the roses growing on it were white, but there were three gardeners at it, busily painting them red. Alice thought this a very curious thing, and she went nearer to watch them, and, just as she came up to them, she heard one of them say "Look out now, Five! Don't go splashing paint over me like that!"

"I couldn't help it," said Five, in a sulky tone. "Seven jogged my elbow."

On which Seven looked up and said "That's right, Five! Always lay the blame on others!"

"*You'd* better not talk!" said Five. "I heard the Queen say only yesterday you deserved to be beheaded."

"What for?" said the one who had spoken first.

"That's none of *your* business, Two!" said Seven.

"Yes, it *is* his business!" said Five. "And I'll tell him—it was for bringing the cook tulip-roots instead of onions."[1]

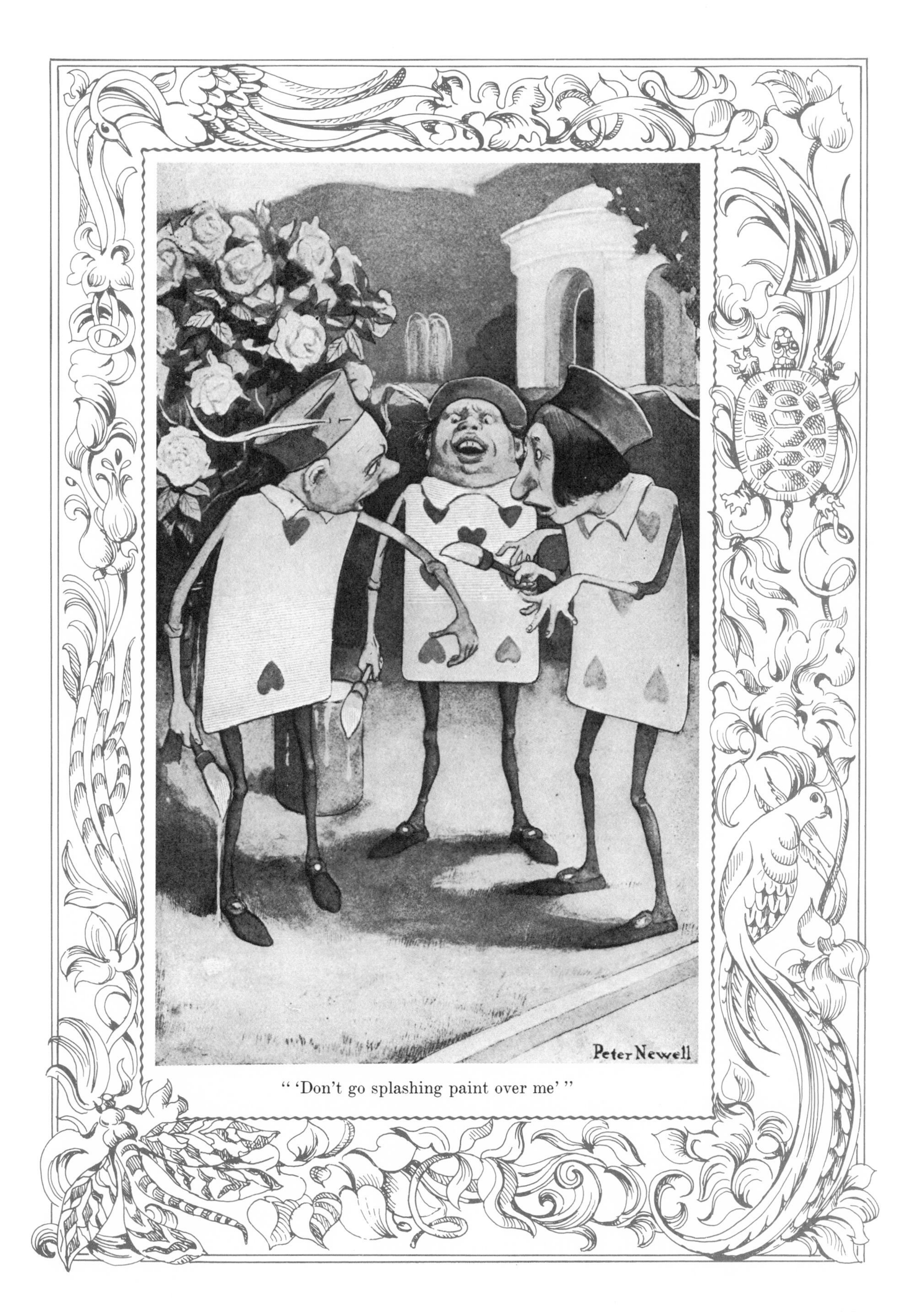

" 'Don't go splashing paint over me' "

Seven flung down his brush, and had just begun "Well, of all the unjust things—" when his eye chanced to fall upon Alice, as she stood watching them, and he checked himself suddenly: the others looked round also, and all of them bowed low.

"Would you tell me, please," said Alice, a little timidly, "why you are painting those roses?"

Five and Seven said nothing, but looked at Two. Two began, in a low voice, "Why, the fact is, you see, Miss, this here ought to have been a *red* rose-tree, and we put a white one in by mistake; and, if the Queen was to find out, we should all have our heads cut off, you know. So you see, Miss, we're doing our best, afore she comes, to—" At this moment, Five, who had been anxiously looking across the garden, called out, "The Queen! The Queen!" and the three gardeners instantly three themselves flat upon their faces. There was a sound of many footsteps, and Alice looked round, eager to see the Queen.

First came ten soldiers carrying clubs: these were all shaped like the three gardeners, oblong and flat, with their hands and feet at the corners: next the ten courtiers: these were ornamented all over with diamonds, and walked two and two, as the soldiers did. After these came the royal children: there were ten of them, and the little dears came jumping merrily along, hand in hand, in couples: they were all ornamented with hearts. Next came the guests, mostly Kings and Queens, and among them Alice recognized the White Rabbit: it was talking in a hurried nervous manner, smiling at everything that was said, and went by without noticing her. Then followed the Knave of Hearts, carrying the King's crown on a crimson velvet cushion; and, last of all this grand procession, came THE KING AND THE QUEEN OF HEARTS.[2]

Alice was rather doubtful whether she ought not to lie down on her face like the three gardeners, but she could not remember ever having heard of such a rule at processions; "and besides, what would be the use of a procession," thought she, "if people had all to lie down on their faces, so that they couldn't see it?" So she stood where she was, and waited.

When the procession came opposite to Alice, they all stopped and looked at her, and the Queen said, severely, "Who is this?" She said it to the Knave of Hearts, who only bowed and smiled in reply.

"Idiot!" said the Queen, tossing her head impatiently; and turning to Alice, she went on: "What's your name, child?"

"My name is Alice, so please your Majesty," said Alice very politely; but she added, to herself, "Why, they're only a pack of cards, after all. I needn't be afraid of them!"

"And who are *these?*" said the Queen, pointing to the three gardeners who were lying round the rose-tree; for, you see, as they were lying on their faces, and the pattern on their backs was the same as the rest of the pack, she could not tell whether they were gardeners, or soldiers, or courtiers, or three of her own children.

"How should *I* know?" said Alice, surprised at her own courage. "It's no business of *mine.*"

The Queen turned crimson with fury, and, after glaring at her for a moment like a wild

2. Tenniel's illustration of this garden scene is admirably analyzed in Michael Hancher's book on Tenniel. The Knave, his nose slightly shaded (see Chapter 12, note 5), is carrying England's official St. Edward's crown. The heads of the King of Hearts and the Knave of Hearts (one of the two one-eyed jacks, as they are known to cardplayers) are of course based on playing cards. Left of the King of Hearts you see the faces of the King of Spades and the King of Clubs, and the one-eyed King of Diamonds, facing east instead of his customary west.

The Queen of Hearts wears a dress patterned like the dress of a queen of spades. Was Tenniel, Hancher asks, identifying her with a card traditionally associated with death? Note the glass dome of a conservatory in the far background.

Puzzle: Find the White Rabbit in the picture.

beast, began screaming "Off with her head! Off with—"

"Nonsense!" said Alice, very loudly and decidedly, and the Queen was silent.

The King laid his hand upon her arm, and timidly said "Consider, my dear: she is only a child!"

The Queen turned angrily away from him, and said to the Knave "Turn them over!"

The Knave did so, very carefully, with one foot.

"Get up!" said the Queen in a shrill, loud voice, and the three gardeners instantly jumped up, and began bowing to the King, the Queen, the royal children, and everybody else.

"Leave off that!" screamed the Queen. "You make me giddy." And then, turning to the rose-tree, she went on "What *have* you been doing here?"

"May it please your Majesty," said Two, in a very humble tone, going down on one knee as he spoke, "we were trying—"

"*I* see!" said the Queen, who had meanwhile been examining the roses. "Off with their heads!" and the procession moved on, three of the soldiers remaining behind to execute the unfortunate gardeners, who ran to Alice for protection.

"You sha'n't be beheaded!" said Alice, and she put them into a large flower-pot that stood near. The three soldiers wandered about for a minute or two, looking for them, and then quietly marched off after the others.

"Are their heads off?" shouted the Queen.

"Their heads are gone, if it please your Majesty!" the soldiers shouted in reply.

" 'Off with her head!' "

"That's right!" shouted the Queen. "Can you play croquet?"

The soldiers were silent, and looked at Alice, as the question was evidently meant for her.

"Yes!" shouted Alice.

"Come on, then!" roared the Queen, and Alice joined the procession, wondering very much what would happen next.

"It's—it's a very fine day!" said a timid voice at her side. She was walking by the White Rabbit, who was peeping anxiously into her face.

"Very," said Alice. "Where's the Duchess?"

"Hush! Hush!" said the Rabbit in a low hurried tone. He looked anxiously over his shoulder as he spoke, and then raised himself upon tiptoe, put his mouth close to her ear, and whispered "She's under sentence of execution."

"What for?" said Alice.

"Did you say 'What a pity!'?" the Rabbit said.

"No, I didn't," said Alice. "I don't think it's at all a pity. I said 'What for?' "

"She boxed the Queen's ears—" the Rabbit began. Alice gave a little scream of laughter. "Oh, hush!" the Rabbit whispered in a frightened tone. "The Queen will hear you! You see she came rather late, and the Queen said—"

"Get to your places!" shouted the Queen in a voice of thunder, and people began running about in all directions, tumbling up against each other: however, they got settled down in a minute or two, and the game began.

Alice thought she had never seen such a curious croquet-ground in her life: it was all ridges and furrows: the croquet balls were live hedgehogs, and the mallets live flamingoes, and the soldiers had to double themselves up and stand on their hands and feet, to make the arches.

The chief difficulty Alice found at first was in managing her flamingo: she succeeded in getting its body tucked away, comfortably enough, under her arm, with its legs hanging down, but generally, just as she had got its neck nicely straightened out, and was going to give the hedgehog a blow with its head, it *would* twist itself round and look up in her face, with such a puzzled expression that she could not help bursting out laughing; and, when she had got its head down, and was going to begin again, it was very provoking to find that the hedgehog had unrolled itself, and was in the act of crawling away: besides all this, there was generally a ridge or a furrow in the way wherever she wanted to send the hedgehog to, and, as the doubled-up soldiers were always getting up and walking off to other parts of the ground, Alice soon came to the conclusion that it was a very difficult game indeed.

The players all played at once, without waiting for turns, quarreling all the while, and fighting for the hedgehogs; and in a very short time the Queen was in a furious passion, and went stamping about, and shouting "Off with his head!" or "Off with her head!" about once in a minute.

Alice began to feel very uneasy: to be sure, she had not as yet had any dispute with the Queen, but she knew that it might happen any minute, "and then," thought she, "what would become of me? They're dreadfully fond of beheading people here: the great wonder is, that there's any one left alive!"

"It *would* twist itself round and look up in her face"

She was looking about for some way of escape, and wondering whether she could get away without being seen, when she noticed a curious appearance in the air: it puzzled her very much at first, but after watching it a minute or two she made it out to be a grin, and she said to herself "It's the Cheshire-Cat: now I shall have somebody to talk to."

"How are you getting on?" said the Cat, as soon as there was mouth enough for it to speak with.

Alice waited till the eyes appeared, and then nodded. "It's no use speaking to it," she thought, "till its ears have come, or at least one of them." In another minute the whole head appeared, and then Alice put down her flamingo, and began an account of the game, feeling very glad she had some one to listen to her. The Cat seemed to think that there was enough of it now in sight, and no more of it appeared.

"I don't think they play at all fairly," Alice began, in rather a complaining tone, "and they all quarrel so dreadfully one ca'n't hear oneself speak—and they don't seem to have any rules in particular: at least, if there are, nobody attends to them—and you've no idea how confusing it is all the things being alive: for instance, there's the arch I've got to go through next walking about at the other end of the ground—and I should have croqueted the Queen's hedgehog just now, only it ran away when it saw mine coming!"

"How do you like the Queen?" said the Cat in a low voice.

"Not at all," said Alice: "she's so extremely—" Just then she noticed that the

Queen was close behind her, listening: so she went on "—likely to win, that it's hardly worth while finishing the game."

The Queen smiled and passed on.

"Who *are* you talking to?" said the King, coming up to Alice, and looking at the Cat's head with great curiosity.

"It's a friend of mine—a Cheshire-Cat," said Alice: "allow me to introduce it."

"I don't like the look of it at all," said the King: "however, it may kiss my hand, if it likes."

"I'd rather not," the Cat remarked.

"Don't be impertinent," said the King, "and don't look at me like that!" He got behind Alice as he spoke.

"A cat may look at a king," said Alice. "I've read that in some book, but I don't remember where."[3]

"Well, it must be removed," said the King very decidedly; and he called to the Queen, who was passing at the moment, "My dear! I wish you would have this cat removed!"

The Queen had only one way of settling all difficulties, great or small. "Off with his head!" she said without even looking around.

"I'll fetch the executioner myself," said the King eagerly, and he hurried off.

Alice thought she might as well go back and see how the game was going on, as she heard the Queen's voice in the distance, screaming with passion. She had already heard her sentence three of the players to be executed for having missed their turns, and she did not like the look of things at all, as the game was in such confusion that she never knew whether it was her

3. Frankie Morris suggests in *Jabberwocky* (Autumn 1985) that the book Alice read could have been *A Cat May Look Upon a King* (London, 1652), a slashing attack on English kings by Sir Archibald Weldon. "A cat may look at a king" is a familiar proverb implying that inferiors have certain privileges in the presence of superiors.

" 'Don't look at me like that' "

turn or not. So she went off in search of her hedgehog.

The hedgehog was engaged in a fight with another hedgehog, which seemed to Alice an excellent opportunity for croqueting one of them with the other: the only difficulty was, that her flamingo was gone across the other side of the garden, where Alice could see it trying in a helpless sort of way to fly up into a tree.

By the time she had caught the flamingo and brought it back, the fight was over, and both the hedgehogs were out of sight: "but it doesn't matter much," thought Alice, "as all the arches are gone from this side of the ground." So she tucked it away under her arm, that it might not escape again, and went back to have a little more conversation with her friend.

When she got back to the Cheshire-Cat, she was surprised to find quite a large crowd collected round it: there was a dispute going on between the executioner, the King, and the Queen, who were all talking at once, while all the rest were quite silent, and looked very uncomfortable.[4]

The moment Alice appeared, she was appealed to by all three to settle the question, and they repeated their arguments to her, though, as they all spoke at once, she found it very hard to make out exactly what they said.

The executioner's argument was, that you couldn't cut off a head unless there was a body to cut it off from: that he had never had to do such a thing before, and he wasn't going to begin at *his* time of life.

The King's argument was that anything that

4. In Tenniel's illustration of this scene he made the executioner, appropriately, the Knave of Clubs:

In Newell's picture of Alice holding the flamingo, you will see the executioner running toward her.

"The hedgehog was engaged in a fight with another hedgehog"

had a head could be beheaded, and that you weren't to talk nonsense.

The Queen's argument was that, if something wasn't done about it in less than no time, she'd have everybody executed, all round. (It was this last remark that had made the whole party look so grave and anxious.)

Alice could think of nothing else to say but "It belongs to the Duchess: you'd better ask *her* about it."

"She's in prison," the Queen said to the executioner: "fetch her here." And the executioner went off like an arrow.

The Cat's head began fading away the moment he was gone, and, by the time he had come back with the Duchess, it had entirely disappeared: so the King and the executioner ran wildly up and down, looking for it, while the rest of the party went back to the game.

CHAPTER IX

THE MOCK TURTLE'S STORY

"You can't think how glad I am to see you again, you dear old thing!" said the Duchess, as she tucked her arm affectionately into Alice's, and they walked off together.

Alice was very glad to find her in such a pleasant temper, and thought to herself that perhaps it was only the pepper that had made her so savage when they met in the kitchen.

"When *I'm* a Duchess," she said to herself (not in a very hopeful tone, though), "I wo'n't have any pepper in my kitchen *at all.* Soup does very well without—Maybe it's always pepper that makes people hot-tempered," she went on, very much pleased at having found out a new kind of rule, "and vinegar that makes them sour—and camomile that makes them bitter—and—and barley-sugar and such things that make children sweet-tempered. I only wish people knew *that:* then they wouldn't be so stingy about it, you know—"

She had quite forgotten the Duchess by this

time, and was a little startled when she heard her voice close to her ear. "You're thinking about something, my dear, and that makes you forget to talk. I ca'n't tell you just now what the moral of that is, but I shall remember it in a bit."

"Perhaps it hasn't one," Alice ventured to remark.

"Tut, tut, child!" said the Duchess. "Everything's got a moral, if only you can find it."[1] And she squeezed herself up closer to Alice's side as she spoke.

Alice did not much like her keeping so close to her: first because the Duchess was *very* ugly; and secondly, because she was exactly the right height to rest her chin on Alice's shoulder, and it was an uncomfortably sharp chin. However, she did not like to be rude: so she bore it as well as she could.

"The game's going on rather better now," she said, by way of keeping up the conversation a little.

" 'Tis so," said the Duchess: "and the moral of that is—'Oh, 'tis love, 'tis love, that makes the world go round!' "[2]

"Somebody said," Alice whispered, "that it's done by everybody minding their own business!"

"Ah well! It means much the same thing," said the Duchess, digging her sharp little chin into Alice's shoulder as she added "and the moral of *that* is—'Take care of the sense, and the sounds will take care of themselves.' "

"How fond she is of finding morals in things!" Alice thought to herself.

"I dare say you're wondering why I don't

1. M. J. C. Hodgart called my notice to the following statement in Charles Dickens's novel *Dombey and Son* (Chapter 2): "There's a moral in everything, if we would only avail ourselves of it." James Kincaid, in one of his notes for the Pennyroyal edition of *Through the Looking-Glass* (1983), illustrated by Barry Moser, quotes from Carroll's monograph *The New Belfry of Christ Church, Oxford:* "Everything has a moral if you choose to look for it. In Wordsworth a good half of every poem is devoted to the Moral: in Byron, a smaller proportion: in Tupper, the whole."

2. A popular French song of the time contains the lines "C'est l'amour, l'amour, l'amour / Qui fait le monde à la ronde," but Roger Green thinks the Duchess is quoting the first line of an equally old English song, "The Dawn of Love." He calls attention to the similar statement that closes Dante's *Paradiso.*

" 'Tis love that makes the world go round, my baby," writes Dickens (*Our Mutual Friend,* Book 4, Chapter 4), and there are endless other expressions of the sentiment in English literature.

" 'Tut, tut, child!' said the Duchess"

put my arm round your waist," the Duchess said, after a pause: "the reason is, that I'm doubtful about the temper of your flamingo. Shall I try the experiment?"

"He might bite," Alice cautiously replied, not feeling at all anxious to have the experiment tried.

"Very true," said the Duchess: "flamingoes and mustard both bite. And the moral of that is—'Birds of a feather flock together.' "

"Only mustard isn't a bird," Alice remarked.

"Right, as usual," said the Duchess: "what a clear way you have of putting things!"

"It's a mineral, I *think,*" said Alice.

"Of course it is," said the Duchess, who seemed ready to agree to everything that Alice said: "there's a large mustard-mine near here. And the moral of that is—'The more there is of mine, the less there is of yours.' "[3]

"Oh, I know!" exclaimed Alice, who had not attended to this last remark. "It's a vegetable. It doesn't look like one, but it is."[4]

"I quite agree with you," said the Duchess; "and the moral of that is—'Be what you would seem to be'—or, if you'd like it put more simply—'Never imagine yourself not to be otherwise than what it might appear to others that what you were or might have been was not otherwise than what you had been would have appeared to them to be otherwise.' "

"I think I should understand that better," Alice said very politely, "if I had it written down: but I ca'n't quite follow it as you say it."

"That's nothing to what I could say if I chose," the Duchess replied, in a pleased tone.

3. Carroll seems to have invented this proverb. It describes what in modern game theory is called a two-person zero-sum game—a game in which the payoff to the winner exactly equals the losses of the loser. Poker is a many-person zero-sum game because the total amount of money won equals the total amount of money lost.

4. Alice has gone from animal to mineral to vegetable. As reader Jane Parker writes in a letter, we have here a reference to the popular Victorian parlor game animal, vegetable, mineral, in which players tried to guess what someone was thinking of. The first questions asked were traditionally: Is it animal? Is it vegetable? Is it mineral? Answers had to be yes or no, and the object was to guess correctly in twenty or fewer questions. A more explicit reference to the game can be found in Chapter 7 of the second *Alice* book.

"Pray don't trouble yourself to say it any longer than that," said Alice.

"Oh, don't talk about trouble!" said the Duchess. "I make you a present of everything I've said as yet."

"A cheap sort of present!" thought Alice. "I'm glad people don't give birthday-presents like that!" But she did not venture to say it out loud.

"Thinking again?" the Duchess asked, with another dig of her sharp little chin.

"I've a right to think," said Alice sharply, for she was beginning to feel a little worried.

"Just about as much right," said the Duchess, "as pigs have to fly;[5] and the m——"

But here, to Alice's great surprise, the Duchess's voice died away, even in the middle of her favourite word "moral", and the arm that was linked into hers began to tremble. Alice looked up, and there stood the Queen in front of them, with her arms folded, frowning like a thunderstorm.

"A fine day, your Majesty!" the Duchess began in a low, weak voice.

"Now, I give you fair warning," shouted the Queen, stamping on the ground as she spoke; "either you or your head must be off, and that in about half no time! Take your choice!"

The Duchess took her choice, and was gone in a moment.

"Let's go on with the game," the Queen said to Alice; and Alice was too much frightened to say a word, but slowly followed her back to the croquet-ground.

The other guests had taken advantage of the

5. A reference to flying pigs occurs in Tweedledee's song in the second *Alice* book when the Walrus wonders if pigs have wings. "Pigs may fly," so goes an old Scottish proverb, "but it's not likely." You'll see winged pigs in Henry Holiday's illustration of the Beaver's lesson in *The Hunting of the Snark.*

Queen's absence, and were resting in the shade: however, the moment they saw her, they hurried back to the game, the Queen merely remarking that a moment's delay would cost them their lives.

All the time they were playing the Queen never left off quarreling with the other players, and shouting "Off with his head!" or "Off with her head!" Those whom she sentenced were taken into custody by the soldiers, who of course had to leave off being arches to do this, so that, by the end of half an hour or so, there were no arches left, and all the players, except the King, the Queen, and Alice, were in custody and under sentence of execution.

Then the Queen left off, quite out of breath, and said to Alice "Have you seen the Mock Turtle yet?"

"No," said Alice. "I don't even know what a Mock Turtle is."

"It's the thing Mock Turtle Soup is made from," said the Queen.

"I never saw one, or heard of one," said Alice.

"Come on, then," said the Queen, "and he shall tell you his history."

As they walked off together, Alice heard the King say in a low voice, to the company, generally, "You are all pardoned." "Come, *that's* a good thing!" she said to herself, for she had felt quite unhappy at the number of executions the Queen had ordered.

They very soon came upon a Gryphon, lying fast asleep in the sun.[6] (If you don't know what a Gryphon is, look at the picture.) "Up, lazy thing!" said the Queen, "and take this young

6. Reader James Bethune thinks there is satirical significance in the Gryphon's sleeping. Griffins were supposed to guard fiercely the gold mines of ancient Scythia, and this led to their becoming heraldic emblems of extreme vigilance. See Anne Clark's article "The Griffin and the Gryphon," in *Jabberwocky* (Winter 1977).

I am indebted to Vivien Greene for informing me that the griffin is the emblem of Oxford's Trinity College. It appears on Trinity's main gate, a fact surely familiar to Carroll and the Liddell sisters.

Newell did not provide a picture of the Gryphon; Tenniel's illustration is reproduced here.

lady to see the Mock Turtle, and to hear his history. I must go back and see after some executions I have ordered;" and she walked off, leaving Alice alone with the Gryphon. Alice did not quite like the look of the creature, but on the whole she thought it would be quite as safe to stay with it as to go after that savage Queen: so she waited.

The Gryphon sat up and rubbed its eyes: then it watched the Queen till she was out of sight: then it chuckled. "What fun!" said the Gryphon, half to itself, half to Alice.

"What *is* the fun?" said Alice.

"Why, *she,*" said the Gryphon. "It's all her fancy that: they never executes nobody, you know.[7] Come on!"

"Everybody says 'come on!' here," thought Alice, as she went slowly after it: "I never was so ordered about before, in all my life, never!"

They had not gone far before they saw the Mock Turtle in the distance, sitting sad and lonely on a little ledge of rock, and, as they came nearer, Alice could hear him sighing as if his heart would break. She pitied him deeply. "What is his sorrow?" she asked the Gryphon. And the Gryphon answered, very nearly in the same words as before, "It's all his fancy, that: he hasn't got no sorrow, you know. Come on!"

So they went up to the Mock Turtle, who looked at them with large eyes full of tears, but said nothing.

"This here young lady," said the Gryphon, "she wants for to know your history, she do."

"I'll tell it her," said the Mock Turtle in a deep, hollow tone. "Sit down, both of you, and don't speak a word till I've finished."

7. If the Gryphon's "nobody" is never executed, then Alice may well have seen nobody on the road in Chapter 7 of the second *Alice* book.

So they sat down, and nobody spoke for some minutes. Alice thought to herself "I don't see how he can *ever* finish, if he doesn't begin." But she waited patiently.

"Once," said the Mock Turtle at last, with a deep sigh, "I was a real Turtle."

These words were followed by a very long silence, broken only by an occasional exclamation of "Hjckrrh!" from the Gryphon, and the constant heavy sobbing of the Mock Turtle. Alice was very nearly getting up and saying, "Thank you, Sir, for your interesting story," but she could not help thinking there *must* be more to come, so she sat still and said nothing.

"When we were still little," the Mock Turtle went on at last, more calmly, though still sobbing a little now and then, "we went to school in the sea. The master was an old Turtle—we used to call him Tortoise—"

"Why did you call him Tortoise,[8] if he wasn't one?" Alice asked.

"We called him Tortoise because he taught us," said the Mock Turtle angrily. "Really you are very dull!"

"You ought to be ashamed of yourself for asking such a simple question," added the Gryphon; and then they both sat silent and looked at poor Alice, who felt ready to sink into the earth. At last the Gryphon said to the Mock Turtle "Drive on, old fellow! Don't be all day about it!" and he went on in these words:—

"Yes, we went to school in the sea, though you mayn't believe it—"

"I never said I didn't!" interrupted Alice.

"You did," said the Mock Turtle.[9]

"Hold your tongue!" added the Gryphon,

8. In Alice's day the word "tortoise" was usually given to land turtles to distinguish them from turtles that lived in the sea.

9. As Peter Heath has pointed out in *The Philosopher's Alice,* the Mock Turtle is telling Alice that she has just said "I didn't." Heath reminds us of how Humpty, in the next book, catches Alice in a similar verbal trap by referring to something she *didn't* say.

before Alice could speak again. The Mock Turtle went on.

"We had the best of educations—in fact, we went to school every day—"

"*I've* been to a day-school, too," said Alice. "You needn't be so proud as all that."

"With extras?" asked the Mock Turtle, a little anxiously.

"Yes," said Alice: "we learned French and music."

"And washing?" said the Mock Turtle.

"Certainly not!" said Alice indignantly.

"Ah! Then yours wasn't a really good school," said the Mock Turtle in a tone of great relief. "Now, at *ours,* they had, at the end of the bill, 'French, music, *and washing*—extra.' "

"You couldn't have wanted it much," said Alice; "living at the bottom of the sea."

"I couldn't afford to learn it," said the Mock Turtle with a sigh. "I only took the regular course."

"What was that?" inquired Alice.

"Reeling and Writhing, of course, to begin with," the Mock Turtle replied; "and then the different branches of Arithmetic—Ambition, Distraction, Uglification, and Derision."

"I never heard of 'Uglification,' " Alice ventured to say. "What is it?"

The Gryphon lifted up both its paws in surprise. "Never heard of uglifying!" it exclaimed. "You know what to beautify is, I suppose?"

"Yes," said Alice doubtfully: "it means—to—make—anything—prettier."

"Well, then," the Gryphon went on, "if you don't know what to uglify is, you *are* a simpleton."

Alice did not feel encouraged to ask any more questions about it: so she turned to the Mock Turtle, and said "What else had you to learn?"

"Well, there was Mystery," the Mock Turtle replied, counting off the subjects on his flappers—"Mystery, ancient and modern, with Seaography: then Drawling—the Drawling-master was an old conger-eel, that used to come once a week: *he* taught us Drawling, Stretching, and Fainting in Coils."**10**

"What was *that* like?" said Alice.

"Well, I ca'n't show it you, myself," the Mock Turtle said: "I'm too stiff. And the Gryphon never learnt it."

"Hadn't time," said the Gryphon: "I went to the Classical master, though. He was an old crab, *he* was."

"I never went to him," the Mock Turtle said with a sigh. "He taught Laughing and Grief, they used to say."

"So he did, so he did," said the Gryphon, sighing in his turn; and both creatures hid their faces in their paws.

"And how many hours a day did you do lessons?" said Alice, in a hurry to change the subject.

"Ten hours the first day," said the Mock Turtle: "nine the next, and so on."

"What a curious plan!" exclaimed Alice.

"That's the reason they're called lessons," the Gryphon remarked: "because they lessen from day to day."

This was quite a new idea to Alice, and she thought it over a little before she made her next remark. "Then the eleventh day must have been a holiday?"

10. The "Drawling-master" who came once a week to teach "Drawling, Stretching, and Fainting in Coils" is a reference to none other than the art critic John Ruskin. Ruskin came once a week to the Liddell home to teach drawing, sketching, and painting in oils to the children. They were taught well. It takes only a glance at Alice's many watercolors and those of her brother Henry, and at an oil painting of Alice by her younger sister Violet, to appreciate the talent for art that they inherited from their father. See Colin Gordon's *Behind the Looking Glass* (Harcourt Brace Jovanovich, 1982) for reproductions, many in color, of works of art produced by the Liddells.

Photographs of Ruskin at the time, and a caricature by Max Beerbohm *(below),* show him tall and thin, and strongly resembling a conger-eel. Like Carroll, he was attracted to nymphets precisely because of their sexual purity. His marriage to Euphemia ("Effie") Gray, ten years his junior, was annulled after six miserable years on grounds of "incurable impotency." Effie promptly married young John Millais, whose Pre-Raphaelite paintings Ruskin greatly admired. She bore him eight children, one of whom was the little girl pictured in Millais's famous *My First Sermon.* (See Chapter 3, note 3, of the second *Alice* book.)

Four years later Ruskin fell passionately in love with Rosie La Touche, daughter of an Irish banker, whose wife admired Ruskin's writings. She was then ten, and he was forty-seven. He proposed marriage when she was eighteen, but she turned him down. It was a crushing blow. Ruskin continued to fall in love with little girls as virginal as himself, proposing marriage to one girl when he was seventy. In 1900 he died after ten years of severe manic depression. An autobiography speaks of his admiration for Alice Liddell, but there is no mention of Lewis Carroll.

"Of course it was," said the Mock Turtle.

"And how did you manage on the twelfth?" Alice went on eagerly.[11]

"That's enough about lessons," the Gryphon interrupted in a very decided tone. "Tell her something about the games now."

11. Alice's excellent question rightly puzzles the Gryphon because it introduces the possibility of mysterious negative numbers (a concept that also puzzled early mathematicians), which seem to have no application to hours of lessons in the "curious" educational scheme. On the twelfth day and succeeding days did the pupils start teaching their teacher?

CHAPTER X

THE LOBSTER-QUADRILLE

The Mock Turtle sighed deeply, and drew the back of one flapper across his eyes. He looked at Alice and tried to speak, but, for a minute or two, sobs choked his voice. "Same as if he had a bone in his throat," said the Gryphon; and it set to work shaking him and punching him in the back. At last the Mock Turtle recovered his voice, and, with tears running down his cheeks, he went on again:—

"You may not have lived much under the sea—" ("I haven't," said Alice)—"and perhaps you were never even introduced to a lobster—" (Alice began to say "I once tasted—" but checked herself hastily, and said "No never") "—so you can have no idea what a delightful thing a Lobster-Quadrille is!"[1]

"No, indeed," said Alice. "What sort of a dance is it?"

"Why," said the Gryphon, "you first form into a line along the sea-shore—"

"Two lines!" cried the Mock Turtle. "Seals, turtles, salmon, and so on: then, when you've cleared all the jelly-fish out of the way—"

1. "Lobster Quadrille" could be an intended play on "Lancers Quadrille," a walking square dance for eight to sixteen couples that was enormously popular in English ballrooms at the time Carroll wrote his *Alice* books. A variant of the quadrille, it consisted of five figures, each in a different meter. According to *The Grove Dictionary of Music and Musicians,* the Lancers (as both the dance and its music were called) was invented by a Dublin dancing master and achieved an international following in the 1850s after being introduced in Paris. The Liddell children were taught the dance by a private tutor. The last stanza of the Mock Turtle's song may reflect the popularity of the Lancers in France, and the tossing of the lobsters may allude to the tossing of lances in combat. Whether such tossing played a role in the dance I do not know.

"*That* generally takes some time," interrupted the Gryphon.

"—you advance twice—"

"Each with a lobster as a partner!" cried the Gryphon.

"Of course," the Mock Turtle said: "advance twice, set to partners—"[2]

"—change lobsters, and retire in same order," continued the Gryphon.

"Then, you know," the Mock Turtle went on, "you throw the—"

"The lobsters!" shouted the Gryphon, with a bound into the air.

"—as far out to sea as you can—"

"Swim after them!" screamed the Gryphon.

"Turn a somersault in the sea!" cried the Mock Turtle, capering wildly about.

"Change lobsters again!" yelled the Gryphon at the top of its voice.

"Back to land again, and—that's all the first figure," said the Mock Turtle, suddenly dropping his voice; and the two creatures, who had been jumping about like mad things all this time, sat down again very sadly and quietly, and looked at Alice.

"It must be a very pretty dance," said Alice timidly.

"Would you like to see a little of it?" said the Mock Turtle.

"Very much indeed," said Alice.

"Come, let's try the first figure!" said the Mock Turtle to the Gryphon. "We can do it without lobsters, you know. Which shall sing?"

"Oh, *you* sing," said the Gryphon. "I've forgotten the words."

So they began solemnly dancing round and

2. A British correspondent who signed her letter "R. Reader" pointed out that "set to partners" means to face your partner, hop on one foot, then on the other.

"They began solemnly dancing round and round Alice"

round Alice, every now and then treading on her toes when they passed too close, and waving their fore-paws to mark the time, while the Mock Turtle sang this, very slowly and sadly:—[3]

"Will you walk a little faster?" said a whiting to a snail,
"There's a porpoise close behind us, and he's treading on my tail.

3. In a letter (1886) to Henry Savile Clarke, who adapted the *Alice* books to the stage operetta, Carroll urged that his songs that parodied old nursery rhymes be sung to the traditional tunes, not set to new music. He singled out this song in particular. "It would take a very good composer to write anything better than the old sweet air of 'Will you walk into my parlor, said the Spider to the Fly.' "

Tenniel's political cartoon in *Punch* (March 8, 1899), captioned "Alice in Bumbleland," features the same trio of Alice, Gryphon, and Mock Turtle. Alice represents the prime minister Arthur James Balfour, the Gryphon is London,

See how eagerly the lobsters and the turtles all advance!
They are waiting on the shingle—will you come and join the dance?
Will you, wo'n't you, will you, wo'n't you, will you join the dance?
Will you, wo'n't you, will you, wo'n't you, wo'n't you join the dance?

"You can really have no notion how delightful it will be
When they take us up and throw us, with the lobsters, out to sea!"
But the snail replied "Too far, too far!", and gave a look askance—
Said he thanked the whiting kindly, but he would not join the dance.
Would not, could not, would not, could not, could not join the dance.
Would not, could not, would not, could not, could not join the dance.

"What matters it how far we go?" his scaly friend replied.
"There is another shore, you know, upon the other side.
The further off from England the nearer is to France.
Then turn not pale, beloved snail, but come and join the dance.
Will you, wo'n't you, will you, wo'n't you, will you join the dance?
Will you, wo'n't you, will you, wo'n't you, wo'n't you join the dance?"

"Thank you, it's a very interesting dance to watch," said Alice, feeling very glad that it was over at last: "and I do so like that curious song about the whiting!"

"Oh, as to the whiting," said the Mock Turtle, "they—you've seen them, of course?"

"Yes," said Alice, "I've often seen them at dinn——" she checked herself hastily.

and the weeping Mock Turtle is the city of Westminster. Alice, the Gryphon, and an ordinary turtle appear in Tenniel's earlier cartoon "Alice in Blunderland" (*Punch,* October 30, 1880). Other appearances of Alice in *Punch* are in Tenniel's February 1, 1868, cartoon (Alice represents the United States), and in Tenniel's frontispiece to the bound Volume 46 (1864).

" 'Will you walk a little faster?' said a whiting to a snail"

"I don't know where Dinn may be," said the Mock Turtle; "but, if you've seen them so often, of course you know what they're like?"

"I believe so," Alice replied thoughtfully. "They have their tails in their mouths—and they're all over crumbs."

"You're wrong about the crumbs," said the Mock Turtle: "crumbs would all wash off in the sea. But they *have* their tails in their mouths;

and the reason is—" here the Mock Turtle yawned and shut his eyes. "Tell her about the reason and all that," he said to the Gryphon.

"The reason is," said the Gryphon, "that they *would* go with the lobsters to the dance. So they got thrown out to sea. So they had to fall a long way. So they got their tails fast in their mouths. So they couldn't get them out again. That's all."

"Thank you," said Alice, "it's very interesting. I never knew so much about a whiting before."

"I can tell you more than that, if you like," said the Gryphon. "Do you know why it's called a whiting?"

"I never thought about it," said Alice. "Why?"

"It does the boots and shoes," the Gryphon replied very solemnly.

Alice was thoroughly puzzled. "Does the boots and shoes!" she repeated in a wondering tone.

"Why, what are *your* shoes done with?" said the Gryphon. "I mean, what makes them so shiny?"

Alice looked down at them, and considered a little before she gave her answer. "They're done with blacking, I believe."

"Boots and shoes under the sea," the Gryphon went on in a deep voice, "are done with whiting. Now you know."

"And what are they made of?" Alice asked in a tone of great curiosity.

"Soles and eels, of course," the Gryphon replied, rather impatiently: "any shrimp could have told you that."

"If I'd been the whiting," said Alice, whose thoughts were still running on the song, "I'd have said to the porpoise 'Keep back, please! We don't want *you* with us!' "

"They were obliged to have him with them," the Mock Turtle said. "No wise fish would go anywhere without a porpoise."

"Wouldn't it, really?" said Alice, in a tone of great surprise.

"Of course not," said the Mock Turtle. "Why, if a fish came to *me,* and told me he was going a journey, I should say 'With what porpoise?' "

"Don't you mean 'purpose'?" said Alice.

"I mean what I say," the Mock Turtle replied, in an offended tone. And the Gryphon added "Come, let's hear some of *your* adventures."

"I could tell you my adventures—beginning from this morning," said Alice a little timidly; "but it's no use going back to yesterday, because I was a different person then."

"Explain all that," said the Mock Turtle.

"No, no! The adventures first," said the Gryphon in an impatient tone: "explanations take such a dreadful time."

So Alice began telling them her adventures from the time when she first saw the White Rabbit. She was a little nervous about it, just at first, the two creatures got so close to her, one on each side, and opened their eyes and mouths so *very* wide; but she gained courage as she went on. Her listeners were perfectly quiet till she got to the part about her repeating *"You are old, Father William,"* to the Caterpillar, and the words all coming different, and then the Mock

"Alice began telling them her adventures"

Turtle drew a long breath, and said "That's very curious!"

"It's all about as curious as it can be," said the Gryphon.

"It all came different!" the Mock Turtle repeated thoughtfully. "I should like to hear her try and repeat something now. Tell her to begin." He looked at the Gryphon as if he thought it had some kind of authority over Alice.

"Stand up and repeat *' 'Tis the voice of the sluggard,'* " said the Gryphon.

"How the creatures order one about, and make one repeat lessons!" thought Alice. "I might just as well be at school at once." However, she got up, and began to repeat it, but her head was so full of the Lobster-Quadrille, that she hardly knew what she was saying; and the words came very queer indeed:—

" 'Tis the voice of the Lobster: I heard him declare
'You have baked me too brown, I must sugar my hair.'
As a duck with his eyelids, so he with his nose
Trims his belt and his buttons, and turns out his toes.
When the sands are all dry, he is gay as a lark,
And will talk in contemptuous tones of the Shark:
But, when the tide rises and sharks are around,
His voice has a timid and tremulous sound."

"That's different from what *I* used to say when I was a child," said the Gryphon.

"Well, *I never* heard it before," said the Mock Turtle; "but it sounds uncommon nonsense."

Alice said nothing: she had sat down with her face in her hands, wondering if anything would *ever* happen in a natural way again.

"I should like to have it explained," said the Mock Turtle.

"She ca'n't explain it," said the Gryphon hastily. "Go on with the next verse."

"But about his toes?" the Mock Turtle persisted. "How *could* he turn them out with his nose, you know?"

"It's the first position in dancing," Alice said; but she was dreadfully puzzled by the whole thing, and longed to change the subject.[4]

"Go on with the next verse," the Gryphon repeated: "it begins *'I passed by his garden.'*"

Alice did not dare to disobey, though she felt sure it would all come wrong, and she went on in a trembling voice:—

"I passed by his garden, and marked, with one eye,
How the Owl and the Panther were sharing a pie:
The Panther took pie-crust, and gravy, and meat,
While the Owl had the dish as its share of the treat.
When the pie was all finished, the Owl, as a boon,
Was kindly permitted to pocket the spoon:
While the Panther received knife and fork with a
growl,
And concluded the banquet by—"[5]

"What *is* the use of repeating all that stuff?" the Mock Turtle interrupted, "if you don't explain it as you go on? It's by far the most confusing thing that *I* ever heard!"

"Yes, I think you'd better leave off," said the Gryphon, and Alice was only too glad to do so.

"Shall we try another figure of the Lobster-Quadrille?" the Gryphon went on. "Or would you like the Mock Turtle to sing you another song?"[6]

"Oh, a song, please, if the Mock Turtle would

4. Selwyn Goodacre passed on to me his daughter's observation that Tenniel carefully followed Alice's remark by drawing the lobster with its feet in the first position in ballet.

5. Carrollians have amused themselves by replacing the implied grim ending, "eating the owl," with other phrases, which are reported from time to time in the Lewis Carroll Society's newsletter, *Bandersnatch.* Here are some proposed endings: "taking a prowl," "wiping his jowl," "giving a howl," "taking a trowel," "kissing the fowl," "giving a scowl," and "donning a cowl."

6. In *Alice's Adventures Under Ground* the Mock Turtle sings a song that is not repeated in this book:

"Beneath the waters of the sea
Are lobsters thick as thick can be—
They love to dance with you and me,
My own, my gentle Salmon!"

The Gryphon joins in singing the chorus:

"Salmon come up! Salmon go down!
Salmon come twist your tail around!
Of all the fishes of the sea
There's none so good as Salmon!"

be so kind," Alice replied, so eagerly that the Gryphon said, in a rather offended tone, "Hm! No accounting for tastes! Sing her *'Turtle Soup,'* will you, old fellow?"

The Mock Turtle sighed deeply, and began, in a voice choked with sobs,[7] to sing this:—

"Beautiful Soup, so rich and green,
Waiting in a hot tureen!
Who for such dainties would not stoop?
Soup of the evening, beautiful Soup!
Soup of the evening, beautiful Soup!
Beau—ootiful Soo—oop!
Beau—ootiful Soo—oop!
Soo—oop of the e—e—evening,
Beautiful, beautiful Soup!

"Beautiful Soup! Who cares for fish,
Game, or any other dish?
Who would not give all else for two p
ennyworth only of beautiful Soup?
Pennyworth only of beautiful soup.
Beau—ootiful Soo—oop!
Beau—ootiful Soo—oop!
Soo—oop of the e—e—evening,
Beautiful, beauti—FUL SOUP!"

"Chorus again!" cried the Gryphon, and the Mock Turtle had just begun to repeat it, when a cry of "The trial's beginning!" was heard in the distance.

"Come on!" cried the Gryphon, and, taking Alice by the hand, it hurried off, without waiting for the end of the song.

"What trial is it?" Alice panted as she ran: but the Gryphon only answered "Come on!" and ran the faster, while more and more faintly

The song parodies "Sally Come Up," a Negro minstrel song. In his diary (July 3, 1862) Carroll describes an occasion when the Liddell sisters sang the song "with great spirit." Roger Green, in a note on this entry, provides the song's second verse and chorus:

> *Last Monday night I gave a ball,*
> *And I invite de Niggers all,*
> *The thick, the thin, the short, the tall,*
> *But none came up to Sally!*
>
> *Sally come up! Sally go down!*
> *Sally come twist your heel around!*
> *De old man he's gone down to town—*
> *Oh Sally come down de middle!*
>
> Some verses end 'Dar's not a gal like Sally!'

7. Several readers informed me that marine turtles often appear to weep copiously—especially females, when they make nocturnal egg-laying visits to the shore. One reader, Henry Smith, explained why: Reptilian kidneys are not made to deal efficiently with removing salt from water. Marine turtles are equipped with a special gland that discharges salty water through a duct at the outside corners of each eye. Underwater the secretion washes away, but when the turtle is on land the secretion resembles a flood of tears. Carroll, who had a lively interest in zoology, undoubtedly knew of this phenomenon.

" 'Come on!' cried the Gryphon"

came, carried on the breeze that followed them, the melancholy words:—

"Soo—oop of the e—e—evening,
Beautiful, beautiful Soup!"

CHAPTER XI

WHO STOLE THE TARTS?

The King and Queen of Hearts were seated on their throne when they arrived, with a great crowd assembled about them—all sorts of little birds and beasts, as well as the whole pack of cards: the Knave was standing before them, in chains, with a soldier on each side to guard him; and near the King was the White Rabbit, with a trumpet in one hand, and a scroll of parchment in the other. In the very middle of the court was a table, with a large dish of tarts upon it: they looked so good, that it made Alice quite hungry to look at them—"I wish they'd get the trial done," she thought, "and hand round the refreshments!" But there seemed to be no chance of this; so she began looking at everything about her to pass away the time.

Alice had never been in a court of justice before, but she had read about them in books, and she was quite pleased to find that she knew the name of nearly everything there. "That's the judge," she said to herself, "because of his great wig."

"The King and Queen of Hearts were seated on their throne"

1. For Tenniel's frontispiece, see Chapter 12, note 5.

The judge, by the way, was the King; and, as he wore his crown over the wig (look at the frontispiece if you want to see how he did it),[1] he did not look at all comfortable, and it was certainly not becoming.

"And that's the jury-box," thought Alice; "and those twelve creatures," (she was obliged to say "creatures," you see, because some of them were animals, and some were birds), "I suppose they are the jurors." She said this last word two or three times over to herself, being rather proud of it: for she thought, and rightly too, that very few little girls of her age knew the meaning of it at all. However, "jurymen" would have done just as well.

The twelve jurors were all writing very busily on slates. "What are they doing?" Alice whispered to the Gryphon. "They ca'n't have anything to put down yet, before the trial's begun."

"They're putting down their names," the Gryphon whispered in reply, "for fear they should forget them before the end of the trial."

"Stupid things!" Alice began in a loud indignant voice; but she stopped herself hastily, for the White Rabbit cried out "Silence in the court!", and the King put on his spectacles and looked anxiously round, to make out who was talking.

Alice could see, as well as if she were looking over their shoulders, that all the jurors were writing down "Stupid things!" on their slates, and she could even make out that one of them didn't know how to spell "stupid," and that he had to ask his neighbour to tell him. "A nice muddle their slates'll be in, before the trial's over!" thought Alice.

One of the jurors had a pencil that squeaked. This, of course, Alice could *not* stand, and she went round the court and got behind him, and very soon found an opportunity of taking it away. She did it so quickly that the poor little juror (it was Bill, the Lizard) could not make out at all what had become of it; so, after hunting all about for it, he was obliged to write with one finger for the rest of the day; and this was of very little use, as it left no mark on the slate.

"Herald, read the accusation!" said the King.

On this the White Rabbit blew three blasts on the trumpet, and then unrolled the parchment-scroll, and read as follows:—[2]

"The Queen of Hearts, she made some tarts,
All on a summer day:
The Knave of Hearts, he stole those tarts
And took them quite away!"

"Consider your verdict," the King said to the jury.

"Not yet, not yet!" the Rabbit hastily interrupted. "There's a great deal to come before that!"

"Call the first witness," said the King; and the White Rabbit blew three blasts on the trumpet, and called out "First witness!"

The first witness was the Hatter. He came in with a teacup in one hand and a piece of bread-and-butter in the other. "I beg pardon, your Majesty," he began, "for bringing these in; but I hadn't quite finished my tea when I was sent for."

"You ought to have finished," said the King. "When did you begin?"

The Hatter looked at the March Hare, who

2. As William and Ceil Baring-Gould note in their *Annotated Mother Goose* (Clarkson N. Potter, 1962, p. 149), the White Rabbit reads only the first lines of a four-stanza poem that originally appeared in *The European Magazine* (April 1782). The first stanza found its way into a collection of "Mother Goose" rhymes and probably owes its present fame, as the Baring-Goulds suggest, to its use by Carroll.

Here is the entire poem:

The Queen of Hearts
She made some tarts,
All on a summer's day;
The Knave of Hearts
He stole the tarts,
And took them clean away.
The King of Hearts
Called for the tarts,
And beat the Knave full sore;
The Knave of Hearts
Brought back the tarts,
And vow'd he'd steal no more.

The King of Spades
He kissed the maids,
Which made the Queen full sore;
The Queen of Spades
She beat those maids,
And turned them out of door;
The Knave of Spades
Grieved for those jades,
And did for them implore;
The Queen so gent
She did relent
And vow'd she'd ne'er strike more.

The King of Clubs
He often drubs
His loving Queen and wife;
The Queen of Clubs
Returns his snubs,
And all is noise and strife;
The Knave of Clubs
Gives winks and rubs,
And swears he'll take her part;
For when our kings
Will do such things,
They should be made to smart.

The Diamond King
I fain would sing,
And likewise his fair Queen;
But that the Knave,
A haughty slave,
Must needs step in between;
Good Diamond King,
With hempen string,
The haughty Knave destroy!
Then may your Queen
With mind serene,
Your royal bed enjoy.

3. It has been noticed that the Hatter's bow tie, in Tenniel's illustration for this scene, has its pointed end on his right, as in Newell's pictures. In two earlier Tenniel illustrations the tie points to the Hatter's left. Michael Hancher, in his book on Tenniel, cites this as one of several amusing inconsistencies in Tenniel's art.

had followed him into the court, arm-in-arm with the Dormouse. "Fourteenth of March, I *think* it was," he said.

"Fifteenth," said the March Hare.

"Sixteenth," said the Dormouse.

"Write that down," the King said to the jury; and the jury eagerly wrote down all three dates on their slates, and then added them up, and reduced the answer to shillings and pence.

"Take off your hat," the King said to the Hatter.

"It isn't mine," said the Hatter.

"Stolen!" the King exclaimed, turning to the jury, who instantly made a memorandum of the fact.

"I keep them to sell," the Hatter added as an explanation. "I've none of my own. I'm a Hatter."

Here the Queen put on her spectacles, and began staring hard at the Hatter, who turned pale and fidgeted.

"Give your evidence," said the King: "and don't be nervous, or I'll have you executed on the spot."

This did not seem to encourage the witness at all: he kept shifting from one foot to the other, looking uneasily at the Queen, and in his confusion he bit a large piece out of his teacup instead of the bread-and-butter.[3]

Just at this moment Alice felt a very curious sensation, which puzzled her a good deal until she made out what it was: she was beginning to grow larger again, and she thought at first she would get up and leave the court; but on second thoughts she decided to remain where she was as long as there was room for her.

"I wish you wouldn't squeeze so," said the Dormouse, who was sitting next to her. "I can hardly breathe."

"I ca'n't help it," said Alice very meekly: "I'm growing."

"You've no right to grow *here,*" said the Dormouse.

"Don't talk nonsense," said Alice more boldly: "you know you're growing too."

"Yes, but *I* grow at a reasonable pace," said the Dormouse: "not in that ridiculous fashion." And he got up very sulkily and crossed over to the other side of the court.

All this time the Queen had never left off staring at the Hatter, and, just as the Dormouse crossed the court, she said, to one of the officers of the court, "Bring me the list of the singers in the last concert!" on which the wretched Hatter trembled so, that he shook off both his shoes.

"Give your evidence," the King repeated angrily, "or I'll have you executed, whether you are nervous or not."

"I'm a poor man, your Majesty," the Hatter began, in a trembling voice, "and I hadn't begun my tea—not above a week or so—and what with the bread-and-butter getting so thin—and the twinkling of the tea—"[4]

"The twinkling of *what?*" said the King.

"It *began* with the tea," the Hatter replied.

"Of course twinkling *begins* with a T!" said the King sharply. "Do you take me for a dunce? Go on!"

"I'm a poor man," the Hatter went on, "and most things twinkled after that—only the March Hare said—"

4. If the Hatter had not been interrupted he would have said "tea tray." He is thinking of the song he sang at the Mad Tea-Party about the bat that twinkled in the sky like a tea tray.

"I didn't!" the March Hare interrupted in a great hurry.

"You did!" said the Hatter.

"I deny it!" said the March Hare.

"He denies it," said the King: "leave out that part."

"Well, at any rate, the Dormouse said—" the Hatter went on, looking anxiously around to see if he would deny it too; but the Dormouse denied nothing, being fast asleep.

"After that," continued the Hatter, "I cut some more bread-and-butter—"

"But what did the Dormouse say?" one of the jury asked.

"That I ca'n't remember," said the Hatter.

"You *must* remember," remarked the King, "or I'll have you executed."

The miserable Hatter dropped his teacup and bread-and-butter and went down on one knee. "I'm a poor man, your Majesty," he began.

"You're a *very* poor *speaker,*" said the King.

Here one of the guinea-pigs cheered, and was immediately suppressed by the officers of the court. (As that is rather a hard word, I will just explain to you how it was done. They had a large canvas bag, which tied up at the mouth with strings: into this they slipped the guinea-pig, head first, and then sat upon it.)

"I'm glad I've seen that done," thought Alice. "I've so often read in the newspapers, at the end of trials, 'There was some attempt at applause, which was immediately suppressed by the officers of the court,' and I never understood what it meant till now."

"If that's all you know about it, you may stand down," continued the King.

"'I'm a poor man, your Majesty,' the Hatter began, in a trembling voice"

"I ca'n't go no lower," said the Hatter: "I'm on the floor, as it is."

"Then you may *sit* down," the King replied.

Here the other guinea-pig cheered, and was suppressed.

"Come, that finishes the guinea-pigs!" thought Alice. "Now we shall get on better."

"I'd rather finish my tea," said the Hatter, with an anxious look at the Queen, who was reading the list of singers.

"You may go," said the King, and the Hatter hurriedly left the court, without even waiting to put his shoes on.

"—and just take his head off outside," the Queen added to one of the officers; but the Hatter was out of sight before the officer could get to the door.

"Call the next witness!" said the King.

The next witness was the Duchess's cook. She carried the pepper-box in her hand, and Alice guessed who it was, even before she got into the court, by the way the people near the door began sneezing all at once.

"Give your evidence," said the King.

"Sha'n't," said the cook.

The King looked anxiously at the White Rabbit, who said, in a low voice, "Your Majesty must cross-examine *this* witness."

"Well, if I must, I must," the King said with a melancholy air, and, after folding his arms and frowning at the cook till his eyes were nearly out of sight, he said, in a deep voice, "What are tarts made of?"

"Pepper, mostly," said the cook.

"Treacle," said a sleepy voice behind her.

"Collar that Dormouse!" the Queen shrieked

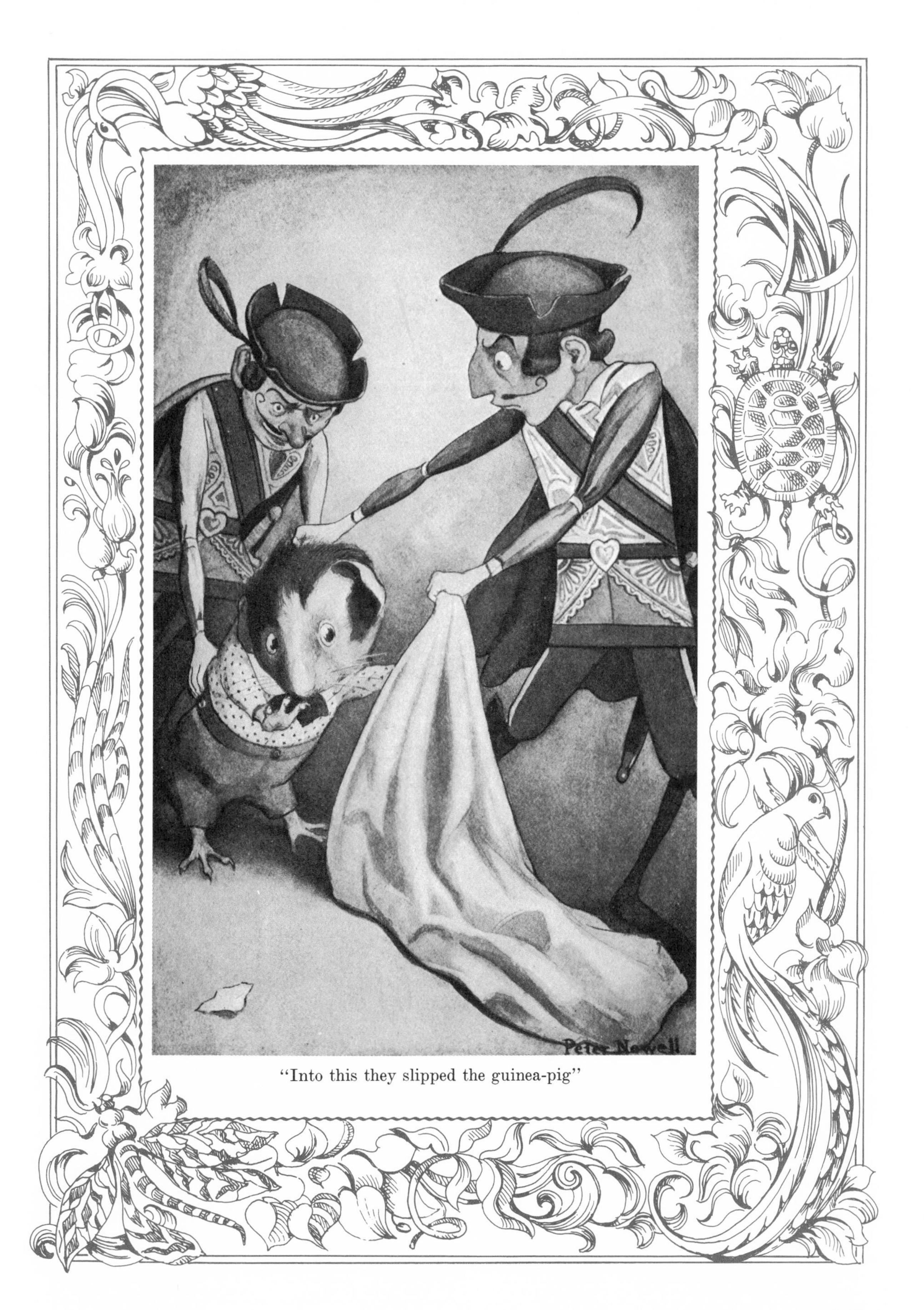

"Into this they slipped the guinea-pig"

out. "Behead that Dormouse! Turn that Dormouse out of court! Suppress him! Pinch him! Off with his whiskers!"

For some minutes the whole court was in confusion, getting the Dormouse turned out, and, by the time they had settled down again, the cook had disappeared.

"Never mind!" said the King with an air of great relief. "Call the next witness." And, he added, in an undertone to the Queen, "Really, my dear, *you* must cross-examine the next witness. It quite makes my forehead ache!"

Alice watched the White Rabbit as he fumbled over the list, feeling very curious to see what the next witness would be like, "—for they haven't got much evidence *yet,*" she said to herself. Imagine her surprise, when the White Rabbit read out, at the top of his shrill little voice, the name "Alice!"

CHAPTER XII

ALICE'S EVIDENCE

"Here!" cried Alice, quite forgetting in the flurry of the moment how large she had grown in the last few minutes, and she jumped up in such a hurry that she tipped over the jury-box with the edge of her skirt, upsetting all the jurymen on to the heads of the crowd below, and there they lay sprawling about, reminding her very much of a globe of gold-fish she had accidentally upset the week before.

"Oh, I *beg* your pardon!" she exclaimed in a tone of great dismay, and began picking them up again as quickly as she could, for the accident of the gold-fish kept running in her head, and she had a vague sort of idea that they must be collected at once and put back into the jury-box, or they would die.

"The trial cannot proceed," said the King, in a very grave voice, "until all the jurymen are back in their proper places—*all,*" he repeated with great emphasis, looking hard at Alice as he said so.

Alice looked at the jury-box, and saw that, in

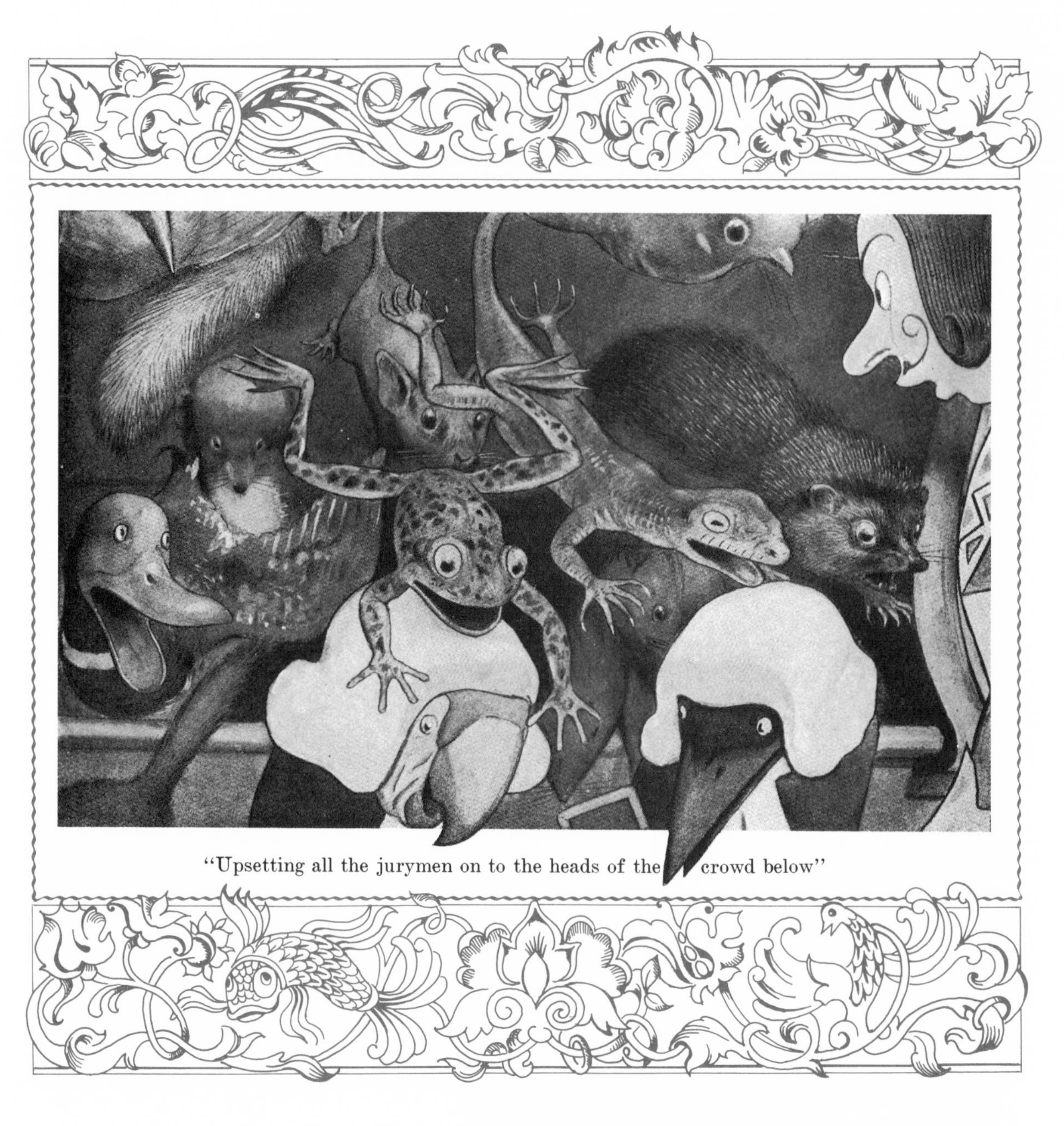

"Upsetting all the jurymen on to the heads of the crowd below"

her haste, she had put the Lizard in head downwards, and the poor little thing was waving its tail about in a melancholy way, being quite unable to move. She soon got it out again, and put it right; "not that it signifies much," she said to herself; "I should think it would be *quite* as much use in the trial one way up as the other."

As soon as the jury had a little recovered from the shock of being upset, and their slates and pencils had been found and handed back to them, they set to work very diligently to write out a history of the accident, all except the Lizard, who seemed too much overcome to do anything but sit with its mouth open, gazing up into the roof of the court.

"What do you know about this business?" the King said to Alice.

"Nothing," said Alice.

"Nothing *whatever?*" persisted the King.

"Nothing whatever," said Alice.

"That's very important," the King said, turning to the jury. They were just beginning to write this down on their slates, when the White Rabbit interrupted: "*Un*important, your Majesty means, of course," he said, in a very respectful tone, but frowning and making faces at him as he spoke.

"*Un*important, of course, I meant," the King hastily said, and went on to himself in an undertone, "important—unimportant—unimportant—important—" as if he were trying which word sounded best.

Some of the jury wrote it down "important," and some "unimportant." Alice could see this, as she was near enough to look over their slates; "but it doesn't matter a bit," she thought to herself.

At this moment the King, who had been for some time busily writing in his note-book, called out "Silence!", and read out from his book, "Rule Forty-two.[1] *All persons more than a mile high to leave the court.*"

Everybody looked at Alice.

"*I'm* not a mile high," said Alice.

"You are," said the King.

"Nearly two miles high," added the Queen.

1. The number forty-two held a special meaning for Carroll. The first *Alice* book had forty-two illustrations but a last-minute change of plans raised the number to fifty. An important nautical rule, Rule 42, is cited in Carroll's preface to *The Hunting of the Snark,* and in fit 1, stanza 7, the Baker comes aboard the ship with forty-two carefully packed boxes. In his poem "Phantasmagoria," canto 1, stanza 16, Carroll gives his age as forty-two although he was five years younger at the time. In *Through the Looking-Glass* the White King sends 4,207 horses and men to restore Humpty Dumpty, and seven is a factor of forty-two. Alice's age in the second book is seven years and six months, and seven times six equals forty-two. It is probably coincidental, but (as Philip Benham has observed) each *Alice* book has twelve chapters, or twenty-four in all, and twenty-four is forty-two backwards.

For more numerology about forty-two—in Carroll's life, in the Bible, in the Sherlock Holmes canon, and elsewhere—see the forty-second issue of *Bandersnatch,* the newsletter of England's Lewis Carroll Society. (The issue was published in January 1942 plus 42.) See also Edward Wakeling's "What I Tell You Forty-two Times Is True!" (*Jabberwocky,* Autumn 1977), his "Further Findings About the Number Forty-two" (*Jabberwocky,* Winter/Spring 1988) and note 32 of my *Annotated Snark* as it appears in *The Hunting of the Snark* (William Kaufmann, Inc., 1981). In Douglas Adams's popular science-fiction novel *The Hitchhiker's Guide to the Galaxy,* forty-two is said to be the answer to the "Ultimate Question about Everything."

"Well, I sha'n't go, at any rate," said Alice; "besides, that's not a regular rule: you invented it just now."

"It's the oldest rule in the book," said the King.

"Then it ought to be Number One," said Alice.

The King turned pale, and shut his note-book hastily. "Consider your verdict," he said to the jury, in a low trembling voice.

"There's more evidence to come yet, please your Majesty," said the White Rabbit, jumping up in a great hurry: "this paper has just been picked up."

"What's in it?" said the Queen.

"I haven't opened it yet," said the White Rabbit; "but it seems to be a letter, written by the prisoner to—to somebody."

"It must have been that," said the King, "unless it was written to nobody, which isn't usual, you know."

"Who is it directed to?" said one of the jurymen.

"It isn't directed at all," said the White Rabbit: "In fact, there's nothing written on the *outside.*" He unfolded the paper as he spoke, and added "It isn't a letter, after all: it's a set of verses."

"Are they in the prisoner's handwriting?" asked another of the jurymen.

"No, they're not," said the White Rabbit, "and that's the queerest thing about it." (The jury all looked puzzled.)

"He must have imitated somebody else's hand," said the King. (The jury all brightened up again.)

"Please, your Majesty," said the Knave, "I didn't write it, and they ca'n't prove that I did: there's no name signed at the end."[2]

2. If the Knave didn't write it, asks Selwyn Goodacre, how did he know it wasn't signed?

"If you didn't sign it," said the King, "that only makes the matter worse. You *must* have meant some mischief, or else you'd have signed your name like an honest man."

There was a general clapping of hands at this: it was the first really clever thing the King had said that day.

"That *proves* his guilt, of course," said the Queen, "so, off with—"

"It doesn't prove anything of the sort!" said Alice. "Why, you don't even know what they're about!"

"Read them," said the King.

The White Rabbit put on his spectacles. "Where shall I begin, please your Majesty?" he asked.

"Begin at the beginning," the King said, very gravely, "and go on till you come to the end: then stop."

There was dead silence in the court, whilst the White Rabbit read out these verses:—

"They told me you had been to her,
And mentioned me to him:
She gave me a good character,
But said I could not swim.

He sent them word I had not gone
(We know it to be true):
If she should push the matter on,
What would become of you?

I gave her one, they gave him two,
You gave us three or more;
They all returned from him to you,
Though they were mine before.

If I or she should chance to be
Involved in this affair,
He trusts to you to set them free,
Exactly as we were.

My notion was that you had been
(Before she had this fit)
An obstacle that came between
Him, and ourselves, and it.

Don't let him know she liked them best,
For this must ever be
A secret, kept from all the rest,
Between yourself and me."

"That's the most important piece of evidence we've heard yet," said the King, rubbing his hands; "so now let the jury—"

"If any one of them can explain it," said Alice, (she had grown so large in the last few minutes that she wasn't a bit afraid of interrupting him,) "I'll give him sixpence.[3] I don't believe there's an atom of meaning in it."

The jury all wrote down, on their slates, "*She* doesn't believe there's an atom of meaning in it," but none of them attempted to explain the paper.

"If there's no meaning in it," said the King, "that saves a world of trouble, you know, as we needn't try to find any. And yet I don't know," he went on, spreading out the verses on his knee, and looking at them with one eye; "I seem to see some meaning in them, after all. '*—said I could not swim—*' you ca'n't swim, can you?" he added, turning to the Knave.

The Knave shook his head sadly. "Do I look like it?" he said. (Which he certainly did *not,* being made entirely of cardboard.)

"All right, so far," said the King; and he

3. "A statement that is a measure of her increasing confidence," comments Selwyn Goodacre (*Jabberwocky,* Spring 1982), "because *we* know she hasn't a coin in her pocket—she told the Dodo she only had the thimble."

went on muttering over the verses to himself: " *'We know it to be true'*—that's the jury, of course—*'If she should push the matter on'*—that must be the Queen—*'What would become of you?'*—What, indeed!—*'I gave her one, they gave him two'*—why, that must be what he did with the tarts, you know—"

"But it goes on *'they all returned from him to you,'* " said Alice.

"Why, there they are!" said the King triumphantly, pointing to the tarts on the table. "Nothing can be clearer than *that.* Then again—*'before she had this fit'*—you never had *fits,* my dear, I think?" he said to the Queen.

"Never!" said the Queen, furiously, throwing an inkstand at the Lizard as she spoke. (The unfortunate little Bill had left off writing on his slate with one finger, as he found it made no mark; but he now hastily began again, using the ink, that was trickling down his face, as long as it lasted.)[4]

"Then the words don't *fit* you," said the King looking round the court with a smile.[5] There was a dead silence.

"It's a pun!" the King added in an angry tone, and everybody laughed. "Let the jury consider their verdict," the King said, for about the twentieth time that day.

"No, no!" said the Queen. "Sentence first—verdict afterwards."

"Stuff and nonsense!" said Alice loudly. "The idea of having the sentence first!"

"Hold your tongue!" said the Queen, turning purple.

"I wo'n't!" said Alice.

4. This is the first of two references to throwing ink on someone's face. In the first chapter of *Through the Looking-Glass,* Alice intends to revive the White King by tossing ink on his face.

5. Tenniel's illustration of the King looking around with a faint smile *(below left)* was clearly intended to show the King only a moment after the scene that appeared in the book's frontispiece *(below right).* The Knave has not altered his defiant stance, although the King (as Selwyn Goodacre noticed) has managed to change his crown, put on spectacles, and discard his orb and scepter, and the three court officials have fallen asleep. Observe that in both pictures Tenniel shaded the Knave's nose to suggest that he is a lush. Victorians thought of criminals as heavy drinkers, and shading noses was a convention among cartoonists then, as it is now, to signify boozers. In *The Nursery "Alice,"* whose illustrations were hand-colored by Tenniel, the tip of the Knave's nose is a rosy color in the frontispiece as well as in the picture in Chapter 8 where the Knave is presenting the King with his crown.

Jeffrey Stern, in *Jabberwocky* (Spring 1978), called attention to many similarities between this frontispiece and the frontispiece of *The Fables of Aesop and Others Translated into Human Nature* (1857), illustrated by Tenniel's fellow *Punch* artist Charles Henry Bennett:

The Court clerk (the owl) has the stunned look of the King, and the Lion has an identical scowl to the Queen's (she is even looking the same way). Some of the jurors and the bewigged bird/lawyers are in similar pose, and the pleading dog is in something of the same position as the Knave. All this would not mean very much but for the fact that Bennett's book appeared in 1857—eight years before *Wonderland.* The fable illustrated, incidentally, is "Man tried at the Court of the Lion for the Ill-treatment of a Horse."

6. In Tenniel's illustration of this scene (*facing page*), the cards have become ordinary playing cards, though three have retained vestigial noses. In Newell's version some even have heads, arms, and legs.

To underscore the return from dream to reality, as Richard Kelly noted in his contribution to *Lewis Carroll: A Celebration,* edited by Edward Guiliano, Tenniel (though not Newell) has undressed the White Rabbit.

"Off with her head!" the Queen shouted at the top of her voice. Nobody moved.

"Who cares for *you?*" said Alice (she had grown to her full size by this time). "You're nothing but a pack of cards!"

At this the whole pack rose up into the air, and came flying down upon her;[6] she gave a little scream, half of fright and half of anger, and tried to beat them off, and found herself lying on the bank, with her head in the lap of her sister, who was gently brushing away some dead leaves that had fluttered down from the trees upon her face.

"Wake up, Alice dear!" said her sister. "Why, what a long sleep you've had!"

"Oh, I've had such a curious dream!" said Alice. And she told her sister, as well as she could remember them, all these strange Adventures of hers that you have just been reading about; when she had finished, her sister kissed her, and said "It *was* a curious dream, dear, certainly; but now run in to your tea: it's getting late." So Alice got up and ran off, thinking while she ran, as well she might, what a wonderful dream it had been.

* * * * *
* * * *
* * * * *

But her sister sat still just as she left her, leaning her head on her hand, watching the setting sun, and thinking of little Alice and all her wonderful Adventures, till she too began dreaming after a fashion, and this was her dream:—

First, she dreamed about little Alice herself: once again the tiny hands were clasped upon her knee, and the bright eager eyes were looking up into hers—she could hear the very tones of her voice, and see that queer little toss of her head to keep back the wandering hair that *would* always get into her eyes—and still as she listened, or seemed to listen, the whole place around her became alive with the strange creatures of her little sister's dream.

The long grass rustled at her feet as the White Rabbit hurried by—the frightened Mouse splashed his way through the neighbouring pool—she could hear the rattle of the teacups as the March Hare and his friends shared their never-ending meal, and the shrill voice of the Queen ordering off her unfortunate guests to execution—once more the pig-baby was sneezing on the Duchess's knee, while plates and dishes crashed around it—once more the shriek of the Gryphon, the squeaking of the Lizard's slate-pencil, and the choking of the suppressed guinea-pigs, filled the air, mixed up with the distant sob of the miserable Mock Turtle.

So she sat on, with closed eyes, and half believed herself in Wonderland, though she knew she had but to open them again, and all would change to dull reality—the grass would be only rustling in the wind, and the pool rippling to the waving of the reeds—the rattling teacups would change to tinkling sheep-bells, and the Queen's shrill cries to the voice of the shepherd-boy—and the sneeze of the baby, the shriek of the Gryphon, and all the other queer noises, would change (she knew) to the confused clamour of the busy farm-yard—while the lowing of the cattle in the distance would take the place of the Mock Turtle's heavy sobs.

Lastly, she pictured to herself how this same little sister of hers would, in the after-time, be

"At this the whole pack rose up into the air"

herself a grown woman; and how she would keep, through all her riper years, the simple and loving heart of her childhood; and how she would gather about her other little children, and make *their* eyes bright and eager with many a strange tale, perhaps even with the dream of Wonderland of long ago; and how she would feel with all their simple sorrows, and find a pleasure in all their simple joys, remembering her own child-life, and the happy summer days.[7]

7. On the last page of Carroll's hand-lettered manuscript of *Alice's Adventures Under Ground,* which he gave to Alice Liddell, he pasted an oval photograph of her face that he had taken in 1859 when she was seven, the age of Alice in the story. It was not until 1977 that Morton Cohen discovered concealed underneath this photograph a drawing of Alice's face. It is the only known sketch Dodgson ever made of the real Alice.

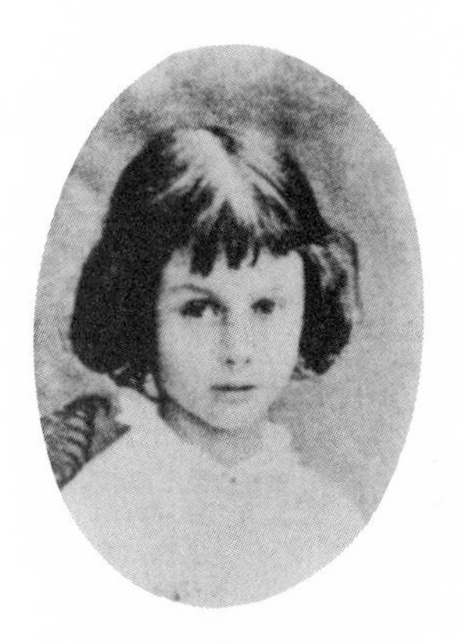

Through the Looking-Glass

and What Alice Found There

THROUGH THE LOOKING-GLASS AND WHAT ALICE FOUND THERE

1. Proofs of the prefatory poem have survived with alterations in Carroll's handwriting. The changes made for the first edition are listed on page 60 of *The Lewis Carroll Handbook* (Oxford, 1931) by Sidney Williams and Falconer Madan. In stanza 4, line 4, "A melancholy maiden" replaced "A wilful weary maiden." In stanza 5, line 1, "Without, the frost, the blinding snow" replaced "Without, the whirling wind and snow," and the next line, "The storm-wind's moody madness" replaced "That lash themselves to madness."

2. "unwelcome bed": A reference to the melancholy maiden's death, with the Christian implication that it will be merely a bedtime slumber, and, as Freudian critics never tire of pointing out, perhaps with subconscious overtones of the marriage bed.

Child of the pure unclouded brow[1]
And dreaming eyes of wonder!
Though time be fleet, and I and thou
Are half a life asunder,
Thy loving smile will surely hail
The love-gift of a fairy-tale.

I have not seen thy sunny face,
Nor heard thy silver laughter:
No thought of me shall find a place
In thy young life's hereafter—
Enough that now thou wilt not fail
To listen to my fairy-tale.

A tale begun in other days,
When summer suns were glowing—
A simple chime, that served to time
The rhythm of our rowing—
Whose echoes live in memory yet,
Though envious years would say "forget."

Come, hearken then, ere voice of dread,
With bitter tidings laden,
Shall summon to unwelcome bed[2]
A melancholy maiden!
We are but older children, dear,
Who fret to find our bedtime near.

Without, the frost, the blinding snow,
The storm-wind's moody madness—
Within, the firelight's ruddy glow,
And childhood's nest of gladness.
The magic words shall hold thee fast:
Thou shalt not heed the raving blast.

And, though the shadow of a sigh
May tremble through the story,
For "happy summer days" gone by,
And vanish'd summer glory—
It shall not touch, with breath of bale,[3]
The pleasance[4] *of our fairy-tale.*

3. "breath of bale": breath of sorrow.

4. "pleasance": The word was "pleasures" in proofs of the book. Carroll cleverly changed it to the archaic "pleasance" so he could introduce Alice Liddell's middle name.

RED

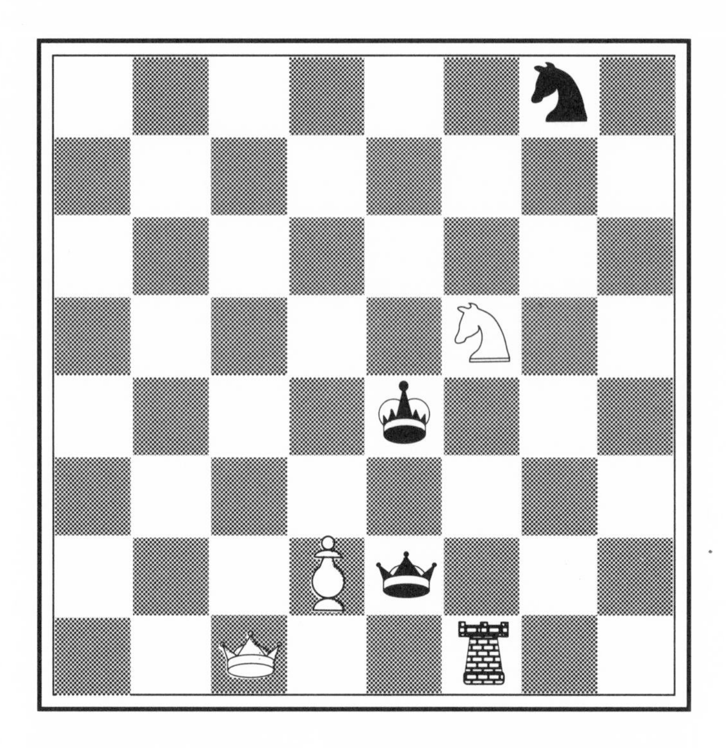

WHITE

White Pawn (Alice) to play, and win in eleven moves.

1. ALICE MEETS R. Q.	1. R. Q. TO K'S 4TH
2. ALICE THROUGH Q'S 3D *(by railway)* TO Q'S 4TH *(Tweedledum and Tweedledee)*	2. W. Q. TO Q. B.'S 4TH *(after shawl)*
3. ALICE MEETS W. Q. *(with shawl)*	3. W. Q. TO Q. B'S 5TH *(becomes sheep)*
4. ALICE TO Q'S 5TH *(shop, river, shop)*	4. W. Q. TO K. B'S 8TH *(leaves egg on shelf)*
5. ALICE TO Q'S 6TH *(Humpty Dumpty)*	5. W. Q. TO Q. B'S 8TH *(flying from R. Kt.)*
6. ALICE TO Q'S 7TH *(forest)*	6. R. KT. TO K'S 2ND *(ch.)*
7. W. KT. TAKES R. KT.	7. W. KT. TO K. B'S 5TH
8. ALICE TO Q'S 8TH *(coronation)*	8. R. Q. TO K'S SQ. *(examination)*
9. ALICE BECOMES QUEEN	9. QUEENS CASTLE
10. ALICE CASTLES *(feast)*	10. W. Q. TO Q. R'S 6TH *(soup)*
11. ALICE TAKES R. Q. & WINS	

PREFACE TO THE 1896 EDITION

As the chess-problem, given on the previous page, has puzzled some of my readers, it may be well to explain that it is correctly worked out, so far as the *moves* are concerned. The *alternation* of Red and White is perhaps not so strictly observed as it might be, and the "castling" of the three Queens is merely a way of saying that they entered the palace;[1] but the "check" of the White King at move 6, the capture of the Red Knight at move 7, and the final "checkmate" of the Red King, will be found, by any one who will take the trouble to set the pieces and play the moves as directed, to be strictly in accordance with the laws of the game.[2]

The new words, in the poem "Jabberwocky," have given rise to some differences of opinion as to their pronunciation: so it may be well to give instructions on *that* point also. Pronounce "slithy" as if it were the two words "sly, the": make the "g" *hard* in "gyre" and "gimble": and pronounce "rath" to rhyme with "bath."

For this sixty-first thousand, fresh electrotypes have been taken from the wood-blocks (which, never having been used for printing from, are in as good condition as when first cut in 1871), and the whole book has been set up afresh with new type. If the artistic qualities of this re-issue fall short, in any particular, of those possessed by the original issue, it will not be for want of painstaking on the part of author, publisher, or printer.

1. There is no chess move in which queens castle. Carroll is here explaining that when the three Queens (the Red Queen, the White Queen, and Alice) have entered the "castle," they have moved to the eighth row, where pawns become queens.

DRAMATIS PERSONAE

(As arranged before commencement of game.)

WHITE		RED	
PIECES	PAWNS	PAWNS	PIECES
Tweedledee	Daisy	Daisy.....	Humpty Dumpty
Unicorn.........	Haigha	Messenger.	Carpenter
Sheep...........	Oyster	Oyster....	Walrus
W. Queen	'Lily'	Tiger-Lily.	R. Queen
W. King	Fawn	Rose	R. King
Aged man	Oyster	Oyster....	Crow
W. Knight	Hatta	Frog	R. Knight
Tweedledum	Daisy	Daisy.....	Lion

2. The above list of dramatis personae appeared in early editions of the book before Carroll replaced it with his 1896 preface. Removing it was wise because it only adds confusion to the chess game. I will cite only one instance. If the Tweedle brothers are the two white rooks, asked Denis Crutch in a lecture on the chess game (published in *Jabberwocky,* Summer 1972), then who is the white rook on the first row of Carroll's diagram?

The arrangement of the words in the starting position of a chess game makes it easy to identify each piece and pawn. Observe that the bishops, never mentioned in the story, are here linked to the Sheep, Aged man, Walrus, and Crow, though for no discernible reason.

I take this opportunity of announcing that the Nursery "Alice," hitherto priced at four shillings, net, is now to be had on the same terms as the ordinary shilling picture-books—although I feel sure that it is, in every quality (except the *text* itself, in which I am not qualified to pronounce), greatly superior to them. Four shillings was a perfectly reasonable price to charge, considering the very heavy initial outlay I had incurred: still, as the Public have practically said "We will *not* give more than a shilling for a picture-book, however artistically got-up," I am content to reckon my outlay on the book as so much dead loss, and, rather than let the little ones, for whom it was written, go without it, I am selling it at a price which is, to me, much the same thing as *giving* it away.

Christmas, 1896

CHAPTER I

LOOKING-GLASS HOUSE

One thing was certain, that the *white* kitten had had nothing to do with it—it was the black kitten's fault entirely. For the white kitten had been having its face washed by the old cat for the last quarter of an hour (and bearing it pretty well, considering): so you see that it *couldn't* have had any hand in the mischief.

The way Dinah washed her children's faces was this: first she held the poor thing down by its ear with one paw, and then with the other paw she rubbed its face all over, the wrong way, beginning at the nose: and just now, as I said, she was hard at work on the white kitten, which was lying quite still and trying to purr—no doubt feeling that it was all meant for its good.

But the black kitten had been finished with earlier in the afternoon, and so, while Alice was sitting curled up in a corner of the great arm-chair, half talking to herself and half asleep, the kitten had been having a grand game of romps with the ball of worsted Alice had been trying to wind up, and had been rolling it up and down till it had all come undone again; and there it was, spread over the hearth-rug, all knots and tangles, with the kitten running after its own tail in the middle.

"Oh, you wicked, wicked little thing!" cried Alice, catching up the kitten, and giving it a little kiss to make it understand that it was in disgrace. "Really, Dinah ought to have taught you better manners! You *ought,* Dinah, you know you ought!" she added, looking reproachfully at the old cat, and speaking in as cross a voice as she could manage—and then she scrambled back into the arm-chair, taking the kitten and the worsted with her, and began winding up the ball again. But she didn't get on very fast, as she was talking all the time, sometimes to the kitten, and sometimes to herself. Kitty sat very demurely on her knee, pretending to watch the progress of the winding, and now and then putting out one paw and gently touching the ball, as if it would be glad to help if it might.

"Do you know what to-morrow is, Kitty?"[1] Alice began. "You'd have guessed if you'd been up in the window with me—only Dinah was making you tidy, so you couldn't. I was watching the boys getting in sticks for the bonfire—and it wants plenty of sticks, Kitty! Only it got so cold, and it snowed so, they had to leave off. Never mind, we'll go and see the bonfire to-morrow." Here Alice wound two or three turns of the worsted round the kitten's neck, just to see how it would look: this led to a scramble, in which the ball rolled down upon the floor, and yards and yards of it got unwound again.

"Do you know, I was so angry, Kitty," Alice went on, as soon as they were comfortably set-

1. Mrs. Mavis Bailey, in her booklet *Alice's Adventures in Oxford* (A Pitkin Pictorial Guide, 1980), argues that the day was March 10, 1863, the wedding day of the Prince of Wales. The occasion was celebrated at Oxford with bonfires and fireworks, and in his diary Carroll tells of taking Alice on an evening tour through the university: "It was delightful to see the thorough abandonment with which Alice enjoyed the whole thing."

My *Annotated Alice* gives several reasons for thinking the day was November 5, Guy Fawkes Day, and additional evidence for this view is the fact that Carroll's diary for March 9 and 10 makes no mention of the snow Alice speaks of. However, Mrs. Bailey's conjecture is supported by the fact that in England snow is very rare in early November and quite common in March.

tled again, "when I saw all the mischief you had been doing, I was very nearly opening the window, and putting you out into the snow! And you'd have deserved it, you little mischievous darling! What have you got to say for yourself? Now don't interrupt me!" she went on, holding up one finger. "I'm going to tell you all your faults. Number one: you squeaked twice while Dinah was washing your face this morning. Now you ca'n't deny it, Kitty: I heard you! What's that you say?" (pretending that the kitten was speaking). "Her paw went into your eye? Well, that's *your* fault, for keeping your eyes open—if you'd shut them tight up, it wouldn't have happened. Now don't make any more excuses, but listen! Number two: you pulled Snowdrop[2] away by the tail just as I had put down the saucer of milk before her! What, you were thirsty, were you? How do you know she wasn't thirsty too? Now for number three: you unwound every bit of the worsted while I wasn't looking!

"That's three faults, Kitty, and you've not been punished for any of them yet. You know I'm saving up all your punishments for Wednesday week[3]—Suppose they had saved up all *my* punishments?" she went on, talking more to herself than the kitten. "What *would* they do at the end of a year? I should be sent to prison, I suppose, when the day came. Or—let me see—suppose each punishment was to be going without a dinner: then, when the miserable day came, I should have to go without fifty dinners at once! Well, I shouldn't mind *that* much! I'd far rather go without them than eat them!

"Do you hear the snow against the window-

2. Kitty and Snowdrop, the black and white kittens, reflect the chessboard's black and white squares, and the red and white pieces of the book's chess game.

3. "Wednesday week": a week after the coming Wednesday.

panes, Kitty? How nice and soft it sounds! I wonder if the snow *loves* the trees and fields, that it kisses them so gently? And then it covers them up snug, you know, with a white quilt; and perhaps it says 'Go to sleep, darlings, till the summer comes again.' And when they wake up in the summer, Kitty, they dress themselves all in green, and dance about—whenever the wind blows—oh, that's very pretty!" cried Alice, dropping the ball of worsted to clap her hands. "And I do so *wish* it was true! I'm sure the woods look sleepy in the autumn, when the leaves are getting brown.

"Kitty, can you play chess? Now, don't smile, my dear. I'm asking it seriously. Because, when we were playing just now, you watched just as if you understood it: and when I said 'Check!' you purred! Well, it *was* a nice check, Kitty, and really I might have won, if it hadn't been for that nasty Knight, that came wriggling down among my pieces. Kitty dear, let's pretend—" And here I wish I could tell you half the things Alice used to say, beginning with her favourite phrase "Let's pretend." She had had quite a long argument with her sister only the day before—all because Alice had begun with "Let's pretend we're kings and queens"; and her sister, who liked being very exact, had argued that they couldn't, because there were only two of them, and Alice had been reduced at last to say "Well, *you* can be one of them, then, and *I'll* be all the rest." And once she had really frightened her old nurse by shouting suddenly in her ear, "Nurse! Do let's pretend that I'm a hungry hyæna, and you're a bone!"

But this is taking us away from Alice's

speech to the kitten. "Let's pretend that you're the Red Queen, Kitty! Do you know, I think if you sat up and folded your arms, you'd look exactly like her. Now do try, there's a dear!" And Alice got the Red Queen off the table, and set it up before the kitten as a model for it to imitate: however, the thing didn't succeed, principally, Alice said, because the kitten wouldn't fold its arms properly. So, to punish it, she held it up to the Looking-glass, that it might see how sulky it was, "—and if you're not good directly," she added, "I'll put you through into Looking-glass House. How would you like *that*?

"Now, if you'll only attend, Kitty, and not talk so much, I'll tell you all my ideas about Looking-glass House.[4] First, there's the room you can see through the glass—that's just the same as our drawing-room, only the things go the other way. I can see all of it when I get upon a chair—all but the bit just behind the fireplace. Oh! I do so wish I could see *that* bit! I want so much to know whether they've a fire in the winter: you never *can* tell, you know, unless our fire smokes, and then smoke comes up in that room too—but that may be only pretence, just to make it look as if they had a fire. Well then, the books are something like our books, only the words go the wrong way: I know *that,* because I've held up one of our books to the glass, and then they hold up one in the other room.

"How would you like to live in Looking-glass House, Kitty? I wonder if they'd give you milk in there? Perhaps Looking-glass milk isn't good to drink—but oh, Kitty! now we come to the passage. You can just see a little *peep* of the

4. R. B. Shaberman, writing on the influence of George MacDonald on Carroll (*Jabberwocky,* Summer 1976), quotes the following passage from Chapter 13 of MacDonald's 1858 novel *Phantastes:*

> What a strange thing a mirror is! And what a wondrous affinity exists between it and a man's imagination! For this room of mine, as I behold it in the glass, is the same and yet not the same. It is not the mere representation of the room I live in, but it looks just as if I were reading about it in a story I like. All its commonness has disappeared. The mirror has lifted it out of the region of fact into the realms of art. . . . I should like to live in that room if I could only get into it.

Allusions to mirror reversals, and to reversals of time, abound in this second of Alice's dreams. Recent nontechnical references on the symmetry and asymmetry of space and time include *Reality's Mirror: Exploring the Mathematics of Symmetry,* by Bryan Bunch (Wiley, 1989); my *New Ambidextrous Universe* (W. H. Freeman, 1990); and "The Handedness of the Universe," by Roger Hegstrom and Dilip Kondepudi, in *Scientific American,* January 1990.

passage in Looking-glass House, if you leave the door of our drawing-room wide open: and it's very like our passage as far as you can see, only you know it may be quite different on beyond. Oh, Kitty, how nice it would be if we could only get through into Looking-glass House! I'm sure it's got, oh! such beautiful things in it! Let's pretend there's a way of getting through into it, somehow, Kitty. Let's pretend the glass has got all soft like gauze, so that we can get through. Why, it's turning into a sort of mist now, I declare! It'll be easy enough to get through—" She was up on the chimney-piece[5] while she said this, though she hardly knew how she had got there. And certainly the glass *was* beginning to melt away, just like a bright silvery mist.

In another moment Alice was through the glass,[6] and had jumped lightly down into the Looking-glass room. The very first thing she did was to look whether there was a fire in the fire-place, and she was quite pleased to find that there was a real one, blazing away as brightly as the one she had left behind. "So I shall be as warm here as I was in the old room," thought Alice: "warmer, in fact, because there'll be no one here to scold me away from the fire. Oh, what fun it'll be, when they see me through the glass in here, and ca'n't get at me!"

Then she began looking about, and noticed that what could be seen from the old room was quite common and uninteresting, but that all the rest was as different as possible. For instance, the pictures on the wall next the fire seemed to be all alive, and the very clock on the chimney-piece (you know you can only see the

5. For American readers: the chimney-piece is the mantel. A number of science-fiction writers have used the mirror as a device for joining our world to a parallel world: Henry S. Whitehead's "The Trap," Donald Wandrei's "The Painted Mirror," and Fritz Leiber's "Midnight in the Mirror World" are three such stories.

6. Tenniel's pictures of Alice passing through the mirror are worth studying. Observe that in the second illustration he added a grinning face to the back of the clock and to the lower part of the vase. It was a Victorian custom to put clocks and artificial flowers under glass bell jars. Less obvious is the gargoyle, sticking out its tongue, in the ornament at the top of the fireplace.

The pictures also show that Alice is not reversed on the other side of the glass. She continues to raise her right arm and to kneel on her right leg.

Note the name "Dalziel" at the bottom of both pictures, as well as on most of Tenniel's illustrations in both *Alice* books. The Dalziel brothers were the wood engravers for all of Tenniel's drawings. Observe also that Tenniel has reversed his monogram in the second picture.

We are told later on that the pictures on the wall near the fire seem to be alive. Observe how Newell has indicated this in his illustration of Alice emerging from

back of it in the Looking-glass) had got the face of a little old man, and grinned at her.

"They don't keep this room so tidy as the other," Alice thought to herself, as she noticed several of the chessmen down in the hearth among the cinders; but in another moment, with a little "Oh!" of surprise, she was down on her hands and knees watching them. The chessmen were walking about, two and two!

"Here are the Red King and the Red Queen," Alice said (in a whisper, for fear of frightening them), "and there are the White King and the White Queen sitting on the edge of the shovel—and here are two Castles walking arm in arm[7]—I don't think they can hear me," she went on, as she put her head closer down, "and I'm nearly sure they ca'n't see me. I feel somehow as if I was getting invisible—"

Here something began squeaking on the table behind Alice, and made her turn her head just in time to see one of the White Pawns roll over and begin kicking: she watched it with great curiosity to see what would happen next.

"It is the voice of my child!" the White Queen cried out, as she rushed past the King, so violently that she knocked him over among the cinders. "My precious Lily! My imperial kitten!" and she began scrambling wildly up the side of the fender.

"Imperial fiddlestick!" said the King, rubbing his nose, which had been hurt by the fall. He had a right to be a *little* annoyed with the Queen, for he was covered with ashes from head to foot.

Alice was very anxious to be of use, and, as the poor little Lily was nearly screaming herself

the mirror. In the 1939 Paramount motion picture the pictures on the wall come alive and talk to Alice.

In all standard editions, the two pictures are on opposite sides of a leaf, as if the leaf itself was the mirror Alice passed through. A Puffin edition (1948) puts the pictures on its front and back covers, making the book the mirror.

7. Although Carroll never mentions bishops (perhaps out of deference to the clergy), they can be seen clearly in one of Tenniel's drawings as well as in Newell's illustration for the same scene. Isaac Asimov's mystery story "The Curious Omission," in his *Tales of the Black Widow Spiders,* derives from Carroll's curious omission of chess bishops.

"In another moment Alice was through the glass"

"The chessmen were walking about, two and two!"

into a fit, she hastily picked up the Queen and set her on the table by the side of her noisy little daughter.

The Queen gasped, and sat down: the rapid journey through the air had quite taken away her breath, and for a minute or two she could do nothing but hug the little Lily in silence. As soon as she had recovered her breath a little, she called out to the White King, who was sitting sulkily among the ashes, "Mind the volcano!"

"What volcano?" said the King, looking up anxiously into the fire, as if he thought that was the most likely place to find one.

"Blew—me—up," panted the Queen, who was still a little out of breath. "Mind you come up—the regular way—don't get blown up!"

Alice watched the White King as he slowly struggled up from bar to bar,[8] till at last she said "Why, you'll be hours and hours getting to the table, at that rate. I'd far better help you, hadn't I?" But the King took no notice of the question: it was quite clear that he could neither hear her nor see her.

So Alice picked him up very gently, and lifted him across more slowly than she had lifted the Queen, that she mightn't take his breath away; but, before she put him on the table, she thought she might as well dust him a little, he was so covered with ashes.

She said afterwards that she had never seen in all her life such a face as the King made, when he found himself held in the air by an invisible hand, and being dusted: he was far too much astonished to cry out, but his eyes and his mouth went on getting larger and larger, and rounder and rounder, till her hand shook so with laughter that she nearly let him drop upon the floor.

"Oh! *please* don't make such faces, my dear!" she cried out, quite forgetting that the King couldn't hear her. "You make me laugh so that I can hardly hold you! And don't keep your mouth so wide open! All the ashes will get into it—there, now I think you're tidy enough!" she added, as she smoothed his hair, and set him upon the table near the Queen.

8. The White King's slow struggle up the fender, from bar to bar, reflects the fact that although a chess king can move in any direction like a queen, it is allowed to move only from one square to the next. A queen can go as far as eight cells in one move, which explains the ability of queens later on to fly through the air, but it takes a king eight moves to go from one side of a chessboard to the other.

"She thought she might as well dust him a little"

The King immediately fell flat on his back, and lay perfectly still;[9] and Alice was a little alarmed at what she had done, and went round the room to see if she could find any water to throw over him. However, she could find nothing but a bottle of ink, and when she got back with it she found he had recovered, and he and the Queen were talking together in a frightened whisper—so low, that Alice could hardly hear what they said.

The King was saying "I assure you, my dear, I turned cold to the very ends of my whiskers!"

To which the Queen replied "You haven't got any whiskers."[10]

"The horror of that moment," the King went on, "I shall never, *never* forget!"

"You will, though," the Queen said, "if you don't make a memorandum of it."

Alice looked on with great interest as the King took an enormous memorandum-book out of his pocket, and began writing. A sudden thought struck her, and she took hold of the end of the pencil, which came some way over his shoulder, and began writing for him.[11]

The poor King looked puzzled and unhappy, and struggled with the pencil for some time without saying anything; but Alice was too strong for him, and at last he panted out "My dear! I really *must* get a thinner pencil. I ca'n't manage this one a bit: it writes all manner of things that I don't intend—"

"What manner of things?" said the Queen, looking over the book (in which Alice had put *'The White Knight is sliding down the poker. He balances very badly'*). "That's not a memorandum of *your* feelings!"

9. In chess play the loser often signifies defeat by turning his king flat on its back. As we soon learn, this is a moment of horror for the King, who naturally turns cold, like a person slain in combat. The Queen's suggestion about making a memorandum of the event suggests the practice of recording chess moves so that a player won't forget the game.

10. American readers have been puzzled by the Queen's remark because Tenniel's illustrations (in contrast to Newell's) show the White King, both here and in Chapter 7, with mustache and beard. As Denis Crutch has pointed out, the Queen meant that the King has no sideburns. Crutch quotes a remark in Carroll's *Sylvie and Bruno* (Chapter 18) about a man's face being "bounded on the North by a fringe of hair, on the East and West by a fringe of whiskers, and on the South by a fringe of beard." In England, "whiskers" customarily means sideburns.

11. Automatic writing, as it was called, was a major aspect of the spiritualist craze in the nineteenth century. A disembodied spirit was believed to seize the hand of a psychic—Conan Doyle's wife was an accomplished automatic writer—and produce messages from the Great Beyond. For my comments about Carroll's interest in the occult, see *Alice in Wonderland,* Chapter 5, note 4, above.

"The poor King looked puzzled and unhappy"

There was a book lying near Alice on the table, and while she sat watching the White King (for she was still a little anxious about him, and had the ink all ready to throw over him, in case he fainted again), she turned over the leaves, to find some part that she could read, "—for it's all in some language I don't know," she said to herself.

It was like this.

JABBERWOCKY

'Twas brillig, and the slithy toves
Did gyre and gimble in the wabe:
All mimsy were the borogoves,
And the mome raths outgrabe.[12]

She puzzled over this for some time, but at last a bright thought struck her. "Why, it's a Looking-glass book, of course! And, if I hold it up to a glass, the words will all go the right way again."

This was the poem that Alice read:

JABBERWOCKY

'Twas brillig, and the slithy toves
Did gyre and gimble in the wabe:
All mimsy were the borogoves,
And the mome raths outgrabe.

"Beware the Jabberwock, my son!
The jaws that bite, the claws that catch!
Beware the Jubjub bird, and shun
The frumious Bandersnatch!"

He took his vorpal sword in hand:
Long time the manxome foe he sought—
So rested he by the Tumtum tree,
And stood awhile in thought.

And, as in uffish thought he stood,
The Jabberwock, with eyes of flame,

12. The mirror reversal of "Jabberwocky" suggests that Alice's brain was not reversed by her passage through the looking glass. There are other reasons for assuming she was not mirror reflected; see Chapter 1, note 6, for example. Many of Tenniel's pictures in the first book show her right-handed, and she continues to be right-handed in his pictures for the second book. Newell's art is ambiguous on this point, though in Chapter 9 his Alice holds a scepter in her left hand, not in her right as Tenniel has it.

Alice has no difficulty reading the Wasp's newspaper in the long-lost "Wasp in a Wig" episode, so presumably, unlike "Jabberwocky," it was not reversed. Brian Kirshaw sent a detailed analysis of the left-right aspects of the book, all of which lead to the conclusion that neither Tenniel nor Carroll was consistent about who or what was mirror-reflected behind the looking glass.

" 'Beware the Jubjub bird, and shun
The frumious Bandersnatch!' "

Came whiffling through the tulgey wood,
And burbled[13] *as it came!*

One, two! One, two! And through and through
The vorpal blade went snicker-snack![14]
He left it dead, and with its head
He went galumphing back.

"And, hast thou slain the Jabberwock?
Come to my arms, my beamish boy!
O frabjous day! Callooh! Callay!"[15]
He chortled in his joy.

'Twas brillig, and the slithy toves
Did gyre and gimble in the wabe:
All mimsy were the borogoves,
And the mome raths outgrabe.[16]

"It seems very pretty," she said when she had finished it, "but it's *rather* hard to understand!"[17] (You see she didn't like to confess, even to herself, that she couldn't make it out at all.) "Somehow it seems to fill my head with ideas—only I don't exactly know what they are! However, *somebody* killed *something:* that's clear, at any rate—"

"But oh!" thought Alice, suddenly jumping up, "if I don't make haste, I shall have to go back through the Looking-glass, before I've seen what the rest of the house is like! Let's have a look at the garden first!" She was out of the room in a moment, and ran down stairs—or, at least, it wasn't exactly running, but a new invention for getting down stairs quickly and easily, as Alice said to herself. She just kept the tips of her fingers on the hand-rail, and floated gently down without even touching the stairs with her feet: then she floated on through the hall, and would have gone straight out at the

13. Observe how Newell, in his picture of the Jabberwock, has interpreted "burbled" to mean blowing bubbles. Correspondent Mrs. Henry Morss, Jr., found a striking similarity between Tenniel's Jabberwock and the dragon being slain by Saint George in a painting by Paolo Uccello, in London's National Gallery. For other pictures of monsters that could have influenced Tenniel, see Chapter 8 of Michael Hancher's *The Tenniel Illustrations to the "Alice" Books.*

14. In my lengthy commentary in *AA* on the nonsense words of "Jabberwocky" I missed a chance to relate "snicker-snack" to "snickersnee," an old word for a large knife. It also means "to fight with a knife." The *Oxford English Dictionary* quotes from *The Mikado,* Act 2: "As I gnashed my teeth, when from its sheath I drew my snicker-snee."

15. Readers Albert Blackwell and Mrs. Carlton Hyman separately pointed out that Carroll may have had in mind two forms of the Greek word *kalos,* meaning "beautiful," "good," or "fair." They would be pronounced "callooh" and "callay" and their meaning would fit the line. Another conjecture, given in my *AA,* refers to an arctic duck called the calloo because of its evening call "Calloo! Calloo!"

16. In a long note on "Jabberwocky" in *AA* I gave a French and a German translation, and indicated where two Latin versions could be found. Here is a quite different French version, from Henri Parisot's 1971 translation of *Through the Looking-Glass:*

JABBERWOCHEUX

Il était reveneure; les slictueux toves
Sur l'allouinde gyraient et vriblaient;

"The Jabberwock, with eyes of flame,
Came whiffling through the tulgey wood,
And burbled as it came!"

Tout flivoreux vaguaient les borogoves;
Les verchons fourgus bourniflaient.

"Au Jabberwoc prends bien garde, mon fils!
A sa griffe qui mord, à sa gueule qui happe!
Gare l'oiseau Jeubjeub, et laisse
En paix le frumieux, le fatal Bandersnatch!"

Le jeune homme, ayant ceint sa vorpaline épée,
Longtemps cherchait le monstre manxiquais,
Puis, arrivé près de l'arbre Tépé,
Pour réfléchir un instant s'arrêtait.

Or, tandis qu'il lourmait de suffèches pensées,
Le Jabberwoc, l'œil flamboyant,
Ruginiflant par le bois touffeté,
Arrivait en barigoulant!

Une, deux! une, deux! Fulgurant, d'outre en outre,
Le glaive vorpalin perce et tranche: flac-vlan!
Il terrasse la bête et, brandissant sa tête,
Il s'en retourne, galomphant.

"Tu as tué le Jabberwoc!
Dans mes bras, mon fils rayonnois!
O jour frableux! callouh! calloc!"
Le vieux glouffait de joie.

Il était reveneure; les sclitueux toves
Sur l'allouinde gyraient et vriblaient;
Tout flivoreux vaguaient les borogoves;
Les verchons fourgus bourniflaient.

August A. Imholtz, Jr., writing on "Latin and Greek Versions of 'Jabberwocky' " in the *Rocky Mountain Review of Language and Literature,* Vol. 41, No. 4 (1987), gives many Latin and Greek translations. Of the Latin ones, he thinks the best was the first to be written. Composed in 1872 by Augustus Arthur Vansittart of Trinity College, Cambridge, it goes like this:

MORS IABROCHII

Coesper erat: tunc lubriciles ultravia circum
Urgebant gyros gimbiculosque tophi:
Moestenui visae borogovides ire meatu:
Et profugi gemitus exgrabuere rathae.

O fuge Iabrochium, sanguis meus! Ille recurvis
Unguibus, estque avidis dentibus ille minax.
Ububae fuge cautus avis vim, gnate! Neque unquam
Faedarpax contra te frumiosus eat!

Vorpali gladio iuvenis succingitur: hostis
Manxumus ad medium quaeritur usque diem:
Iamque via fesso, sed plurima mente prementi,
Tumtumiae frondis suaserat umbra moram.

Consilia interdum stetit egnia mente revolvens:
At gravis in densa fronde susuffrus erat,
Spiculaque ex oculis iacientis flammea, tulscam
Per silvam venit burbur Iabrochii!

Vorpali, semel atque iterum collectus in ictum,
Persnicuit gladio persnacuitque puer:
Deinde glaumphatus, spernens informe cadaver,
Horrendum monstri rettulit ipse caput.

Victor Iabrochii, spoliis insignis opimis
Rursus in amplexus, o radiose, meos!
O frabiose dies! CALLO clamatque CALLA!
Vix potuit laetus chorticulare pater.

Coesper erat: tunc lubriciles ultravia circum
Urgebant gyros gimbiculosque tophi;
Moestenui visae borogovides ire meatu;
Et profugi gemitus exgrabuere rathae.

New translations of the *Alice* books keep coming, and by now there must be more than fifty foreign versions of "Jabberwocky" in almost as many languages. Charles and Stephanie Lovett, a husband-and-wife team of Carroll scholars who run Lovett and Lovett, a rare-books store in Winston-Salem, North Carolina, and who own a fine collection of Carrolliana, have kindly supplied me with the following selection:

An Italian version by Adriana Crespi (1974):

IL CIARLESTRONE

Era brillosto, e gli alacridi tossi
succhiellavano scabbi nel pantúle:
Méstili eran tutti i paparossi,
e strombavan musando i tartarocchi.

"Attento al Ciarlestrone, figlio mio!
Fauci che azzannano, fauci che ti artigliano,
attento all'uccel Giuggio e attento ancora
Al fumibondo chiappabana!"

Afferrò quello la sua vorpi da lama
a lungo il manson nemico cercò . . .
Cosí sostò presso l'albero Touton
e riflettendo alquanto dimorò.

E mentre il bellico pensier si trattenea,
il Ciarlestrone con occhiali brage
venne sifflando nella fulgida selva,
sbollentando nella sua avanzata.

Un, due! Un, due! E dentro e dentro
scattò saettante la vorpida lama!
Ei lo lasciò cadavere, e col capo
Se ne venne al ritorno galumpando.

"E hai tu ucciso il Ciarlestrone?
Fra le mie braccia, o raggioso fanciullo!
O giorno fragoroso, Callò, Callài!"
stripetò quello dalla gioia.

Era brillosto, e gli alacridi tossi
succhiellavano scabbi nel pantúle:
méstili eran tutti i papparossi,
e strombavan musando i tartarocchi.

A Spanish version by Adolfo de Alba (1978):

El Jabberwocky

Era la asarvesperia y los flexilimosos toves
giroscopiaban taledrando en el vade;
debilmiseros estaban los borogoves;
bramatchisilban los verdilechos parde.

¡Cuidado con el Jabberwocky, hijo mío!
¡Cuídate de las mandíbulas que muerden.
de las garras que apresan!
Cuídate del pájaro Rapiña y del altanero
Halcón.

Empuñó él su tajante espada,
y contempló a su terrible enemigo largo rato.
Se puso a la sombra del árbol tumtum
y duró un rato cavilando.

Luego, de un brinco, púsose presto,
y la mala bestia, con ojos fulgurantes
llegó resoplando por el sombrío bosque,
y al acercarse aullaba.

¡Uno, dos! ¡Uno, dos! Sin cesar
la filosa espada daba tajos.
Muerto lo dejó, y, cortándole la cabeza,
de allí se alejó presto.

—¿Mataste al fin a la mala bestia,
al tremendo Jabberwocky?
¡Ven a mis brazos, niño querido!
¡Hermoso día! ¡Hurra! ¡Hurra!
—gritaba con alegría.

Era la asarvesperia y los flexilimosos toves
giroscopiaban taledrando en el vade;
debilmiseros estaban los borogoves;
bramatchisilban los verdilechos parde.

A Russian version by U. L. Oryol (1980), with a transliteration:

УМЗАРИ

Сверкалось . . . Скойкие сюды
Волчились у развел.
Дрожжали в лужасе грозды,
И крюх засвиревел.

Ты Умзара страшись, мой сын!
Его следов искать не смей
И помни: не ходи один
Ловить Сплетнистых Змей!

Свой чудо-юдоострый меч
Он взял и дринулся вперед,
Но—нолон дум—он под Зум-Зум
Раскидитый идет.

И вот, пока ои скрепко шпал,
Явился Умзар огневой
И он на Рыбцаря напал:
Ты слышишь, зронкий вой?

Да, чудо-юдоострый меч
Сильнее Умзара стократ!
Зверой побрит, Геройспешит
Спешит споржественно иазад.

"Я побредил его, Старик!
Позволь, тебя я обниму!"
"Вот это час, вот это миг!"
Отец сказал ему.

Сверкалось . . . Скойкие сюды
Волчились у развел.
Дрожжали в лужасе грозды,
И крюх засвиревел.

Umzari

Sverkalos' . . . Skoykie syudy
Volchilis' u razvel.
Drozhzhali v luzhasye grozdy,
I kryukh zasvirevel.

"Ty Umzara strashis', moy syn!
Yevo sledov iskat' ne smey.
I pomni: ne khodi odin
Lovit' Spletnistykh Zmey!"

Svoy chudo-yudoostryy mech
On vzyal i drinulsya vpered,
No—nolon dum—on pod Zum-Zum
Raskidistyy idet.

I vot, poka on skrepko shpal,
Yavilsya Umzar ognevoy
I on na Rybtsarya napal:
Ty slyshish' zronkiy voy?

Da, chudo-yudoostryy mech
Sil'neye Umzara stokrat!
Zveroy pobrit, Geroy speshit
Speshit sporzhestvenno nazad.

"Ya pobredil yevo, Starik!
Pozvol', tebya ya obnimu!"
"Vot eto chas, vot eto mig!"
Otets skazal yemu.

Sverkalos' . . . Skoykie syudy
Volchilis' u razvel.
Drozhzhali v luzhasye grozdy,
I kryukh zasvirevel.

A Welsh version by Selyf Roberts (1984):

Siaberwoci

Mae'n brydgell ac mae'r brochgim stwd
Yn gimblo a gyrian yn y mhello:

Pob cólomrws yn féddabwd,
A'r hoch oma'n chwibruo.

Gwylia'r hen Siaberwoc, fy mab!
Y brathiad llym a'r crafanc tynn!
A rhed pan weli'r Gwbigab
A'r ofnynllyd Barllyn!

Cym'rodd ei gleddyf yn ei law
I geisio ei fanawaidd brae—
A gorffwys ger y goeden Taw,
I feddwl—fel pe tae.

A thra pendronai ymhlith y coed
Y Siaberwoc a'i lygaid fflam
A ddaeth, mor wallgof ag erioed
Gan ffrwtian gam a cham!

Un, dau! Un, dau! drwy'r awyr oer
Aeth min y cledd ysgiw, ysgôl!
Fe'i lladdodd, a chan gludo'i ben
Hwblamodd yn ei ôl.

"A leddaist ti y Siaberwoc?
Tyrd yma, hapllon fachgen!
O jiwblus ddydd! Hwrê! Hwroc!"
Gan wenu arno'n llawen.

Mae'n brydgell ac mae'r brochgim stwd
Yn gimblo a gyrian yn y mhello:
Pob cólomrws yn féddabwd,
A'r hoch oma'n chwibruo.

17. In *Useful and Instructive Poetry,* written by Carroll when he was thirteen (it was his first book), there is a parody of a passage from Shakespeare's *Henry the Fourth, Second Part,* in which the Prince of Wales uses the word "biggen." In Carroll's version he explains to the puzzled king that the word "means a kind of woolen nightcap." Later he introduces the word "rigol."

"What meaneth 'rigol'?" asks the king.

"My liege, I know not," the prince replies, "save that it doth enter most apt into the metre."

"True, it doth," the king agrees. "But wherefore use a word which hath no meaning?"

The prince's answer has a prophetic reference to the nonsense words of "Jabberwocky": "My lord, the word is said, for it hath passed my lips, and all the powers upon this earth cannot unsay it."

door in the same way, if she hadn't caught hold of the doorpost. She was getting a little giddy with so much floating in the air, and was rather glad to find herself walking again in the natural way.

CHAPTER II
THE GARDEN OF LIVE FLOWERS

"I should see the garden far better," said Alice to herself, "if I could get to the top of that hill: and here's a path that leads straight to it—at least, no, it doesn't do *that*—" (after going a few yards along the path, and turning several sharp corners), "but I suppose it will at last. But how curiously it twists! It's more like a corkscrew[1] than a path! Well, *this* turn goes to the hill, I suppose—no, it doesn't! This goes straight back to the house! Well then, I'll try it the other way."

And so she did: wandering up and down, and trying turn after turn, but always coming back to the house, do what she would. Indeed, once, when she turned a corner rather more quickly than usual, she ran against it before she could stop herself.

"It's no use talking about it," Alice said, looking up at the house and pretending it was arguing with her. "I'm *not* going in again yet. I know I should have to get through the Looking-glass again—back into the old room—and there'd be an end of all my adventures!"

1. Corkscrews are mentioned several times in *Through the Looking-Glass.* Carroll knew, of course, that corkscrews are helices, asymmetric three-dimensional curves that spiral the "other way" in the mirror. Humpty Dumpty tells Alice that the "toves" in "Jabberwocky" look something like corkscrews. He recites a poem in which he speaks of using a corkscrew to wake up the fish, and in Chapter 9 the White Queen recalls his coming to her door, corkscrew in hand, looking for a hippopotamus.

So, resolutely turning her back upon the house, she set out once more down the path, determined to keep straight on till she got to the hill. For a few minutes all went on well, and she was just saying. "I really *shall* do it this time—" when the path gave a sudden twist and shook itself (as she described it afterwards), and the next moment she found herself actually walking in at the door.

"Oh, it's too bad!" she cried. "I never saw such a house for getting in the way! Never!"

However, there was the hill full in sight, so there was nothing to be done but start again. This time she came upon a large flower-bed, with a border of daisies, and a willow-tree growing in the middle.

"O Tiger-lily!" said Alice, addressing herself to one that was waving gracefully about in the wind, "I *wish* you could talk!"

"We *can* talk," said the Tiger-lily, "when there's anybody worth talking to."

Alice was so astonished that she couldn't speak for a minute: it quite seemed to take her breath away. At length, as the Tiger-lily only went on waving about, she spoke again, in a timid voice—almost in a whisper. "And can *all* the flowers talk?"

"As well as *you* can," said the Tiger-lily. "And a great deal louder."

"It isn't manners for us to begin, you know," said the Rose, "and I really was wondering when you'd speak! Said I to myself, 'Her face has got *some* sense in it, though it's not a clever one!' Still, you're the right colour, and that goes a long way."

"I don't care about the colour," the Tiger-lily

"'We *can* talk,' said the Tiger-lily"

remarked. "If only her petals curled up a little more, she'd be all right."

Alice didn't like being criticized, so she began asking questions. "Aren't you sometimes frightened at being planted out here, with nobody to take care of you?"

"There's the tree in the middle," said the Rose. "What else is it good for?"

"But what could it do, if any danger came?" Alice asked.

"It could bark," said the Rose.

"It says 'Boughwough!'" cried a Daisy. "That's why its branches are called boughs!"

"Didn't you know *that?*" cried another Daisy. And here they all began shouting together, till the air seemed quite full of little shrill voices. "Silence, every one of you!" cried the Tiger-lily, waving itself passionately from side to side, and trembling with excitement. "They know I ca'n't get at them!" it panted, bending its quivering head towards Alice, "or they wouldn't dare to do it!"

"Never mind!" Alice said in a soothing tone, and, stooping down to the daisies, who were just beginning again, she whispered "If you don't hold your tongues, I'll pick you!"

There was silence in a moment, and several of the pink daisies turned white.[2]

"That's right!" said the Tiger-lily. "The daisies are worst of all. When one speaks, they all begin together, and it's enough to make one wither to hear the way they go on!"

"How is it you can all talk so nicely?" Alice said, hoping to get it into a better temper by a compliment. "I've been in many gardens before, but none of the flowers could talk."

2. Robert Hornback (in an article cited in Chapter 5, note 3, of *Alice in Wonderland*) suggests that the daisies are varieties of the wild English daisy: "They have ray petals that are white on top and reddish underneath. When these unfold in the morning, the daisies appear to change from pink to white."

"Put your hand down, and feel the ground," said the Tiger-lily. "Then you'll know why."

Alice did so. "It's very hard," she said; "but I don't see what that has to do with it."

"In most gardens," the Tiger-lily said, "they make the beds too soft—so that the flowers are always asleep."

This sounded a very good reason, and Alice was quite pleased to know it. "I never thought of that before!" she said.

"It's *my* opinion that you never think *at all,*" the Rose said, in a rather severe tone.

"I never saw anybody that looked stupider," a Violet said, so suddenly, that Alice quite jumped; for it hadn't spoken before.

"Hold *your* tongue!" cried the Tiger-lily. "As if *you* ever saw anybody! You keep your head under the leaves, and snore away there, till you know no more what's going on in the world, than if you were a bud!"

"Are there any more people in the garden besides me?" Alice said, not choosing to notice the Rose's last remark.

"There's one other flower in the garden that can move about like you," said the Rose. "I wonder how you do it—" ("You're always wondering," said the Tiger-lily), "but she's more bushy than you are."

"Is she like me?" Alice asked eagerly, for the thought crossed her mind, "There's another little girl in the garden, somewhere!"

"Well, she has the same awkward shape as you," the Rose said: "but she's redder—and her petals are shorter, I think."

"They're done up close, like a dahlia," said the Tiger-lily: "not tumbled about, like yours."

3. In the first edition of *Through the Looking-Glass* the sentence "She's one of the kind that has nine spikes . . ." read "She's one of the thorny kind." The "spikes" refer to the nine points on the Red Queen's crown. Tenniel's queens, in contrast to Newell's, all have nine-pointed crowns, and when Alice reaches the eighth square and becomes a queen, her gold crown has nine points as well.

"But that's not *your* fault," the Rose added kindly. "You're beginning to fade, you know—and then one ca'n't help one's petals getting a little untidy."

Alice didn't like this idea at all: so, to change the subject, she asked "Does she ever come out here?"

"I daresay you'll see her soon," said the Rose. "She's one of the kind that has nine spikes, you know."[3]

"Where does she wear them?" Alice asked with some curiosity.

"Why, all round her head, of course," the Rose replied. "I was wondering *you* hadn't got some too. I thought it was the regular rule."

"She's coming!" cried the Larkspur. "I hear her footstep, thump, thump, along the gravel-walk!"

Alice looked round eagerly and found that it was the Red Queen. "She's grown a good deal!" was her first remark. She had indeed: when Alice first found her in the ashes, she had been only three inches high—and here she was, half a head taller than Alice herself!

"It's the fresh air that does it," said the Rose: "wonderfully fine air it is, out here."

"I think I'll go and meet her," said Alice, for, though the flowers were interesting enough, she felt that it would be far grander to have a talk with a real Queen.

"You ca'n't possibly do that," said the Rose: "*I* should advise you to walk the other way."

This sounded nonsense to Alice, so she said nothing, but set off at once towards the Red Queen. To her surprise she lost sight of her in a moment, and found herself walking in at the front-door again.

A little provoked, she drew back, and, after looking everywhere for the Queen (whom she spied out at last, a long way off), she thought she would try the plan, this time, of walking in the opposite direction.

It succeeded beautifully. She had not been walking a minute before she found herself face to face with the Red Queen, and full in sight of the hill she had been so long aiming at.

"Where do you come from?" said the Red Queen. "And where are you going? Look up, speak nicely, and don't twiddle your fingers all the time."

Alice attended to all these directions, and explained, as well as she could, that she had lost her way.

"I don't know what you mean by *your* way," said the Queen: "all the ways about here belong to *me*—but why did you come out here at all?" she added in a kinder tone. "Curtsey while you're thinking what to say. It saves time."

Alice wondered a little at this, but she was too much in awe of the Queen to disbelieve it. "I'll try it when I go home," she thought to herself, "the next time I'm a little late for dinner."

"It's time for you to answer now," the Queen said looking at her watch: "open your mouth a *little* wider when you speak, and always say 'your Majesty.' "

"I only wanted to see what the garden was like, your Majesty—"

"That's right," said the Queen, patting her on the head, which Alice didn't like at all:

"though, when you say 'garden'—*I've* seen gardens, compared with which this would be a wilderness."

Alice didn't dare to argue the point, but went on: "—and I thought I'd try and find my way to the top of that hill—"

"When you say 'hill'," the Queen interrupted, "*I* could show you hills, in comparison with which you'd call that a valley."

"No, I shouldn't," said Alice, surprised into contradicting her at last: "a hill *ca'n't* be a valley, you know. That would be nonsense—"

The Red Queen shook her head. "You may call it 'nonsense' if you like," she said, "but *I've* heard nonsense, compared with which that would be as sensible as a dictionary!"

Alice curtseyed again, as she was afraid from the Queen's tone that she was a *little* offended: and they walked on in silence till they got to the top of the little hill.

For some minutes Alice stood without speaking, looking out in all directions over the country—and a most curious country it was. There were a number of tiny little brooks running straight across it from side to side, and the ground between was divided up into squares by a number of little green hedges, that reached from brook to brook.

"I declare it's marked out just like a large chess-board!" Alice said at last. "There ought to be some men moving about somewhere—and so there are!" she added in a tone of delight, and her heart began to beat quick with excitement as she went on. "It's a great huge game of chess that's being played—all over the world—if this *is* the world at all, you know. Oh, what

" 'Where do you come from?' said the Red Queen"

" 'I declare it's marked out just like a large chess-board!' Alice said at last"

fun it is! How I *wish* I was one of them! I wouldn't mind being a Pawn, if only I might join—though of course I should *like* to be a Queen, best."

She glanced rather shyly at the real Queen as she said this, but her companion only smiled pleasantly, and said "That's easily managed. You can be the White Queen's Pawn, if you like, as Lily's too young to play: and you're in the Second Square to begin with: when you get to the Eighth Square you'll be a Queen—" Just at this moment, somehow or other, they began to run.

Alice never could quite make out, in thinking it over afterwards, how it was that they began: all she remembers is, that they were running hand in hand, and the Queen went so fast that it was all she could do to keep up with her: and still the Queen kept crying "Faster! Faster!" but Alice felt she *could not* go faster, though she had no breath left to say so.

The most curious part of the thing was, that the trees and the other things round them never changed their places at all: however fast they went, they never seemed to pass anything. "I wonder if all the things move along with us?" thought poor puzzled Alice. And the Queen seemed to guess her thoughts, for she cried "Faster! Don't try to talk!"

Not that Alice had any idea of doing *that.* She felt as if she would never be able to talk again, she was getting so much out of breath: and still the Queen cried "Faster! Faster!" and dragged her along. "Are we nearly there?" Alice managed to pant out at last.

"Nearly there!" the Queen repeated. "Why, we passed it ten minutes ago! Faster!" And they ran on for a time in silence, with the wind whistling in Alice's ears, and almost blowing her hair off her head, she fancied.

"Now! Now!" cried the Queen. "Faster! Faster!" And they went so fast that at last they seemed to skim through the air, hardly touching the ground with their feet, till suddenly, just as

" 'Now! Now!' cried the Queen. 'Faster! Faster!' "

Alice was getting quite exhausted, they stopped, and she found herself sitting on the ground, breathless and giddy.

The Queen propped her up against a tree, and said kindly, "You may rest a little now."

Alice looked round her in great surprise. "Why, I do believe we've been under this tree the whole time! Everything's just as it was!"

"Of course it is," said the Queen. "What would you have it?"

"Well, in *our* country," said Alice, still panting a little, "you'd generally get to somewhere else—if you ran very fast for a long time as we've been doing."

"A slow sort of country!" said the Queen. "Now, *here,* you see, it takes all the running *you* can do, to keep in the same place. If you want to get somewhere else, you must run at least twice as fast as that!"

"I'd rather not try, please!" said Alice. "I'm quite content to stay here—only I *am* so hot and thirsty!"

"I know what *you'd* like!" the Queen said good-naturedly, taking a little box out of her pocket. "Have a biscuit?"

Alice thought it would not be civil to say "No," though it wasn't at all what she wanted. She took it, and ate it as well as she could: and it was *very* dry: and she thought she had never been so nearly choked in all her life.

"While you're refreshing yourself," said the Queen, "I'll just take the measurements." And she took a ribbon out of her pocket, marked in inches, and began measuring the ground, and sticking little pegs in here and there.

"At the end of two yards," she said, putting

in a peg to mark the distance, "I shall give you your directions—have another biscuit?"

"No, thank you," said Alice: "one's *quite* enough!"

"Thirst quenched, I hope?" said the Queen.

Alice did not know what to say to this, but luckily the Queen did not wait for an answer, but went on. "At the end of *three* yards I shall repeat them—for fear of your forgetting them. At the end of *four,* I shall say good-bye. And at the end of *five,* I shall go!"

She had got all the pegs put in by this time, and Alice looked on with great interest as she returned to the tree, and then began slowly walking down the row.

At the two-yard peg she faced round, and said "A pawn goes two squares in its first move, you know. So you'll go *very* quickly through the Third Square—by railway, I should think—and you'll find yourself in the Fourth Square in no time. Well, *that* square belongs to Tweedledum and Tweedledee—the Fifth is mostly water—the Sixth belongs to Humpty Dumpty—But you make no remark?"

"I—I didn't know I had to make one—just then," Alice faltered out.

"You *should* have said," the Queen went on in a tone of grave reproof, " 'It's extremely kind of you to tell me all this'—however, we'll suppose it said—the Seventh Square is all forest—however, one of the Knights will show you the way—and in the Eighth Square we shall be Queens together, and it's all feasting and fun!" Alice got up and curtseyed, and sat down again.

At the next peg the Queen turned again, and this time she said "Speak in French when you ca'n't think of the English for a thing—turn out your toes as you walk—and remember who you are!"[4] She did not wait for Alice to curtsey, this time, but walked on quickly to the next peg, where she turned for a moment to say "Good-bye," and then hurried on to the last.

How it happened, Alice never knew, but exactly as she came to the last peg, she was gone. Whether she vanished into the air, or whether she ran quickly into the wood ("and she *can* run very fast!" thought Alice), there was no way of guessing, but she was gone, and Alice began to remember that she was a Pawn, and that it would soon be time for her to move.

4. Gerald M. Weinberg, in a letter, made two interesting observations about the Queen's advice. Because she is instructing Alice on how to behave as a pawn, "Speak in French when you ca'n't think of the English for a thing" could refer to pawns capturing *en passant* (there is no English term for this ploy), and "turn out your toes" could indicate the way pawns capture by forward diagonal moves to the left or right.

"In fact, it was an elephant—as Alice soon found out"

CHAPTER III
LOOKING-GLASS INSECTS

Of course the first thing to do was to make a grand survey of the country she was going to travel through. "It's something very like learning geography," thought Alice, as she stood on tiptoe in hopes of being able to see a little further. "Principal rivers—there *are* none. Principal mountains—I'm on the only one, but I don't think it's got any name. Principal towns—why, what *are* those creatures, making honey down there? They ca'n't be bees—nobody ever saw bees a mile off, you know—" and for some time she stood silent, watching one of them that was bustling about among the flowers, poking its proboscis into them, "just as if it was a regular bee," thought Alice.

However, this was anything but a regular bee: in fact, it was an elephant[1]—as Alice soon found out, though the idea quite took her breath away at first. "And what enormous flowers they must be!" was her next idea. "Something like cottages with the roofs taken off, and stalks put to them—and what quantities

1. A. S. M. Dickins, in his article on the Looking-Glass chess game (see Chapter 9, note 1), mentions that the letter *B* (aside from being a favorite of Carroll's) is the symbol for a chess bishop, and that some six hundred years ago the chess bishop was called an elephant. "*Alfil* in Muslim, *Hasti* in Indian, and *Kin* or *Siang* in Chinese Chess. The Russians still to this day call it *Slon,* which means Elephant. So in this curious paragraph Lewis Carroll does introduce the Bishop into the story, but wrapped up in a very disguised code-name."

In a charming half-nonsense tale called "Isa's Visit to Oxford," written for his child-friend Isa Bowman, who reprints it in her book *The Story of Lewis Carroll* (J. M. Dent, 1899), Carroll speaks of walking with Isa through the gardens of Worcester College. They failed to "see the swans (who ought to have been on the Lake), nor the hippopotamus, who ought not to have been walking about among the flowers, gathering honey like a busy bee."

of honey they must make! I think I'll go down and—no, I wo'n't go *just* yet," she went on, checking herself just as she was beginning to run down the hill, and trying to find some excuse for turning shy so suddenly. "It'll never do to go down among them without a good long branch to brush them away—and what fun it'll be when they ask me how I liked my walk. I shall say 'Oh, I liked it well enough—' (here came the favourite little toss of the head), 'only it *was* so dusty and hot, and the elephants *did* tease so!' "

"I think I'll go down the other way," she said after a pause; "and perhaps I may visit the elephants later on. Besides, I *do* so want to get into the Third Square!"

So, with this excuse, she ran down the hill, and jumped over the first of the six little brooks.

"Tickets, please!" said the Guard, putting his head in at the window. In a moment everybody was holding out a ticket: they were about the same size as the people, and quite seemed to fill the carriage.

"Now then! Show your ticket, child!" the Guard went on, looking angrily at Alice. And a great many voices all said together ("like the chorus of a song," thought Alice) "Don't keep him waiting, child! Why, his time is worth a thousand pounds a minute!"

"I'm afraid I haven't got one," Alice said in a frightened tone: "there wasn't a ticket-office where I came from." And again the chorus of voices went on. "There wasn't room for one where she came from. The land there is worth a thousand pounds an inch!"

"Don't make excuses," said the Guard: "you should have bought one from the engine-driver." And once more the chorus of voices went on with "The man that drives the engine. Why, the smoke alone is worth a thousand pounds a puff!"[2]

Alice thought to herself "Then there's no use in speaking." The voices didn't join in, *this* time, as she hadn't spoken, but, to her great surprise, they all *thought* in chorus (I hope you understand what thinking in chorus means—for I must confess that *I* don't) "Better say nothing at all. Language is worth a thousand pounds a word!"

"I shall dream about a thousand pounds to-night, I know I shall!" thought Alice.

All this time the Guard was looking at her, first through a telescope, then through a microscope, and then through an opera-glass.[3] At last he said "You're traveling the wrong way," and shut up the window, and went away. "So young a child," said the gentleman sitting opposite to her, (he was dressed in white paper), "ought to know which way she's going, even if she doesn't know her own name!"

A Goat, that was sitting next to the gentleman in white, shut his eyes and said in a loud voice, "She ought to know her way to the ticket-office, even if she doesn't know her alphabet!"

There was a Beetle sitting next the Goat (it was a very queer carriage-full of passengers altogether), and, as the rule seemed to be that they should all speak in turn, *he* went on with "She'll have to go back from here as luggage!"

2. *Jabberwocky* (March 1970) published my query: "Perhaps one of your readers can clear up what for me is one of the biggest mysteries yet unsolved about the *Alice* books. In the railway carriage scene the phrase 'worth a thousand ——— a ———' (with different words where the blanks are) is repeated several times. I feel certain Carroll was referring here to something familiar to his readers then (an advertising slogan?) but I have been unable to discover what it was."

The consensus among respondents, in the next issue, was that the phrase referred to a popular slogan for Beecham's pills: "worth a guinea a box." R. B. Shaberman and Denis Crutch, in *Under the Quizzing Glass,* offer a different theory. They think it echoes a well-known phrase used by Tennyson when he described the freshness of air on the Isle of Wight as "worth sixpence a pint."

Still another conjecture, in a letter from Wilfred Shepherd, ties the thousand pounds to the enormous publicity that surrounded the building of the *Great Eastern,* a British ship that was gigantic for its time (it was launched in 1858). The *Encyclopaedia Britannica* speaks of it as "perhaps the most discussed steamship that has ever been built, and the most historic failure." Shepherd found an account of the affair in a book called *The Great Iron Ship* (1953) by James Duggan. It is filled with references to costs of a thousand pounds—a thousand pounds a foot to launch the ship, an investment on capital of a thousand pounds a day, and so on. Perhaps someone should check the newspaper accounts Carroll would have read to see if there are references to "a thousand pounds a puff."

3. Tenniel's illustration for this scene may have been a deliberate parody of *My First Sermon,* a famous painting by John Everett Millais. The resemblance in the way the two girls are dressed is remarkable: porkpie hat with feather, striped stockings, a skirt with rows of tucks at the bottom, pointed black shoes, and a muff. A purse beside Alice takes the place of a Bible at the left of the girl in the church pew. In his diary (April 7, 1864) Carroll records a visit to Millais's house, where he met his six-year-old daughter, Effie, the original of the girl in the painting.

Spencer D. Brown was the first to spot the resemblance of Tenniel's Alice in the train to Millais's girl at church. The parallels are even more striking if Tenniel's drawing is taken as a composite of *My First Sermon* and a later picture, *My Second Sermon,* showing the same girl sleeping in the pew.

My First Sermon was widely reproduced in England. In the United States, Currier and Ives sold a copy in black and white (some were hand-colored) titled *Little Ella.* It is an exact replica of the Millais painting except that it is mirror-reversed (Carroll would have been amused) and the girl's face has been altered to make it more doll-like. The date of the Currier and Ives print is unknown, as is the name of the artist who modified it. Nor is it known whether the picture was pirated, or if Currier and Ives obtained permission to copy it.

Roger Green convinced me that the resemblance of Tenniel's drawing to the two Millais paintings may have been coincidental. He referred me to pictures of the day in *Punch* that show little girls in railway carriages dressed exactly like Alice, with their hands in muffs. Michael Hearn sent a similar picture from Walter Crane's 1869 book *Little Annie and Jack in London.*

Still, the resemblance of Tenniel's Alice to Millais's daughter in church is so striking that it is impossible to believe Tenniel was not at least aware of it. You can form your own opinion by studying the three pictures reproduced below.

Charles Lovett informed me that Carroll owned a telescope, a microscope, and an opera glass, and often amused his child-friends by letting them look through them.

Alice couldn't see who was sitting beyond the Beetle, but a hoarse voice spoke next. "Change engines—"[4] it said, and there it choked and was obliged to leave off.

"It sounds like a horse," Alice thought to herself. And an extremely small voice, close to her ear, said "You might make a joke on that—something about 'horse' and 'hoarse,' you know."[5]

Then a very gentle voice in the distance said, "She must be labeled 'Lass, with care,' you know—"

And after that other voices went on ("What a number of people there are in the carriage!" thought Alice), saying "She must go by post, as she's got a head on her—"[6] "She must be sent as a message by the telegraph—" "She must draw the train herself the rest of the way—," and so on.

But the gentleman dressed in white paper leaned forwards and whispered in her ear, "Never mind what they all say, my dear, but take a return-ticket every time the train stops."

"Indeed I sha'n't!" Alice said rather impatiently. "I don't belong to this railway journey at all—I was in a wood just now—and I wish I could get back there!"

"You might make a joke on *that,*" said the little voice close to her ear: "something about 'you *would* if you could,' you know."[7]

"Don't tease so," said Alice, looking about in vain to see where the voice came from. "If you're so anxious to have a joke made, why don't you make one yourself?"

The little voice sighed deeply.[8] It was *very* unhappy, evidently, and Alice would have said something pitying to comfort it, "if it would

4. It is easy to overlook the humor in having a horse passenger call out not "change horses" but "change engines."

5. There *is* an old joke based on this pun. "I'm a little hoarse," a person says, then adds, "I have a little colt."

6. "Head" was Victorian slang for a postage stamp. Because Alice has a head, the voices suggest she should be posted. Note the grim suggestion of a post with an enemy's severed head on top.

7. Carroll may have intended this as a quote of the first line of a Mother Goose melody:

> *I would, if I could,*
> *If I couldn't how could I?*
> *I couldn't, without I could, could I?*
> *Could you, without you could, could ye?*
> *Could ye? could ye?*
> *Could you, without you could, could ye?*

8. In the "Wasp in a Wig" episode (reprinted in this book) the aged Wasp's long sigh may have expressed Carroll's sadness over the gulf time had placed between himself and Alice. George Garcin says in a letter that he thinks the Gnat's sigh carries similar overtones. Time, symbolized by the train, is carrying Alice (his "dear friend, and an old friend") the "wrong way"—toward womanhood, when she will soon be lost to him. This passage of time may be the "shadow of a sigh" in the last stanza of Carroll's prefatory poem.

Fred Madden, writing on "Orthographic Transformations in Through the Looking-Glass," in *Jabberwocky* (Autumn 1985), has an intriguing explanation of why Carroll put a gnat in the railway carriage alongside a goat. In Carroll's game of Doublets, the word "gnat" becomes "goat" by the change of a single letter. Madden supports this contention by referring to a word ladder that actually appears in Carroll's pamphlet *Doublets: A Word Puzzle* (Macmillan, third edition, 1880, page 31), in which Carroll changed GNAT to BITE in six steps: GNAT, GOAT, BOAT, BOLT, BOLE, BILE, BITE.

"At last he said, 'You're traveling the wrong way' "

only sigh like other people!" she thought. But this was such a wonderfully small sigh, that she wouldn't have heard it at all, if it hadn't come *quite* close to her ear. The consequence of this was that it tickled her ear very much, and quite took off her thoughts from the unhappiness of the poor little creature.

"I know you are a friend," the little voice went on: "a dear friend, and an old friend. And you wo'n't hurt me, though I *am* an insect."

"What kind of insect?" Alice inquired, a little anxiously. What she really wanted to know was, whether it could sting or not, but she thought this wouldn't be quite a civil question to ask.

"What, then you don't—" the little voice began, when it was drowned by a shrill scream from the engine, and everybody jumped up in alarm, Alice among the rest.

The Horse, who had put his head out of the window, quietly drew it in and said "It's only a brook we have to jump over." Everybody seemed satisfied with this, though Alice felt a little nervous at the idea of trains jumping at all. "However, it'll take us into the Fourth Square, that's some comfort!" she said to herself. In another moment she felt the carriage rise straight up into the air, and in her fright she caught at the thing nearest to her hand, which happened to be the Goat's beard.

*   *   *   *   *
  *   *   *   *
*   *   *   *   *

But the beard seemed to melt away as she touched it, and she found herself sitting quietly under a tree—while the Gnat (for that was the insect she had been talking to) was balancing itself on a twig just over her head, and fanning her with its wings.

It certainly was a *very* large Gnat: "about the size of a chicken," Alice thought. Still, she couldn't feel nervous with it, after they had been talking together so long.

"—then you don't like *all* insects?" the Gnat went on, as quietly as if nothing had happened.

"I like them when they can talk," Alice said. "None of them ever talk, where *I* come from."

"What sort of insects do you rejoice in, where *you* come from?" the Gnat inquired.

"I don't *rejoice* in insects at all," Alice explained, "because I'm rather afraid of them—at least the large kinds. But I can tell you the names of some of them."

"Of course they answer to their names?" the Gnat remarked carelessly.

"I never knew them do it."

"What's the use of their having names," the Gnat said, "if they wo'n't answer to them?"

"No use to *them,*" said Alice; "but it's useful to the people that name them, I suppose. If not, why do things have names at all?"

"I ca'n't say," the Gnat replied. "Further on, in the wood down there, they've got no names—however, go on with your list of insects: you're wasting time."

"Well, there's the Horse-fly," Alice began, counting off the names on her fingers.

"All right," said the Gnat. "Half way up that bush, you'll see a Rocking-horse-fly, if you look. It's made entirely of wood, and gets about by swinging itself from branch to branch."

"What does it live on?" Alice asked, with great curiosity.

"While the Gnat was balancing itself on a twig"

"Sap and sawdust," said the Gnat. "Go on with the list."

Alice looked at the Rocking-horse-fly with great interest, and made up her mind that it must have been just repainted, it looked so bright and sticky; and then she went on.

"And there's the Dragon-fly."

"Look on the branch above your head," said the Gnat, "and there you'll find a Snap-dragon-fly. Its body is made of plum-pudding, its wings of holly-leaves, and its head is a raisin burning in brandy."

"And what does it live on?" Alice asked, as before.

"Frumenty and mince-pie," the Gnat replied; "and it makes its nest in a Christmas-box."

"And then there's the Butterfly," Alice went on, after she had taken a good look at the insect with its head on fire, and had thought to herself, "I wonder if that's the reason insects are so fond of flying into candles—because they want to turn into Snap-dragon-flies!"

"Crawling at your feet," said the Gnat (Alice drew her feet back in some alarm), "you may observe a Bread-and-butter-fly. Its wings are thin slices of bread-and-butter, its body is a crust, and its head is a lump of sugar."

"And what does *it* live on?"

"Weak tea with cream in it."

A new difficulty came into Alice's head. "Supposing it couldn't find any?" she suggested.

"Then it would die, of course."

"But that must happen very often," Alice remarked thoughtfully.

"It always happens," said the Gnat.

After this, Alice was silent for a minute or

two, pondering. The Gnat amused itself meanwhile by humming round and round her head: at last it settled again and remarked "I suppose you don't want to lose your name?"

"No, indeed," Alice said, a little anxiously.

"And yet I don't know," the Gnat went on in a careless tone: "only think how convenient it would be if you could manage to go home without it! For instance, if the governess wanted to call you to your lessons, she would call out 'Come here—,' and there she would have to leave off, because there wouldn't be any name for her to call, and of course you wouldn't have to go, you know."

"That would never do, I'm sure," said Alice: "the governess would never think of excusing me lessons for that. If she couldn't remember my name, she'd call me 'Miss,' as the servants do."

"Well, if she said 'Miss,' and didn't say anything more," the Gnat remarked, "of course you'd miss your lessons. That's a joke. I wish *you* had made it."

"Why do you wish *I* had made it?" Alice asked. "It's a very bad one."

But the Gnat only sighed deeply while two large tears came rolling down its cheeks.

"You shouldn't make jokes," Alice said, "if it makes you so unhappy."

Then came another of those melancholy little sighs, and this time the poor Gnat really seemed to have sighed itself away, for, when Alice looked up, there was nothing whatever to be seen on the twig, and, as she was getting quite chilly with sitting still so long, she got up and walked on.

9. Queen Victoria, Charles Lovett informed me, owned a spaniel named Dash that was well known in England. The queen was often photographed and painted with Dash at her side or on her lap.

She very soon came to an open field, with a wood on the other side of it: it looked much darker than the last wood, and Alice felt a little timid about going into it. However, on second thoughts, she made up her mind to go on: "for I certainly won't go *back,*" she thought to herself, and this was the only way to the Eighth Square.

"This must be the wood," she said thoughtfully to herself, "where things have no names. I wonder what'll become of *my* name when I go in? I shouldn't like to lose it at all—because they'd have to give me another, and it would be almost certain to be an ugly one. But then the fun would be, trying to find the creature that has got my old name! That's just like the advertisements, you know, when people lose dogs—*'answers to the name of "Dash":*[9] *had on a brass collar'*—just fancy calling everything you met 'Alice,' till one of them answered! Only they wouldn't answer at all, if they were wise."

She was rambling on in this way when she reached the wood: it looked very cool and shady. "Well, at any rate it's a great comfort," she said as she stepped under the trees, "after being so hot, to get into the—into the—into *what?*" she went on, rather surprised at not being able to think of the word. "I mean to get under the—under the—under *this,* you know!" putting her hand on the trunk of the tree. "What *does* it call itself, I wonder? I do believe it's got no name—why, to be sure it hasn't!"

She stood silent for a minute, thinking: then she suddenly began again. "Then it really *has* happened, after all! And now, who am I? I *will* remember, if I can! I'm determined to do it!" But being determined didn't help her much, and all she could say, after a great deal of puzzling was "L, I *know* it begins with L!"[10]

Just then a Fawn[11] came wandering by: it looked at Alice with its large gentle eyes, but didn't seem at all frightened. "Here then! Here then!" Alice said, as she held out her hand and tried to stroke it; but it only started back a little, and then stood looking at her again.

"What do you call yourself?" the Fawn said at last. Such a soft sweet voice it had!

"I wish I knew!" thought poor Alice. She answered, rather sadly, "Nothing, just now."

"Think again," it said: "that wo'n't do."

Alice thought, but nothing came of it. "Please, would you tell me what *you* call yourself?" she said timidly. "I think that might help a little."

"I'll tell you, if you'll come a little further on," the Fawn said. "I ca'n't remember *here.*"

So they walked on together through the wood, Alice with her arms clasped lovingly round the soft neck of the Fawn, till they came out into another open field, and here the Fawn gave a sudden bound into the air, and shook itself free from Alice's arm. "I'm a Fawn!" it cried out in a voice of delight. "And, dear me! you're a human child!" A sudden look of alarm came into its beautiful brown eyes, and in another moment it had darted away at full speed.

Alice stood looking after it, almost ready to cry with vexation at having lost her dear little fellow-traveler so suddenly. "However, I know my name now," she said: "that's *some* comfort. Alice—Alice—I won't forget it again. And now, which of these finger-posts ought I to follow, I wonder?"

10. Alice may be thinking of Lily, the name of the white pawn whose place she has taken, and also of her own last name, Liddell. Perhaps, as readers Josephine van Dyk and Mrs. Carlton Hyman independently proposed, Alice is vaguely recalling the sound of her first name, which seems to begin with an *L*—"*L*-is." Ada Brown supported this conjecture by sending the following lines from "Bruno's Picnic," a chapter in Carroll's *Sylvie and Bruno Concluded:* "What *does* an Apple-Tree begin with, when it wants to speak?" asks Sylvie. The narrator replies: "Doesn't 'Apple-Tree' always begin with 'Eh!'?"

In *Language and Lewis Carroll* (Mouton, 1970), Robert Sutherland points out that the theme of forgetting one's name is common in Carroll's writings. "Who are you?" the Caterpillar asks Alice, and she is too confused to answer; the Red Queen admonishes Alice, "Remember who you are!"; the man in white paper tells her, "So young a child ought to know where she's going, even if she doesn't know her name"; the White Queen is so frightened by thunder that she forgets her name; the Baker forgets his name in *The Hunting of the Snark,* and so does the Professor in *Sylvie and Bruno.* Perhaps this theme reflects Carroll's own confusion over whether he is Charles Dodgson, the Oxford professor, or Lewis Carroll, writer of fantasy and nonsense.

11. Fred Madden (see this chapter's note 8) observes that Alice, a pawn, is here meeting a fawn, and that in Carroll's game of doublets the change of a single letter turns "pawn" to "fawn." According to Carroll's *Dramatis Personae,* at the beginning of the book, the fawn is actually a pawn in the chess game. Presumably the two pawns, both white, are now adjacent to each other.

"Alice with her arms clasped lovingly round
the soft neck of the Fawn"

It was not a very difficult question to answer, as there was only one road through the wood, and the two finger-posts both pointed along it. "I'll settle it," Alice said to herself, "when the road divides and they point different ways."

But this did not seem likely to happen. She went on and on, a long way, but wherever the road divided, there were sure to be two finger-posts pointing the same way, one marked "TO TWEEDLEDUM'S HOUSE," and the other "TO THE HOUSE OF TWEEDLEDEE."

"I do believe," said Alice at last, "that they live in the *same* house![12] I wonder I never thought of that before—But I ca'n't stay there long. I'll just call and say 'How d'ye do?' and ask them the way out of the wood. If I could only get to the Eighth Square before it gets dark!" So she wandered on, talking to herself as she went, till, on turning a sharp corner, she came upon two fat little men, so suddenly that she could not help starting back, but in another moment she recovered herself, feeling sure that they must be

12. Reader Greg Stone called my attention to the way "house" and the names of the Tweedle brothers are left-right reversed on these signs, in keeping with the fact that Carroll intended the brothers to be mirror images of each other.

CHAPTER IV

TWEEDLEDUM AND TWEEDLEDEE

They were standing under a tree, each with an arm round the other's neck, and Alice knew which was which in a moment, because one of them had 'DUM' embroidered on his collar, and the other 'DEE.' "I suppose they've each got 'TWEEDLE' round at the back of the collar," she said to herself.

They stood so still that she quite forgot they were alive, and she was just going round to see if the word 'TWEEDLE' was written at the back of each collar, when she was startled by a voice coming from the one marked 'DUM.'

"If you think we're wax-works," he said, "you ought to pay, you know. Wax-works weren't made to be looked at for nothing. Nohow!"

"Contrariwise," added the one marked 'DEE,' "if you think we're alive, you ought to speak."

"I'm sure I'm very sorry," was all Alice could say; for the words of the old song kept ringing through her head like the ticking of a clock, and she could hardly help saying them out loud:—

> *"Tweedledum and Tweedledee*
> *Agreed to have a battle;*
> *For Tweedledum said Tweedledee*
> *Had spoiled his nice new rattle.*
>
> *Just then flew down a monstrous crow,*
> *As black as a tar-barrel;*
> *Which frightened both the heroes so,*
> *They quite forgot their quarrel."*

"I know what you're thinking about," said Tweedledum; "but it isn't so, nohow."

"Contrariwise," continued Tweedledee, "if it was so, it might be; and if it were so, it would be; but as it isn't, it ain't. That's logic."

"I was thinking," Alice said politely, "which is the best way out of this wood: it's getting so dark. Would you tell me, please?"

But the fat little men only looked at each other and grinned.

They looked so exactly like a couple of great schoolboys,[1] that Alice couldn't help pointing her finger at Tweedledum, and saying "First Boy!"

"Nohow!" Tweedledum cried out briskly, and shut his mouth up again with a snap.

"Next Boy!" said Alice, passing on to Tweedledee, though she felt quite certain he would only shout out "Contrariwise!" and so he did.

"You've begun wrong!" cried Tweedledum. "The first thing in a visit is to say 'How d'ye do?' and shake hands!" And here the two brothers gave each other a hug, and then they held out the two hands that were free, to shake hands with her.

Alice did not like shaking hands with either

1. Tenniel's Tweedle brothers, in their schoolboy skeleton suits, as they were called, strongly resemble his drawings of John Bull in *Punch.* See the first chapter of Michael Hancher's *The Tenniel Illustrations to the "Alice" Books.*

of them first, for fear of hurting the other one's feelings; so, as the best way out of the difficulty, she took hold of both hands at once: the next moment they were dancing round in a ring. This seemed quite natural (she remembered afterwards), and she was not even surprised to hear music playing: it seemed to come from the tree under which they were dancing, and it was done (as well as she could make it out) by the branches rubbing one across the other, like fiddles and fiddle-sticks.

"But it certainly *was* funny," (Alice said afterwards, when she was telling her sister the history of all this), "to find myself singing *'Here we go round the mulberry bush.'* I don't know when I began it, but somehow I felt as if I'd been singing it a long long time!"

The other two dancers were fat, and very soon out of breath. "Four times round is enough for one dance," Tweedledum panted out, and they left off dancing as suddenly as they had begun: the music stopped at the same moment.

Then they let go of Alice's hands, and stood looking at her for a minute: there was a rather awkward pause, as Alice didn't know how to begin a conversation with people she had just been dancing with. "It would never do to say 'How d'ye do?' *now,*" she said to herself: "we seem to have got beyond that, somehow!"

"I hope you're not much tired?" she said at last.

"Nohow. And thank you *very* much for asking," said Tweedledum.

"So *much* obliged!" added Tweedledee. "You like poetry?"

"The next moment they were dancing round in a ring"

"Ye-es, pretty well—*some* poetry," Alice said doubtfully. "Would you tell me which road leads out of the wood?"

"What shall I repeat to her?" said Tweedledee, looking round at Tweedledum with great solemn eyes, and not noticing Alice's question.

" *'The Walrus and the Carpenter'* is the longest," Tweedledum replied, giving his brother an affectionate hug.

Tweedledee began instantly:

"The sun was shining—"

Here Alice ventured to interrupt him. "If it's *very* long," she said, as politely as she could, "would you please tell me first which road—"

Tweedledee smiled gently, and began again:[2]

"The sun was shining on the sea,
Shining with all his might:
He did his very best to make
The billows smooth and bright—
And this was odd, because it was
The middle of the night.

The moon was shining sulkily,
Because she thought the sun
Had got no business to be there
After the day was done—
'It's very rude of him,' she said,
'To come and spoil the fun!'

The sea was wet as wet could be,
The sands were dry as dry.
You could not see a cloud, because
No cloud was in the sky:
No birds were flying overhead—
There were no birds to fly.

The Walrus and the Carpenter
Were walking close at hand:[3]
They wept like anything to see
Such quantities of sand:
'If this were only cleared away,'
They said, 'it would be grand!'

'If seven maids with seven mops
Swept it for half a year,
Do you suppose,' the Walrus said,
'That they could get it clear?'
'I doubt it,' said the Carpenter,
And shed a bitter tear.

2. "In composing 'The Walrus and the Carpenter,'" Carroll wrote to an uncle in 1872, "I had no particular poem in my mind. The metre is a common one, and I don't think 'Eugene Aram' [a poem by Thomas Hood] suggested it more than the many other poems I have read in the same metre" (*The Letters of Lewis Carroll,* edited by Morton Cohen, Vol. 1, page 177).

3. At Tenniel's suggestion this line was altered from "Were walking hand in hand."

" 'If this were only cleared away,'
They said, 'it would be grand!' "

'O Oysters, come and walk with us!'
The Walrus did beseech.
'A pleasant walk, a pleasant talk,
Along the briny beach:
We cannot do with more than four,
To give a hand to each.'

The eldest Oyster looked at him,
But never a word he said:
The eldest Oyster winked his eye,
And shook his heavy head—
Meaning to say he did not choose
To leave the oyster-bed.

But four young Oysters hurried up,
All eager for the treat:
Their coats were brushed, their faces washed,
Their shoes were clean and neat—
And this was odd, because, you know,
They hadn't any feet.

Four other Oysters followed them,
And yet another four;
And thick and fast they came at last,
And more, and more, and more—
All hopping through the frothy waves,
And scrambling to the shore.

The Walrus and the Carpenter
Walked on a mile or so,
And then they rested on a rock
Conveniently low:
And all the little Oysters stood
And waited in a row.

'The time has come,' the Walrus said,
'To talk of many things:
Of shoes—and ships—and sealing wax—
Of cabbages—and kings—[4]
And why the sea is boiling hot—
And whether pigs have wings.'

'But wait a bit,' the Oysters cried,
'Before we have our chat;
For some of us are out of breath,
And all of us are fat!'

4. Jane O'Connor Creed wrote to point out how Carroll's lines echo the following portion of King Richard's speech in Shakespeare's *Richard the Second,* Act 3, Scene 2:

Let's talk of graves, of worms, and epitaphs;
Make dust our paper, and with rainy eyes
Write sorrow on the bosom of the earth.
Let's choose executors and talk of wills;
. . . .
For God's sake, let us sit upon the ground
And tell sad stories of the death of kings.

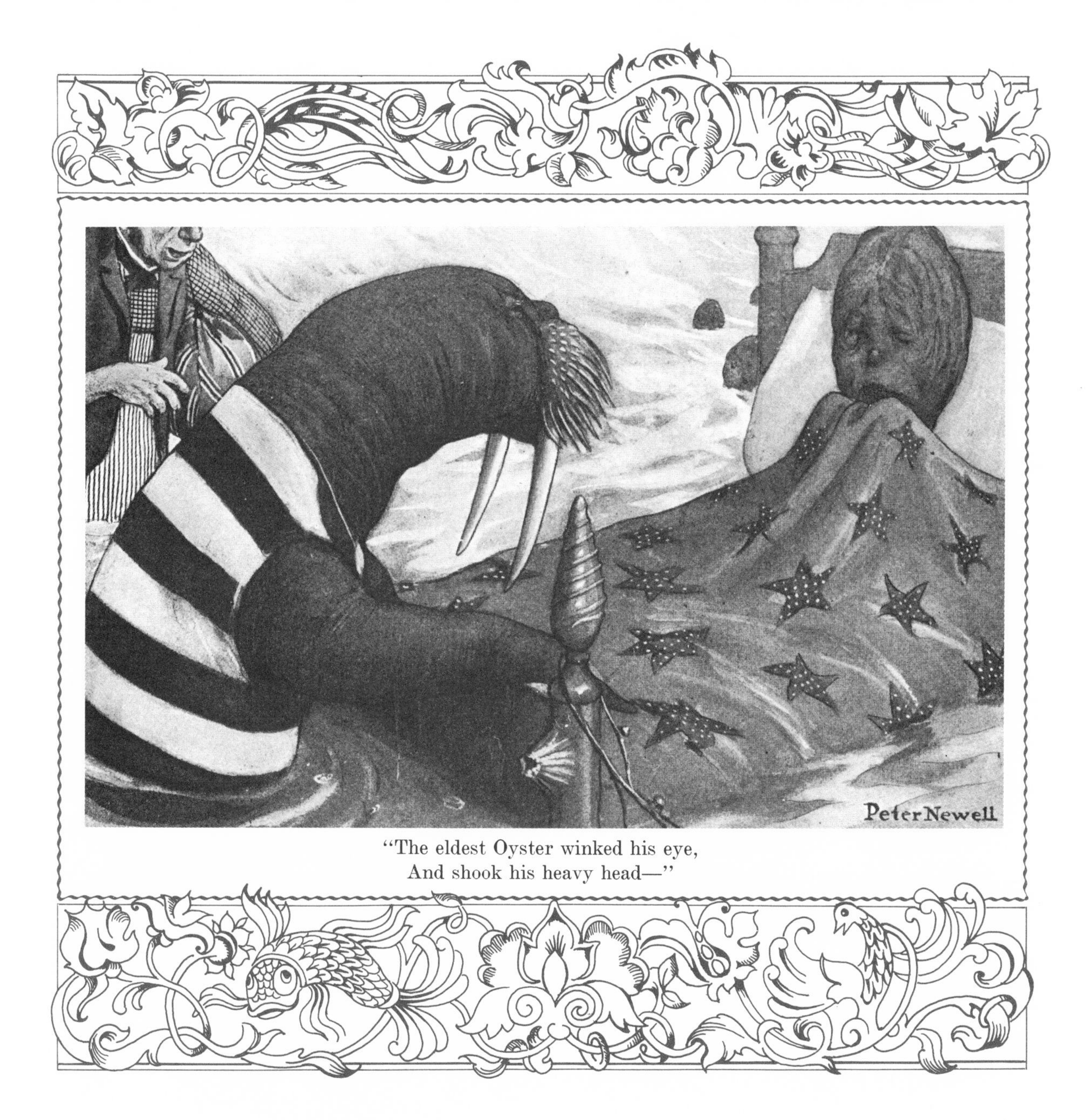

"The eldest Oyster winked his eye,
And shook his heavy head—"

'No hurry!' said the Carpenter.
They thanked him much for that.

'A loaf of bread,' the Walrus said,
'Is what we chiefly need:
Pepper and vinegar besides
Are very good indeed—
Now, if you're ready, Oysters dear,
We can begin to feed.'

'But not on us!' the Oysters cried,
Turning a little blue.
'After such kindness, that would be

A dismal thing to do!'
'The night is fine,' the Walrus said.
'Do you admire the view?

'It was so kind of you to come!
And you are very nice!'
The Carpenter said nothing but
'Cut us another slice.
I wish you were not quite so deaf—
I've had to ask you twice!'

'It seems a shame,' the Walrus said,
'To play them such a trick,
After we've brought them out so far,
And made them trot so quick!'
The Carpenter said nothing but
'The butter's spread too thick!'

'I weep for you,' the Walrus said:
'I deeply sympathize.'
With sobs and tears he sorted out
Those of the largest size,
Holding his pocket-handkerchief
Before his streaming eyes.

'O Oysters,' said the Carpenter,
'You've had a pleasant run!
Shall we be trotting home again?'
But answer came there none—
And this was scarcely odd, because
They'd eaten every one."

"I like the Walrus best," said Alice: "because he was a *little* sorry for the poor oysters."

"He ate more than the Carpenter, though," said Tweedledee. "You see he held his handkerchief in front, so that the Carpenter couldn't count how many he took: contrariwise."

"That was mean!" Alice said indignantly. "Then I like the Carpenter best—if he didn't eat so many as the Walrus."

"But he ate as many as he could get," said Tweedledum.

" 'I weep for you,' the Walrus said:
'I deeply sympathize' "

This was a puzzler. After a pause, Alice began, "Well! They were *both* very unpleasant characters—" Here she checked herself in some alarm, at hearing something that sounded to her like the puffing of a large steam-engine in the wood near them, though she feared it was more likely to be a wild beast. "Are there any lions or tigers about here?" she asked timidly.

"It's only the Red King snoring," said Tweedledee.

"Come and look at him!" the brothers cried, and they each took one of Alice's hands, and led her up to where the King was sleeping.

"Isn't he a *lovely* sight?" said Tweedledum.

Alice couldn't say honestly that he was. He had a tall red night-cap on, with a tassel, and he was lying crumpled up into a sort of untidy heap, and snoring loud—"fit to snore his head off!" as Tweedledum remarked.

"I'm afraid he'll catch cold with lying on the damp grass," said Alice, who was a very thoughtful little girl.

"He's dreaming now," said Tweedledee: "and what do you think he's dreaming about?"

Alice said "Nobody can guess that."

"Why, about *you*!" Tweedledee exclaimed, clapping his hands triumphantly. "And if he left off dreaming about you, where do you suppose you'd be?"

"Where I am now, of course," said Alice.

"Not you!" Tweedledee retorted contemptuously. "You'd be nowhere. Why, you're only a sort of thing in his dream!"[5]

"If that there King was to wake," added Tweedledum, "you'd go out—bang!—just like a candle!"[6]

5. James Branch Cabell, in *Smire,* the last novel of his *Smirt, Smith, Smire* trilogy, introduces the same circular paradox of two persons, each dreaming the other. Smire and Smike confront one another in Chapter 9, each claiming to be asleep and dreaming the other. In a preface to his trilogy, Cabell described it as a "full-length dream story" that attempts "to extend the naturalism of Lewis Carroll."

The Red King sleeps throughout the entire narrative until he is checkmated at the close of Chapter 9 by Queen Alice when she captures the Red Queen. No chess player needs reminding that kings tend to sleep throughout most chess games, sometimes not moving after castling. Tournament games are occasionally played in which a king remains on its starting square throughout the entire game.

6. This remark of Tweedledum's was anticipated by Alice in the first chapter of the previous book where she wonders if her shrinking size might result in her "going out altogether, like a candle."

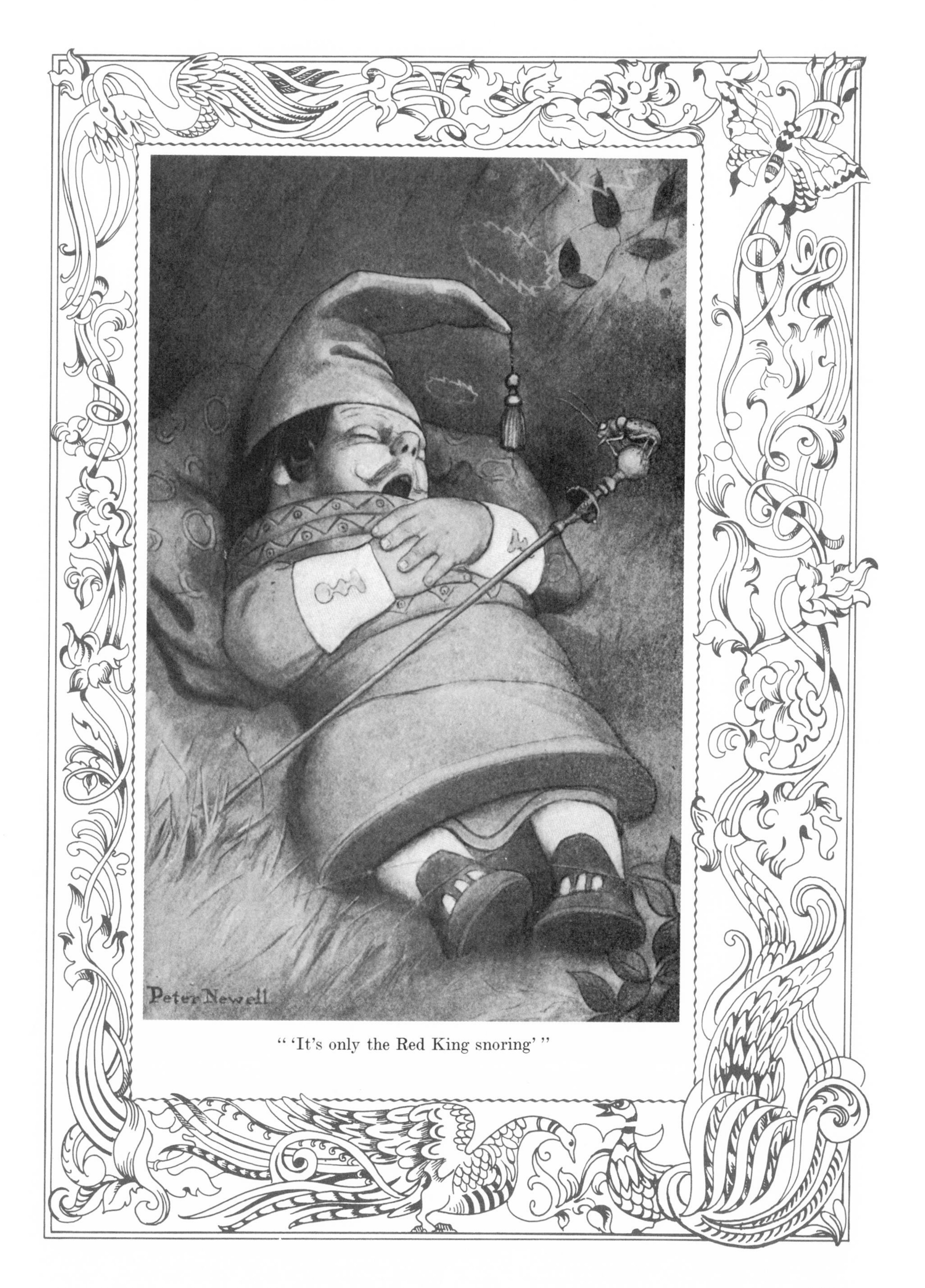

" 'It's only the Red King snoring' "

"I shouldn't!" Alice exclaimed indignantly. "Besides, if *I'm* only a sort of thing in his dream, what are *you,* I should like to know?"

"Ditto," said Tweedledum.

"Ditto, ditto!" cried Tweedledee.

He shouted this so loud that Alice couldn't help saying "Hush! You'll be waking him, I'm afraid, if you make so much noise."

"Well, it's no use *your* talking about waking him," said Tweedledum, "when you're only one of the things in his dream. You know very well you're not real."

"I *am* real!" said Alice, and began to cry.

"You wo'n't make yourself a bit realler by crying," Tweedledee remarked: "there's nothing to cry about."

"If I wasn't real," Alice said—half laughing through her tears, it all seemed so ridiculous—"I shouldn't be able to cry."

"I hope you don't suppose those are *real* tears?" Tweedledum interrupted in a tone of great contempt.

"I know they're talking nonsense," Alice thought to herself: "and it's foolish to cry about it." So she brushed away her tears, and went on, as cheerfully as she could, "At any rate, I'd better be getting out of the wood, for really it's coming on very dark. Do you think it's going to rain?"

Tweedledum spread a large umbrella over himself and his brother, and looked up into it. "No, I don't think it is," he said: "at least—not under *here.* Nohow."

"But it may rain *outside?*"

"It may—if it chooses," said Tweedledee: "we've no objection. Contrariwise."

"Selfish things!" thought Alice, and she was just going to say "Good-night" and leave them, when Tweedledum sprang out from under the umbrella, and seized her by the wrist.

"Do you see *that?*" he said, in a voice choking with passion, and his eyes grew large and yellow all in a moment, as he pointed with a trembling finger at a small white thing lying under the tree.

"It's only a rattle," Alice said, after a careful examination of the little white thing. "Not a rattle-*snake,* you know," she added hastily, thinking that he was frightened: "only an old rattle—quite old and broken."

"I knew it was!" cried Tweedledum, beginning to stamp about wildly and tear his hair. "It's spoilt, of course!" Here he looked at Tweedledee, who immediately sat down on the ground, and tried to hide himself under the umbrella.

Alice laid her hand upon his arm and said, in a soothing tone, "You needn't be so angry about an old rattle."

"But it *isn't* old!" Tweedledum cried, in a greater fury than ever. "It's *new,* I tell you—I bought it yesterday—my nice NEW RATTLE!"[7] and his voice rose to a perfect scream.

All this time Tweedledee was trying his best to fold up the umbrella, with himself in it: which was such an extraordinary thing to do, that it quite took off Alice's attention from the angry brother. But he couldn't quite succeed, and it ended in his rolling over, bundled up in the umbrella, with only his head out: and there he lay, opening and shutting his mouth and his

7. The broken rattle can be seen on the ground in Tenniel's illustration for this scene. In a letter to Henry Savile Clark (November 29, 1886) Carroll complained about how Tenniel had slyly drawn a watchman's rattle: "Mr. Tenniel has introduced a false 'reading' in his picture of the quarrel of Tweedledum and Tweedledee. I am certain that 'my nice new rattle' meant, in the old nursery-song, a child's rattle, not a watchman's rattle as he has drawn it."

In those days a watchman's rattle consisted of a thin wooden strip that vibrated against the teeth of a ratchet wheel when the rattle was whirled, producing a loud clacking noise that sounded an alarm. They are sold today mainly as party noisemakers. As reader H. P. Young pointed out in a letter, they are fragile and easily broken.

In her shrewd analysis of the objects attached to the White Knight's horse in Chapter 8, Janis Lull identifies a large watchman's rattle at the front of the horse. It is visible in three pictures, as well as in the book's frontispiece. Tenniel had earlier drawn such a rattle in the *Punch* cartoon (January 19, 1856) shown below.

large eyes—"looking more like a fish than anything else," Alice thought.

"Of course you agree to have a battle?" Tweedledum said in a calmer tone.

"I suppose so," the other sulkily replied, as he crawled out of the umbrella: "only *she* must help us to dress up, you know."

So the two brothers went off hand-in-hand into the wood, and returned in a minute with their arms full of things—such as bolsters, blankets, hearth-rugs, table-cloths, dish-covers, and coal-scuttles. "I hope you're a good hand at pinning and tying strings?" Tweedledum remarked. "Every one of these things has got to go on, somehow or other."

Alice said afterwards she had never seen such a fuss made about anything in all her life—the way those two bustled about—and the quantity of things they put on—and the trouble they gave her in tying strings and fastening buttons—"Really they'll be more like bundles of old clothes than anything else, by the time they're ready!" she said to herself, as she arranged a bolster round the neck of Tweedledee, "to keep his head from being cut off," as he said.[8]

"You know," he added very gravely, "it's one of the most serious things that can possibly happen to one in a battle—to get one's head cut off."

Alice laughed loud: but she managed to turn it into a cough, for fear of hurting his feelings.

"Do I look very pale?" said Tweedledum, coming up to have his helmet tied on. (He *called* it a helmet, though it certainly looked much more like a saucepan.)

8. Tenniel's illustration of this scene seems to show Alice arranging a bolster around Tweedledee's neck, which would make the other brother Tweedledum. But if you look closely you will see a string in both her hands. The twin on the left is Tweedledum, and Alice is tying a pot on his head. As Michael Hancher points out in his book on the Tenniel pictures, the artist apparently made a mistake here in giving the wooden sword to Tweedledee.

"Alice laughed loud: but she managed to turn it into a cough"

"Well—yes—a *little,*" Alice replied gently.

"I'm very brave, generally," he went on in a low voice: "only to-day I happen to have a headache."

"And *I've* got a toothache!" said Tweedledee, who had overheard the remark. "I'm far worse than you!"

"Then you'd better not fight to-day," said Alice, thinking it a good opportunity to make peace.

"We *must* have a bit of a fight, but I don't care about going on long," said Tweedledum. "What's the time now?"

Tweedledee looked at his watch, and said "Half-past four."

"Let's fight till six, and then have dinner," said Tweedledum.

"Very well," the other said, rather sadly: "and *she* can watch us—only you'd better not come *very* close," he added: "I generally hit every thing I can see—when I get really excited."

"And *I* hit every thing within reach," cried Tweedledum, "whether I can see it or not!"

Alice laughed. "You must hit the *trees* pretty often, I should think," she said.

Tweedledum looked round him with a satisfied smile. "I don't suppose," he said, "there'll be a tree left standing, for ever so far round, by the time we've finished!"

"And all about a rattle!" said Alice, still hoping to make them a *little* ashamed of fighting for such a trifle.

"I shouldn't have minded it so much," said Tweedledum, "if it hadn't been a new one."

"I wish the monstrous crow would come!" thought Alice.

"There's only one sword, you know," Tweedledum said to his brother: "but *you* can have the umbrella—it's quite as sharp. Only we must begin quick. It's getting as dark as it can."

"And darker," said Tweedledee.

It was getting dark so suddenly that Alice thought there must be a thunderstorm coming on. "What a thick black cloud that is!" she said. "And how fast it comes! Why, I do believe it's got wings!"[9]

"It's the crow!" Tweedledum cried out in a shrill voice of alarm; and the two brothers took to their heels and were out of sight in a moment.

Alice ran a little way into the wood, and stopped under a large tree. "It can never get at me *here,*" she thought: "it's far too large to squeeze itself in among the trees. But I wish it wouldn't flap its wings so—it makes quite a hurricane in the wood—here's somebody's shawl being blown away!"

9. J. B. S. Haldane, in his book *Possible Worlds* (Chapter 2), thinks that the monstrous black crow of the nursery rhyme is a way of describing a solar eclipse:

> Every one, for example, has heard of Tweedledum and Tweedledee, whose battle was interrupted by a monstrous crow as big as a tar-barrel. The true story of these heroes is as follows: King Alyattes of Lydia, father of the celebrated Croesus, had been engaged for five years in a war with Cyaxares, king of the Medes. In its sixth year, on May 28, 585 B.C., as we now know, a battle was interrupted by a total eclipse of the sun. The kings not only stopped the battle, but accepted mediation. One of the two mediators was no less a person than Nebuchadnezzar, who in the preceding year had destroyed Jerusalem and led its people into captivity.

CHAPTER V

WOOL AND WATER

She caught the shawl as she spoke, and looked about for the owner: in another moment the White Queen came running wildly through the wood, with both arms stretched out wide, as if she were flying, and Alice very civilly went to meet her with the shawl.

"I'm very glad I happened to be in the way," Alice said, as she helped her to put on her shawl again.

The White Queen only looked at her in a helpless frightened sort of way, and kept repeating something in a whisper to herself that sounded like "Bread-and-butter, bread-and-butter,"[1] and Alice felt that if there was to be any conversation at all, she must manage it herself. So she began rather timidly: "Am I addressing the White Queen?"

"Well, yes, if you call that a-dressing," the Queen said. "It isn't *my* notion of the thing, at all."

Alice thought it would never do to have an argument at the very beginning of their conversation, so she smiled and said "If your Majesty

1. Edwin Marsden recalled in a letter that when growing up in Massachusetts he was taught to whisper "Bread and butter, bread and butter" whenever he was being circled by a wasp, bee, or other insect. The phrase was intended to keep one from being stung. If this was a custom in Victorian England, it may explain the White Queen's use of the phrase while being pursued by the giant crow.

It is also possible that the Queen, who is running with outstretched arms "as if she were flying," is imagining that she is one of the Bread-and-butter-flies encountered by Alice in Chapter 3. "Bread and butter" seems to be much on her mind. In Chapter 9 she asks Alice: "Divide a loaf by a knife—what's the answer to *that?*" The Red Queen interrupts Alice to answer this problem in division with the reply "Bread-and-butter, of course," meaning that after cutting a slice of bread, you butter it.

In the United States a more common use of "bread and butter" occurs when two people, walking together, are forced to "divide" and go on both sides of a tree, post, or similar obstruction.

will only tell me the right way to begin, I'll do it as well as I can."

"But I don't want it done at all!" groaned the poor Queen. "I've been a-dressing myself for the last two hours."

It would have been all the better, as it seemed to Alice, if she had got some one else to dress her, she was so dreadfully untidy. "Every single thing's crooked," Alice thought to herself, "and she's all over pins!—May I put your shawl straight for you?" she added aloud.

"I don't know what's the matter with it!" the Queen said, in a melancholy voice. "It's out of temper, I think. I've pinned it here, and I've pinned it there, but there's no pleasing it!"

"It *ca'n't* go straight, you know, if you pin it all on one side," Alice said as she gently put it right for her; "and dear me, what a state your hair is in!"

"The brush has got entangled in it!" the Queen said with a sigh. "And I lost the comb yesterday."

Alice carefully released the brush, and did her best to get the hair into order. "Come, you look rather better now!" she said, after altering most of the pins. "But really you should have a lady's maid!"

"I'm sure I'll take *you* with pleasure!" the Queen said. "Two pence a week, and jam every other day."

Alice couldn't help laughing, as she said "I don't want you to hire *me*—and I don't care for jam."

"It's very good jam," said the Queen.

"Well, I don't want any *to-day,* at any rate."

"You couldn't have it if you *did* want it," the

Queen said. "The rule is, jam to-morrow and jam yesterday—but never jam *to-day.*"[2]

"It *must* come sometimes to 'jam to-day,'" Alice objected.

"No, it ca'n't," said the Queen. "It's jam every *other* day: to-day isn't any other day, you know."

"I don't understand you," said Alice. "It's dreadfully confusing!"

"That's the effect of living backwards," the Queen said kindly: "it always makes one a little giddy at first—"

"Living backwards!" Alice repeated in great astonishment. "I never heard of such a thing!"[3]

"—but there's one great advantage in it, that one's memory works both ways."

"I'm sure *mine* only works one way," Alice remarked. "I ca'n't remember things before they happen."

"It's a poor sort of memory that only works backwards," the Queen remarked.

"What sort of things do *you* remember best?" Alice ventured to ask.

"Oh, things that happened the week after next," the Queen replied in a careless tone. "For instance, now," she went on, sticking a large piece of plaster on her finger as she spoke, "there's the King's Messenger.[4] He's in prison now, being punished: and the trial doesn't even begin till next Wednesday: and of course the crime comes last of all."

"Suppose he never commits the crime?" said Alice.

"That would be all the better, wouldn't it?" the Queen said, as she bound the plaster round her finger with a bit of ribbon.

2. In *AA* I completely missed the way Carroll plays on the Latin word *iam* (*i* and *j* are interchangeable in classical Latin), which means "now." The word *iam* is used in the past and future tenses, but in the present tense the word for "now" is *nunc.* I received more letters about this than about any other oversight, mostly from Latin teachers. They tell me that the Queen's remark is often used in class as a mnemonic for recalling the proper usage of the word.

3. In Carroll's *Sylvie and Bruno Concluded* there is a wild episode in which events go backwards in time in response to turning the "reversal peg" on the German professor's Outlandish Watch.

Carroll was as fascinated by time reversal as he was by mirror reversals. In *The Story of Lewis Carroll,* Isa Bowman tells of Carroll's fondness for playing tunes backwards on music boxes to produce what he called "music standing on its head." In Chapter 5 of Carroll's "Isa's Visit to Oxford," he speaks of playing an orguinette backward. This American device operated with a perforated roll of paper like the roll of a player piano, which could be rotated by turning a handle:

> They put one [roll] in wrong end first, and had a tune backwards, and soon found themselves in the day before yesterday. So they dared not go on, for fear of making Isa so young she would not be able to talk. The A.A.M. [Aged Aged Man] does not like visitors who only howl, and get red in the face, from morning to night.

In a letter (November 30, 1879) to child-friend Edith Blakemore, Carroll said he was so busy and tired that he would go back to bed the minute after he got up, "and sometimes I go to bed again a minute *before* I get up."

4. In keeping with the whimsical idea that Tenniel anticipated the face of Bertrand Russell when he drew the Mad Hatter, Peter Heath claims that the picture of the Hatter in prison (*facing page, top*) shows Russell, circa 1918, working on his *Introduction to Mathematical Philosophy* while in a British prison for opposing England's entry into the First World War. Evidently Carroll asked Tenniel to redraw this picture, because a

Alice felt there was no denying *that.* "Of course it would be all the better," she said: "but it wouldn't be all the better his being punished."

"You're wrong *there,* at any rate," said the Queen. "Were *you* ever punished?"

"Only for faults," said Alice.

"And you were all the better for it, I know!" the Queen said triumphantly.

"Yes, but then I *had* done the things I was punished for," said Alice: "that makes all the difference."

"But if you *hadn't* done them," the Queen said, "that would have been better still; better, and better, and better!" Her voice went higher with each "better," till it got quite to a squeak at last.

Alice was just beginning to say "There's a mistake somewhere—," when the Queen began screaming, so loud that she had to leave the sentence unfinished. "Oh, oh, oh!" shouted the Queen, shaking her hand about as if she wanted to shake it off. "My finger's bleeding! Oh, oh, oh, oh!"

Her screams were so exactly like the whistle of a steam-engine, that Alice had to hold both her hands over her ears.

"What *is* the matter?" she said, as soon as there was a chance of making herself heard. "Have you pricked your finger?"

"I haven't pricked it *yet,*" the Queen said, "but I soon shall—oh, oh, oh!"

"When do you expect to do it?" Alice said, feeling very much inclined to laugh.

"When I fasten my shawl again," the poor Queen groaned out: "the brooch will come un-

different version of it has survived. It is reproduced below from Michael Hearn's article "Alice's Other Parent: Sir John Tenniel as Lewis Carroll's Illustrator," in the *American Book Collector* (May-June 1983).

Why is the Mad Hatter being punished? It seems to be for a crime he has yet to commit, but behind the mirror time can go either way. Perhaps he has had a stay of execution for "murdering the time"—that is, singing out of rhythm at a concert given by the Queen of Hearts in the previous book (Chapter 7). You will recall that the Queen had ordered him beheaded.

done directly. Oh, oh!" As she said the words the brooch flew open, and the Queen clutched wildly at it, and tried to clasp it again.

"Take care!" cried Alice. "You're holding it all crooked!" And she caught at the brooch; but it was too late: the pin had slipped, and the Queen had pricked her finger.

"That accounts for the bleeding, you see," she said to Alice with a smile. "Now you understand the way things happen here."

"But why don't you scream *now*?" Alice asked, holding her hands ready to put over her ears again.

"Why, I've done all the screaming already," said the Queen. "What would be the good of having it all over again?"

By this time it was getting light. "The crow must have flown away, I think," said Alice: "I'm so glad it's gone. I thought it was the night coming on."

"I wish *I* could manage to be glad!" the Queen said. "Only I never can remember the rule. You must be very happy, living in this wood, and being glad whenever you like!"

"Only it is so *very* lonely here!" Alice said in a melancholy voice; and, at the thought of her loneliness, two large tears came rolling down her cheeks.

"Oh, don't go on like that!" cried the poor Queen, wringing her hands in despair. "Consider what a great girl you are. Consider what a long way you've come to-day. Consider what o'-clock it is. Consider anything, only don't cry!"

Alice could not help laughing at this, even in the midst of her tears. "Can *you* keep from crying by considering things?" she asked.

"That's the way it's done," the Queen said with great decision: "nobody can do two things at once, you know. Let's consider your age to begin with—how old are you?"

"I'm seven and a half, exactly."

"You needn't say 'exactly,' " the Queen remarked. "I can believe it without that. Now I'll give *you* something to believe. I'm just one hundred and one, five months and a day."

"I ca'n't believe *that*!" said Alice.

"Ca'n't you?" the Queen said in a pitying tone. "Try again: draw a long breath, and shut your eyes."

Alice laughed. "There's no use trying," she said: "one *ca'n't* believe impossible things."

"I daresay you haven't had much practice," said the Queen. "When I was your age, I always did it for half-an-hour a day. Why, sometimes I've believed as many as six impossible things before breakfast. There goes the shawl again!"

The brooch had come undone as she spoke, and a sudden gust of wind blew the Queen's shawl across a little brook. The Queen spread out her arms again and went flying after it, and this time she succeeded in catching it herself. "I've got it!" she cried in a triumphant tone. "Now you shall see me pin it on again, all by myself!"

"Then I hope your finger is better now?" Alice said very politely, as she crossed the little brook after the Queen.

* * * * *
* * * *
* * * * *

"Oh, much better!" cried the Queen, her voice rising into a squeak as she went on. "Much be-etter! Be-etter! Be-e-e-etter! Be-e-ehh!" The last word ended in a long bleat, so like a sheep that Alice quite started.

She looked at the Queen, who seemed to have suddenly wrapped herself up in wool. Alice rubbed her eyes, and looked again. She couldn't make out what had happened at all. Was she in a shop? And was that really—was it really a *sheep* that was sitting on the other side of the counter? Rub as she would, she could make nothing more of it: she was in a little dark shop,[5] leaning with her elbows on the counter, and opposite to her was an old Sheep, sitting in an arm-chair, knitting, and every now and then leaving off to look at her through a great pair of spectacles.

"What is it you want to buy?" the Sheep said at last, looking up for a moment from her knitting.

"I don't *quite* know yet," Alice said very gently. "I should like to look all round me first, if I might."

"You may look in front of you, and on both sides, if you like," said the Sheep; "but you ca'n't look *all* round you—unless you've got eyes at the back of your head."

But these, as it happened, Alice had *not* got: so she contented herself with turning round, looking at the shelves as she came to them.

The shop seemed to be full of all manner of curious things—but the oddest part of it all was that, whenever she looked hard at any shelf, to make out exactly what it had on it, that particular shelf was always quite empty, though the others round it were crowded as full as they could hold.

5. The little shop pictured here can be found at 83 Saint Aldate's Street, Oxford; it is now called The Alice in Wonderland Shop, and one can buy books and items of all sorts related to the *Alice* books there. Tenniel faithfully copied the shop's interior—it was then a grocery store—except for giving it a mirror reversal.

"Opposite to her was an old Sheep, sitting in an arm-chair, knitting"

"Things flow about so here!"[6] she said at last in a plaintive tone, after she had spent a minute or so in vainly pursuing a large bright thing that looked sometimes like a doll and sometimes like a work-box, and was always in the shelf next above the one she was looking at. "And this one is the most provoking of all—but I'll tell you what—" she added, as a sudden thought struck her. "I'll follow it up to the very top shelf of all. It'll puzzle it to go through the ceiling, I expect!"

But even this plan failed: the 'thing' went through the ceiling as quietly as possible, as if it were quite used to it.

"Are you a child or a teetotum?" the Sheep said, as she took up another pair of needles. "You'll make me giddy soon, if you go on turning round like that." She was now working with fourteen pairs at once, and Alice couldn't help looking at her in great astonishment.

"How *can* she knit with so many?" the puzzled child thought to herself. "She gets more and more like a porcupine every minute!"

"Can you row?" the Sheep asked, handing her a pair of knitting-needles as she spoke.

"Yes, a little—but not on land—and not with needles—" Alice was beginning to say, when suddenly the needles turned into oars in her hands, and she found they were in a little boat, gliding along between banks: so there was nothing for it but to do her best.

"Feather!" cried the Sheep, as she took up another pair of needles.

This didn't sound like a remark that needed any answer: so Alice said nothing, but pulled away. There was something very queer about

6. Carroll was a great admirer of Pascal's *Pensées*. Jeffrey Stern, writing on "Lewis Carroll and Blaise Pascal" (in *Jabberwocky,* Spring 1983), quotes a passage that Carroll may well have had in mind when he wrote about how things flow about in the Sheep's little shop:

> [We are] incapable of certain knowledge or absolute ignorance. We are floating in a medium of vast extent, always drifting uncertainly, blown to and fro; whenever we think we have a fixed point to which we can cling and make fast, it shifts and leaves us behind; if we follow it, it eludes our grasp, slips away, and flees eternally before us. Nothing stands still for us. This is our natural state and yet the state most contrary to our inclinations. We burn with desire to find a firm footing, an ultimate, lasting base on which to build a tower rising up to infinity, but our whole foundation cracks.

the water, she thought, as every now and then the oars got fast in it, and would hardly come out again.

"Feather! Feather!" the Sheep cried again, taking more needles. "You'll be catching a crab directly."[7]

"A dear little crab!" thought Alice. "I should like that."

"Didn't you hear me say 'Feather'?" the Sheep cried angrily, taking up quite a bunch of needles.

"Indeed I did," said Alice: "you've said it very often—and very loud. Please, where *are* the crabs?"

"In the water, of course!" said the Sheep, sticking some of the needles into her hair, as her hands were full. "Feather, I say!"

"*Why* do you say 'Feather' so often?" Alice asked at last, rather vexed. "I'm not a bird!"

"You are," said the Sheep: "you're a little goose."

This offended Alice a little, so there was no more conversation for a minute or two, while the boat glided gently on, sometimes among beds of weeds (which made the oars stick fast in the water, worse than ever), and sometimes under trees, but always with the same tall river-banks frowning over their heads.

"Oh, please! There are some scented rushes!" Alice cried in a sudden transport of delight. "There really are—and *such* beauties!"

"You needn't say 'please' to *me* about 'em," the Sheep said, without looking up from her knitting: "I didn't put 'em there, and I'm not going to take 'em away."

"No, but I meant—please, may we wait and

7. "Catching a crab" is rowing slang for a faulty stroke in which the oar is dipped so deeply in the water that the boat's motion, if rapid enough, can send the oar handle against the rower's chest with sufficient force to unseat him. This actually happens to Alice later on. "The phrase probably originated," says the *Oxford English Dictionary,* "in the humorous suggestion that the rower had caught a crab, which was holding his oar down under water." The phrase is sometimes used (improperly) for other rowing errors that can unseat the rower.

pick some?" Alice pleaded. "If you don't mind stopping the boat for a minute."

"How am *I* to stop it?" said the Sheep. "If you leave off rowing, it'll stop of itself."

So the boat was left to drift down the stream as it would, till it glided gently in among the waving rushes. And then the little sleeves were carefully rolled up, and the little arms were plunged in elbow-deep, to get hold of the rushes a good long way down before breaking them off—and for a while Alice forgot all about the Sheep and the knitting, as she bent over the side of the boat, with just the ends of her tangled hair dipping into the water—while with bright eager eyes she caught at one bunch after another of the darling scented rushes.

"I only hope the boat wo'n't tipple over!" she said to herself. "Oh, *what* a lovely one! Only I couldn't quite reach it." And it certainly *did* seem a little provoking ("almost as if it happened on purpose," she thought) that, though she managed to pick plenty of beautiful rushes as the boat glided by, there was always a more lovely one that she couldn't reach.

"The prettiest are always further!" she said at last with a sigh at the obstinacy of the rushes in growing so far off, as, with flushed cheeks and dripping hair and hands, she scrambled back into her place, and began to arrange her new-found treasures.

What mattered it to her just then that the rushes had begun to fade, and to lose all their scent and beauty, from the very moment that she picked them? Even real scented rushes, you know, last only a very little while—and these, being dream-rushes, melted away almost like

"The little arms were plunged in elbow-deep"

snow, as they lay in heaps at her feet—but Alice hardly noticed this, there were so many other curious things to think about.

They hadn't gone much farther before the blade of one of the oars got fast in the water and *wouldn't* come out again (so Alice explained it afterwards), and the consequence was that the handle of it caught her under the chin, and, in spite of a series of little shrieks of "Oh, oh, oh!" from poor Alice, it swept her straight off the seat, and down among the heap of rushes.

However, she wasn't a bit hurt, and was soon up again: the Sheep went on with her knitting all the while, just as if nothing had happened. "That was a nice crab you caught!" she remarked, as Alice got back into her place, very much relieved to find herself still in the boat.

"Was it? I didn't see it," said Alice, peeping cautiously over the side of the boat into the dark water. "I wish it hadn't let go—I should so like a little crab to take home with me!" But the Sheep only laughed scornfully, and went on with her knitting.

"Are there many crabs here?" said Alice.

"Crabs, and all sorts of things," said the Sheep: "plenty of choice, only make up your mind. Now, what *do* you want to buy?"

"To buy!" Alice echoed in a tone that was half astonished and half frightened—for the oars, and the boat, and the river, had vanished all in a moment, and she was back again in the little dark shop.

"I should like to buy an egg, please," she said timidly. "How do you sell them?"

"Fivepence farthing for one—twopence for two," the Sheep replied.

"Then two are cheaper than one?" Alice said in a surprised tone, taking out her purse.

"Only you *must* eat them both, if you buy two," said the Sheep.

"Then I'll have *one,* please," said Alice, as she put the money down on the counter. For she thought to herself, "They mightn't be at all nice, you know."

The Sheep took the money, and put it away in a box: then she said "I never put things into people's hands—that would never do—you must get it for yourself." And so saying, she went off to the other end of the shop, and set the egg upright on a shelf.[8]

"I wonder *why* it wouldn't do?" thought Alice, as she groped her way among the tables and chairs, for the shop was very dark towards the end. "The egg seems to get further away the more I walk towards it. Let me see, is this a chair? Why, it's got branches, I declare! How very odd to find trees growing here! And actually here's a little brook! Well, this is the very queerest shop I ever saw!"

*   *   *   *   *

*   *   *   *

*   *   *   *   *

So she went on, wondering more and more at every step, as everything turned into a tree the moment she came up to it, and she quite expected the egg to do the same.

8. Note that the Sheep places the egg *upright* on the shelf—not an easy thing to do without adopting Columbus's stratagem of tapping the egg on a table to crack its lower end slightly.

CHAPTER VI
HUMPTY DUMPTY

1. Michael Hancher, in his book on Tenniel's art, calls attention to a subtlety in Tenniel's picture of Humpty that shows how extremely narrow the top of the wall is. At the right of the drawing you can see the wall in cross-section. It is topped by an almost pointed coping!

However, the egg only got larger and larger, and more and more human: when she had come within a few yards of it, she saw that it had eyes and a nose and a mouth; and, when she had come close to it, she saw clearly that it was HUMPTY DUMPTY himself. "It ca'n't be anybody else!" she said to herself. "I'm as certain of it, as if his name were written all over his face!"

It might have been written a hundred times, easily, on that enormous face. Humpty Dumpty was sitting, with his legs crossed like a Turk, on the top of a high wall—such a narrow one that Alice quite wondered how he could keep his balance[1]—and, as his eyes were steadily fixed in the opposite direction, and he didn't take the least notice of her, she thought he must be a stuffed figure after all.

"And how exactly like an egg he is!" she said aloud, standing with her hands ready to catch him, for she was every moment expecting him to fall.

"It's *very* provoking," Humpty Dumpty said after a long silence, looking away from Alice as he spoke, "to be called an egg—*very*!"

"I said you *looked* like an egg, Sir," Alice gently explained. "And some eggs are very pretty, you know," she added, hoping to turn her remark into a sort of compliment.

"Some people," said Humpty Dumpty, looking away from her as usual, "have no more sense than a baby!"

Alice didn't know what to say to this: it wasn't at all like conversation, she thought, as he never said anything to *her;* in fact, his last remark was evidently addressed to a tree—so she stood and softly repeated to herself:—

"Humpty Dumpty sat on a wall:
Humpty Dumpty had a great fall.
All the King's horses and all the King's men
Couldn't put Humpty Dumpty in his place again."

"That last line is much too long for the poetry," she added, almost out loud, forgetting that Humpty Dumpty would hear her.

"Don't stand chattering to yourself like that," Humpty Dumpty said, looking at her for the first time, "but tell me your name and your business."

"My *name* is Alice, but—"

"It's a stupid name enough!" Humpty Dumpty interrupted impatiently. "What does it mean?"

"*Must* a name mean something?" Alice asked doubtfully.

"Of course it must," Humpty Dumpty said with a short laugh: "*my* name means the shape

I am—and a good handsome shape it is, too. With a name like yours, you might be any shape, almost."

"Why do you sit out here all alone?" said Alice, not wishing to begin an argument.

"Why, because there's nobody with me!" cried Humpty Dumpty. "Did you think I didn't know the answer to *that?* Ask another."

"Don't you think you'd be safer down on the ground?" Alice went on, not with any idea of making another riddle, but simply in her good-natured anxiety for the queer creature. "That wall is so *very* narrow!"

"What tremendously easy riddles you ask!" Humpty Dumpty growled out. "Of course I don't think so! Why, if ever I *did* fall off—which, there's no chance of—but *if* I did—" Here he pursed up his lips, and looked so solemn and grand that Alice could hardly help laughing. "*If* I *did* fall," he went on, "*the King has promised me*—ah, you may turn pale, if you like! You didn't think I was going to say that, did you? *The King has promised me—with his very own mouth*—to—to—"

"To send all his horses and all his men," Alice interrupted, rather unwisely.

"Now I declare that's too bad!" Humpty Dumpty cried, breaking into a sudden passion. "You've been listening at doors—and behind trees—and down chimneys—or you couldn't have known it!"

"I haven't indeed!" Alice said very gently. "It's in a book."

"Ah, well! They may write such things in a *book,*" Humpty Dumpty said in a calmer tone. "That's what you call a History of England, that is. Now, take a good look at me! I'm one that has spoken to a King, *I* am: mayhap you'll never see such another: and, to show you I'm not proud, you may shake hands with me!" And he grinned almost from ear to ear, as he leant forwards (and as nearly as possible fell off the wall in doing so) and offered Alice his hand. She watched him a little anxiously as she took it. "If he smiled much more the ends of his mouth might meet behind," she thought: "And then I don't know *what* would happen to his head! I'm afraid it would come off!"

"Yes, all his horses and all his men," Humpty Dumpty went on. "They'd pick me up again in a minute, *they* would! However, this conversation is going on a little too fast: let's go back to the last remark but one."

"I'm afraid I ca'n't quite remember it," Alice said, very politely.

"In that case we start afresh," said Humpty Dumpty, "and it's my turn to choose a subject—" ("He talks about it just as if it was a game!" thought Alice.) "So here's a question for you. How old did you say you were?"

Alice made a short calculation, and said "Seven years and six months."

"Wrong!" Humpty Dumpty exclaimed triumphantly. "You never said a word like it!"

"I thought you meant 'How old *are* you?' " Alice explained.

"If I'd meant that, I'd have said it," said Humpty Dumpty.

Alice didn't want to begin another argument, so she said nothing.

"Seven years and six months!" Humpty Dumpty repeated thoughtfully. "An uncom-

"And he grinned almost from ear to ear"

fortable sort of age. Now if you'd asked *my* advice, I'd have said 'Leave off at seven'—but it's too late now."

"I never ask advice about growing," Alice said indignantly.

"Too proud?" the other enquired.

Alice felt even more indignant at this suggestion. "I mean," she said, "that one ca'n't help growing older."

"*One* ca'n't, perhaps," said Humpty Dumpty; "but *two* can. With proper assistance, you might have left off at seven."

"What a beautiful belt you've got on!" Alice suddenly remarked. (They had had quite enough of the subject of age, she thought: and, if they really were to take turns in choosing subjects, it was *her* turn now.) "At least," she corrected herself on second thoughts, "a beautiful cravat, I should have said—no, a belt, I mean—I beg your pardon!" she added in dismay, for Humpty Dumpty looked thoroughly offended, and she began to wish she hadn't chosen that subject. "If only I knew," she thought to herself, "which was neck and which was waist!"

Evidently Humpty Dumpty was very angry, though he said nothing for a minute or two. When he *did* speak again, it was in a deep growl.

"It is a—*most—provoking*—thing," he said at last, "when a person doesn't know a cravat from a belt!"

"I know it's very ignorant of me," Alice said, in so humble a tone that Humpty Dumpty relented.

"It's a cravat, child, and a beautiful one, as

you say. It's a present from the White King and Queen. There now!"

"Is it really?" said Alice, quite pleased to find that she *had* chosen a good subject after all.

"They gave it me," Humpty Dumpty continued thoughtfully as he crossed one knee over the other and clasped his hands round it, "they gave it me—for an un-birthday present."

"I beg your pardon?" Alice said with a puzzled air.

"I'm not offended," said Humpty Dumpty.

"I mean, what *is* an un-birthday present?"

"A present given when it isn't your birthday, of course."

Alice considered a little. "I like birthday presents best," she said at last.

"You don't know what you're talking about!" cried Humpty Dumpty. "How many days are there in a year?"

"Three hundred and sixty-five," said Alice.

"And how many birthdays have you?"

"One."

"And if you take one from three hundred and sixty-five what remains?"

"Three hundred and sixty-four, of course."

Humpty Dumpty looked doubtful. "I'd rather see that done on paper," he said.

Alice couldn't help smiling as she took out her memorandum-book, and worked the sum for him:

$$\begin{array}{r} 365 \\ \underline{1} \\ \underline{364} \end{array}$$

Humpty Dumpty took the book and looked at it carefully. "That seems to be done right—" he began.

"You're holding it upside down!" Alice interrupted.

"To be sure I was!" Humpty Dumpty said gaily as she turned it round for him. "I thought it looked a little queer. As I was saying, that *seems* to be done right—though I haven't time to look it over thoroughly just now—and that shows that there are three hundred and sixty-four days when you might get un-birthday presents—"

"Certainly," said Alice.

"And only *one* for birthday presents, you know. There's glory for you!"

"I don't know what you mean by 'glory,' " Alice said.

Humpty Dumpty smiled contemptuously. "Of course you don't—till I tell you. I meant 'there's a nice knock-down argument for you!' "

"But 'glory' doesn't mean 'a nice knock-down argument,' "[2] Alice objected.

"When *I* use a word," Humpty Dumpty said, in rather a scornful tone, "it means just what I choose it to mean—neither more nor less."[3]

"The question is," said Alice, "whether you *can* make words mean so many different things."

"The question is," said Humpty Dumpty, "which is to be master—that's all."

Alice was too much puzzled to say anything; so after a minute Humpty Dumpty began again. "They've a temper, some of them—particularly verbs: they're the proudest—adjectives you can do anything with, but not verbs—however, *I* can manage the whole lot of them! Impenetrability! That's what *I* say!"

2. In "Humpty Dumpty and Heresy; Or, the Case of the Curate's Egg," in *The Western Humanities Review* (Spring 1968), Wilbur Gaffney argues that Humpty's definition of "glory" may have been influenced by a passage in a book by that egotistical British egghead, philosopher Thomas Hobbes:

> *Sudden glory,* is the passion which maketh those *grimaces* called LAUGHTER; and is caused either by some sudden act of their own, that pleaseth them [such as, obviously, coming out with a nice knock-down argument]; or by the apprehension of some deformed thing in another, by comparison whereof they suddenly applaud themselves. And it is incident most to them, that are conscious of the fewest abilities in themselves; who are forced to keep themselves in their own favour, by observing the imperfections of others.

Janis Lull, in *Lewis Carroll: A Celebration,* observes that the White Knight declares his "knock-down" dispute with the Red Knight in Chapter 8 a "glorious victory."

Remove the *l* from "glory," Carroll observes at the end of the sixth knot in *A Tangled Tale,* and you get "gory." An adjective describing the end of a knock-down argument?

3. In his article "The Stage and the Spirit of Reverence," Carroll put it this way: "no word has a meaning *inseparably* attached to it; a word means what the speaker intends by it, and what the hearer understands by it, and that is all. . . . This thought may serve to lessen the horror of some of the language used by the lower classes, which, it is a comfort to remember, is often a mere collection of unmeaning *sounds,* so far as speaker and hearer are concerned."

"Would you tell me please," said Alice, "what that means?"

"Now you talk like a reasonable child," said Humpty Dumpty, looking very much pleased. "I meant by 'impenetrability' that we've had enough of that subject, and it would be just as well if you'd mention what you mean to do next, as I suppose you don't mean to stop here all the rest of your life."

"That's a great deal to make one word mean," Alice said in a thoughtful tone.

"When I make a word do a lot of work like that," said Humpty Dumpty, "I always pay it extra."

"Oh!" said Alice. She was too much puzzled to make any other remark.

"Ah, you should see 'em come round me of a Saturday night," Humpty Dumpty went on, wagging his head gravely from side to side, "for to get their wages, you know."

(Alice didn't venture to ask what he paid them with; and so you see I ca'n't tell *you.*)

"You seem very clever at explaining words, Sir," said Alice. "Would you kindly tell me the meaning of the poem called 'Jabberwocky'?"

"Let's hear it," said Humpty Dumpty. "I can explain all the poems that ever were invented—and a good many that haven't been invented just yet."

This sounded very hopeful, so Alice repeated the first verse:—

" 'Twas brillig, and the slithy toves
Did gyre and gimble in the wabe:
All mimsy were the borogoves,
And the mome raths outgrabe."

"That's enough to begin with," Humpty Dumpty interrupted: "there are plenty of hard words there. *'Brillig'* means four o'clock in the afternoon—the time when you begin *broiling* things for dinner."

"That'll do very well," said Alice: "and *'slithy'*?"

"Well, *'slithy'* means 'lithe and slimy.' 'Lithe' is the same as 'active.' You see it's like a portmanteau—there are two meanings packed up into one word."

"I see it now," Alice remarked thoughtfully: "and what are *'toves'*?"

"Well *'toves'* are something like badgers—they're something like lizards—and they're something like corkscrews."

"They must be very curious-looking creatures."

"They are that," said Humpty Dumpty; "also they make their nests under sun-dials—also they live on cheese."

"And what's to *'gyre'* and to *'gimble'*?"

"To *'gyre'* is to go round and round like a gyroscope. To *'gimble'* is to make holes like a gimlet."

"And *'the wabe'* is the grass-plot round a sun-dial, I suppose?" said Alice, surprised at her own ingenuity.

"Of course it is. It's called *'wabe,'* you know, because it goes a long way before it, and a long way behind it—"

"And a long way beyond it on each side," Alice added.

"Exactly so. Well then, *'mimsy'* is 'flimsy and miserable' (there's another portmanteau for you). And a *'borogove'* is a thin shabby-looking bird with its feathers sticking out all round—something like a live mop."

"And then *'mome raths'*?" said Alice. "I'm afraid I'm giving you a great deal of trouble."

"Well, a *'rath'* is a sort of green pig: but *'mome'* I'm not certain about. I think it's short for 'from home'—meaning that they'd lost their way, you know."

"And what does *'outgrabe'* mean?"

"Well, *'outgribing'* is something between bellowing and whistling, with a kind of sneeze in the middle: however, you'll hear it done, maybe—down in the wood yonder—and, when you've once heard it, you'll be *quite* content. Who's been repeating all that hard stuff to you?"

"I read it in a book," said Alice. "But I *had* some poetry repeated to me much easier than that, by—Tweedledee, I think it was."

"As to poetry, you know," said Humpty Dumpty, stretching out one of his great hands, "*I* can repeat poetry as well as other folk, if it comes to that—"

"Oh, it needn't come to that!" Alice hastily said, hoping to keep him from beginning.

"The piece I'm going to repeat," he went on without noticing her remark, "was written entirely for your amusement."

Alice felt that in that case she really *ought* to listen to it; so she sat down, and said "Thank you" rather sadly.

"In winter, when the fields are white,
I sing this song for your delight—[4]

only I don't sing it," he added, as an explanation.

4. Neil Phelps sent me a possible inspiration for Humpty's song, a poem called "Summer Days" by a forgotten Victorian poet, Wathen Mark Wilks Call (1817–1870). The poem is anonymous in many Victorian anthologies. The following version is from *Everyman's Book of Victorian Verse* (1982), edited by J. R. Watson:

In summer, when the days were long,
We walked, two friends, in field and wood,
Our heart was light, our step was strong,
And life lay round us, fair as good,
In summer, when the days were long.

We strayed from morn till evening came,
We gathered flowers, and wove us crowns,
We walked mid poppies red as flame,
Or sat upon the yellow downs,
And always wished our life the same.

In summer, when the days were long,
We leapt the hedgerow, crossed the brook;
And still her voice flowed forth in song,
Or else she read some graceful book,
In summer, when the days were long.

And then we sat beneath the trees,
With shadows lessening in the noon;
And in the sunlight and the breeze,
We revelled, many a glorious June,
While larks were singing o'er the leas.

In summer, when the days were long,
We plucked wild strawberries, ripe and red,
Or feasted, with no grace but song,
On golden nectar, snow-white bread,
In summer, when the days were long.

We loved, and yet we knew it not,
For loving seemed like breathing then,
We found a heaven in every spot,
Saw angels, too, in all good men,
And dreamt of gods in grove and grot.

In summer, when the days are long,
Alone I wander, muse alone;
I see her not, but that old song,
Under the fragrant wind is blown,
In summer, when the days are long.

Alone I wander in the wood,
But one fair spirit hears my sighs;
And half I see the crimson hood,
The radiant hair, the calm glad eyes,
That charmed me in life's summer mood.

In summer, when the days are long,
I love her as I loved of old;
My heart is light, my step is strong,
For love brings back those hours of gold,
In summer, when the days are long.

"I see you don't," said Alice.

"If you can *see* whether I'm singing or not, you've sharper eyes than most," Humpty Dumpty remarked severely. Alice was silent.

"In spring, when woods are getting green,
I'll try and tell you what I mean:"

"Thank you very much," said Alice.

"In summer, when the days are long,
Perhaps you'll understand the song:

In autumn, when the leaves are brown,
Take pen and ink, and write it down."

"I will, if I can remember it so long," said Alice.

"You needn't go on making remarks like that," Humpty Dumpty said: "they're not sensible, and they put me out."

"I sent a message to the fish:
I told them 'This is what I wish.'

The little fishes of the sea,
They sent an answer back to me.

The little fishes' answer was
'We cannot do it, Sir, because—' "

"I'm afraid I don't quite understand," said Alice.

"It gets easier further on," Humpty Dumpty replied.

"I sent to them again to say
'It will be better to obey.'

The fishes answered, with a grin,
'Why, what a temper you are in!'

I told them once, I told them twice:
They would not listen to advice.

I took a kettle large and new,
Fit for the deed I had to do.

My heart went hop, my heart went thump:
I filled the kettle at the pump.

Then some one came to me and said
'The little fishes are in bed.'

I said to him, I said it plain,
'Then you must wake them up again.'

I said it very loud and clear:
I went and shouted in his ear."

Humpty Dumpty raised his voice almost to a scream as he repeated this verse, and Alice thought, with a shudder, "I wouldn't have been the messenger for *anything*!"

"But he was very stiff and proud:
He said, 'You needn't shout so loud!'[5]

And he was very proud and stiff:
He said 'I'd go and wake them, if—'

I took a corkscrew from the shelf:
I went to wake them up myself.

And when I found the door was locked,
I pulled and pushed and kicked and knocked.

And when I found the door was shut,
I tried to turn the handle, but—"[6]

There was a long pause.

"Is that all?" Alice timidly asked.

"That's all," said Humpty Dumpty. "Good-bye."

This was rather sudden, Alice thought: but, after such a *very* strong hint that she ought to be going, she felt that it would hardly be civil to

5. In his book on Tenniel, Michael Hancher calls attention to how closely Tenniel's illustration for these lines resembles a gigantic gooseberry in his *Punch* cartoon of July 15, 1871.

THE GIGANTIC GOOSEBERRY.

6. "This has to be the worst poem in the *Alice* books," writes Richard Kelly, in *Lewis Carroll* (Twayne, 1977). "The language is flat and prosaic, the frustrated story line is without interest, the couplets are uninspired and fail to surprise or delight, and there are almost no true elements of nonsense present, other than in the unstated wish of the narrator and the lack of a conclusion to the work."

Beverly Lyon Clark, in her contribution to *Soaring with the Dodo* (Lewis Carroll Society of North America, 1982), edited by Edward Guiliano and James Kincaid, calls attention to how the

"I said it very loud and clear:
I went and shouted in his ear"

stay. So she got up, and held out her hand. "Good-bye, till we meet again!" she said as cheerfully as she could.

"I shouldn't know you again if we *did* meet," Humpty Dumpty replied in a discontented tone, giving her one of his fingers to shake:[7] "you're so exactly like other people."

"The face is what one goes by, generally," Alice remarked in a thoughtful tone.

"That's just what I complain of," said Humpty Dumpty. "Your face is the same as everybody has—the two eyes, so—" (marking their places in the air with his thumb) "nose in the middle, mouth under. It's always the same. Now if you had the two eyes on the same side of the nose, for instance—or the mouth at the top—that would be *some* help."

"It wouldn't look nice," Alice objected. But Humpty Dumpty only shut his eyes, and said "Wait till you've tried."

Alice waited a minute to see if he would speak again, but, as he never opened his eyes or took any further notice of her, she said "Good-bye!" once more, and, getting no answer to this, she quietly walked away: but she couldn't help saying to herself, as she went, "of all the unsatisfactory—" (she repeated this aloud, as it was a great comfort to have such a long word to say) "of all the unsatisfactory people I *ever* met—" She never finished the sentence, for at this moment a heavy crash shook the forest from end to end.[8]

abrupt endings of the poem's lines are echoed in Humpty's abrupt "Good-bye" to Alice, and Alice's unfinished comment in the chapter's last paragraph: "Of all the unsatisfactory people I *ever* met—"

7. John Q. Rutherford called my attention to the unpleasant habit, among some members of the Victorian aristocracy, of proffering two fingers when shaking hands with social inferiors. In his pride, Humpty carries this practice to its ultimate.

8. A fourteen-stanza poem titled "The Headstrong Man," written by Carroll when he was thirteen, anticipates Humpty's mighty fall. The poem appeared in Carroll's first book, *Useful and Instructive Poetry,* written for his younger siblings, and published posthumously in 1954. The poem begins:

There was a man who stood on high,
Upon a lofty wall;
And every one who passed him by,
Called out "I fear you'll fall."

A strong wind blows the man off the wall. Next day he climbs a tree, the branch breaks, and he falls again. In the Pennyroyal edition of *Through the Looking-Glass,* Barry Moser drew Humpty with the face of Richard Nixon.

CHAPTER VII

THE LION AND THE UNICORN

The next moment soldiers came running through the wood, at first in twos and threes, then ten or twenty together, and at last in such crowds that they seemed to fill the whole forest. Alice got behind a tree, for fear of being run over, and watched them go by.

She thought that in all her life she had never seen soldiers so uncertain on their feet: they were always tripping over something or other, and whenever one went down, several more always fell over him, so that the ground was soon covered with little heaps of men.

Then came the horses. Having four feet, these managed rather better than the foot-soldiers; but even *they* stumbled now and then; and it seemed to be a regular rule that, whenever a horse stumbled, the rider fell off instantly. The confusion got worse every moment, and Alice was very glad to get out of the wood into an open place, where she found the White King seated on the ground, busily writing in his memorandum-book.

"She had never seen soldiers so uncertain on their feet"

"I've sent them all!" the King cried in a tone of delight, on seeing Alice. "Did you happen to meet any soldiers, my dear, as you came through the wood?"

"Yes, I did," said Alice: "several thousand, I should think."

"Four thousand two hundred and seven, that's the exact number," the King said, referring to his book. "I couldn't send all the horses, you know, because two of them are wanted in the game. And I haven't sent the two Messengers, either. They're both gone to the town. Just look along the road, and tell me if you can see either of them."

"I see nobody on the road," said Alice.

"I only wish *I* had such eyes," the King remarked in a fretful tone. "To be able to see Nobody![1] And at that distance too! Why, it's as much as *I* can do to see real people, by this light!"

All this was lost on Alice, who was still looking intently along the road, shading her eyes with one hand. "I see somebody now!" she exclaimed at last. "But he's coming very slowly—and what curious attitudes he goes into!" (For the Messenger kept skipping up and down, and wriggling like an eel, as he came along, with his great hands spread out like fans on each side.)

"Not at all," said the King. "He's an Anglo-Saxon Messenger—and those are Anglo-Saxon attitudes. He only does them when he's happy. His name is Haigha." (He pronounced it so as to rhyme with 'mayor.')[2]

"I love my love with an H," Alice couldn't help beginning, "because he is Happy. I hate him with an H, because he is Hideous. I fed him with—with—with Ham-sandwiches and Hay. His name is Haigha, and he lives—"

"He lives on the Hill," the King remarked simply, without the least idea that he was joining in the game, while Alice was still hesitating for the name of a town beginning with H. "The other Messenger's called Hatta. I must have *two,* you know—to come and go. One to come, and one to go."

"I beg your pardon?" said Alice.

1. Mathematicians, logicians, and some metaphysicians like to treat zero, the null class, and Nothing as if they were Something, and Carroll was no exception. In the first *Alice* book the Gryphon tells Alice that "they never executes nobody." Here we encounter the unexecuted Nobody walking along the road, and later we learn that Nobody walks slower or faster than the Messenger. "If you see Nobody come into the room," Carroll wrote to one of his child-friends, "please give him a kiss for me." In Carroll's book *Euclid and His Modern Rivals,* we meet Herr Niemand, a German professor whose name means "nobody." When did Nobody first enter the *Alice* books? At the Mad Tea-Party. "Nobody asked *your* opinion," Alice said to the Mad Hatter. He turns up again in the book's last chapter when the White Rabbit produces a letter that he says the Knave of Hearts has written to "somebody." "Unless it was written to nobody," comments the King, "which isn't usual, you know."

Critics have recalled how Ulysses deceived the one-eyed Polyphemus by calling himself Noman before putting out the giant's eye. When Polyphemus cried out, "Noman is killing me!," no one took this to mean that someone was actually attacking him.

2. Hatta is the Mad Hatter, newly released from prison, and Haigha, whose name, when pronounced to rhyme with "mayor," sounds like "Hare," is of course the March Hare. In his book *Carroll's Alice* (Columbia University, 1936), Harry Morgan Ayres suggests that Carroll may have had in mind Daniel Henry Haigh, a noted nineteenth-century expert on Saxon runes and the author of two scholarly books about the Saxons.

It is curious that Alice fails to recognize either of her two old friends.

Just why Carroll disguised the Hatter and the Hare as Anglo-Saxon Messengers (and Tenniel underscored this whimsy by dressing them as Anglo-Saxons and giving them "Anglo-Saxon attitudes") continues to be puzzling. "In the context of Alice's dream," writes Robert Sutherland in *Language and Lewis Carroll* (Mouton, 1970), "they come like ghosts to trouble scholars' joy."

The presence in Alice's dream of the chess-men, the characters from nursery rhymes, the talking animals, the various more bizarre creatures is easily explained. They either have their counterparts in Alice's waking experience or are the fantastic creations of a little girl's dreaming mind. But the Anglo-Saxon Messengers! They are not mentioned in the first chapter, where various aspects of the dream are foreshadowed in Alice's drawing-room. Are we to assume on Alice's part a reading of Anglo-Saxon history in her schoolbooks? Or is the presence of the Anglo-Saxon Messengers a gratuitous addition of Carroll's, constituting a minor flaw in the otherwise consistently conceived structure of the book? Is their presence an intrusion of a private joke at the expense of contemporary Anglo-Saxon scholarship, and a reflection of his own interest in British antiquity? The question of Dodgson's intentions in creating the Anglo-Saxon Messengers is a vexed problem which will remain obscure until further information comes to light.

Roger Green (in *Jabberwocky,* Autumn 1971) offers the following guess. Carroll recorded in his diary (December 5, 1863) his attendance at a Christ Church theatrical that included a burlesque skit called "Alfred the Great." Mrs. Liddell was there with her children. Green surmises that the skit included Anglo-Saxon settings and costumes, which may have given Carroll the idea of turning the Hatter and the Hare into Anglo-Saxon Messengers.

3. "sal-volatile": smelling salts.

"It isn't respectable to beg," said the King.

"I only meant that I didn't understand," said Alice. "Why one to come and one to go?"

"Don't I tell you?" the King repeated impatiently. "I must have *two*—to fetch and carry. One to fetch, and one to carry."

At this moment the Messenger arrived: he was far too much out of breath to say a word, and could only wave his hands about, and make the most fearful faces at the poor King.

"This young lady loves you with an H," the King said, introducing Alice in the hope of turning off the Messenger's attention from himself—but it was of no use—the Anglo-Saxon attitudes only got more extraordinary every moment, while the great eyes rolled wildly from side to side.

"You alarm me!" said the King. "I feel faint—Give me a ham-sandwich!"

On which the Messenger, to Alice's great amusement, opened a bag that hung round his neck, and handed a sandwich to the King, who devoured it greedily.

"Another sandwich!" said the King.

"There's nothing but hay left now," the Messenger said, peeping into the bag.

"Hay, then," the King murmured in a faint whisper.

Alice was glad to see that it revived him a good deal. "There's nothing like eating hay when you're faint," he remarked to her, as he munched away.

"I should think throwing cold water over you would be better," Alice suggested: "—or some sal-volatile."[3]

"I didn't say there was nothing *better,*" the

“ ‘You alarm me!’ said the King. ‘I feel faint!’ ”

King replied. “I said there was nothing *like* it.” Which Alice did not venture to deny.

“Who did you pass on the road?” the King went on, holding out his hand to the Messenger for some hay.

“Nobody,” said the Messenger.

“Quite right,” said the King: “this young lady saw him too. So of course Nobody walks slower than you.”

“I do my best,” the Messenger said in a sullen tone. "I'm sure nobody walks much faster than I do!"

"He ca'n't do that," said the King, "or else he'd have been here first. However, now you've got your breath, you may tell us what's happened in the town."

"I'll whisper it," said the Messenger, putting his hands to his mouth in the shape of a trumpet and stooping so as to get close to the King's ear. Alice was sorry for this, as she wanted to hear the news too. However, instead of whispering, he simply shouted, at the top of his voice, "They're at it again!"

"Do you call *that* a whisper?" cried the poor King, jumping up and shaking himself. "If you do such a thing again, I'll have you buttered! It went through and through my head like an earthquake!"

"It would have to be a very tiny earthquake!" thought Alice. "Who are at it again?" she ventured to ask.

"Why the Lion and the Unicorn, of course," said the King.

"Fighting for the crown?"

"Yes, to be sure," said the King: "and the best of the joke is, that it's *my* crown all the while! Let's run and see them." And they trotted off, Alice repeating to herself, as she ran, the words of the old song:—

"The Lion and the Unicorn were fighting for the crown:
The Lion beat the Unicorn all round the town.
Some gave them white bread, some gave them brown:
Some gave them plum-cake and drummed them out of town."

"Does—the one—that wins—get the crown?" she asked, as well as she could, for the run was putting her quite out of breath.[4]

"Dear me, no!" said the King. "What an idea!"

"Would you—be good enough—" Alice panted out, after running a little further, "to stop a minute—just to get—one's breath again?"

"I'm *good* enough," the King said, "only I'm not *strong* enough. You see, a minute goes by so fearfully quick. You might as well try to stop a Bandersnatch!"

Alice had no more breath for talking; so they trotted on in silence, till they came into sight of a great crowd, in the middle of which the Lion and Unicorn were fighting. They were in such a cloud of dust, that at first Alice could not make out which was which; but she soon managed to distinguish the Unicorn by his horn.

They placed themselves close to where Hatta, the other Messenger, was standing watching the fight, with a cup of tea in one hand and a piece of bread-and-butter in the other.

"He's only just out of prison, and he hadn't finished his tea when he was sent in," Haigha whispered to Alice: "and they only give them oyster-shells in there—so you see he's very hungry and thirsty. How are you, dear child?" he went on, putting his arm affectionately round Hatta's neck.

Hatta looked round and nodded, and went on with his bread-and-butter.

"Were you happy in prison, dear child?" said Haigha.

Hatta looked round once more, and this time

4. For reasons not clear, the White King, by running to see the Lion and Unicorn fight, violates his slow square-by-square way of moving in a chess game.

" 'How are you, dear child?' he went on"

a tear or two trickled down his cheek; but not a word would he say.

"Speak, ca'n't you!" Haigha cried impatiently. But Hatta only munched away, and drank some more tea.

"Speak, wo'n't you!" cried the King. "How are they getting on with the fight?"

Hatta made a desperate effort, and swallowed a large piece of bread-and-butter. "They're getting on very well," he said in a choking voice: "each of them has been down about eighty-seven times."

"Then I suppose they'll soon bring the white bread and the brown?" Alice ventured to remark.

"It's waiting for 'em now," said Hatta; "this is a bit of it as I'm eating."

There was a pause in the fight just then, and the Lion and the Unicorn sat down, panting, while the King called out "Ten minutes allowed for refreshments!" Haigha and Hatta set to work at once, carrying round trays of white and brown bread. Alice took a piece to taste, but it was *very* dry.

"I don't think they'll fight any more to-day," the King said to Hatta: "go and order the drums to begin." And Hatta went bounding away like a grasshopper.

For a minute or two Alice stood silent, watching him. Suddenly she brightened up. "Look, look!" she cried, pointing eagerly. "There's the White Queen running across the country! She came flying out of the wood over yonder—How fast those Queens *can* run!"

"There's some enemy after her, no doubt,"

the King said, without even looking round. "That wood's full of them."

"But aren't you going to run and help her?" Alice asked, very much surprised at his taking it so quietly.

"No use, no use!" said the King. "She runs so fearfully quick. You might as well try to catch a Bandersnatch! But I'll make a memorandum about her, if you like—She's a dear good creature," he repeated softly to himself, as he opened his memorandum-book. "Do you spell 'creature' with a double 'e'?"

At this moment the Unicorn sauntered by them, with his hands in his pockets. "I had the best of it this time?" he said to the King, just glancing at him as he passed.

"A little—a little," the King replied, rather nervously. "You shouldn't have run him through with your horn, you know."

"It didn't hurt him," the Unicorn said carelessly, and he was going on, when his eye happened to fall upon Alice: he turned round instantly, and stood for some time looking at her with an air of the deepest disgust.

"What—is—this?" he said at last.

"This is a child!" Haigha replied eagerly, coming in front of Alice to introduce her, and spreading out both his hands towards her in an Anglo-Saxon attitude. "We only found it to-day. It's as large as life, and twice as natural!"

"I always thought they were fabulous monsters!" said the Unicorn. "Is it alive?"

"It can talk," said Haigha solemnly.

The Unicorn looked dreamily at Alice, and said "Talk, child."

Alice could not help her lips curling up into a smile as she began: "Do you know, I always thought Unicorns were fabulous monsters, too? I never saw one alive before!"

"Well, now that we *have* seen each other," said the Unicorn, "if you'll believe in me, I'll believe in you. Is that a bargain?"

"Yes, if you like," said Alice.

"Come, fetch out the plum-cake, old man!" the Unicorn went on, turning from her to the King. "None of your brown bread for me!"

"Certainly—certainly!" the King muttered, and beckoned to Haigha. "Open the bag!" he whispered. "Quick! Not that one—that's full of hay!"

Haigha took a large cake out of the bag, and gave it to Alice to hold, while he got out a dish and carving-knife. How they all came out of it Alice couldn't guess. It was just like a conjuring-trick, she thought.

The Lion had joined them while this was going on: he looked very tired and sleepy, and his eyes were half shut. "What's this!" he said, blinking lazily at Alice, and speaking in a deep hollow tone that sounded like the tolling of a great bell.[5]

"Ah, what *is* it, now?" the Unicorn cried eagerly. "You'll never guess! *I* couldn't."

The Lion looked at Alice wearily. "Are you animal—or vegetable—or mineral?"[6] he said, yawning at every other word.

"It's a fabulous monster!" the Unicorn cried out, before Alice could reply.

"Then hand round the plum-cake, Monster," the Lion said, lying down and putting his chin

5. After the union of England and Scotland, the British lion and the Scottish unicorn faced each other on the British coat of arms, a common sight on buildings in Oxford. Did Tenniel intend the beasts to caricature Gladstone and Disraeli, who often sparred with each other? Michael Hancher, in his book on Tenniel's art, maintains that neither Carroll nor Tenniel had such resemblances in mind. He reproduces one of Tenniel's *Punch* cartoons, showing a Scottish unicorn and a British lion, both drawn almost exactly like those in *Alice,* confronting one another.

6. See Chapter 9, note 4, of *Alice's Adventures in Wonderland.*

on his paws. "And sit down, both of you," (to the King and the Unicorn): "fair play with the cake, you know!"

The King was evidently very uncomfortable at having to sit down between the two great creatures; but there was no other place for him.

"What a fight we might have for the crown *now*!" the Unicorn said, looking slyly up at the crown, which the poor King was nearly shaking off his head, he trembled so much.

"I should win easy," said the Lion.

"I'm not so sure of that," said the Unicorn.

"Why, I beat you all round the town, you chicken!" the Lion replied angrily, half getting up as he spoke.

Here the King interrupted, to prevent the quarrel going on: he was very nervous, and his voice quite quivered. "All round the town?" he said. "That's a good long way. Did you go by the old bridge, or the market-place? You get the best view by the old bridge."

"I'm sure I don't know," the Lion growled out as he lay down again. "There was too much dust to see anything. What a time the Monster is, cutting up that cake!"

Alice had seated herself on the bank of a little brook, with the great dish on her knees, and was sawing away diligently with the knife. "It's very provoking!" she said, in reply to the Lion (she was getting quite used to being called 'the Monster'). "I've cut several slices already, but they always join on again!"

"You don't know how to manage Looking-glass cakes," the Unicorn remarked. "Hand it round first, and cut it afterwards."

This sounded nonsense, but Alice very obedi-

" 'What's this!' he said, blinking lazily at Alice"

ently got up, and carried the dish round, and the cake divided itself into three pieces as she did so. "*Now* cut it up," said the Lion, as she returned to her place with the empty dish.

"I say, this isn't fair!" cried the Unicorn, as Alice sat with the knife in her hand, very much puzzled how to begin. "The Monster has given the Lion twice as much as me!"

"She's kept none for herself, anyhow," said the Lion. "Do you like plum-cake, Monster?"

But before Alice could answer him, the drums began.

Where the noise came from, she couldn't make out: the air seemed full of it, and it rang through and through her head till she felt quite deafened. She started to her feet and sprang across the little brook in her terror, and had

* * * * *
* * * *
* * * * *

just time to see the Lion and the Unicorn rise to their feet, with angry looks at being interrupted in their feast, before she dropped to her knees, and put her hands over her ears, vainly trying to shut out the dreadful uproar.

"If *that* doesn't 'drum them out of town,'" she thought to herself, "nothing ever will!"

CHAPTER VIII

"IT'S MY OWN INVENTION"

After a while the noise seemed gradually to die away, till all was dead silence, and Alice lifted up her head in some alarm. There was no one to be seen, and her first thought was that she must have been dreaming about the Lion and the Unicorn and those queer Anglo-Saxon Messengers. However, there was the great dish still lying at her feet, on which she had tried to cut the plum-cake, "So I wasn't dreaming, after all," she said to herself, "unless—unless we're all part of the same dream. Only I do hope it's *my* dream, and not the Red King's! I don't like belonging to another person's dream," she went on in a rather complaining tone: "I've a great mind to go and wake him, and see what happens!"

At this moment her thoughts were interrupted by a loud shouting of "Ahoy! Ahoy! Check!" and a Knight, dressed in crimson armour, came galloping down upon her, brandishing a great club. Just as he reached her, the horse stopped suddenly: "You're my prisoner!" the Knight cried, as he tumbled off his horse.

Startled as she was, Alice was more frightened for him than for herself at the moment, and watched him with some anxiety as he mounted again. As soon as he was comfortably in the saddle, he began once more "You're my—" but here another voice broke in "Ahoy! Ahoy! Check!" and Alice looked round in some surprise for the new enemy.

This time it was a White Knight.[1] He drew up at Alice's side, and tumbled off his horse just as the Red Knight had done: then he got on again, and the two Knights sat and looked at each other for some time without speaking. Alice looked from one to the other in some bewilderment.

"She's *my* prisoner, you know!" the Red Knight said at last.

"Yes, but then *I* came and rescued her!" the White Knight replied.

"Well, we must fight for her, then," said the Red Knight, as he took up his helmet (which hung from the saddle, and was something the shape of a horse's head) and put it on.

"You will observe the Rules of Battle, of course?" the White Knight remarked, putting on his helmet too.

"I always do," said the Red Knight, and they began banging away at each other with such fury that Alice got behind a tree to be out of the way of the blows.

"I wonder, now, what the Rules of Battle are," she said to herself, as she watched the fight, timidly peeping out from her hiding-place. "One Rule seems to be, that if one Knight hits the other, he knocks him off his horse; and, if he misses, he tumbles off himself—and an-

1. Although most Carrollians agree that Carroll intended the White Knight to represent himself (see my discussion of this in *AA*), other candidates have been proposed. Don Quixote is an obvious choice, and the parallels are ably defended in John Hinz's "Alice Meets the Don," in the *South Atlantic Quarterly* (Vol. 52, 1953, pages 253–266), reprinted in *Aspects of Alice* (Vanguard, 1971), edited by Robert Phillips.

Charles Edwards wrote to tell me about a passage in Cervantes's novel (Part 2, Chapter 4) in which the Don asks a poet to write an acrostic poem, the initial letters of its lines to spell "Dulcinea del Toboso." The poet finds seventeen letters awkward for a poem with regular stanzas because seventeen is a prime number with no divisors. The Don advises him to work hard on it because "no woman will believe that those verses were made for her where her name is not plainly discerned." "Alice Pleasance Liddell" has twenty-one letters. This made it possible for Carroll, in his acrostic terminal poem, to have seven stanzas of three lines each.

Another candidate for the White Knight is a chemist and inventor who was a friend of Carroll's and is often mentioned in Carroll's diary. See "The Chemist in Allegory: Augustus Vernon Harcourt and the White Knight," by M. Christine King, *Journal of Chemical Education* (March 1983). Other candidates are considered in Chapter 7 of Michael Hancher's *The Tenniel Illustrations to the "Alice" Books*. Because Tenniel in later life had a handlebar mustache (and his nose resembled that of the White Knight), it has been suggested that Tenniel drew the Knight as a caricature of himself. This seems farfetched because at the time that he drew the White Knight he did not wear a mustache.

Tenniel's frontispiece picture of the White Knight in many ways resembles Albrecht Dürer's etching of the Knight in the presence of Death and the Devil. Was this intentional? When I wrote to Michael Hancher for his opinion, he called my attention to Tenniel's cartoon in *Punch* (March 5, 1887), titled "The Knight and His Companion (Suggested by Dürer's famous picture)." The Knight represents Bismarck and his companion is Socialism. "Obviously Tenniel had a copy of the Dürer in front of him when he drew this cartoon," Hancher wrote. "My hunch is that he

other Rule seems to be that they hold their clubs with their arms, as if they were Punch and Judy—What a noise they make when they tumble! Just like a whole set of fire-irons falling into the fender! And how quiet the horses are! They let them get on and off them just as if they were tables!"

Another Rule of Battle, that Alice had not noticed, seemed to be that they always fell on their heads; and the battle ended with their both falling off in this way, side by side. When they got up again, they shook hands, and then the Red Knight mounted and galloped off.

"It was a glorious victory, wasn't it?" said the White Knight, as he came up panting.

"I don't know," Alice said doubtfully. "I don't want to be anybody's prisoner. I want to be a Queen."

"So you will, when you've crossed the next brook," said the White Knight. "I'll see you safe to the end of the wood—and then I must go back, you know. That's the end of my move."

"Thank you very much," said Alice. "May I help you off with your helmet?" It was evidently more than he could manage by himself: however, she managed to shake him out of it at last.

"Now one can breathe more easily," said the Knight, putting back his shaggy hair with both hands, and turning his gentle face and large mild eyes to Alice. She thought she had never seen such a strange-looking soldier in all her life.

He was dressed in tin armour, which seemed to fit him very badly, and he had a queer-shaped little deal box fastened across his shoulders, up-

did not when he drew the *Looking-Glass* frontispiece, but that he called it up out of his remarkable visual memory."

"The White Knight," Carroll wrote to Tenniel, "must not have whiskers; he must not be made to look old." Nowhere in the text does Carroll mention a mustache, nor does he indicate the knight's age. Tenniel's handlebar mustache and Newell's bushy mustache were the artists' additions. Perhaps Tenniel, sensing that the White Knight was Carroll, gave him a balding, elderly look to contrast his age with that of Alice.

"They began banging away at each other"

side-down, and with the lid hanging open. Alice looked at it with great curiosity.

"I see you're admiring my little box," the Knight said in a friendly tone. "It's my own invention—to keep clothes and sandwiches in. You see I carry it upside-down, so that the rain ca'n't get in."

"But the things can get *out,*" Alice gently remarked. "Do you know the lid's open?"

"I didn't know it," the Knight said, a shade of vexation passing over his face. "Then all the things must have fallen out! And the box is no use without them." He unfastened it as he spoke, and was just going to throw it into the bushes, when a sudden thought seemed to strike him, and he hung it carefully on a tree. "Can you guess why I did that?" he said to Alice.

Alice shook her head.

"In hopes some bees may make a nest in it—then I should get the honey."

"But you've got a bee-hive—or something like one—fastened to the saddle," said Alice.

"Yes, it's a very good bee-hive," the Knight said in a discontented tone, "one of the best kind. But not a single bee has come near it yet. And the other thing is a mouse-trap. I suppose the mice keep the bees out—or the bees keep the mice out, I don't know which."

"I was wondering what the mouse-trap was for," said Alice. "It isn't very likely there would be any mice on the horse's back."

"Not very likely, perhaps," said the Knight; "but, if they *do* come, I don't choose to have them running all about."

"You see," he went on after a pause, "it's as

well to be provided for *everything.* That's the reason the horse has all those anklets round his feet."

"But what are they for?" Alice asked in a tone of great curiosity.

"To guard against the bites of sharks," the Knight replied. "It's an invention of my own. And now help me on. I'll go with you to the end of the wood—What's that dish for?"

"It's meant for plum-cake," said Alice.

"We'd better take it with us," the Knight said. "It'll come in handy if we find any plum-cake. Help me to get it into this bag."

This took a long time to manage, though Alice held the bag open very carefully, because the Knight was so *very* awkward in putting in the dish: the first two or three times that he tried he fell in himself instead. "It's rather a tight fit, you see," he said, as they got it in at last; "there are so many candlesticks in the bag." And he hung it to the saddle, which was already loaded with bunches of carrots, and fire-irons, and many other things.[2]

"I hope you've got your hair well fastened on?" he continued, as they set off.

"Only in the usual way," Alice said, smiling.

"That's hardly enough," he said, anxiously. "You see the wind is so *very* strong here. It's as strong as soup."

"Have you invented a plan for keeping the hair from being blown off?" Alice enquired.

"Not yet," said the Knight. "But I've got a plan for keeping it from *falling* off."

"I should like to hear it, very much."

"First you take an upright stick," said the

2. Janis Lull, in *Lewis Carroll: A Celebration,* argues that Carroll and Tenniel together loaded the steed with objects closely related to things mentioned or pictured elsewhere in the *Alice* books: the wooden sword and the umbrella are similar to the sword and umbrella owned by the Tweedle brothers; the watchman's rattle looks like the rattle over which the brothers fought; the beehive recalls the elephant bees in Chapter 3; the mouse-trap stands for the mouse in the first *Alice* book; the candlesticks allude to the candles that go off like fireworks at the end of Chapter 9; the spring bell suggests the two bells on the door in Chapter 9; the fire irons and bellows are like those in Alice's living room below the mirror; the shark anklets could be identified with the sharks in Alice's recitation in Chapter 10 of the previous book; the two brushes are related to the hair-brush with which Alice combs the White Queen's hair in Chapter 5; the plum-cake dish is, of course, the one that the March Hare produces like magic from his small bag when the Lion and Unicorn are fighting for the crown; the carrots may be there as food for the March Hare; and the wine bottle, perhaps empty, suggests the nonexistent wine that the March Hare asked Alice to drink at the Mad Tea-Party, as well as the real wine at the feast in Chapter 9.

"The Knight is a sort of property master," Lull summarizes, "whose furniture both recapitulates what has gone before and anticipates what will come."

Knight. "Then you make your hair creep up it, like a fruit-tree. Now the reason hair falls off is because it hangs *down*—things never fall *upwards,* you know. It's a plan of my own invention. You may try it if you like."

It didn't sound a comfortable plan, Alice thought, and for a few minutes she walked on in silence, puzzling over the idea, and every now and then stopping to help the poor Knight, who certainly was *not* a good rider.

Whenever the horse stopped (which it did very often), he fell off in front; and, whenever it went on again (which it generally did rather suddenly), he fell off behind. Otherwise he kept on pretty well, except that he had a habit of now and then falling off sideways; and, as he generally did this on the side on which Alice was walking, she soon found that it was the best plan not to walk *quite* close to the house.

"I'm afraid you've not had much practice in riding," she ventured to say, as she was helping him up from his fifth tumble.

The Knight looked very much surprised, and a little offended at the remark. "What makes you say that?" he asked, as he scrambled back into the saddle, keeping hold of Alice's hair with one hand, to save himself from falling over on the other side.

"Because people don't fall off quite so often, when they've had much practice."

"I've had plenty of practice," the Knight said very gravely: "plenty of practice!"

Alice could think of nothing better to say than "Indeed?" but she said it as heartily as she could. They went on a little way in silence after this, the Knight with his eyes shut, muttering to himself, and Alice watching anxiously for the next tumble.

"The great art of riding," the Knight suddenly began in a loud voice, waving his right arm as he spoke, "is to keep—" Here the sentence ended as suddenly as it had begun, as the Knight fell heavily on the top of his head exactly in the path where Alice was walking. She was quite frightened this time, and said in an anxious tone, as she picked him up, "I hope no bones are broken?"

"None to speak of," the Knight said, as if he didn't mind breaking two or three of them. "The great art of riding, as I was saying, is—to keep your balance properly. Like this, you know—"

He let go the bridle, and stretched out both his arms to show Alice what he meant, and this time he fell flat on his back, right under the horse's feet.

"Plenty of practice!" he went on repeating, all the time that Alice was getting him on his feet again. "Plenty of practice!"

"It's too ridiculous!" cried Alice, losing all her patience this time. "You ought to have a wooden horse on wheels, that you ought!"

"Does that kind go smoothly?" the Knight asked in a tone of great interest, clasping his arms round the horse's neck as he spoke, just in time to save himself from tumbling off again.

"Much more smoothly than a live horse," Alice said, with a little scream of laughter, in spite of all she could do to prevent it.

"I'll get one," the Knight said thoughtfully to himself. "One or two—several."

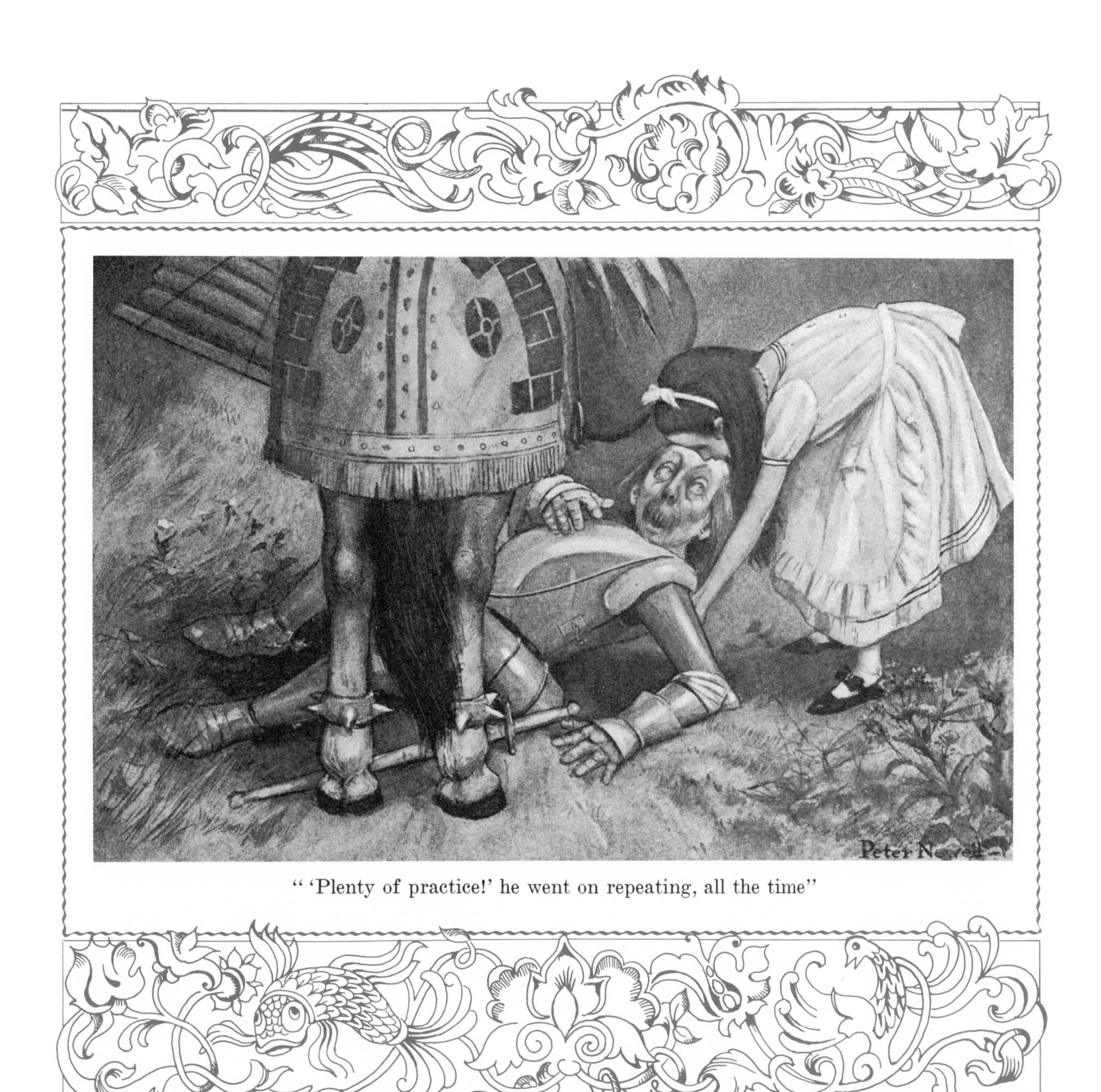

" 'Plenty of practice!' he went on repeating, all the time"

There was a short silence after this, and then the Knight went on again. "I'm a great hand at inventing things. Now, I daresay you noticed, the last time you picked me up, that I was looking rather thoughtful?"

"You *were* a little grave," said Alice.

"Well, just then I was inventing a new way of getting over a gate—would you like to hear it?"

"Very much indeed," Alice said politely.

"I'll tell you how I came to think of it," said the Knight. "You see, I said to myself 'The only difficulty is with the feet: the *head* is high enough already.' Now, first I put my head on the top of the gate—then the head's high enough—then I stand on my head—then the feet are high enough, you see—then I'm over, you see."

"Yes, I suppose you'd be over when that was done," Alice said thoughtfully: "but don't you think it would be rather hard?"

"I haven't tried it yet," the Knight said, gravely; "so I ca'n't tell for certain—but I'm afraid it *would* be a little hard."

He looked so vexed at the idea, that Alice changed the subject hastily. "What a curious helmet you've got!" she said cheerfully. "Is that your invention too?"

The Knight looked down proudly at his helmet, which hung from the saddle. "Yes," he said; "but I've invented a better one than that—like a sugar-loaf. When I used to wear it, if I fell off the horse, it always touched the ground directly. So I had a *very* little way to fall, you see—But there *was* the danger of falling *into* it, to be sure. That happened to me once—and the worst of it was, before I could get out again, the other White Knight came and put it on. He thought it was his own helmet."

The Knight looked so solemn about it that Alice did not dare to laugh. "I'm afraid you must have hurt him," she said in a trembling voice, "being on the top of his head."

"I had to kick him, of course," the Knight said, very seriously. "And then he took the helmet off again—but it took hours and hours to get me out. I was as fast as—as lightning, you know."

"But that's a different kind of fastness," Alice objected.

The Knight shook his head. "It was all kinds of fastness with me, I can assure you!" he said. He raised his hands in some excitement as he said this, and instantly rolled out of the saddle, and fell headlong into a deep ditch.

Alice ran to the side of the ditch to look for him. She was rather startled by the fall, as for some time he had kept on very well, and she was afraid that he really *was* hurt this time. However, though she could see nothing but the soles of his feet, she was much relieved to hear that he was talking on in his usual tone. "All kinds of fastness," he repeated: "but it was careless of him to put another man's helmet on—with the man in it, too."

"How *can* you go on talking so quietly, head downwards?" Alice asked, as she dragged him out by the feet, and laid him in a heap on the bank.

The Knight looked surprised at the question. "What does it matter where my body happens to be?" he said. "My mind goes on working all the same. In fact, the more head-downwards I am, the more I keep inventing new things."

"Now the cleverest thing of the sort that I ever did," he went on after a pause, "was inventing a new pudding during the meat-course."

"In time to have it cooked for the next course?" said Alice. "Well, that *was* quick work, certainly!"

"Well, not the *next* course," the Knight said

" 'How *can* you go on talking so quietly, head downwards?' "

in slow thoughtful tone: "no, certainly not the next *course.*"

"Then it would have to be the next day. I suppose you wouldn't have two pudding-courses in one dinner?"

"Well, not the *next* day," the Knight repeated as before: "not the next *day.* In fact," he went on, holding his head down, and his voice getting lower and lower, "I don't believe that pudding ever *was* cooked! In fact, I don't believe that pudding ever *will* be cooked! And yet it was a very clever pudding to invent."[3]

"What did you mean it to be made of?" Alice asked, hoping to cheer him up, for the poor Knight seemed quite low-spirited about it.

"It began with blotting-paper," the Knight answered with a groan.

"That wouldn't be very nice, I'm afraid—"

"Not very nice *alone,*" he interrupted, quite eagerly: "but you've no idea what a difference it makes, mixing it with other things—such as gunpowder and sealing-wax. And here I must leave you." They had just come to the end of the wood.

Alice could only look puzzled: she was thinking of the pudding.

"You are sad," the Knight said in an anxious tone: "let me sing you a song to comfort you."

"Is it very long?" Alice asked, for she had heard a good deal of poetry that day.

"It's long," said the Knight, "but it's very, *very* beautiful. Everybody that hears me sing it—either it brings the *tears* into their eyes, or else—"

"Or else what?" said Alice, for the Knight had made a sudden pause.

3. Is Carroll alluding to the proverb "The proof of the pudding is in the eating"?

"Or else it doesn't, you know. The name of the song is called *'Haddocks' Eyes.'* "

"Oh, that's the name of the song, is it?" Alice said, trying to feel interested.

"No, you don't understand," the Knight said, looking a little vexed. "That's what the name is called. The name really *is 'The Aged Aged Man.'* "

"Then I ought to have said 'That's what the *song* is called'?" Alice corrected herself.

"No, you oughtn't: that's quite another thing! The *song* is called *'Ways and Means'*:[4] but that's only what it's *called,* you know!"

"Well, what *is* the song, then?" said Alice, who was by this time completely bewildered.

"I was coming to that," the Knight said. "The song really *is 'A-sitting On A Gate':* and the tune's my own invention."

So saying, he stopped his horse and let the reins fall on its neck: then, slowly beating time with one hand, and with a faint smile lighting up his gentle foolish face, as if he enjoyed the music of his song, he began.

Of all the strange things that Alice saw in her journey Through The Looking-Glass, this was the one that she always remembered most clearly. Years afterwards she could bring the whole scene back again, as if it had been only yesterday—the mild blue eyes and kindly smile of the Knight—the setting sun gleaming through his hair, and shining on his armour in a blaze of light that quite dazzled her—the horse quietly moving about, with the reins hanging loose on his neck, cropping the grass at her feet—and the black shadows of the forest

4. In his diary (August 5, 1862) Carroll wrote: "After dinner Harcourt and I went to the Deanery to arrange about the river tomorrow, and stayed to play a game of 'Ways and Means' with the children." I am told that Carroll's relatives own a set of rules in Carroll's handwriting, but no one seems to know if the game was invented by Carroll or by someone else.

"With a faint smile lighting up his gentle foolish face, . . . he began"

behind—all this she took in like a picture, as, with one hand shading her eyes, she leant against a tree, watching the strange pair, and listening, in a half-dream, to the melancholy music of the song.[5]

"But the tune *isn't* his own invention," she said to herself: "it's *'I give thee all, I can no more.'* " She stood and listened very attentively, but no tears came into her eyes.

"I'll tell thee everything I can:
There's little to relate.
I saw an aged aged man,
A-sitting on a gate.
'Who are you, aged man?' I said.
'And how is it you live?'
And his answer trickled through my head,
Like water through a sieve.

He said 'I look for butterflies
That sleep among the wheat:
I make them into mutton-pies,
And sell them in the street.
I sell them unto men,' he said,
'Who sail on stormy seas;
And that's the way I get my bread—
A trifle, if you please.'

But I was thinking of a plan
To dye one's whiskers green,
And always use so large a fan
That they could not be seen.
So, having no reply to give
To what the old man said,
I cried 'Come, tell me how you live!'
And thumped him on the head.

His accents mild took up the tale:
He said 'I go my ways,
And when I find a mountain-rill,
I set it in a blaze;
And thence they make a stuff they call
Rowland's Macassar-Oil—

5. The White Knight's song is an expanded version of "Upon the Lonely Moor," a poem by Carroll that appeared anonymously in a magazine called *The Train* (1856). (See *AA* for the full text of this poem, as well as Wordsworth's "Resolution and Independence," the subject matter of which Carroll travestied.) "Upon the Lonely Moor" was written for Tennyson's son Lionel. Here is Carroll's account of its origin, from an April 1862 entry in his diary. The entry was in a portion of the diary now missing, but Stuart Collingwood quotes it in his biography of Carroll.

> After luncheon I went to the Tennysons, and got Hallam and Lionel to sign their names in my album. Also I made a bargain with Lionel, that he was to give me some MS. of his verses, and I was to send him some of mine. It was a very difficult bargain to make; I almost despaired of it at first, he put in so many conditions—first, I was to play a game of chess with him; this, with much difficulty we reduced to twelve moves on each side; but this made little difference, as I checkmated him at the sixth move. Second, he was to be allowed to give me one blow on the head with a mallet (this he at last consented to give up). I forget if there were others, but it ended in my getting the verses, for which I have written out 'The Lonely Moor' for him.

" 'Sitting on a Gate' *is* a parody," Carroll said in a letter (see *The Letters of Lewis Carroll,* edited by Morton Cohen, Vol. 1, page 177), "though not as to style or metre—but its plot is borrowed from Wordsworth's 'Resolution and Independence,' a poem that has always amused me a good deal (though it is by no means a comic poem) by the absurd way in which the poet goes on questioning the poor old leech-gatherer, making him tell his history over and over again, and never attending to what he says. Wordsworth ends with a moral—an example I have *not* followed."

Carroll surely identified himself with the song's "aged aged man," a man even further removed in age from Alice than was the White Knight. In "Isa's Visit to Oxford," Carroll calls himself "the Aged Aged Man," abbreviating it throughout the diary as the A.A.M. Carroll was then fifty-eight. He often referred to himself in letters to child-friends as an aged, aged man.

Yet twopence-halfpenny is all
They give me for my toil.'

But I was thinking of a way
To feed oneself on batter,
And so go on from day to day
Getting a little fatter.
I shook him well from side to side,
Until his face was blue:
'Come, tell me how you live,' I cried,
'And what it is you do!'

He said 'I hunt for haddocks' eyes
Among the heather bright,
And work them into waistcoat-buttons
In the silent night.
And these I do not sell for gold
Or coin of silvery shine,
But for a copper halfpenny,
And that will purchase nine.

'I sometimes dig for buttered rolls,
Or set limed twigs for crabs:
I sometimes search the grassy knolls
For wheels of Hansom-cabs.[6]
And that's the way' (he gave a wink)
'By which I get my wealth—
And very gladly will I drink
Your Honour's noble health.'

I heard him then, for I had just
Completed my design
To keep the Menai bridge from rust
By boiling it in wine.
I thanked him much for telling me
The way he got his wealth,
But chiefly for his wish that he
Might drink my noble health.

And now, if e'er by chance I put
My fingers into glue,
Or madly squeeze a right-hand foot
Into a left-hand shoe,[7]
Or if I drop upon my toe
A very heavy weight,
I weep, for it reminds me so

6. "Hansom-cabs": Covered carriages with two wheels and an elevated seat for the driver in the back. They were the taxicabs of Victorian England.

7. It is an ancient superstition, reader Tim Healey tells me, that putting one's right foot into a left shoe is an omen of bad luck. He quotes a passage from Samuel Butler's *Hudibras* which speaks of Augustus Caesar making this mistake:

> *Augustus, having by an oversight*
> *Put on his left shoe for his right,*
> *And like to have been slain that day*
> *By soldiers mutineering for pay.*

" 'I shook him well from side to side,
Until his face was blue' "

Of that old man I used to know—
Whose look was mild, whose speech was slow,
Whose hair was whiter than the snow,
Whose face was very like a crow,
With eyes, like cinders, all aglow,[8]
Who seemed distracted with his woe,
Who rocked his body to and fro,
And muttered mumblingly and low,
As if his mouth were full of dough,
Who snorted like a buffalo—
That summer evening long ago,
A-sitting on a gate."

As the Knight sang the last words of the ballad, he gathered up the reins, and turned his horse's head along the road by which they had come. "You've only a few yards to go," he said, "down the hill and over that little brook, and then you'll be a Queen—But you'll stay and see me off first?" he added as Alice turned with an eager look in the direction to which he pointed. "I sha'n't be long. You'll wait and wave your handkerchief when I get to that turn in the road? I think it'll encourage me, you see."

"Of course I'll wait," said Alice: "and thank you very much for coming so far—and for the song—I liked it very much."

"I hope so," the Knight said doubtfully: "but you didn't cry so much as I thought you would."

So they shook hands, and then the Knight rode slowly away into the forest. "It wo'n't take long to see him *off,* I expect," Alice said to herself, as she stood watching him. "There he goes! Right on his head as usual! However, he gets on again pretty easily—that comes of having so many things hung round the horse—" So she went on talking to herself, as she watched the

8. Physicist David Frisch called my attention to the following lines—the last two lines of stanza 12 in Wordsworth's poem before he revised them for a later printing:

He answer'd me with pleasure and surprise
And there was, while he spake, a fire about his eyes.

" 'And what *is* this on my head?' she exclaimed"

horse walking leisurely along the road, and the Knight tumbling off, first on one side and then on the other. After the fourth or fifth tumble he reached the turn, and then she waved her handkerchief to him, and waited till he was out of sight.[9]

"I hope it encouraged him," she said, as she turned to run down the hill: "and now for the last brook, and to be a Queen! How grand it sounds!" A very few steps brought her to the edge of the brook.[10] "The Eighth Square at last!" she cried as she bounded across, and

* * * * *
* * * *
* * * * *

threw herself down to rest on a lawn as soft as moss, with little flowerbeds dotted about it here and there. "Oh, how glad I am to get here! And what *is* this on my head?" she exclaimed in a tone of dismay, as she put her hands up to something very heavy, that fitted tight all around her head.

"But how *can* it have got there without my knowing it?" she said to herself, as she lifted it off, and set it on her lap to make out what it could possibly be.

It was a golden crown.

9. Because knight moves are L-shaped, the White Knight's move is the "turn in the road" to which he referred a few paragraphs earlier.

This scene, in which Carroll clearly intends to describe how he hopes Alice will feel after she grows up and says goodbye, is one of the great poignant episodes of English literature. No one has written more eloquently about it than Donald Rackin in his essay "Love and Death in Carroll's *Alices*" (in *Soaring with the Dodo: Essays on Lewis Carroll's Life and Art,* edited by Edward Guiliano and James Kincaid): "The fleeting love that whispers through this scene is, therefore, complex and paradoxical: it is a love between a child all potential, freedom, flux, and growing up and a man all impotence, imprisonment, stasis, and falling down."

10. This is the spot where Carroll originally intended to place his episode about the Wasp in a Wig. Although Tenniel, in his letter to Carroll urging that the episode be omitted, called it a chapter, all evidence indicates it was to be a lengthy section in a chapter that even without it became the longest in the book. The complete episode, with my introduction and notes, is reprinted in this book.

CHAPTER IX
QUEEN ALICE

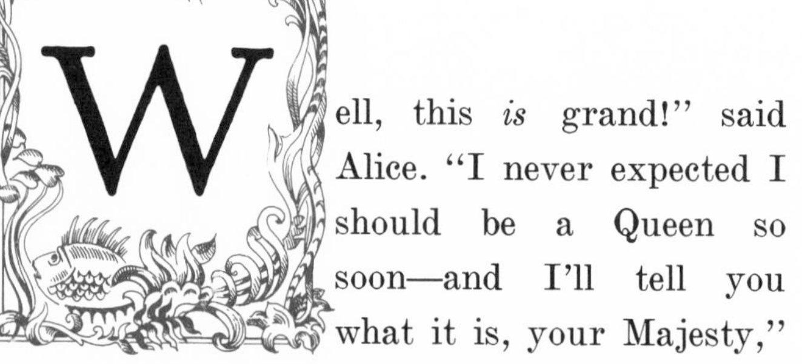

"Well, this *is* grand!" said Alice. "I never expected I should be a Queen so soon—and I'll tell you what it is, your Majesty," she went on, in a severe tone (she was always rather fond of scolding herself), "it'll never do for you to be lolling about on the grass like that! Queens have to be dignified, you know!"

So she got up and walked about—rather stiffly just at first, as she was afraid that the crown might come off: but she comforted herself with the thought that there was nobody to see her, "and if I really am a Queen," she said as she sat down again, "I shall be able to manage it quite well in time."

Everything was happening so oddly that she didn't feel a bit surprised at finding the Red Queen and the White Queen sitting close to her, one on each side:[1] she would have liked very much to ask them how they came there, but she feared it would not be quite civil. However, there would be no harm, she thought, in asking

1. Ivor Davies, writing on "Looking-Glass Chess" in *The Anglo-Welsh Review* (Autumn 1970), has an explanation of why no one notices that the White King has been placed in check by the Red Queen's move to the King's square. One of the chess books in Carroll's library was *The Art of Chess-Play* (1846) by George Walker. The book's Law 20 states: "When you give check, you must apprize your adversary by saying aloud 'check'; or he need not notice it, but may move as though check were not given."

"The Red Queen did not say 'Check,' " comments Davies. "Her silence was entirely logical because, at the moment of her arrival at King one, she said to Alice . . . 'Speak when you're spoken to!' Since no one had spoken to *her* she would have been breaking her own rule had she said 'check.' "

Another informative paper on the book's chess game is "Alice in Fairyland" by A. S. M. Dickins, in *Jabberwocky* (Winter 1976). A world expert on "fairy chess," Dickins analyzes Carroll's game as a mélange of fairy chess rules. He calls attention to Walker's Law 14, which, incredibly, allows a player to make a series of consecutive moves in one turn provided the opponent doesn't object!

if the game was over. "Please, would you tell me—" she began, looking timidly at the Red Queen.

"Speak when you're spoken to!" the Queen sharply interrupted her.

"But if everybody obeyed that rule," said Alice, who was always ready for a little argument, "and if you only spoke when you were spoken to, and the other person always waited for *you* to begin, you see nobody would ever say anything, so that—"

"Ridiculous!" cried the Queen. "Why, don't you see, child—" here she broke off with a frown, and, after thinking for a minute, suddenly changed the subject of the conversation. "What do you mean by 'If you really are a Queen'? What right have you to call yourself so? You ca'n't be a Queen, you know, till you've passed the proper examination. And the sooner we begin it, the better."

"I only said 'if'!" poor Alice pleaded in a piteous tone.

The two Queens looked at each other, and the Red Queen remarked, with a little shudder. "She *says* she only said 'if'—"

"But she said a great deal more than that!" the White Queen moaned, wringing her hands. "Oh, ever so much more than that!"

"So you did, you know," the Red Queen said to Alice. "Always speak the truth—think before you speak—and write it down afterwards."

"I'm sure I didn't mean—" Alice was beginning, but the Red Queen interrupted her impatiently.

"That's just what I complain of! You *should* have meant! What do you suppose is the use of a child without any meaning? Even a joke should have some meaning—and a child's more important than a joke, I hope. You couldn't deny that, even if you tried with both hands."

"I don't deny things with my *hands,*" Alice objected.

"Nobody said you did," said the Red Queen. "I said you couldn't if you tried."

"She's in that state of mind," said the White Queen, "that she wants to deny *something*—only she doesn't know what to deny!"

"A nasty, vicious temper," the Red Queen remarked; and then there was an uncomfortable silence for a minute or two.

The Red Queen broke the silence by saying, to the White Queen, "I invite you to Alice's dinner-party this afternoon."

The White Queen smiled feebly, and said "And I invite *you.*"

"I didn't know I was to have a party at all," said Alice; "but, if there *is* to be one, I think *I* ought to invite the guests."

"We gave you the opportunity of doing it," the Red Queen remarked: "but I daresay you've not had many lessons in manners yet."

"Manners are not taught in lessons," said Alice. "Lessons teach you to do sums, and things of that sort."

"Can you do Addition?" the White Queen asked. "What's one and one and one and one and one and one and one and one and one and one?"

"I don't know," said Alice. "I lost count."

"She ca'n't do Addition," the Red Queen interrupted. "Can you do Subtraction? Take nine from eight."

" 'She's in that state of mind,' said the White Queen, 'that she wants to deny *something*' "

"Nine from eight I ca'n't, you know," Alice replied very readily: "but—"

"She ca'n't do Subtraction," said the White Queen. "Can you do Division? Divide a loaf by a knife—what's the answer to *that?*"

"I suppose—" Alice was beginning, but the Red Queen answered for her. "Bread-and-butter, of course. Try another Subtraction sum. Take a bone from a dog: what remains?"

Alice considered. "The bone wouldn't remain, of course, if I took it—and the dog wouldn't remain: it would come to bite me—and I'm sure *I* shouldn't remain!"

"Then you think nothing would remain?" said the Red Queen.

"I think that's the answer."

"Wrong, as usual," said the Red Queen: "the dog's temper would remain."

"But I don't see how—"

"Why, look here!" the Red Queen cried. "The dog would lose its temper, wouldn't it?"

"Perhaps it would," Alice replied cautiously.

"Then if the dog went away, its temper would remain!" the Queen exclaimed triumphantly.

Alice said, as gravely as she could, "They might go different ways." But she couldn't help thinking to herself "What dreadful nonsense we *are* talking!"

"She ca'n't do sums a *bit!*" the Queens said together, with great emphasis.

"Can *you* do sums?" Alice said, turning suddenly on the White Queen, for she didn't like being found fault with so much.

The Queen gasped and shut her eyes. "I can do Addition," she said, "if you give me time—

but I ca'n't do Subtraction under *any* circumstances!"

"Of course you know your ABC?" said the Red Queen.

"To be sure I do," said Alice.

"So do I," the White Queen whispered: "we'll often say it over together, dear. And I'll tell you a secret—I can read words of one letter! Isn't *that* grand? However, don't be discouraged. You'll come to it in time."

Here the Red Queen began again. "Can you answer useful questions?" she said. "How is bread made?"

"I know *that*!" Alice cried eagerly. "You take some flour—"

"Where do you pick the flower?" the White Queen asked: "In a garden or in the hedges?"

"Well, it isn't *picked* at all;" Alice explained: "it's *ground*—"

"How many acres of ground?" said the White Queen. "You mustn't leave out so many things."

"Fan her head!" the Red Queen anxiously interrupted. "She'll be feverish after so much thinking." So they set to work and fanned her with bunches of leaves, till she had to beg them to leave off, it blew her hair about so.

"She's all right again now," said the Red Queen. "Do you know Languages? What's the French for fiddle-de-dee?"

"Fiddle-de-dee's not English," Alice replied gravely.

"Who ever said it was?" said the Red Queen.

Alice thought she saw a way out of the difficulty, this time. "If you'll tell me what language 'fiddle-de-dee' is, I'll tell you the French for it!" she exclaimed triumphantly.

But the Red Queen drew herself up rather stiffly, and said "Queens never make bargains."

"I wish Queens never asked questions," Alice thought to herself.

"Don't let us quarrel," the White Queen said in an anxious tone. "What is the cause of lightning?"

"The cause of lightning," Alice said very decidedly, for she felt quite certain about this, "is the thunder—no, no!" she hastily corrected herself. "I meant the other way."

"It's too late to correct it," said the Red Queen: "when you've once said a thing, that fixes it, and you must take the consequences."[2]

"Which reminds me—" the White Queen said, looking down and nervously clasping and unclasping her hands, "we had *such* a thunderstorm last Tuesday—I mean one of the last set of Tuesdays, you know."

Alice was puzzled. "In *our* country," she remarked, "there's only one day at a time."

The Red Queen said "That's a poor thin way of doing things. Now *here,* we mostly have days and nights two or three at a time, and sometimes in the winter we take as many as five nights together—for warmth, you know."

"Are five nights warmer than one night, then?" Alice ventured to ask.

"Five times as warm, of course."

"But they should be five times as *cold,* by the same rule—"

"Just so!" cried the Red Queen. "Five times as warm, *and* five times as cold—just as I'm five

2. Is the Red Queen, as conjectured by Selwyn Goodacre and several other correspondents, alluding to the fact that no move in chess can be taken back? Once it is made "you must take the consequences." Modern chess rules are even more strict. If a piece is merely touched, it must be moved.

times as rich as you are, *and* five times as clever!"

Alice sighed and gave it up. "It's exactly like the riddle with no answer!"[3] she thought.

"Humpty Dumpty saw it too," the White Queen went on in a low voice, more as if she were talking to herself. "He came to the door with a corkscrew in his hand—"

"What did he want?" said the Red Queen.

"He said he *would* come in," the White Queen went on, "because he was looking for a hippopotamus. Now, as it happened, there wasn't such a thing in the house, that morning."

"Is there generally?" Alice asked in an astonished tone.

"Well, only on Thursdays," said the Queen.

"I know what he came for," said Alice: "he wanted to punish the fish, because—"[4]

Here the White Queen began again. "It was *such* a thunderstorm, you ca'n't think!" ("She *never* could, you know," said the Red Queen.) "And part of the roof came off, and ever so much thunder got in—and it went rolling round the room in great lumps—and knocking over the tables and things—till I was so frightened, I couldn't remember my own name!"

Alice thought to herself "I never should *try* to remember my name in the middle of an accident! Where would be the use of it?" but she did not say this aloud, for fear of hurting the poor Queen's feelings.

"Your Majesty must excuse her," the Red Queen said to Alice, taking one of the White Queen's hands in her own, and gently stroking it: "she means well, but she ca'n't help saying foolish things as a general rule."

3. "riddle with no answer": such as the Mad Hatter's unanswered riddle about the raven and the writing desk.

4. Alice may not have been interrupted in her remark. She may simply be recalling Humpty's poem in Chapter 6 with its inconclusive couplet:

> *The little fishes' answer was*
> *"We cannot do it, Sir, because—"*

5. "papers": papers around which locks of hair are wound for curling.

The White Queen looked timidly at Alice, who felt she *ought* to say something kind, but really couldn't think of anything at the moment.

"She never was really well brought up," the Red Queen went on: "but it's amazing how good-tempered she is! Pat her on the head, and see how pleased she'll be!" But this was more than Alice had courage to do.

"A little kindness—and putting her hair in papers[5]—would do wonders with her—"

The White Queen gave a deep sigh, and laid her head on Alice's shoulder. "I *am* so sleepy!" she moaned.

"She's tired, poor thing!" said the Red Queen. "Smoothe her hair—lend her your nightcap—and sing her a soothing lullaby."

"I haven't got a nightcap with me," said Alice, as she tried to obey the first direction: "and I don't know any soothing lullabies."

"I must do it myself, then," said the Red Queen, and she began:—

"Hush-a-by lady, in Alice's lap!
Till the feast's ready, we've time for a nap.
When the feast's over, we'll go to the ball—
Red Queen, and White Queen, and Alice, and all!

"And now you know the words," she added, as she put her head down on Alice's other shoulder, "just sing it through to *me.* I'm getting sleepy, too." In another moment both Queens were fast asleep, and snoring loud.

"What *am* I to do?" exclaimed Alice, looking about in great perplexity, as first one round head, and then the other, rolled down from her

"First one round head, and then the other,
rolled down from her shoulder"

6. As Michael Hancher points out in his book, cited so often in previous notes, the Romanesque doorway in Tenniel's picture of this scene (*below*) is identical with a doorway he drew for the title page of the bound volume of *Punch,* July–December, 1853. Hancher also reproduces the illustration as Tenniel originally drew it (*bottom*), showing Alice with a crinoline skirt that resembles the lower part of chess queens, in keeping with her crown, which is identical with the crowns of the chess pieces. Carroll, who is on record as saying "I hate crinoline fashion," objected to five pictures by Tenniel that showed Alice in a crinoline skirt after she became a queen. Tenniel complied with Carroll's request by redrawing all five pictures.

shoulder, and lay like a heavy lump in her lap. "I don't think it *ever* happened before, that any one had to take care of two Queens asleep at once! No, not in all the History of England—it couldn't, you know, because there never was more than one Queen at a time. Do wake up, you heavy things!" she went on in an impatient tone; but there was no answer but a gentle snoring.

The snoring got more distinct every minute, and sounded more like a tune: at last she could even make out words, and she listened so eagerly that, when the two great heads suddenly vanished from her lap, she hardly missed them.

She was standing before an arched doorway, over which were the words "QUEEN ALICE" in large letters, and on each side of the arch there was a bell-handle; one was marked "Visitors' Bell," and the other "Servants' Bell."

"I'll wait till the song's over," thought Alice, "and then I'll ring the—the—*which* bell must I ring?" she went on, very much puzzled by the names. "I'm not a visitor, and I'm not a servant. There *ought* to be one marked 'Queen,' you know—"

Just then the door opened a little way, and a creature with a long beak put its head out for a moment and said "No admittance till the week after next!" and shut the door again with a bang.

Alice knocked and rang in vain for a long time; but at last a very old Frog, who was sitting under a tree, got up and hobbled slowly towards her: he was dressed in bright yellow, and had enormous boots on.[6]

"What is it, now?" the Frog said in a deep hoarse whisper.

Alice turned round, ready to find fault with anybody. "Where's the servant whose business it is to answer the door?" she began angrily.

"Which door?" said the Frog.

Alice almost stamped with irritation at the slow drawl in which he spoke. "*This* door, of course!"

The Frog looked at the door with his large dull eyes for a minute: then he went nearer and rubbed it with his thumb, as if he were trying whether the paint would come off: then he looked at Alice.

"To answer the door?" he said. "What's it been asking of?" He was so hoarse that Alice could scarcely hear him.[7]

"I don't know what you mean," she said.

"I speaks English, doesn't I?" the Frog went on. "Or are you deaf? What did it ask you?"

"Nothing!" Alice said impatiently. "I've been knocking at it!"

"Shouldn't do that—shouldn't do that—" the Frog muttered. "Wexes[8] it, you know." Then he went up and gave the door a kick with one of his great feet. "You let *it* alone," he panted out, as he hobbled back to his tree, "and it'll let *you* alone, you know."

At this moment the door was flung open, and a shrill voice was heard singing:—

"To the Looking-Glass world it was Alice that said
'I've a sceptre in hand, I've a crown on my head.
Let the Looking-Glass creatures, whatever they be,
Come and dine with the Red Queen, the White Queen,
and me!' "

The same Norman arched doorway, Charles Lovett tells me, with its characteristic zigzag pattern, was drawn by Tenniel in his first commissioned book illustrations, the second series of the *Book of British Ballads.* The arch appears in the background of a scene accompanying a ballad called "King Estmere."

In her booklet *Alice's Adventures in Oxford* (1980) Mavis Batey says that the door is "clearly the door of her [Alice's] father's Chapter House"—the house where the business of Christ Church's cathedral is conducted.

7. The Frog has a frog in his throat.

8. Victorian Cockneys had a habit of exchanging initial *w*s for *v*s and *v*s for *w*s. "Wexes" is how Mr. Pickwick's servant Sam Weller pronounces "vexes" in *Pickwick Papers.*

"Then he went nearer and rubbed it with his thumb"

And hundreds of voices joined in the chorus:—

"Then fill up the glasses as quick as you can,
And sprinkle the table with buttons and bran:
Put cats in the coffee, and mice in the tea—
And welcome Queen Alice with thirty-times-three!"

Then followed a confused noise of cheering, and Alice thought to herself "Thirty times three makes ninety. I wonder if any one's counting?" In a minute there was silence again, and the same shrill voice sang another verse:—

" 'O Looking-Glass creatures,' quoth Alice, 'draw near!
'Tis an honour to see me, a favour to hear:
'Tis a privilege high to have dinner and tea
Along with the Red Queen, the White Queen, and me!' "

Then came the chorus again:—

"Then fill up the glasses with treacle and ink,
Or anything else that is pleasant to drink:
Mix sand with the cider, and wool with the wine—
And welcome Queen Alice with ninety-times-nine!"

"Ninety times nine!" Alice repeated in despair. "Oh, that'll never be done! I'd better go in at once—" and in she went, and there was a dead silence the moment she appeared.

Alice glanced nervously along the table, as she walked up the large hall, and noticed that there were about fifty guests, of all kinds: some were animals, some birds, and there were even a few flowers among them. "I'm glad they've come without waiting to be asked," she thought: "I should never have known who were the right people to invite!"

There were three chairs at the head of the table: the Red and White Queens had already taken two of them, but the middle one was empty. Alice sat down in it, rather uncomfortable at the silence, and longing for some one to speak.

At last the Red Queen began. "You've missed the soup and fish," she said. "Put on the joint!" And the waiters set a leg of mutton before Alice, who looked at it rather anxiously, as she had never had to carve a joint before.

"You look a little shy: let me introduce you to that leg of mutton," said the Red Queen. "Alice—Mutton: Mutton—Alice." The leg of mutton got up in the dish and made a little bow to Alice; and Alice returned the bow, not knowing whether to be frightened or amused.

"May I give you a slice?" she said, taking up the knife and fork, and looking from one Queen to the other.

"Certainly not," the Red Queen said, very decidedly: "it isn't etiquette to cut any one you've been introduced to.[9] Remove the joint!" And the waiters carried it off, and brought a large plum-pudding in its place.

"I won't be introduced to the pudding, please," Alice said rather hastily, "or we shall get no dinner at all. May I give you some?"

But the Red Queen looked sulky, and growled "Pudding—Alice: Alice—Pudding. Remove the pudding!" and the waiters took it away so quickly that Alice couldn't return its bow.

However, she didn't see why the Red Queen should be the only one to give orders; so, as an experiment, she called out "Waiter! Bring back the pudding!" and there it was again in a mo-

9. No Victorian reader would miss the pun. "To cut" is to ignore someone you know. *Brewer's Dictionary of Phrase and Fable* distinguishes four kinds of cuts: the cut direct (staring at an acquaintance and pretending not to know him or her); the cut indirect (pretending not to see someone); the cut sublime (admiring something, such as the top of a building, until an acquaintance has walked by); and the cut informal (stooping to adjust a shoelace).

"The leg of mutton got up in the dish and made a little bow to Alice"

10. Roger Green thought Alice's dialogue with the pudding might have been suggested to Carroll by a cartoon in *Punch* (January 19, 1861) showing a plum pudding standing up in its dish and saying to a diner, "Allow me to disagree with you." Michael Hancher reproduces the *Punch* cartoon in his book on Tenniel, and points out the reappearance of the pudding, its legs in the air, at the lower left corner of the chapter's last Tenniel illustration.

ment, like a conjuring-trick. It was so large that she couldn't help feeling a *little* shy with it, as she had been with the mutton; however, she conquered her shyness by a great effort, and cut a slice and handed it to the Red Queen.

"What impertinence!" said the Pudding. "I wonder how you'd like it, if I were to cut a slice out of *you,* you creature!"[10]

It spoke in a thick, suety sort of voice, and Alice hadn't a word to say in reply: she could only sit and look at it and gasp.

"Make a remark," said the Red Queen: "it's ridiculous to leave all the conversation to the pudding!"

"Do you know, I've had such a quantity of poetry repeated to me to-day," Alice began, a little frightened at finding that, the moment she opened her lips, there was dead silence, and all eyes were fixed upon her; "and it's a very curious thing, I think—every poem was about fishes in some way. Do you know why they're so fond of fishes, all about here?"

She spoke to the Red Queen, whose answer was a little wide of the mark. "As to fishes," she said, very slowly and solemnly, putting her mouth close to Alice's ear, "her White Majesty knows a lovely riddle—all in poetry—all about fishes. Shall she repeat it?"

"Her Red Majesty's very kind to mention it," the White Queen murmured into Alice's other ear, in a voice like the cooing of a pigeon. "It would be *such* a treat! May I?"

"Please do," Alice said very politely.

The White Queen laughed with delight, and stroked Alice's cheek. Then she began:

"'First, the fish must be caught.'
That is easy: a baby, I think, could have caught it.
'Next, the fish must be bought.'
That is easy: a penny, I think, could have bought it.

'Now cook me the fish!'
That is easy, and will not take more than a minute.
'Let it lie in a dish!'
That is easy, because it already is in it.

'Bring it here! Let me sup!'
It is easy to set such a dish on the table.
'Take the dish-cover up!'
Ah, that *is so hard that I fear I'm unable!*

For it holds it like glue—
Holds the lid to the dish, while it lies in the middle:
Which is easiest to do,
Un-dish-cover the fish, or dishcover the riddle?"

"Take a minute to think about it, and then guess," said the Red Queen. "Meanwhile, we'll drink your health—Queen Alice's health!" she screamed at the top of her voice, and all the guests began drinking it directly, and very queerly they managed it: some of them put their glasses upon their heads like extinguishers, and drank all that trickled down their faces—others upset the decanters, and drank the wine as it ran off the edges of the table—and three of them (who looked like kangaroos) scrambled into the dish of roast mutton, and began eagerly lapping up the gravy, "just like pigs in a trough!" thought Alice.

"You ought to return thanks in a neat speech," the Red Queen said, frowning at Alice as she spoke.

"We must support you, you know," the White Queen whispered, as Alice got up to do it, very obediently, but a little frightened.

"Thank you very much," she whispered in reply, "but I can do quite well without."

"That wouldn't be at all the thing," the Red Queen said very decidedly: so Alice tried to submit to it with good grace.

("And they *did* push so!" she said afterwards, when she was telling her sister the history of her feast. "You would have thought they wanted to squeeze me flat!")

In fact it was rather difficult for her to keep in her place while she made her speech: the two Queens pushed her so, one on each side, that they nearly lifted her up into the air. "I rise to return thanks—" Alice began: and she really *did* rise as she spoke, several inches; but she got hold of the edge of the table, and managed to pull herself down again.

"Take care of yourself!" screamed the White Queen, seizing Alice's hair with both her hands. "Something's going to happen!'

And then (as Alice afterwards described it) all sorts of things happened in a moment. The candles all grew up to the ceiling, looking something like a bed of rushes with fireworks at the top. As to the bottles, they each took a pair of plates, which they hastily fitted on as wings, and so, with forks for legs, went fluttering about in all directions: "and very like birds they look," Alice thought to herself, as well as she could in the dreadful confusion that was beginning.

At this moment she heard a hoarse laugh at her side, and turned to see what was the matter with the White Queen; but, instead of the Queen, there was the leg of mutton sitting in the chair. "Here I am!" cried a voice from the soup-tureen, and Alice turned again, just in time to see the Queen's broad good-natured face grinning at her for a moment over the edge of the tureen, before she disappeared into the soup.

There was not a moment to be lost. Already several of the guests were lying down in the dishes, and the soup ladle was walking up the table towards Alice's chair, and beckoning to her impatiently to get out of its way.

"I ca'n't stand this any longer!" she cried, as she jumped up and seized the tablecloth with both hands: one good pull, and plates, dishes, guests, and candles came crashing down together in a heap on the floor.

"And as for *you,*" she went on, turning fiercely upon the Red Queen, whom she considered as the cause of all the mischief—but the Queen was no longer at her side—she had suddenly dwindled down to the size of a little doll, and was now on the table, merrily running round and round after her own shawl, which was trailing behind her.

At any other time, Alice would have felt surprised at this, but she was far too much excited to be surprised at anything *now.* "As for *you,*" she repeated, catching hold of the little creature in the very act of jumping over a bottle which had just lighted upon the table, "I'll shake you into a kitten, that I will!"

"Dishes, guests, and candles came crashing down together in a heap on the floor"

CHAPTER X

SHAKING

She took her off the table as she spoke, and shook her backwards and forwards with all her might.

The Red Queen made no resistance whatever: only her face grew very small, and her eyes got large and green: and still, as Alice went on shaking her, she kept on growing shorter—and fatter—and softer—and rounder—and—

CHAPTER XI
WAKING

—it really *was* a kitten, after all.[1]

1. Rose Franklin, one of Carroll's child-friends, recalled in a memoir that Carroll had said to her, "I cannot decide what to make the Red Queen turn into." Rose replied: "She looks so cross, please turn her into the Black Kitten."

"That will do splendidly," Carroll is reported to have said, "and the White Queen shall be the White Kitten."

Recall that in Chapter 1, before she fell asleep, Alice said to the black kitten, "Let's pretend that you're the Red Queen."

CHAPTER XII

WHICH DREAMED IT?

Your Red Majesty shouldn't purr so loud," Alice said, rubbing her eyes, and addressing the kitten, respectfully, yet with some severity. "You woke me out of oh! such a nice dream! And you've been along with me, Kitty—all through the Looking-glass world. Did you know it, dear?"

It is a very inconvenient habit of kittens (Alice had once made the remark) that, whatever you say to them, they *always* purr. "If they would only purr for 'yes,' and mew for 'no,' or any rule of that sort," she had said, "so that one could keep up a conversation! But how *can* you talk with a person if they *always* say the same thing?"[1]

On this occasion the kitten only purred: and it was impossible to guess whether it meant "yes" or "no."

So Alice hunted among the chessmen on the table till she had found the Red Queen: then she went down on her knees on the hearth-rug, and put the kitten and the Queen to look at each

1. Alice's point is fundamental in information theory, Gerald Weinberg says in a letter. There is no one-value logic—no way to record or transmit information without at least a binary distinction between yes and no, or true and false. In computers the distinction is handled by the on-off switches of their circuitry.

" 'Now, Kitty!' she cried, clapping her hands triumphantly"

other. "Now Kitty!" she cried, clapping her hands triumphantly. "Confess that was what you turned into!"

("But it wouldn't look at it," she said, when she was explaining the thing afterwards to her sister: "it turned away its head, and pretended not to see it: but it looked a *little* ashamed of itself, so I think it *must* have been the Red Queen.")

"Sit up a little more stiffly, dear!" Alice cried

with a merry laugh. "And curtsey while you're thinking what to—what to purr. It saves time, remember!" And she caught it up and gave it one little kiss, "just in honour of its having been a Red Queen."

"Snowdrop, my pet!" she went on, looking over her shoulder at the White Kitten, which was still patiently undergoing its toilet, "when *will* Dinah have finished with your White Majesty, I wonder? That must be the reason you were so untidy in my dream—Dinah! Do you know that you're scrubbing a White Queen? Really, it's most disrespectful of you!

"And what did *Dinah* turn to, I wonder?" she prattled on, as she settled comfortably down, with one elbow on the rug, and her chin in her hand, to watch the kittens. "Tell me, Dinah, did you turn to Humpty Dumpty?[2] I *think* you did—however, you'd better not mention it to your friends just yet, for I'm not sure.

"By the way, Kitty, if only you'd been really with me in my dream, there was one thing you *would* have enjoyed—I had such a quantity of poetry said to me, all about fishes![3] To-morrow morning you shall have a real treat. All the time you're eating your breakfast, I'll repeat 'The Walrus and the Carpenter' to you; and then you can make believe it's oysters, dear!

"Now, Kitty, let's consider who it was that dreamed it all. This is a serious question, my dear, and you should *not* go on licking your paw like that—as if Dinah hadn't washed you this morning! You see, Kitty, it *must* have been either me or the Red King. He was part of my dream, of course—but then I was part of his dream, too! *Was* it the Red King, Kitty? You

2. Why did Alice think Humpty was Dinah? Ellis Hillman, writing on "Dinah, the Cheshire Cat, and Humpty Dumpty," in *Jabberwocky* (Winter 1977), offers an ingenious theory. "I'm one that has spoken to a King, *I* am," Humpty said to Alice. As we know from the old proverb that Alice quoted in Chapter 8 of the previous book, a cat may look at a king.

Fred Madden, in his article cited in Chapter 3, notes 8 and 11, points out that when the initials of Humpty Dumpty are reversed, they become D. H., the first and last letters of "Dinah."

3. The term "queer fish," meaning someone considered odd, was current in Carroll's day. In stressing fish in this book, was Carroll thinking of all the odd fish it contained? Or that there is something "fishy" about his nonsense? Coincidentally, "fish" is slang in the United States for a mediocre chess player.

were his wife, my dear, so you ought to know—Oh, Kitty, *do* help to settle it! I'm sure your paw can wait!" But the provoking kitten only began on the other paw, and pretended it hadn't heard the question.

Which do *you* think it was?

A boat, beneath a sunny sky
Lingering onward dreamily
In an evening of July—

Children three that nestle near,
Eager eye and willing ear,
Pleased a simple tale to hear—

Long has paled that sunny sky:
Echoes fade and memories die:
Autumn frosts have slain July.

Still she haunts me, phantomwise.
Alice moving under skies
Never seen by waking eyes.

Children yet, the tale to hear,
Eager eye and willing ear,
Lovingly shall nestle near.

In a Wonderland they lie,
Dreaming as the days go by,
Dreaming as the summers die:

Ever drifting down the stream—
Lingering in the golden gleam—
Life, what is it but a dream?[1]

1. Matthew Hodgart wrote from England to suggest that in this stanza of his acrostic poem Carroll was consciously echoing the sentiments of that anonymous canon, well known in England at the time:

> *Row, row, row your boat*
> *Gently down the stream;*
> *Merrily, merrily, merrily, merrily,*
> *Life is but a dream.*

Ralph Lutts, a correspondent who made the same suggestion, pointed out that "merrily" in the canon links to the "merry crew" in the prefatory poem of the first *Alice* book.

The real world and the "eerie" state of dreaming alternate throughout Carroll's two *Sylvie and Bruno* books. "Either I've been dreaming about Sylvie," he says to himself in Chapter 2 of the first book, "and this is reality. Or else I've been with Sylvie, and this is the dream! Is Life itself a dream, I wonder?"

The prefatory poem of *Sylvie and Bruno,* an acrostic on the name of Isa Bowman, conveys the same theme:

> *Is all our Life, then, but a dream*
> *Seen faintly in the golden gleam*
> *Athwart Time's dark resistless stream?*
>
> *Bowed to the earth with bitter woe,*
> *Or laughing at some raree-show,*
> *We flutter idly to and fro.*
>
> *Man's little Day in haste we spend,*
> *And, from its merry noontide, send*
> *No glance to meet the silent end.*

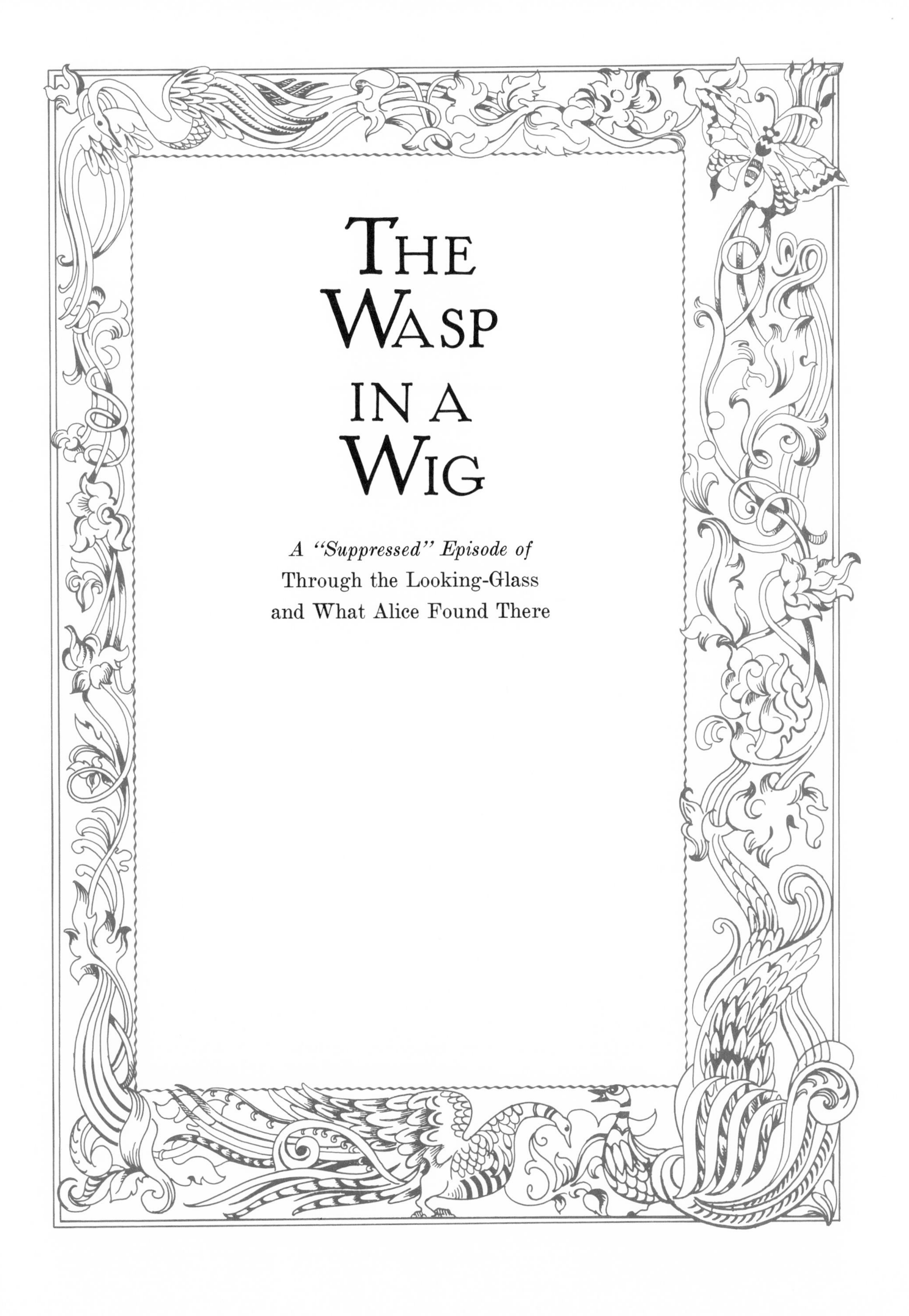

The Wasp in a Wig

A "Suppressed" Episode of
Through the Looking-Glass
and What Alice Found There

CONTENTS

PREFACE

In 1974 the London auctioneering firm of Sotheby Parke Bernet and Company listed, inconspicuously, the following item in their June 3 catalog:

> Dodgson (C.L.) "Lewis Carroll." Galley proofs for a suppressed portion of "Through the Looking-Glass," slip 64–67 and portions of 63 and 68, with autograph revisions in black ink and note in the author's purple ink that the extensive passage is to be omitted.
>
> The present portion contains an incident in which Alice meets a bad-tempered wasp, incorporating a poem of five stanzas, beginning "When I was young, my ringlets waved." It was to have appeared following "A very few steps brought her to the edge of the brook" on page 183 of the first edition. The proofs were bought at the sale of the author's furniture, personal effects, and library, Oxford, 1898, and are apparently unrecorded and unpublished.

The word "apparently" in the last sentence was an understatement. Not only had the suppressed portion not been published, but Carroll experts did not even know it had been set in type, let alone preserved. The discovery that it still existed was an event of major significance to Carrollians—indeed, to all students of English literature. Now, more than one hundred years after *Through the Looking-Glass* was first set in type, the long-lost episode receives its first major publication.

Until 1974 nothing was known about the missing portion beyond what Stuart Dodgson Collingwood, a nephew of Lewis Carroll, had said about it in his 1898 biography of his uncle, *The Life and Letters of Lewis Carroll.* Collingwood wrote:

> The story, as originally written, contained thirteen chapters, but the published book consisted of twelve only. The omitted chapter introduced a

wasp, in the character of a judge or barrister, I suppose, since Mr. Tenniel wrote that "a *wasp* in a *wig* is altogether beyond the appliances of art." Apart from difficulties of illustration, the "wasp" chapter was not considered to be up to the level of the rest of the book, and this was probably the principal reason of its being left out.

These remarks were followed by a facsimile of a letter, dated June 1, 1870, that John Tenniel had sent to Carroll. (The letter is here reproduced on pages 331–33.) In Tenniel's sketch for the railway carriage scene, Alice sits opposite a goat and a man dressed in white paper while the Guard observes Alice through opera glasses. In his final drawing Tenniel gave the man in the paper hat the face of Benjamin Disraeli, the British prime minister he so often caricatured in *Punch.*

Carroll accepted both of Tenniel's suggestions. The "old lady," presumably a character in the original version of Chapter 3, vanished from the chapter and from Tenniel's illustration, and the Wasp vanished from the book. In *The Annotated Alice* my note on this ends: "Alas, nothing of the missing chapter has survived." Collingwood himself had not read the episode. We know this because he assumed, mistakenly as it turned out, that if the Wasp wore a wig he must have been a judge or lawyer.

Carroll left no record of his own final opinion of the episode or the poem it contained. He did, however, carefully preserve the galleys, and it seems likely that he intended to do something with them someday. It was Carroll himself, remember, who decided to publish his first version of *Alice in Wonderland,* the manuscript he had hand-lettered and illustrated for Alice Liddell. Many of his early poems, printed in obscure periodicals or not published at all, found their way eventually into his books. Even if Carroll had no specific plans for making use of the Wasp episode or its poem, it is hard to believe he would not have been pleased to know it would find eventual publication.

After Carroll's death in 1898 the galleys were bought by an unknown person and—for the present at least—we know little about who owned them until Sotheby's put them up for auction. They are not listed in the 1898 catalogs of Carroll's effects, apparently because they were included in a miscellaneous lot of unidentified items. "The property of a gentleman" is how Sotheby's labeled them in its catalog. Sotheby's does not disclose the identities of vendors who desire to remain anonymous, but they tell me that the galleys had been passed on to the vendor by an older member of his family.

The galleys were bought by John Fleming, a Manhattan rare book dealer, for Norman Armour, Jr., also of New York City. It was Mr. Armour's gracious consent to permit publication of these galleys that makes this book possible. What more need be said in the way of thanks?

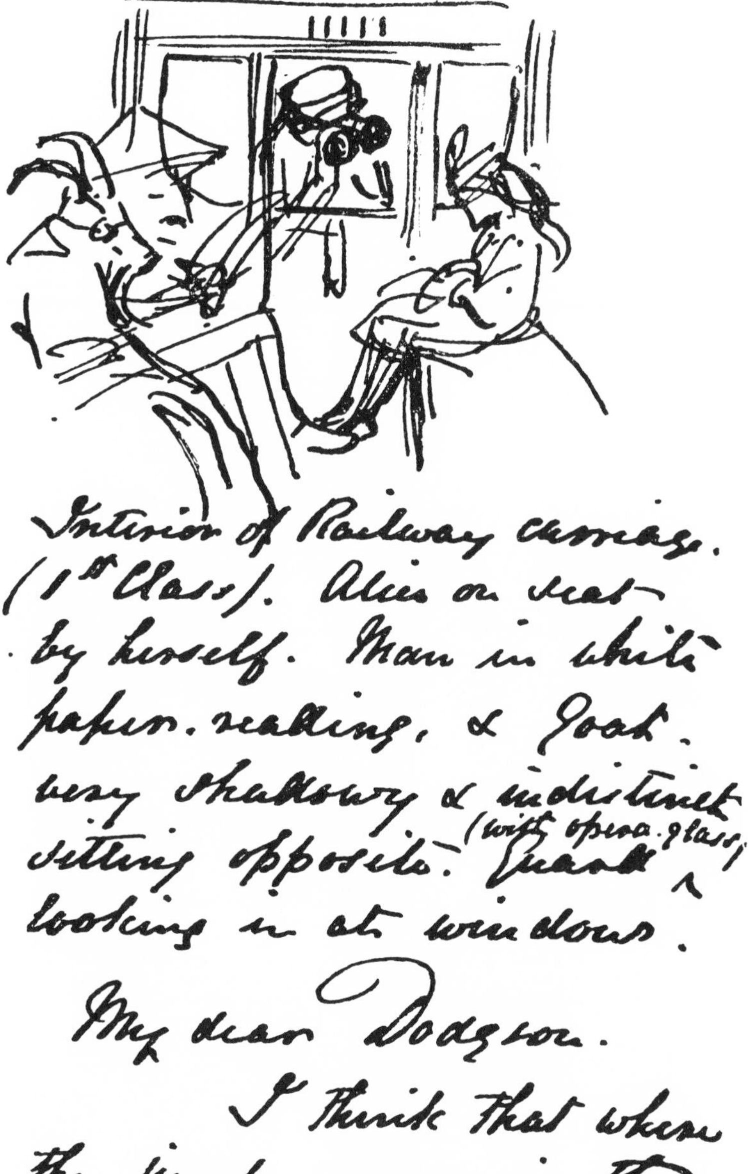

4823

Interior of Railway carriage. (1st Class). Alice on seat by herself. Man in white paper. reading. & Goat. very shadowy & indistinct sitting opposite. Guard (with opera-glass) looking in at window.

My dear Dodgson.

I think that where the jump occurs in the

Railway scene you might
very well make Alice lay
hold of the Goat's beard
as being the object nearest
to her hand – instead of
the old lady's hair. The
jerk would naturally
throw them together.
Don't think me brutal, but
I am bound to say that
the 'wasp' chapter doesn't
interest me in the least, &
~~that~~ I can't see my way
to a picture. If you
want to shorten the book,

I can't help thinking —
with all submission —
that there is your oppor-
tunity.
In an agony of haste
Yours sincerely
J Tenniel.

Portsdown Road.
June 1. 1870

Facsimile of Tenniel's letter to Dodgson, with a transcription

My dear Dodgson.

I think that when the *jump* occurs in the Railway scene you might very well make Alice lay hold of the Goat's *beard* as being the object nearest to her hand—instead of the old lady's hair. The jerk would naturally throw them together.

Don't think me brutal, but I am bound to say that the *'wasp'* chapter doesn't interest me in the least, & I can't see my way to a picture. If you want to shorten the book, I can't help thinking—with all submission—that *there* is your opportunity.

In an agony of haste

Yours sincerely
J. Tenniel.

Portsdown Road.
June 1, 1870

INTRODUCTION

Before the Wasp episode came to light, most students of Carroll assumed that the lost episode was adjacent to, at least not far from, the railway carriage scene. This was because Tenniel, in his letter of complaint, seemed to link the two incidents. In Chapter 3, where Alice leaps the first brook and the train jumps over the second, Alice encounters a variety of insects, including bees the size of elephants. Was it not appropriate that she would meet a wasp in this region of the chessboard?

That Carroll did not intend Alice to come upon the Wasp so early in the chess game is evident at once from the numbers on the galleys, and from what Alice thought when the Wasp told her how his ringlets used to wave. "A curious idea came into Alice's head. Almost every one she had met had repeated poetry to her, and she thought she would try if the Wasp couldn't do it too." The first person to recite poetry to Alice is Tweedledee, and the second is Humpty Dumpty. The lost episode, therefore, had to occur later than Chapter 6.

The incomplete first line of the galleys (see p. 349) leaves no doubt that Sotheby's catalog correctly indicates where Carroll had intended the Wasp episode to go. (The spot is shown by the arrow in the reproduction of page 183 of the first edition of *Through the Looking-Glass,* here printed on page 342.) Alice has just waved her final farewell to the White Knight, then gone down the hill to leap the last brook and become a Queen. "A very few steps brought her to the edge of the brook." Instead of a period there was a comma. The sentence continued as at the top of the first galley: "and she was just going to spring over, when she heard a deep sigh, which seemed to come from the wood behind her."

Both Tenniel and Collingwood called the episode a "chapter," but there are difficulties with this view. The galleys give no indication that they are anything but an excerpt from Chapter 8, and it seems unlikely that Carroll would have wanted his second *Alice* book to have thirteen chapters when the first book had twelve. It is Morton Cohen's belief that Tenniel, writing "in an agony of haste," used the word "chapter" when he meant episode. Collingwood's remarks are easily explained as elaborations of how he interpreted Tenniel's letters. (There must have been at least one other Tenniel letter available to him, because the remark of Tenniel's that he quotes about a wasp in a wig being "beyond the appliances of art" does not appear in the letter he reproduces in facsimile.)

One might argue that had the Wasp episode belonged to the White Knight chapter, the chapter would have been uncommonly long, and would not Tenniel have written that the episode should be removed to "shorten the chapter" rather than "shorten the book"? On the other hand, the fact that the chapter was too long may have been another reason why Carroll was willing to excise the episode. Unfortunately no other galleys for the book are known to have survived, so we are forced to rely on indirect evidence for deciding which view is correct.

Edward Guiliano favors the view that Tenniel had "episode" in mind. He supports the arguments already presented, and also feels that the incidents of the episode would have added thematic unity to the White Knight chapter. After conversing with the White Knight, an upper-class gentleman still in his vigor, Alice meets a lower-class worker in his declining years.* She waves good-bye to the White Knight with a handkerchief; the Wasp has a handkerchief around his face. The White Knight talks about bees and honey; the Wasp thinks Alice is a bee and asks her if she has any honey. Even the pun about the comb, Guiliano believes, is not quite so feeble in the context of the chapter as originally planned. These and other incidents in the Wasp episode link it to the White Knight chapter in ways that suggest it was not intended to stand alone.

Was the Wasp episode worth preserving? It was, of course, eminently worth saving for historical reasons, but that is not what I mean. Does it have intrinsic merit? Tenniel said it did not interest him in the least, and many who have recently read the episode agree that it is not (in Collingwood's words) "up to the level of the rest of the book." Peter Heath feels that one reason the episode lacks the vivacity of other parts of the book is that it repeats so many themes that occur elsewhere. Alice had a previous conversation with an unhappy insect, the Gnat, in Chapter 3. In the chapter following the Wasp episode Alice converses with another elderly lower-class male, the Frog. The Wasp's criticisms of Alice's face are reminiscent of Humpty Dumpty's criticisms. Alice's attempts to repair the Wasp's disheveled appearance parallel her attempts to remedy the untidyness of the White Queen in Chapter 5. There are other echoes of familiar themes that

*The White Knight, so far as Carroll's text alone is concerned, could have been a young man in his twenties. Tenniel, with Carroll's approval, drew him as an elderly gentleman, though certainly not as old as the "aged aged man" about whom the Knight sings.

Professor Heath has noted. "It's as if Carroll's inventiveness was flagging a bit," he writes in a letter, "and the momentum of the narrative had temporarily been lost."

All this may be true, but I am convinced that if the episode is read carefully, then reread several times on later occasions, its merit will steadily become more apparent. First of all it is unmistakably Carrollian in its general tone, its humor, its wordplay, and its nonsense. The Wasp's remark "Let it stop there!" and his observation that Alice's eyes are so close together (compared with his own, of course) that she could have done as well with one eye instead of two are both pure Carroll. The wordplay may not be up to Carroll's best, but we must remember that he frequently had a book set in type long before he began to work in earnest on revisions. If the Wasp episode was removed from the book before Carroll began to polish the galleys, that would explain why the writing seems cruder at times than elsewhere in the book.

Two features of the episode impress me as having special interest: the extraordinary skill with which Carroll, in just a few pages of dialogue, brings out the personality of a waspish but somehow lovable old man, and Alice's unfailing gentleness toward him.

Although Alice is usually kind and respectful toward the curious creatures she meets in her two dreams, no matter how unpleasant the creatures are, this is not always the case. In the pool of tears she twice offends the Mouse, by telling him that her cat chases mice and that a neighbor's dog likes to kill rats. A short time later, after the Caucus-race, she forgets herself again and insults the assembled birds by remarking on how much her cat likes to eat birds. And remember Alice's sharp kick that sends Bill, the Lizard, out the chimney? ("There goes Bill!")

In *Through the Looking-Glass,* Alice (now six months older) is not quite so thoughtless, but there is no episode in the book in which she treats a disagreeable creature with such remarkable patience. In no other episode, in either book, does her character come through so vividly as that of an intelligent, polite, considerate little girl. It is an episode in which extreme youth confronts extreme age. Although the Wasp is constantly critical of Alice, not once does she cease to sympathize with him.

Need I spell it out? We are told how much Alice, the white pawn, longs to become a Queen. We know how easily she could have leaped the final brook to occupy the last row of the chessboard. Yet Alice does not make the move when she hears the sigh of distress behind her. When the Wasp responds crossly to her kind remarks, she excuses his ill-temper with the understanding that it is his pain that makes him cross. After she has helped him around the tree to a warmer side, his response is "Can't you leave a body alone?" Unoffended, Alice offers to read to him from the wasp newspaper at his feet.

Although the Wasp continues to criticize, when Alice leaves him she is "quite pleased that she had gone back and given a few minutes to making the poor old creature comfortable." Carroll surely must have wanted to show Alice performing a final deed of charity that would justify her approaching coronation, a reward that Carroll, a pious Christian and patriotic Englishman, would have regarded as a crown of righteousness. Alice comes through as such an admirable, appealing little girl that Professor Guiliano discovered to his surprise that reading the episode altered a bit his response to the entire book.

The old man, with his waspish temper and his aching bones, is also, of course, a genuine insect. Female wasps (queens and workers) prey on other insects, such as caterpillars, spiders, and flies, which they first paralyze by stinging them. With their strong mandibles they remove the victim's head, legs, and wings; then the body is chewed to a pulp to give as food to their larvae. It may not be accidental that Carroll's insect belongs to a social structure that includes fierce, powerful queens, like the queens of chess and many former queens of England.

In contrast, male wasps (drones) do not sting. In some species the male, if you seize him in your hand, will try to frighten you into dropping him by going through all the movements of stinging. (John Burroughs likened this bluffing to a soldier in battle who tries to frighten the enemy by firing blank cartridges.) Male wasps, like Carroll's Wasp, although they look formidable, resemble the kings of chess. They are amiable, harmless creatures.

Except for a few hibernating queens, wasps are summer insects and do not survive the winter. During the hot months they work furiously to provide for their offspring; then they stiffen and die with the approach of autumn's cold winds. This is how Oliver Goldsmith phrases it in his marvelous, now-forgotten *History of the Earth and Animated Nature:*

> While the summer heats continue, they [wasps] are bold, voracious, and enterprising; but as the sun withdraws, it seems to rob them of their courage and activity. In proportion as the cold increases, they are seen to become more domestic; they seldom leave the nest, they make but short adventures from home, they flutter about in the noon-day heats, and soon after return chilled and feeble. . . . As the cold increases they no longer find sufficient warmth in their nests, which grow hateful to them, and they fly to seek it in the corners of houses, and places that receive an artificial heat. But the winter is still insupportable; and, before the new year begins, they wither and die."

Like so many elderly people, the Wasp has happy memories of a childhood when his tresses waved. In five stanzas of doggerel he tells Alice about his terrible mistake of allowing friends to persuade him to shave his head for a wig. All his subsequent unhappiness is blamed on this foolish indiscretion. He knows his present appearance is ridiculous. His wig does not fit. He fails to keep it neat. He resents being laughed at. The Wasp is Oliver Wendell Holmes's "last leaf," enduring the community's ridicule as he clings "to the old forsaken bough."

Although the Wasp pretends not to want Alice to help him in any way, his spirits are lifted by her visit and the opportunity to tell his sad tale. Indeed, before Alice leaves he has become animated and talkative. When she finally says good-bye he responds with "Thank ye." It is the only thanks Alice gets from anyone she meets on the mirror's other side.

The fashion of wearing wigs reached absurd heights in France and England in the seventeenth and eighteenth centuries. During Queen Anne's reign almost every upper-class man and woman in England wore a wig, and one could instantly tell a man's profession by the kind of wig he sported. Some male wigs hung below the shoulders to cover both back and chest. The craze began to fade under Queen Victoria. In Carroll's time it had all but vanished, except for the ceremonial wigs of judges and barristers, the wigs of actors, and the wearing of wigs to conceal baldness. The Wasp's wig is clearly a mark of his advanced age even though he started wearing it when young.

Why a yellow wig? If the Wasp's ringlets were yellow it would be natural for him to substitute a yellow wig, but Carroll seems to emphasize the color for other reasons. He calls it "bright yellow." And when Alice first meets the Wasp his wig is covered by a yellow handkerchief tied around his head and face.

Both *Alice* books contain inside jokes about persons the real Alice, Alice Liddell, knew. It is possible, I suppose, that Carroll's Wasp pokes fun at someone, perhaps an elderly tradesman in the area, who sported an unkempt yellow wig that resembled seaweed.

Another theory has to do with the yellow color of many wasps in England. The American term "yellow-jackets," for a large class of social insects that were (and are) called hornets, may have been in Carroll's mind. The term had spread to England, and numerous varieties of British wasps have bright yellow stripes circling their black bodies. Wasp antennae are composed of tiny joints that also could be called ringlets. A young wasp's antennae would certainly wave, curl, and crinkle, as the poem has it. If cut off, perhaps they would not grow again.

There may have been wasps in Oxford, familiar to Carroll and Alice Liddell, with black heads circled by a yellow stripe that would look for all the world like a yellow handkerchief tied around the insect's face. Even aside from a yellow stripe, a wasp's face does resemble a human face done up in a handkerchief, the knot's ends sticking up from the top of the head like two antennae.* Professor Heath recalls having had just such thoughts himself when he was a child in England.

A third theory is that the Wasp, with his yellow handkerchief above a yellow wig, parallels Alice after she becomes a queen—the gold crown on top of her flaxen hair.

A fourth theory (of course these theories are not mutually exclusive) is that Carroll chose yellow because of its long association in literature and common speech with autumn and old age. Yellow is the complexion of the elderly, especially if they suffer from jaundice. It is the color of fall leaves, of ripe corn, of paper "yellowed with age." "Sorrow, thought, and great distress," wrote Chaucer (in *Romance of the Rose*), "made her full yellow."

Shakespeare frequently used yellow as a symbol of age. Professor Cohen reports that Carroll, at least twice in his letters, quotes the following remark from *Macbeth:* "My way of life is fallen into the sere, the yellow leaf." These lines from Shakespeare's Sonnet 73 are particularly apt:

That time of year thou mayst in me behold
When yellow leaves, or none, or few, do hang
Upon those boughs which shake against the cold . . .

Through the Looking-Glass opens and closes with poems that speak of winter and death. The dream itself probably occurs in November, while Alice sits in front of a blazing fire and snow is "kissing" the windowpanes. "Autumn frosts have slain July" is how Carroll puts it in his terminal poem, recalling that sunny July 4 boating trip on the Isis when he first told Alice the story of her trip to Wonderland.

Although Carroll was not yet forty when he wrote his second *Alice* book, he was twenty years older than Alice Liddell, the child-friend he adored above any other. In the book's prefatory poem he speaks of himself and Alice as "half a life asunder." He reminds Alice that it will not be long until the "bitter tidings" summon her to "unwelcome bed," and he likens himself to an older child fretting at the approach of the final bedtime.

Carroll scholars believe that Carroll intended his White Knight—that awkward, inventive gentleman with the mild blue eyes and kindly smile who treated Alice with such uncharacteristic courtesy for someone behind the mirror—to be a parody of himself. Is it possible that Carroll regarded his Wasp as a parody of himself forty years later? Professor Cohen has convinced me that it is not possible. Carroll prided himself on being a Victorian gentleman. Under no circumstances would he have associated him-

*Lewis Carroll's library at the time of his death included a book by John G. Wood called *A World of Little Wonders: or Insects at Home.* The chapter on wasps describes a common variety of social wasp as having antennae with a first joint that is "yellow in front."

self with a lower-class drone. Nonetheless, it seems to me that Carroll could not have written this episode without being acutely aware of the fact that the chasm of age between Alice and the Wasp resembled the chasm that separated Alice Liddell from the middle-aged teller of the story.

I am persuaded that Carroll, perhaps not consciously, spoke through his Wasp like a ventriloquist talking through a dummy when he has the Wasp exclaim—in a way that seems strangely out of place in the dialogue—"Worrity, worrity! There never was such a child!"

Where Carroll intended the episode to appear (reproduction of first edition)

"IT'S MY OWN INVENTION." 183

comes of having so many things hung round the horse——" So she went on talking to herself, as she watched the horse walking leisurely along the road, and the Knight tumbling off, first on one side and then on the other. After the fourth or fifth tumble he reached the turn, and then she waved her handkerchief to him, and waited till he was out of sight.

"I hope it encouraged him," she said, as she turned to run down the hill: "and now for the last brook, and to be a Queen! How grand it sounds!" A very few steps brought her to the edge of the brook. "The Eighth Square at last!" she cried as she bounded across,

* * * * * *

* * * * *

* * * * * *

and threw herself down to rest on a lawn as soft as moss, with little flower-beds dotted about it here and there. "Oh, how glad I am to get here! And what *is* this on my head?" she

THE WASP IN A WIG

. . . and she was just going to spring over, when she heard a deep sigh, which seemed to come from the wood behind her.

"There's somebody *very* unhappy there," she thought, looking anxiously back to see what was the matter. Something like a very old man (only that his face was more like a wasp) was sitting on the ground, leaning against a tree, all huddled up together, and shivering as if he were very cold.

"I don't *think* I can be of any use to him," was Alice's first thought, as she turned to spring over the brook:—"but I'll just ask him what's the matter," she added, checking herself on the very edge. "If I once jump over, everything will change, and then I can't help him."[1]

So she went back to the Wasp—rather unwillingly, for she was *very* anxious to be a Queen.

"Oh, my old bones, my old bones!" he was grumbling as Alice came up to him.

"It's rheumatism, I should think," Alice said to herself, and she stooped over him, and said very kindly, "I hope you're not in much pain?"

The Wasp only shook his shoulders, and turned his head away. "Ah, dreary me!" he said to himself.

1. The abrupt changes of scenery that take place whenever Alice leaps a brook resemble the changes that occur in a chess game whenever a move is made, as well as the sudden transitions that occur in dreams.

"Can I do anything for you?" Alice went on. "Aren't you rather cold here?"

"How you go on!" the Wasp said in a peevish tone. "Worrity, worrity! There never was such a child!"[2]

Alice felt rather offended at this answer, and was very nearly walking on and leaving him, but she thought to herself "Perhaps it's only pain that makes him so cross." So she tried once more.

"Won't you let me help you round to the other side? You'll be out of the cold wind there."

The Wasp took her arm, and let her help him round the tree, but when he got settled down again he only said, as before, "Worrity, worrity! Can't you leave a body alone?"

"Would you like me to read you a bit of this?" Alice went on, as she picked up a newspaper which had been lying at his feet.[3]

"You may read it if you've a mind to," the Wasp said, rather sulkily. "Nobody's hindering you, that *I* know of."

So Alice sat down by him, and spread out the paper on her knees, and began. *"Latest News. The Exploring Party have made another tour in the Pantry, and have found five new lumps of white sugar, large and in fine condition. In coming back—"*

"Any brown sugar?" the Wasp interrupted.

Alice hastily ran her eye down the paper and said "No. It says nothing about brown."

"No brown sugar!" grumbled the Wasp. "A nice exploring party!"[4]

"In coming back," Alice went on reading, *"they found a lake of treacle. The banks of the lake*

2. "Worrit" was a slang noun in Carroll's time for worry or mental distress. The *Oxford English Dictionary* quotes Mr. Bumble (in Dickens's *Oliver Twist*): "A porochial life, ma'am, is a life of worrit and vexation and hardihood." "Worrity" was another form of the noun commonly used by British lower classes.

3. If any insect had a newspaper it would be the social wasp. Wasps are great paper makers. Their thin paper nests, usually in hollow trees, are made from a pulp which they produce by chewing leaves and wood fiber.

4. "brown sugar": Wasps are fond of all kinds of man-made sweets, especially sugar. Morton Cohen points out that the Wasp's preference for brown sugar is characteristic of Victorian lower classes, who found it cheaper than the refined white.

were blue and white, and looked like china. While tasting the treacle, they had a sad accident: two of their party were engulphed—"

"Were *what?*" the Wasp asked in a very cross voice.

"En-gulph-ed," Alice repeated, dividing the word into syllables.[5]

"There's no such word in the language!" said the Wasp.

"It's in this newspaper, though," Alice said a little timidly.

"Let it stop there!" said the Wasp, fretfully turning away his head.

Alice put down the newspaper. "I'm afraid you're not well," she said in a soothing tone. "Can't I do anything for you?"

"It's all along of the wig,"[6] the Wasp said in a much gentler voice.

"Along of the wig?" Alice repeated, quite pleased to find that he was recovering his temper.

"You'd be cross too, if you'd a wig like mine," the Wasp went on. "They jokes at one. And they worrits one.[7] And then I gets cross. And I gets cold. And I gets under a tree. And I gets a yellow handkerchief.[8] And I ties up my face—as at the present."

Alice looked pityingly at him. "Tying up the face is very good for the toothache," she said.[9]

"And it's very good for the conceit," added the Wasp.

Alice didn't catch the word exactly. "Is that a kind of toothache?" she asked.

The Wasp considered a little. "Well, no," he said: "it's when you hold up your head—*so*—without bending your neck."

5. "Engulph" was a common spelling of "engulf" in the sixteenth and seventeenth centuries. It was occasionally seen in Carroll's time, and the Wasp may be voicing Carroll's personal dislike of the spelling. Perhaps it is Alice's incorrect pronunciation, "en-gulph-ed" (three syllables instead of two), that the Wasp finds so outlandish. Donald L. Hotson suggests that Carroll may here be playing on a university slang expression of the time. According to *The Slang Dictionary* (Chatto & Windus, 1974), "gulfed" (sometimes spelled "gulphed") was "originally a Cambridge term, denoting that a man is unable to enter for the classical examination from having failed in the mathematical. . . . The expression is common now in Oxford as descriptive of a man who goes in for honours, and only gets a pass."

6. "all along of": all because of. Another lower-class expression of the day.

7. "worrits": The word was also vulgarly used as a verb. "Don't worrit your poor mother," says Mrs. Saunders in Dickens's *Pickwick Papers.* The Wasp's speech marks him clearly as a drone in the wasp social structure.

Carroll not only identified his cantankerous aged man with a creature universally feared and hated, he also made him lower class, in sharp contrast to Alice's upper-class background—facts that make her kindness toward the insect all the more remarkable.

8. A yellow silk handkerchief, colloquially called a "yellowman," was fashionable in Victorian England.

9. Tying a handkerchief around the face, with a poultice inside, was in Carroll's time believed around the world to provide relief from a toothache. Persons who considered themselves good-looking must have frequently been seen in this condition, and their appearance surely would not have strengthened their conceit.

"Oh, you mean stiff-neck,"[10] said Alice.

The Wasp said "That's a new-fangled name. They called it conceit in my time."

"Conceit isn't a disease at all," Alice remarked.

"It is, though," said the Wasp: "wait till you have it, and then you'll know. And when you catches it, just try tying a yellow handkerchief round your face. It'll cure you in no time!"

He untied the handkerchief as he spoke, and Alice looked at his wig in great surprise. It was bright yellow like the handkerchief,[11] and all tangled and tumbled about like a heap of seaweed. "You could make your wig much neater," she said, "if only you had a comb."

"What, you're a Bee, are you?" the Wasp said, looking at her with more interest. "And you've got a comb.[12] Much honey?"

"It isn't that kind," Alice hastily explained. "It's to comb hair with—your wig's so *very* rough, you know."

"I'll tell you how I came to wear it," the Wasp said. "When I was young, you know, my ringlets used to wave—"

A curious idea came into Alice's head. Almost every one she had met had repeated poetry to her, and she thought she would try if the Wasp couldn't do it too. "Would you mind saying it in rhyme?" she asked very politely.

"It aint what I'm used to," said the Wasp: "however I'll try; wait a bit." He was silent for a few moments, and then began again—

"When I was young, my ringlets waved[13]
And curled and crinkled on my head:

10. A stiff neck is a bodily ailment as well as the bearing of a haughty, proud, or conceited person. Perhaps the Wasp is warning Alice of the danger of becoming a haughty Queen, as stiff-necked as an ivory chess queen. Indeed, as soon as Alice finds the gold crown on her head she walks about "rather stiffly" to keep the crown from falling off. In the last chapter she commands the black kitten to "sit up a little more stiffly" like the Red Queen she fancied the kitten to have been in her dream. Compare also with the "proud and stiff" messenger in Humpty Dumpty's poem.

Professor Cohen observes that the Wasp reverses history when he calls "stiff-neck" a new-fangled name. It is a much older word than "conceit." "You are a stiff-necked people," the Lord commanded Moses to tell the Israelites (Exodus 33:5).

11. "bright yellow": The phrase is used again by Carroll in Chapter 9, where it is also associated with advanced age. A "very old frog" is dressed in "bright yellow."

12. "comb": another pun. Note that if Alice is a bee, she is about to become a Queen bee.

13. Is this poem, like so many of the others in both *Alice* books, a parody? Many poems and songs of the time begin "When I was young . . ." but I could find none that seemed a probable basis for this poem. Carroll may have been aware that the phrase "ringlets waved" occurs in John Milton's beautiful description of the naked Eve (*Paradise Lost,* Book 4):

She, as a veil down to the slender waist,
Her unadorned golden tresses wore
Dishevelled, but in wanton ringlets waved
As the vine curls her tendrils . . .

And there is the following line from Alexander Pope's "Sappho":

No more my locks, in ringlets, curled . . .

However, since ringlets always curl and wave, the parallels may be coincidental.

It may be worth pointing out that the word "ringlets" usually refers not to short curls but to long locks in helical form, like the vines mentioned by Milton. As a mathematician Carroll knew

And then they said 'You should be shaved,
And wear a yellow wig instead.'

But when I followed their advice,
And they had noticed the effect,
They said I did not look so nice
As they had ventured to expect.

They said it did not fit, and so
It made me look extremely plain:
But what was I to do, you know?
My ringlets would not grow again.

So now that I am old and gray,
And all my hair is nearly gone,
They take my wig from me and say
'How can you put such rubbish on?'

And still, whenever I appear,
They hoot at me and call me 'Pig!'[14]
And that is why they do it, dear,
Because I wear a yellow wig."

"I'm very sorry for you," Alice said heartily: "and I think if your wig fitted a little better, they wouldn't tease you quite so much."

"*Your* wig fits very well," the Wasp murmured, looking at her with an expression of admiration: "it's the shape of your head as does it. Your jaws aint well shaped, though—I should think you couldn't bite well?"

Alice began with a little scream of laughter, which she turned into a cough as well as she could.[15] At last she managed to say gravely, "I can bite anything I want."[16]

"Not with a mouth as small as that," the Wasp persisted. "If you was a-fighting, now—could you get hold of the other one by the back of the neck?"

"I'm afraid not," said Alice.

"Well, that's because your jaws are too

that the helix is an asymmetrical structure which (in Alice's words) "goes the other way" in the mirror.

As mentioned earlier, it is no accident that the second *Alice* book is filled with references to mirror reversals and asymmetric objects. The helix itself is mentioned several times. Humpty Dumpty compares the toves to corkscrews, and Tenniel drew them with helical tails and snouts. Humpty also speaks in a poem about waking up fish with a corkscrew, and in Chapter 9 the White Queen recalls that Humpty had a corkscrew in hand when he was looking for a hippopotamus. In Tenniel's pictures the unicorn and the goat have helical horns. The road that leads up the hill in Chapter 3 twists like a corkscrew. Carroll must have realized that the young (perhaps then conceited?) Wasp, admiring himself in a mirror, would have seen his ringlets curl "the other way."

Any way you look at it, the poem itself is a strange one to appear in a book for children, though no more so, perhaps, than the inscrutable poem recited by Humpty in Chapter 6. The cutting off of hair, like decapitation and teeth extraction, is a familiar Freudian symbol of castration. Interesting interpretations of the poem by psychoanalytically oriented critics are possible.

14. In the Pig and Pepper chapter of *Alice in Wonderland,* Alice at first thinks that "Pig!," shouted by the Duchess, is addressed to her. It turns out that the Duchess is hurling the epithet at the baby boy she is nursing, who soon turns into an actual pig. The use of "pig" as a derisive name for a person, says the *OED,* was common in Victorian England. Surprisingly, even then it was an epithet often used against police officers. An 1874 slang dictionary adds: "The word is almost exclusively applied by London thieves to a plain-clothes man."

J. A. Lindon, a British writer of comic verse, suggests that it is the Wasp's baldness (cf. the baldness of the Duchess's baby) that prompts the epithet; and he recalls the association of pig and wig in "piggywiggy," which the *OED* says is applied to both a little pig and a child. In "The Owl and the Pussycat," Edward Lear writes:

And there in a wood a Piggy-wig stood,
With a ring at the end of its nose.

short," the Wasp went on: "but the top of your head is nice and round." He took off his own wig as he spoke, and stretched out one claw towards Alice,[17] as if he wished to do the same for her, but she kept out of reach, and would not take the hint. So he went on with his criticisms.

"Then your eyes—they're too much in front, no doubt. One would have done as well as two, if you *must* have them so close—"[18]

Alice did not like having so many personal remarks made on her, and as the Wasp had quite recovered his spirits, and was getting very talkative, she thought she might safely leave him. "I think I must be going on now," she said. "Good-bye."

"Good-bye, and thank-ye," said the Wasp, and Alice tripped down the hill again, quite pleased that she had gone back and given a few minutes to making the poor old creature comfortable.

15. Alice changed her "little scream of laughter" at the Wasp to a discreet cough. A short time before she had tried unsuccessfully to hold back a "little scream of laughter" at the White Knight. We cannot be sure, of course, that all parallels such as this were in the original text. After removing the Wasp episode, Carroll may have borrowed some of its phrases and images for use elsewhere when he polished the rest of the galleys.

16. Alice once frightened her nurse by shouting in her ear, "Do let's pretend that I'm a hungry hyaena, and you're a bone!" (*Through the Looking-Glass,* Chapter 1).

17. This somewhat terrifying scene, a large wasp reaching out a "claw" to remove Alice's hair, recalls three other episodes in the book. The White Knight, mounting his horse, steadies himself by holding Alice's hair. The White Queen grabs Alice's hair with both hands in Chapter 9. And, in a reversal of ages, Carroll planned to have Alice seize the hair of an old lady sitting near her when the railway carriage jumps the second brook, as we know from Tenniel's letter.

18. Unlike Alice, wasps have bulbous compound eyes on the sides of their heads and large strong jaws. Like Alice's, their heads are "nice and round." Other Looking-Glass creatures (the Rose, the Tiger-lily, the Unicorn) size up Alice in similar fashion, in the light of their own physical attributes.

Tenniel, at the age of twenty, lost the sight of one eye in a fencing bout with his father. The button accidentally dropped from his father's foil, and the blade's tip flicked across his right eye with a sudden pain that must have felt like a wasp's sting. One can understand why Tenniel might have been offended by the Wasp's remark; if so, it could have colored his attitude toward the episode.

FACSIMILE OF CORRECTED GALLEY PROOFS

Reproduced here are the corrected galley proofs of the suppressed portion of *Through the Looking-Glass* (part of Slip 63, Slips 64–67, and part of Slip 68). Carroll's revisions are in black ink. On Slip 63 the order to "omit to middle of Slip 68," the cross striking out the section's opening, and the curved line on the left are in the author's purple ink, as are the line on the left and the order to "Omit" on Slip 68.

and she was just going to spring over, when she heard a deep sigh, which seemed to come from the wood behind her.

"There's somebody *very* unhappy there," she thought, ~~and she went a little way~~ looking anxiously back ~~again~~ to see what was the matter. Something like a very old man (only that his face was more like a wasp) was sitting on the ground, leaning against a tree, all huddled up together, and shivering as if he were very cold.

Omit to middle of Slip 68—

64

"I don't *think* I can be of any use to him," was Alice's first thought, as she turned to spring over the brook:——"but I'll just ask him what's the matter," she added, checking herself on the very edge. "If I once jump over, everything will change, and then I can't help him."

So she went back to the Wasp——rather unwillingly, for she was *very* anxious to be a Queen.

"Oh, my old bones, my old bones!" he was grumbling on, as Alice came up to him.

"It's rheumatism, I should think," Alice said to herself, and she stooped over him, and said very kindly, "I hope you're not in much pain?"

The Wasp only shook his shoulders, and turned his head away. "Ah, deary me!" he said to himself.

"Can I do anything for you?" Alice went on. "Aren't you rather cold here?"

"How you go on!" the Wasp said in a peevish tone. "Worrity, worrity! There never was such a child!"

Alice felt rather offended at this answer, and was very nearly walking on and leaving him, but she thought to herself "Perhaps it's only pain that makes him so cross." So she tried once more.

"Won't you let me help you round to the

other side? You'll be out of the cold wind there."

The Wasp took her arm, and let her help him round the tree, but when he got settled down again he only said, as before, "Worrity, worrity! Can't you leave a body alone?"

"Would you like me to read you a bit of this?" Alice went on, as she picked up a newspaper which had been lying at his feet.

"You may read it if you've a mind to," the Wasp said, rather sulkily. "Nobody's hindering you, that *I* know of."

So Alice sat down by him, and spread out the paper on her knees, and began. "*Latest News. The Exploring Party have made another tour in the Pantry, and have found five new lumps of white sugar, large and in fine condition. In coming back——*"

"Any brown sugar?" the Wasp interrupted.

Alice hastily ran her eye down the paper and said "No; it says nothing about brown."

"No brown sugar!" grumbled the Wasp. "A nice exploring party!"

"*In coming back,*" Alice went on reading, "*they found a lake of treacle. The banks of the lake were blue and white, and looked like china. While tasting the treacle, they had a sad accident: two of their party were engulphed——*"

"Were *what?*" the Wasp asked in a very cross voice.

"En-gulph-ed," Alice repeated, dividing the word into syllables.

"There's no such word in the language!" said the Wasp.

"It's in this newspaper though," Alice said a little timidly.

"Let it stop there!" said the Wasp, fretfully turning away his head.

Alice put down the newspaper. "I'm afraid you're not well," she said in a soothing tone. "Can't I do anything for you?"

"It's all along of the wig," the Wasp said in a much gentler voice.

"Along of the wig?" Alice repeated, quite pleased to find that he was recovering his temper.

"You'd be cross too, if you'd a wig like

mine," the Wasp went on. "They jokes; at one. And they worrits one. And then I gets cross. And I gets cold. And I gets under a tree. And I gets a yellow handkerchief. And I ties up my face——as at the present."

Alice looked pityingly at him. "Tying up the face is very good for the toothache," she said.

"And it's very good for the conceit," added the Wasp.

Alice didn't catch the word exactly. "Is that a kind of toothache?" she asked.

The Wasp considered a little. "Well, no," he said: "it's when you hold up your head——*so*——without bending your neck."

"Oh, you mean stiff-neck," said Alice.

The Wasp said "That's a new-fangled name. They called it conceit in my time."

"Conceit isn't a disease at all," Alice remarked.

66

"It is though," said the Wasp: "wait till you have it, and then you'll know. And when you catches it, just try tying a yellow handkerchief round your face. It'll cure you in no time!"

He untied the handkerchief as he spoke, and Alice looked at his wig in great surprise. It was bright yellow like the handkerchief, and all tangled and tumbled about like a heap of sea-weed. "You could make your wig much neater," she said, "if only you had a comb."

"What, you're a Bee, are you?" the Wasp said, looking at her with more interest. "And you've got a comb. Much honey?"

"It isn't that kind," Alice hastily explained. "It's to comb hair with——your wig's so *very* rough, you know."

"I'll tell you how I came to wear it," the Wasp said. "When I was young, you know, my ringlets used to wave——"

A curious idea came into Alice's head. Almost every one she had met had repeated poetry to her, and she thought she would try if the Wasp couldn't do it too. "Would you mind saying it in rhyme?" she asked very politely.

"It aint what I'm used to," said the Wasp: "however I'll try; wait a bit." He was silent for a few moments, and then began again—

"When I was young, my ringlets waved
And curled and crinkled on my head:
And then they said 'You should be shaved,
And wear a yellow wig instead.'

"But when I followed their advice,
And they had noticed the effect,
They said I did not look so nice
As they had ventured to expect.

"They said it did not fit, and so
It made me look extremely plain:
But what was I to do, you know?
My ringlets would not grow again.

"So now that I am old and gray,
And all my hair is nearly gone,
They take my wig from me and say
'How can you put such rubbish on?'

67

"And still, whenever I appear,
They hoot at me and call me 'Pig!'
And that is why they do it, dear,
Because I wear a yellow wig."

"I'm very sorry for you," Alice said heartily: "and I think if your wig fitted a little better, they wouldn't tease you quite so much."

"*Your* wig fits very well," the Wasp murmured, looking at her with an expression of admiration: "it's the shape of your head as does it. Your jaws aint well shaped, though—— I should think you couldn't bite well?"

Alice began with a little scream of laughing, which she turned into a cough as well as she could: at last she managed to say gravely "I can bite anything I want."

"Not with a mouth as small as that," the Wasp persisted. "If you was a-fighting, now ——could you get hold of the other one by the back of the neck?"

"I'm afraid not," said Alice.

"Well, that's because your jaws are too short," the Wasp went on: "but the top of your head is nice and round." He took off his own wig as he spoke, and stretched out one claw towards Alice, as if he wished to do the same for her, but she kept out of reach, and would not take the hint. So he went on with his criticisms.

Omit

68

"Then your eyes——they're too much in front, no doubt. One would have done as well as two, if you *must* have them so close——"

Alice did not like having so many personal remarks made on her, and as the Wasp had quite recovered his spirits, and was getting very talkative, she thought she might safely leave him. "I think I must be going on now," she said. "Good-bye."

"Good-bye, and thank-ye," said the Wasp, and Alice tripped down the hill again, quite pleased that she had gone back and given a few minutes to making the poor old creature comfortable.

A NOTE ABOUT THE LEWIS CARROLL SOCIETY

The Lewis Carroll Society of North America is a nonprofit organization that encourages the study of the life, work, times, and influence of Charles Lutwidge Dodgson. The Society was founded in 1974 and has grown from several dozen members to several hundred members, drawn from across North America and from abroad. Current members include leading authorities on Carroll, collectors, students, general enthusiasts, and libraries. The Society is making a concerted professional effort to become the center for Carroll activities and studies.

The Society meets twice a year, usually in the fall and in the spring, at the site of an important Carroll collection in the eastern United States. Meetings have featured distinguished speakers and outstanding exhibitions.

The Society maintains an active publications program, administered by a distinguished committee interested in publishing and assisting in the publication of materials dealing with the life and work of Lewis Carroll. Members receive the Society's newsletter, the *Knight-Letter,* chapbooks in the Society's series, *Carroll Studies,* and other special publications. *The Wasp in a Wig* was first published as part of this series.

Further information can be obtained by writing to The Secretary, Maxine Schaefer, Lewis Carroll Society of North America, 617 Rockford Road, Silver Spring, Maryland 20902.

ABOUT THE AUTHORS

CHARLES LUTWIDGE DODGSON was a shy, stammering teacher of mathematics at Oxford University who became a charming storyteller in the presence of little girls and, under the pseudonym Lewis Carroll, invented humorous fantasy stories to amuse them. Two of his fictional works, *Alice in Wonderland* and *Through the Looking-Glass,* have become classics of English literature.

MARTIN GARDNER is best known as a popularizer of mathematics and science, though his more than forty books also include volumes on philosophy and literature. For twenty-five years he wrote the Mathematical Games column in *Scientific American,* and he shares with Lewis Carroll a love of recreational mathematics and wordplay.

Grateful acknowledgment is made to the following for permission
to reprint previously published material:

A. P. Watt Ltd and Macmillan London Ltd: "The Wasp in a Wig" by Lewis Carroll. Reprinted by permission of A. P. Watt Limited on behalf of The Trustees of the C. L. Dodgson Estate, The Lewis Carroll Society of North America, and Martin Gardner and Macmillan London and Basingstoke.

Clarkson N. Potter, Inc.: Preface, Introduction, and Notes by Martin Gardner from *The Wasp in a Wig* by Lewis Carroll. Copyright © 1977 by Martin Gardner. Reprinted by permission of Clarkson N. Potter, Inc.

Harcourt Brace Jovanovich, Inc., and Faber and Faber Limited: Fourteen lines from "Burnt Norton" from *Four Quartets* by T. S. Eliot. Copyright 1943 by T. S. Eliot. Copyright renewed 1971 by Esme Valerie Eliot; two lines from "Morning at the Window" from *Collected Poems 1909–1962* by T. S. Eliot. Copyright 1936 by Harcourt Brace Jovanovich, Inc. Copyright © 1964, 1963 by T. S. Eliot. World rights excluding the United States are controlled by Faber and Faber Limited. Reprinted by permission of Harcourt Brace Jovanovich, Inc., and Faber and Faber Limited.

Michael Patrick Hearn: Essay on Peter Newell. Michael Patrick Hearn's essay on Peter Newell originally appeared in *Dictionary of Literary Biography,* Volume 42: *American Writers for Children Before 1900,* edited by Glenn E. Estes. Copyright © 1985 by Gale Research Company. Reprinted by permission of the publisher and Michael Patrick Hearn. Gale, 1985.

Robert Hornback: Excerpts from "Garden Tour of Wonderland" by Robert Hornback from *Pacific Horticulture,* Fall 1983, Volume 44, pages 9–13. Copyright © Robert Hornback. Reprinted by permission of Robert Hornback.

Jabberwocky: Excerpt from an article about Alice's hands by Selwyn Goodacre, from the Spring 1982 issue of *Jabberwocky.* Copyright © 1982 by The Lewis Carroll Society. Reprinted by permission.

Lewis Carroll Society of North America: Excerpt from *Soaring with the Dodo,* edited by Edward Giuliano and James R. Kincaid. Reprinted courtesy of The Lewis Carroll Society of North America and Morton Cohen.